## WEAVERS

"Come," the Inquestor [...]
the magic in this darkness, the [...]
He pointed at the circling wall.

"There are four million shades of darkness, it is said . . .
and not one of them the true darkness. You start with filaments
of color, and you strand and unstrand them so that they cancel
and uncancel each other out, and you get a field of darkness
such as one of these—but look more carefully! Suddenly, when
you're least expecting it, when you've stared at the darkness
until you can't bear it any longer, you'll catch a glimpse of color,
a rainbow's edge. Do you see?"

She stared at the wall, squinting hard. And suddenly . . .
it was like bursting through into a joyous universe where light
danced wildly . . . her heart almost stopped beating. And then
it was gone. . . .

### High praise for Somtow Sucharitkul:

Other books by Somtow Sucharitkul

STARSHIP & HAIKU
MALLWORLD
THE AQUILIAD
FIRE FROM A WINE-DARK SEA
*The Inquestor Series:*
   LIGHT ON THE SOUND
   THE THRONE OF MADNESS
VAMPIRE JUNCTION (as S.P. Somtow)

# UTOPIA HUNTERS

## Chronicles of the High Inquest

## Somtow Sucharitkul

**BANTAM BOOKS**
TORONTO · NEW YORK · LONDON · SYDNEY · AUCKLAND

UTOPIA HUNTERS
*A Bantam Book / December 1984*

*Parts of* Utopia Hunters *have appeared in somewhat different form under the following titles and dates:*

*"Rainbow King,"* Isaac Asimov's Science Fiction Magazine, *February, 1981, "The Web Dancer,"* Isaac Asimov's Science Fiction Magazine, *December, 1979, "The Dust,"* Isaac Asimov's Science Fiction Magazine, *August, 1981, "Remembrances,"* Isaac Asimov's Science Fiction Magazine, *March, 1982, "Scarlet Snow,"* Isaac Asimov's Science Fiction Magazine, *May, 1982, "The Comet that Cried for its Mother,"* Amazing, *September, 1984.*

ISBN 0-553-24526-0

*Published simultaneously in the United States and Canada*

PRINTED IN THE UNITED STATES OF AMERICA

H      0 9 8 7 6 5 4 3 2 1

# Contents

**ONE** The Book of Children's Dreams     1
*The Story of the Rainbow King*     22

**TWO** The Book of Shapers and Visionaries     55
*The Story of the Dust-Sculptress*     66
*The Story of the Web Dancer*     98

**THREE** The Book of Rememberers and Warriors     127
*The Rememberer's Story*     138
*The Comet's Story*     166

**FOUR** The Book of Three Young Inquestors     189
*The Myth of Mother Vara*     194
*The Myth of the Windbringers*     201
*The Story of Young Arryk*     211

**FIVE** The Book of the Darkweaver     233

# UTOPIA
# HUNTERS

# ONE

# The Book of Children's Dreams

*eih! asheveraín*
*am-plánzhet ka dhánd-erúden;*
*eih! skrikám, skrikám:*
*pu eyáh chítarans hyémadh?*

　　　　　　　—ek shéntraran Sájiti

Ai! after the Dispersal of Man
We wept for the dead earth;
Ai! we cried, we cried:
"Where is the homeworld of the heart?"

　　　　　　　—*from the Songs of Sajit*

# I

In time she would come to understand that they were not all alike, those tapestries of seamless-seeming shadow that hung in the gallery of the darkweavers in the seventh arrondissement of the city of Ikshatra. But that first day, fleeing her friends in an ecstacy of childish rage, popping heedless through the displacement plates of the city until she had completely lost her way, flinging herself into the foyer of the museum for fear of the mankilling plants chained up, tended by grim servocorpses, in the knot garden that ringed the arrondissement like a snake swallowing its tail . . . that first day they came upon her as a profound mystery.

Perhaps, too, it was because of the Inquestor.

She knew he must be one. The entrance hall was hung with darkweavings, and *he* was wearing a shimmercloak, a matrix of furry light that blushed rose against a dark blue deep as the evening sea. She stood transfixed, a girl not yet past puberty who had never set foot off Essondras. His back was turned to her at first; she saw only the crimson ripple of the cloak. He cast about him a terrible grief, like an aura. She would have been afraid if she had known how. But words like *rulers of the Dispersal of Man, galactic tyrant, lord of compassion* were just formulas to her, things you repeated in school.

What could she say? Already a museum guard was advancing from the entranceway, fingers wagging in a soundless tsk-tsk. Why, the girl thought, she is afraid to admonish me aloud, lest the Inquestor be displeased. All the rules have been suspended. . . .

It was then that she decided to address the Inquestor. But what could she say? Didn't the Inquestors speak only the highspeech? And all she knew was *"Hokh'Ton."* There. She'd blurted it out. The Inquestor turned: white hair flaming like the mane of a snow lion: the guard dumbstruck, not daring to come forward. What else could she say? Only the words of the Inquestral anthem, learned by rote, the meanings only half-grasped: *"Dhelyá sarnáng z tóraka z níshis . . .* I, a slave, a chattel, a nothing, throw down before you all my heart, my thoughts, the works of my hands, O you who bask in the High Compassion. . . ."

Her words trailed away. But because she did not know yet how much she must be afraid, she did not cast down her eyes when his met hers; and she saw in them not the cold awe of eternity but softness and laughter. And when he spoke it was in the lowspeech of Essondras: *"Keshwelati, dawekek. Temweminit. Ki kiamwati?* Console yourself, little girl. Do not fear me. What is your name?"

"Jeni. Will you take me to a rainbow castle?" It was something she'd heard in an old story, or an old song, or something.

The Inquestor laughed sadly. "No, Jenjen, I cannot." He called her not by childname but gave it the reduplicated inflection proper to the names of grown-up women. It was strange to be thus addressed; for her it was the first time. The palace guard, sensing that a crisis had been averted, sighed with relief. "Why did you come here?" the Inquestor said.

"I don't know, *hokh'Ton.* Why did you come to this arrondissment?"

"To meditate on the colors of darkness." He reached down to play with a strand of her hair. Jeni saw a look of terror, instantly masked, flicker across the face of the palace guard.

"Darkness? I don't understand."

"Come, child."

He took her by the hand and led her through a second entranceway into a long hall hung with sheets of darkness. Some, frameless, suspended from the ceiling by golden wires, seemed like transdimensional windows. Some had ornate borders, friezes in precious metals, stranded rainbow-stuff, a pattern of wavering laser-threads like cilia of a microscopic animal or the edge of a frayed carpet. Jeni said, "I think the frames are more interesting, don't you?"

He laughed. "I used to too, at first, when I was young. But their brash, dissonant colors serve only to heighten the illusion, you see. Tell me, can you read their names?"

Beside each sheet of darkness was a plaque with the artwork's name, both in High Inquestral and Essondran. One said *Tembarangkier,* and beneath it, in the lowspeech, *Anwero di Temwara, City of Darkness.* Another: *Iriskning: Kishtrawo d'Erwislinge: The Rainbow King.* She read aloud for the Inquestor the liquid polysyllables of the lowspeech and tried to wrap her tongue around the resonant harsh music of the highspeech. He smiled at her. He did not have that worried, creased-faced look that her schoolteacher always seemed to wear; his expression was benign, fatherly; and this directly contradicted what her teachers had taught her to believe about the High Inquest. And she asked him—just as she might have asked her own father—"But they are only sheets of darkness. Why must they have these silly names? What do people see in them?"

"Dear child. I suppose you know the story of the Emperor's clothes?"

"Of course. Even *little* kids know that one."

"Come."

Displacement plates; chamber after chamber with the tapestries; but now their shapes were ever more regular, and few of them had the complicated frame designs that had characterized the darkweavings in the outer halls. Jeni became more and more puzzled. Officials of the museum came, genuflected before the Inquestor, and ushered them the way to the next chamber. Some stared strangely at her. Each official seemed even more resplendently dressed than the last, and to be even more obsequious, even more fearful. "Curators and palace guards!" the Inquestor said to one of them. "Could I not meet a single true artist in this palace of art?" The person addressed scurried away; presently there came three or four darkweavers, each robed in a filmy, almost living darkness, who prostrated themselves abjectly in front of him. They stood now in a huge exhibit room; a wall of darkness encircled them completely. The artists and the young girl and the Inquestor each stood isolated in a puddle of light that followed him as he moved.

There followed a strained conversation. The darkweavers spoke in turn, in carefully rehearsed platitudes and highspeech formulas. Their words seemed empty to the young girl; and as she gazed into the Inquestor's face she understood that they hurt him with their fear of him, and that he must always mask that hurt. . . . She saw that the Inquestor did not wish to continue, but that for decency's sake he must. His life is not his own, she thought. And though she knew that the Inquestors held in their hands the power of life and death not only over men but over whole planets and star systems, yet she knew too that she did not envy him.

They were alone now. And it was then that the little girl said, "You are so lonely, *hokh'Ton*. And so sad. I wish there was something I could do for you."

At first he did not answer. But then he said, "Come, I will show you the magic in this darkness, the magic the dark-weavers wove." He pointed at the circling wall. "There are four million shades of darkness, it is said . . . and not one of them the true darkness. You start with filaments of color, and you strand and unstrand them so that they cancel and uncancel each other out, and you get a field of darkness such as one of these, but look more carefully! Suddenly, when you're least expecting it . . . when you've stared at the darkness until you can't bear it any longer . . . you'll catch a glimpse of color, a rainbow's edge. Do you see?"

She stared at the wall, squinting hard. "No, *hokh'Ton*," she said.

"Again. Concentrate. Lose yourself. Suddenly . . . a fleeting transience . . ."

And suddenly . . . it was like bursting through into a joyous universe where light danced wildly. . . . Her heart almost stopped beating. And it was gone. "I think I saw something," she said. For a split second she has danced on alien worlds and breathed air from another planet. . . .

"What did you see?" asked the Inquestor.

"I can't say. But it . . . it must have been very beautiful, *hokh'Ton*."

"I think so too. Now you must leave me, my child."

And the Inquestor stepped into the wall and vanished. But when she stared harder she saw that there was a black circle where he had sunk into the tapestry, and the circle was shifting, that it was a ball of utter blackness, against which the dark tapestry had acquired a faint luminescence. A tachyon bubble!

For she knew that that was how Inquestors traveled, and that only such bubbles possessed true darkness, for they were not even of this universe, but were literally droplets of non-existence. . . .

And dimly she began to understand how there might be many darknesses, and how the weaving of a darkness might be called an art by some.

But when she stepped from the museum into the garden's evening air, that epiphany was already losing its clarity. Indeed it was not until years later, when she was a grown woman, that she was to know for certain that it had not all been a dream.

2

To those who sailed the space between spaces, Essondras might justly be called a backwater. But Jenjen had nothing to compare it with. And if anyone had been so curious as to ask the little girl what she thought of the High Inquest, or of man's dispersal over the million known worlds, or about the delphinoid shipminds whose quickpaths threaded the overcosm and united man under the Inquest's unimaginable power . . . the girl would probably just have shrugged. You never thought about such cosmic events when you lived on a backworld like Essondras.

Ikshatra was the only city of consequence; it had been the capital ever since the Inquest had declared the planet open and the people bins had been unloaded, almost a millennium ago. It was said that under modern Ikshatra lay an older Ikshatra, and beneath that an older one still, and so on, and that they were separated from each other only by ceilings of force thrown up as foundations for each spate of fresh building. Before the displacement plate system had been installed, Ikshatra had shot upwards, not outwards; but now it sprawled towards the sea, a jigsaw of arrondissements. The old city center, a necessary gathering place in the days before displacement plates, was now frequented only by necrodrama audiences and, occasionally, tourists from other worlds.

As Jenjen grew older she became fascinated by the art of

lightweaving. Her parents moved to the forty-ninth arrondissment, which bordered on the seventh, where stood the gallery
where she had met the Inquestor; it was a long time before she
dared walk past the knot garden of the chained man-eating
plants.

In school, she learned much more about the Inquest. She
knew that the man whom she had innocently questioned could
have ordered her execution with a flick of the finger, or even
the destruction of her world. And so the encounter seemed
more and more dreamlike until at last it faded from her consciousness.

She went to a school for lightweavers; a dozen or so
youngsters were always to be found there. She loved her artwork; conversely, it was often said that she found it difficult to
love people. But there was something so soothing about being
enfolded in the forcecocoon at the center of a tapestry, of feeling
the electrical tingle as she directed the filaments of multi-
colored light. She would point abruptly at a spot, subvocalize
to the thinkhive in the lightloom, and strands of light would
shoot from her fingers, twist together, braid into patterns
around her. And when she had finished her exercises for the
day she took almost as much pleasure in unweaving them, in
watching the firelines dissipate into the bare white walls of the
studio.

But most of all, she loved lightweaving because she could
be alone, dreaming of scenes at once childish and cosmic. And
no one would dare disturb her at her loom. Even the studio's
weavemaster would tiptoe past the lightloom, for on Essondras
everyone knew what a high place must be accorded art, as
witness their necrotheaters, holotheaters, the mist-sculptures
drifting from offshore island centers over the bay of Ikshatra,
the lavish gardens in every arrondissement, the somber splendor of the city's mnemothanasions.

It was when Jenjen was ten that she first saw one of these.
A cross-cousin of hers had died, not someone she had known
well or much liked. But Pei Sarsar was an important familial
elder who possessed many of the family's trophies, including
the heads of some important ancestors. These relics would, by
family custom, be apportioned to the surviving relatives. . . .

She was not permitted into the mnemothanasion proper,
though she felt a certain curiosity about it. The children were

all clustered around the facade, chattering; it was a bright night, cloudless, all the moons out. She watched dubiously as her parents, their rented mourning capes billowing cumulously behind them, cautioned her not to stray and told her she might be upset if she went inside with the adults; then they joined the stream of mourners. A frenzied ululating punctuated by deathdrums came from within; even at her age she suspected hypocrisy. She looked around for someone to play with.

"Who are you?" one of the kids asked her.

"Jeni."

"The lightweaver's apprentice!" said a boy about her age. "She's strange, that one."

"Why are you talking about me as if I wasn't there? And how do you know what I do? I don't even know your names."

"Oh, I'm Paryk, your left-branch cross-maternal cousin. But you wouldn't know any of this stuff. They say you sit at a lightloom all day. And you only ten years old, with three summers behind you, sitting around with rancid old women! My mother says lightweaving's not an honest profession."

"So? And what are *you* going to be?"

"I shall be a childsoldier! I've already passed the test." And Paryk strutted back and forth on the flagstones before the facade of the mnemothanasion, as if he were already invested with the iridium gravi-boots and the dark cloak and the citrine laser-slitty eyes. And the other children applauded, except one, younger than the rest, who looked so like Paryk that Jenjen thought she must be his sister.

The little girl said, "You'll go 'way, and we'll never see you again. . . . You'll go kill people for the In-inquest." And the others' eyes went wide, and they clustered around Paryk, content to bask in the glow of his glamorous future.

"That's nothing," Jenjen said. "I *talked* to an Inquestor once."

The others just scoffed and turned to play a round of skip-the-flagstones. I suppose they just can't imagine it, the very idea, thought Jenjen. *Talking* to one of the gods themselves. And yet Paryk's going to die for them—as good as die, because we'll never see him again. Not that I like him much.

She found herself sneaking away from the gaggle of chattering children, and drawn to the quadrangle of blue light that emanated from the threshold of the mnemothanasion. She put her ear to the door: cool metal, moonlit, on her skin, made bumpy by a bas-relief that showed scenes of joyful city life: marketplaces, gardens, lovers by the Blue Canal, a flock of kashanthras—you could almost hear their plaintive squawking—heading towards a sewer trough beside the Temple of Mother Vara. Nothing to remind the visitor of death.

A voice, abruptly startling her, with a metallic after-echo: *What do you want, Jenjen, daughter of Jarrys and Wanwan? Is there a loved one you wish to remember?*

"Oh, you're the building's thinkhive. How did you recognize me?"

*I am joined to the planetary thinkhive, child,* said the thinkhive sentinel. *What a foolish question. As you touched your cheek to my metal hide, I read your DNA and matched to that of the millions that inhabit our world. . . . Where did you go to school, if you don't even know how a gate-guardian works? Now, answer my question.*

"I'm sorry, I'm not that well educated. . . . I'm apprenticed to a lightweaver. . . . I spend my days dreaming by the loom. Are you angry?"

*Of course not. You can come in if you like. You know there is nothing to fear. No evil can cross the threshold of a mnemothanasion. It is a place of peace.* And the doorway accordioned a crack, wide enough to admit her slight body. She slipped inside.

There was a vestibule devoid of ornament, dark-walled; at its center, a signpost with many hundred arrows, spiraling from floor to ceiling, like a gigantic strand of DNA or like the spinal column of an ancient sea monster. Above each arrow were words in Essondran and in High Inquestral: *Devotees of Mother Vara. Followers of the Way of Darkness.* Names of religions . . . when she looked where the arrows pointed she saw hundreds of shadowy staircases, spiraling up from a mist whose swirling tendrils hid from view the walls, if any, of the vestibule. Which way could her parents have gone? Frightened, she looked for the exit, but it has disappeared . . . only the signpost in a pool of light, and the staircases draped in mist. Stairways to a hundred heavens. Which way had they gone? They were orthodox atheists, weren't they? She found the right arrow and headed for its staircase. Footsteps dulled by gloom and oppressive heaviness. As she reached the first of the steps, they began to bear her upward in a shaft of reddish light. Around her moans, wails, imprecations in some dead tongue. . . . Surely this must be the wrong funeral. Skulls tall as buildings leered at her. A threnody on screech-shrill high-woods. Skulls that wept blood. Skulls that cackled.

"Despair, despair!" A giant of a man waving a straw doll, dancing . . . in a room reeking with incense, and mourners flagellating each other, drinking blood that dripped from the eye sockets of a corpse on an altar laden with decaying fruits and wilted flowers—

She turned, she ran, past rooms where one or two wept silently, past rooms where orgiasts writhed or bonzes chanted or dancers mimicked totem animals. She ran wildly, breathlessly. She had to find the exit—

But instead she ran into the arms of a boy barely older than herself. The room: well-lit. Around, in concentric pews, sat men and women in white robes. One by one they were standing up to say a few words. No corpse was anywhere in sight. "Who are you?" she said.

"It might be more proper," said the boy, "for us to ask *you* that question. But we are Rememberers, of the Clan of Tash. Today we are remembering one of us, untimely taken. You can stay if you like."

"Who—"

"I never knew him. He died two hundred years ago. But the remembrance lingers on." He smiled a little. A boy this young, she thought, should not be so solemn. He was nothing like Paryk, strutting and boasting.

"What does a Rememberer do?" she said, for she had never encountered one.

"Work for the Inquest." He had lively eyes. He always seemed to be absorbing some detail. She felt she could trust him, somehow.

"Like the childsoldiers?" Would this stranger, like Paryk, suddenly be called skyward, to die in some war parsecs away?

He laughed. "No. Sometimes we can even stop wars."

"You? A few people in white robes, who do nothing but remember people who've been dead for centuries? Can't be a very useful occupation. I met one once, you know."

"An Inquestor?" But he did not seem to disbelieve her.

"Yes. I don't think someone like *you* could have changed his mind about anything. Oh, he had power in him."

"But power is why we exist, we Rememberers. We are

frail; some of us are even blind, that our remembrance may be more vivid, unfettered by the present. But without us the Inquestors would forget that power is not always a good thing. . . ."

At that moment the ceremony came to an end and the mourners began to file out of the room. She overheard them talking among themselves.

One said, "The *falling beyond* has been averted, I think. But I don't know how we can forestall the riots."

Another: "Revolutionaries! Can't they ever learn they are powerless without at least the tacit support of factions within the Inquest? This Shadow Inquest now—"

Another: "Be quiet! They have ears everywhere." Suddenly he saw Jenjen. "Who's this, one of their spies? Gava, get her out of here! Powers of powers blast that Inquest with its interminable meddlings and its—" He stopped, seeing he had said too much. The others stared at him. Gava—that was the name, it transpired, of the boy she had been talking to—started to hustle her out of the room, and she found herself once more within the vestibule of the mists and stairways.

"Don't mind that ancient," Gava said. "Old *hokh'Tash* Harratash! He's completely paranoid—thinks whenever he says something mildly subversive they'll reach down and strike him dead with a thunderbolt! He can't quite understand the Inquest's monumental indifference—to him, to this planet, to the whole damned galaxy."

She saw a sudden fire in his eyes; abruptly it seemed to douse itself. "Revolutions, revolutions," the boy said, "just a game." He looked nervously about for a few moments, and Jenjen realized that he had become as paranoid as the old man Harratash had earlier.

"You're scared too," she said, with the tactlessness of childhood.

"Yes, I suppose." He turned abruptly away. "Where is everyone? I have to get back—" he closed his eyes and subvocalized a command. . . . She grabbed his arm lightly, wanting to ask him some other question, but he must have given the thinkhive the exit command, for the safety rebound took hold of her too, and they were both standing outside the mnemothanasion. She looked up: her parents were there. Her mother was clutching a package shaped like a human head. Her father seemed furious.

"We've looked for you all over! The funeral's finished now. Come on, Jeni."

Her mother stared at the young Rememberer beside her. The boy bolted. When she was sure he was out of earshot, her mother whispered angrily: "You should know better than to associate with the likes of him! Don't talk to a whiterobed person like that. . . . Cross the street to avoid him if you must!"

"Why, Mother, why?" Jenjen was astonished at her mother's intensity.

"When the whiterobed ones come forth from the House of Tash," her father said, as though repeating some formula, "it will mean that Essondras has *fallen beyond*."

"But what is to *fall beyond*?"

"It is—"

"No. You'll give the child nightmares," her mother said. She was grateful for that. "You don't need to know these things." They started to walk toward the displacement plate, which lay at the end of a pathway that ran through landscaped gardens. It was night; still the moons shone, lending a pearl-like luster to the flat-leaved groundvines that clustered at the footpath's edges. Mother and Father walked ahead. She could hear them talking quietly. They didn't know she could over-hear them. They were talking of various relatives and how the funeral had gone, dull things; in her mind she was already back at the lightloom.

But she heard her mother say something that startled her from her reverie: "Jarrys, dear, what do you know about the Prince of Shadow?"

"I have no idea." But he sounded distinctly uneasy.

"I heard a rumor of it . . . something to do with a revolution or something. . . ."

"Be quiet, woman!" her father whispered harshly. "You could get us killed!" He looked nervously behind. At that moment Jenjen caught up with her parents, and they looked guiltily away from her.

What did it all mean? She felt the tingle of displacement; suddenly they were many klomets away, walking down an alley toward one of the city squares and a rank of communal dis-placement plates. She caught a quick glimpse of some moon-worshipping festival, and determined to weave it into her next lightloom exercise.

# 3

On her eighteenth birthday she wove a lightwall on a base of gold with a hundred hues of blue. From some angles it was a pure abstraction; from others it seemed to be stitched from the wings of kashanthra-birds; from still others it resembled the sea beside the city. She worked on the lightwall for almost a year, oblivious to the young people's gossip about the latest necrodramas or the new craze for monopole skating. Only when she'd put on the finishing touches did she realize that a young man had been staring at her for several hours. Indeed, he had been watching her at work, on and off, for weeks.

"Who are you?" she said. It was almost an afterthought.

"I'm Zalo. I've written a play. It is about love and other romantic things. Will you come?"

They fell in love.

Although it was from school that Jenjen learned about the Inquest's unimaginable power, its unbroken twenty millennia of rule over the million worlds of the Dispersal of Man, and the consonant-rich cadence of the high Inquestral tongue, it was Zalo who taught her of the Inquest's magic, its mythic figures, its bizarre barbaric grandeur. As she wove he would tell her stories. . . . The stories were from the necrodrama. He was apprenticed to Karnofara, grandmaster of the dancing corpses. All the material of necrodrama was to be found in the Inquestral myths.

He would say, "Have you heard of the Rainbow King?"

"No." And touched a finger to the lightwoof, warping it with the stuff of rainbow.

"He was a mad Inquestor who made a necrodrama of an entire planet. And the story contains two children, childsoldier and princeling, who rode to the rainbow castle on the backs of pteratygers. . . ."

He would go on; sometimes she would listen; often, though she did not listen, his words caused strange new colors

14

to creep into her tapestries. Perhaps that was how her work became so quickly famous. Zalo developed much more slowly; he was still at the stage of contorting his lyrics into the elaborate scansion-schemes of verses to be uttered by the dead.

Jenjen believed that he was hampered by his obstinate refusal to learn the highspeech. Even at twenty, all he knew of the Inquestral tongue was a speech-tag or two, a catch-phrase to be found in the necrodrama. Otherwise he was ignorant as any peasant. Sometimes they quarreled about it.

"You can't get anywhere without the Inquest," she would say. "Don't you ever want to visit other worlds?"

"I visit them already," he said stubbornly. Or, "I want to speak *my* language, not the language of distant overlords."

It was a paradox to her. For when he told the stories— always in the homely language of Essondras—the Inquest seemed beautiful, compassionate. Zalo transformed the stuff of legend into the stories of real people, passionate, suffering. She knew that he possessed genius, although few could see it yet. Her opinion was confirmed when Karnofara named Zalo his successor, a most controversial decision which catapulted the young man into planetary notoriety. Suddenly the couple was constantly in demand.

It hardly came as a surprise when a summons from the Inquest arrived at the academy where Jenjen had studied and where she still maintained her studio. But when she saw that it was addressed to her alone she felt a sudden foreboding.

Quickly she tore open the enclosure sealed with a circle of shimmerfur. There was a message disk inside. It read simply:

> *Given at Varezhdur, the Seat of Ton Elloran n'Taanyel Tath, Inquestor and Princeling.*
> *Child that is called Jenjen, daughter of Jarrys and Wanwan Ikshatriskindrah, it is Our pleasure that you be named to the Clan of Ir, and that you accompany the messenger who awaits outside to Our palace now in orbit about Essondras, that we may continue a conversation once begun in your childhood.*

Zalo burst in at that moment. "What does this mean?" he cried. "The news is all over the building. A link-boy in the garden told me! What is this Ton Elloran, a secret lover?"

"No. You don't understand. . . ." Behind them the light-wall she had been crafting glittered, burned. . . . She was going to name it *Zalo's Heart*. "Do you know what the clan of Ir is?"

"You know I never learned the highspeech," Zalo said resentfully.

"It is . . . it is the clan of Darkweavers!"

She stood before her creation, firedance of mating sunlight, bursting of giant stars. . . . Zalo understood at last. "It's like a death sentence!" he shouted. "He's condemning you to turn your back on all this beauty . . . to dream only the darkness now. . . . How can he do this? I'll fight him. He can't take you away from me. . . ."

"You can't fight him," Jenjen said.

"They're cruel, capricious gods. Just when you and I are on the verge of fame, just when we have each other. Powers of powers, aren't you angry, Jeni? They can't do this to us!"

But she turned away from him, for all at once that childhood memory surfaced, and she remembered staring into that Inquestor's eyes, and knowing not only the splendor of the god, but the loneliness of the man. And though Zalo wept bitterly, and stormed extravagantly around the studio, and kicked down walls of light so that they twisted into kaleidoscope jumbles on the stone floor, yet Jenjen could feel no such transports of youthful emotion. For this moment had been preordained, and she could not resist it now.

# 4

And so at last Jenjen came to Varezhdur, Elloran's palace, and waited for an audience outside the throneroom. There was a door; a strange door, its wood not a holosculpt veneer that would iris open with a simple subvocalized command, but firm, solid, forbidding. It was her first day in the golden palace that sailed the overcosm, and she was not used to doors that did not melt away when you thought *open, open,* at them. She waited, pacing back and forth, idly watching the animated murals, scenes from the palace's millennial past, trying to count the fluted columns, each capped with purple flame, that lined the gold-walled hallway.

A sennet sounded, many corridors away. Nearer now. Soundlessly the massive door pulled open, and she was in the presence of Ton Elloran n'Taanyel Tath.

The throne seemed so far away . . . gold everywhere. A throng of suppliants surging around him, many of them Essondras's most high-ranking oligarchs. Above, on floaters railinged with tapestries, hovering, darting, consorts of shimmerviols and screechstones and plangitars and whisperlyres, and flying carpets on which knelt choirs of neuterchildren, their high voices keening. The sounds, sensuous and sweet, rang out over the mutterings of the crowd. Amid the splendor, the Inquestor sat unmoving, like a doll; only his shimmercloak, flamed by an artwind, billowed about him, a storm of crimson and ultramarine.

Their eyes met across the vast throneroom. It was the same Inquestor; how could she doubt that? The Inquestor she had dared to pity, when she was a child and knew no better. As she went up to him, the crowd parted. The Inquestor lifted his hand for the music to subside.

Jenjen was angry now. She abandoned all propriety. She did not care if he sentenced her to death; this would only confirm Zalo's notions about the Inquest's gratuitous cruelty. She said: "Why have you called me here, *hokh'Ton*? Didn't you know you were tearing me away from all that made me happy, my work, my lover, and compelling me to work with the darkness I hate so much?" But how could he know all this? He was an Inquestor, busily engaged in the destruction of worlds and in *makrúgh*, that deadly game of diplomacy and deceit that usually ended with a planet's *falling beyond*.

"Don't be sad, Jenjen. A clan-name is not so bad a thing to possess. With it comes the right to travel to other worlds, to breathe ever new airs and experience new colors of light—"

"But to labor forever in the naming of darknesses!"

"Don't be afraid, Jenjen." He beckoned for her to approach the throne, to come up to him on the gold steps friezed with pteratygers. "A dark wind is blowing through the Inquest now. Do you remember the day we stood together and I showed you darkness after darkness?"

"You said," the memory surfaced suddenly, "there were

four million shades of darkness, and not one of them the true one."

"Yes." Once again she felt his ancient sadness.

"But why do you come back now, after all these years, and pluck me from Essondras? You could have summoned me when I was still a child, still pliable."

"You are not clay, you are not a sequence of lightstrands that I should weave together as I would, but a woman," Elloran said. "And besides, it was only yesterday that I saw you as a child. Since then I have sailed the overcosm to play at *shtezhnat* with Ton Karakaël; when I came back for you, time dilation had affected me, and made twenty years elapse to my single day. . . ."

She knew then how different their worlds were, and she was afraid.

Elloran said, "I understand why you are angry. You thought that you would always be a weaver of bright colors. You're an impulsive woman; you threw yourself into your lightloom . . . but all the time you were fleeing *me*! For when we met in that museum, you did not see me as others see me: a god, immutable, omnipotent. You saw instead the darkness and the grief. You saw a great truth. . . . And this truth is a darkness that once seen can never be escaped. And because you have seen the true darkness . . . you may one day become the greatest of all darkweavers. You must not fear your destiny, Ir Jenjen. Do you understand?"

"No, Lord." But her mind was racing back to her childhood . . . the same eyes of clear gray, compassionate and sad. *How could I have forgotten?* she thought. But of course she had never forgotten. Even tucked in the womblike lightloom, with lattice after lattice of laser brilliance exploding from her fingertips, something had troubled her. Was it dread of this meeting to come that had imbued her work with its much-admired urgency, its fiery fervor? "I do understand," she said suddenly. And looked into his eyes. And felt once more that pity. Why? How could you pity a man who bestrode worlds like a god?

And Elloran said, "I was a child, too, once. Have you ever heard the story of the Rainbow King?"

"Yes, *hokh'Ton*. It is a very famous myth."

"Myth!" And Ton Elloran began to laugh quietly to himself. Sensing that the interview was over, Jenjen slipped away. A steward found her an apartment beside the palace aviary.

She stood around feeling helpless. The apartment was the largest she had ever seen, although the steward kept apologizing for it. The floors and walls contoured themselves to accommodate her whenever she leaned on them; when she clapped her hands, a lightloom descended from the ceiling; it was a model she had never seen, with a lightfont of ten billion colors. The steward was already bowing to her and backing away toward the displacement plate, but she beckoned him to stay.

"Steward—"

"Yes, Lady?"

"What are my duties? I see no equipment for weaving darknesses. . . . On the contrary, they've furnished me with a luxurious lightloom. Am I supposed to create something on it?"

"No instructions, Lady. But . . . when you get to know Ton Elloran better . . . you'll realize that you're not going to be commanded to create anything before you're ready."

"I don't know about that! It was pretty highhanded, the way he brought me here."

"Highhanded! Lady, he's an *Inquestor.* He can do anything he wants. He's showing you unheard of favor. The palace has been buzzing with news about you ever since yesterday."

"Yesterday—"

"Yesterday you were still a little girl, or course. Our time."

"How can I learn more about him?"

"Go on to the Rememberers. Ask for Tash Tievar; he knows everything." And the steward was gone.

She found him, at last, after many days' search. It was a room all walled in white, austere; an old man sat in a hoverchair, asleep. He wore the white robes of the Clan of Tash. A woman, similarly clothed, whispered in his ear. He started; he stared at Jenjen for a long time. She was not surprised; she had learned that this was the art of Rememberers. He studied her, appraising, noting every feature of her, so that he might one day recall it as a remembrance. In turn, she regarded him, waiting.

"Such a labyrinth, Varezhdur! Hm," said the old man. "So you've come at last. You know who I am?"

"Tash Tievar, senior Rememberer," Jenjen said, "here in the palace of Varezhdur."

"Took you long enough to find me. But then, mine is the most hated room in the palace."

"Surely not—"

"I seem so harmless! You were about to say that, weren't you?"

"Yes." But she remembered too how her parents had once reacted, long ago, to the sight of a mere boy in the clan's white robes.

"Listen then. One day, perhaps your world Essondras will *fall beyond* in *makrúgh*, the High Inquestral game of life and death. Well, on every world there is a House of Tash, where adepts are trained for this final contingency. We, the Rememberers. When a world is to be visited by the fire-death, each Inquestor who has participated in the planet's death must take with him one of us. . . . It is we who must remember for him the sounds, the fragrances, the textures of the dead world . . . who must remind him that though he lives in splendor he must not abandon compassion, or he will become less, not more, than human. My world, for instance—"

"It's—"

"Gone, without trace! At least, all civilization has been wiped out from my world. And perhaps the planet itself destroyed! And its people scattered, in their people bins throughout the overcosm, waiting for a new world to open up! Oh, my dead world! Its cities buried beneath child-created mountains, its seas poisoned by the childsoldiers' breath!"

"And he keeps you here as a macabre memento of it!" More than ever she wanted to leave, to renounce her clan-name, to return to Zalo and the backworld. "I suppose that's what *I* am too—something to remind him of a cute conversation he once had twenty years ago!"

"No. He needs us, Jenjen. At first I was angry too. I too felt—plucked away, helpless, resentful. For all you know, by the time you go home your whole world will have been destroyed, the people you once loved dead for centuries . . . for when we sail the overcosm the real universe ages in a few instants. Soon Varezhdur itself will depart Essondras's orbit and dart from star to star like a tadpole. One of the hardest lessons

I learned—I, a Rememberer—was forgetting! But you are so much younger than I. And more resilient than you think you are."

Jenjen sat down on the floorfur, which wrapped itself about her knees. "They tell me," she said, "that you know many stories."

"Yes. We're not just the Inquest's slaves, you know. We have our own traditions. For the Inquestors, tales of long-dead planets; for ourselves. . . . We tell stories about the Inquest: its glories, its spectacles, its dark secrets. Ton Elloran has given you the freedom of the palace. You will wander the labyrinth as you please; you will see many beautiful and cruel things in the universe of the powerful. Adepts such as I will fashion remembrances; you will doubtless find ways of weaving them into tapestries of light. And in time you will come to understand much, and there will be stories that you alone can tell. . . ."

"Once, when I was a child, I met the Inquestor in a place dedicated to darkness."

"Ton Elloran too was a child once—"

"So he told me. I could not believe it. He seems old as the stars themselves."

"Listen, child. I will tell you a tale of Ton Elloran and the great musician Sajit, when they were both children. You know the story of the Rainbow King?"

"It is a famous myth."

"Let me tell you what *really* happened."

And so it was that Tash Tievar, master of remembrances, began to tell Ir Jenjen tales of the Inquest. No longer were they ancient myths and dusty fables. Such was the Rememberer's art that the gods of Jenjen's childhood took on flesh. And at last she would come to understand the great grief she had seen so long ago in the eyes of the Inquestor . . . and she would begin her journey towards the darkness and the light that lay beyond it, and she would know the wisdom of Elloran's summoning.

Tievar spoke of a childsoldier and a burning starship. . . .

# 5

# The Story of the Rainbow King

No use thinking of glory. No use thinking of distant star-ships that seemed to stand still against the starlight. No use thinking of a girl's charred body, gift-wrapped in ribbons of warped steel.

Sajit turned his back on the fire and shook off the memories. There wasn't any time. The flames were gaining on him, hissing down the corridors of the doomed starship.

He ran. His fursoles pattered on the mirror metal, the only sound save the fire's whisper in this worm's gullet of a corridor that twisted away from the ship's heart, bypassing the weaponry levels and the living levels and the observing levels. It wasn't meant for people—only for maintenance equipment. Ahead, reflected in the curve of the wall, the fire behind him danced. He'd found the corridor his first day aboard the ship. He hadn't told anyone. Sajit was a survivor.

He had grown up fleecing the *dorezdas* in the junglestreets of Aírang on his homeworld and he'd fought his way through two terrible wars.

*I can't die now!* he was thinking. *I've already been through too much!* He was twelve years old.

He flung his cloak behind him, sacrificing it to the fire. *That'll slow you down!* He threw out all his weapons, until he was down to the bundle he had packed away in case it ever came to this. If it would only stop to consume the cloak and the weapons and not catch up with him—

And there was the hatch he wanted. He shoved at it with his whole body—he had not much weight to put into it—but it wouldn't give. It was too cramped to make a dash and crash it open, and he felt the heat behind him, he felt his blood ready to boil and the sweat streaming—

An idea. He turned his laser-irises on the doorway and sizzled the metal with a lethal stare, then wriggled through a stomach-wrenching gravity reversal—

And landed lightly on his feet. He was where he hoped he'd be. The launch hangar of the Inquestors. A wide ledge that extended outside the delphinoid starship, protected from empty space by an insubstantial dome of force. Above, the stars shone. Straight ahead, so far that they looked like toys, three dead ships floated, three silver amulets hanging in the blackness. When he craned his neck he could see how the upper levels of his own ship had been pried open and shredded by the attackers. Whoever they had been. It had been one side or the other, waiting in ambush at the transdimensional nexus as they burst blind out of the overcosm into realspace. It didn't matter who it had been. The Inquestral mission had failed.

And here on the hangar, just as Sajit had hoped, shiny-new and sleek as a wild silverdove, was the Inquestral landing craft.

If things had gone as they should have this lander would have come to Ymvyrsh and the Inquestors would have stood in the parched fields of the razed planet, tall, their shimmercloaks blushing in the wind, their faces serene, old, unruffled as they dictated the terms of the Inquestral peace upon the warring worlds of Ymvyrsh and Ainverell. Sajit could see the scene now: the Inquestors standing, calm and compassionate, while husks of old buildings fell burning to the ground. . . . It was not to be. No Inquestor would come to Ymvyrsh now. Only a young boy who wanted to be alive.

He clutched his bundle under his arm. It seemed thinner than before, and something metal was digging into his side, cold. The starlight, unseen for the three subjective months of overcosm travel, was strange to him; here too there was coldness. He moved quickly to the landing craft, shivering. He didn't want to admit the cold was fear.

He found the entrance and opened it, sliding his slight body easily down the shaft. There were two rooms, like pears joined at the stems: the one he was in was wide enough for two or three adults. Half-light, bluish and diffuse, played over shelves of provisions. That was good—he'd have to learn to operate the lander somehow, he'd have to find Ymvyrsh—he'd need food.

*I'll find Ymvyrsh somehow. A world's a world, even when*

*it's at war,* he thought fiercely. *I'll sing for a few cheap meals, or if they're too poor I'll find something less honorable to do. . . .*

He crept towards the passageway that led to the control room. If the lander was at all like a standard short-range vessel, there would be no problem, but—

The lander lurched to life! Sajit was jerked forward into the control cabin. He felt violent pain in his foot and wondered distantly whether it was broken. For a moment he closed his eyes. The lander had been on automatic! His plans were ruined!

When he opened his eyes he saw a swath of blue fur that rippled, the hem of a robe that shimmered pink against the dark blue. . . .

"Lord Inquestor!" he whispered, knowing he must be in the presence of one of the rulers of the Dispersal of Man. He did not dare look up. When he tried to move his foot, pain stabbed him. He had to say something. "I am Sajit-without-a-clan, born on the world Alykh and three years a soldier of the Inquest," he said, keeping his eyes fixed on the hem of the shimmercloak. The shimmercloak sparkled, a million jewel facets in the living cloth. He was almost hypnotized by it.

The Inquestor said nothing for a long time. When he spoke it was not the authoritative voice of an old man. It was a young voice, a voice that struggled to master terror. "I am," said the Inquestor, "Ton Elloran n'Taanyel Tath, Inquestor-that-is-to-be."

Sajit looked up. Above the sparkling raiment was the face of a boy, perhaps only a year or two older than Sajit himself. "You're a boy!" Sajit burst out, and then bit his tongue.

"Yes," Ton Elloran said. "Get up, Sajit-without-a-clan."

"I've hurt my foot."

The other boy knelt down beside him and half-lifted him so that he was leaning against the wall of the passageway. Sajit saw into his eyes then; but he could not understand anything that he saw. They were clear, gray eyes that seemed to mask a terrible loneliness. They did not speak for a while, and the lander sped on, steadying itself, knowing its destination.

Elloran said, "I have to try to finish the mission, you know."

"Why, Inquestor, why?"

"When we saw that the ship was doomed, the Inquestors

in command chose me, the youngest, to survive. They decided that they had lived long enough. . . ."

"And how will you do what four Inquestral warships couldn't do?" Sajit said softly.

"We will land on Ymvyrsh. I am an Inquestor and inviolate. We will find the Inquestor who rules on Ymvyrsh, make arrangements for the war to end, and I shall return to Uran s'Varek. The Inquestor-in-power will surely have access to a tachyon bubble system. . . ." He spoke, Sajit noticed, like a textbook. Didn't he know how impossible it would be? You couldn't go charging down to a war-torn planet and make peace. "I know what you're thinking!" he went on, sounding very young suddenly. "You think you should stop me or something. You think I can't do this. You didn't exactly have this in mind when you sneaked aboard this lander instead of dying with the ship as was your duty."

"I didn't come this far to die."

"Why don't you kill me, then? Then you wouldn't be troubled by a meddlesome apprentice Inquestor—"

"Ton Elloran, I didn't say anything about killing—"

"Listen. You are a soldierchild of the Inquest, aren't you? You have laser-irises, implanted at the time of your induction, and you could kill me at any time with a glance and a subvocalized command. The ship is yours for the taking."

Sajit looked at the older boy, and he knew he couldn't kill him. You just *couldn't* kill an Inquestor. It went against everything—

"I told you, Sajit-without-a-clan. To harm me would be to harm yourself. Even a rebel like you can't resist a truth so deeply ingrained. I *can* perform the Inquest's mission on Ymvyrsh. . . ." Elloran looked away, then got up and clapped his hands, blanking the metal wallshields so that the stars shone on them. It must be at least a day's journey to the star Darronderrik around which Ymvyrsh and Ainverell revolved, twin worlds locked in a slow pavane around the same star, in one orbit . . . yet never at peace. Sajit could make nothing of the starstream; he was not one of those to whom the night sky sang. He liked cities. Blackness and stars meant bleakness and war to him.

His foot still ached. He struggled to get up, propped himself against the wall of the linking corridor, and thought: *So much for my clever plans.*

He clenched back a tear. When he saw that Ton Elloran was not looking, he let that tear trickle down, tickling his cheek. Then he tried to stand up and winced with pain and the bundle he'd wedged under his arm slipped and clattered to the floor, spilling its contents—

Elloran turned, startled.

. . . untuned strings jangling . . . a sussurant sigh . . . a silvery breathy keening . . . glint of metal and polished wood and intagliate agates . . .

Sajit said, half to himself, "At least I haven't lost everything from my past, then."

He picked it up—the whisperlyre, the only thing that linked him to his homeworld and to his nameless father—and cradled it in his arms. Sounds, random, an almost-harmony, cascaded; but he did not play.

For no song came.

The two of them traveled on for two or three sleeps, not speaking much, distrusting one another. Through the crystalline shipwalls shone unrecognized stars; and the star Darronderrik grew from pinpoint to topaz cabochon, fireball-brilliant. Sajit slept mostly. But dreams of the past haunted him, and to sleep was as restive as to stay awake. . . .

. . . Aírang, a city of mazes within mazes, chief city of the pleasure-world Alykh, where tall spires stung the violet sky, where the tired and the rootless and the jaded came and bought love and release, where they rode the varigrav coasters until they had purged all their pain, where they came for a sleep or two and were wooed by the splendor and awed by the glitter and did not see the hovels of those who called this their homeworld; that was Alykh. A tapestry stitched with jewels and seamed with sewers. . . .

. . . hurt old eyes that could not quite meet his own, old eyes in a fresh new face, the eternal fresh face of the Alykhish pleasure girl, sung of in a thousand songs, perfect face unlined by worry, face replaced each summer for the new season before the blemishes could come . . . the voice: *Leave, Sajit! Leave before I don't have the heart to kick you out. Take the whisperlyre. Take anything you want. I don't want anything left here to remind me of the* dorezda *who spawned you in my womb* . . . tall figure of a man waiting. A new *dorezda*.

. . . growing up in a small room with moulting walls, the

displacement plate at the street corner was defunct and overgrown with weeds and you had to walk the four klomets to the streets of the strutting starmen. . . .

. . . and the whisperlyre. There was a metal-wood harpframe that supported the seven strings for plucking and the sixty-eight sympathetic strings; and in the body of the frame were the thousands of tiny whisperpassages where the ionized wind rushed and re-echoed and transmuted the ping of the string into lonely mountains' wuthering and surf-shatter of abandoned shores, the wind that gave the whisperlyre its name, that drew its energy from the heat of your body, so that when you threw all your passion and all your heart into the song you would become cold, like a statue, like a corpse. . . .

. . . *Please sir, take me with you, you're a singer like my father. I'm an orphan sir, help. . . .*

. . . beaten and abandoned amid the fireshows of Ont. . . .

. . . voice of the tall Inquestor, grip of the restraint-field— *Don't run anymore, boy. It's over. You'll go to the wars like every other child, and if you return you'll be initiated into a profession and perhaps your singing will stand you in good stead and you'll find a good musicians' clan even. . . .*

. . . fingertingle of a taut string, shimmerfade of an afterwhisper, a dying strain, fading, fading. . . .

Sajit woke, clutching his whisperlyre. He wrapped his arms around it, recharging it, feeling warmth steal away from his body. He was about to play—

"Come quickly!" the voice of Ton Elloran from the other room.

Sajit limped through the passageway. A planet shone in the darkness, blue-green wisp-streaked with white. ". . . Ymvyrsh?"

"You don't understand. Ainverell, Ainverell—it's gone!"

"What do you mean?"

"There's only one planet here when there should be two!"

Sajit went up to the other boy. He touched the edge of an untouchable loneliness and shied away. Elloran said, "It is the right place. The lander doesn't make mistakes. Ainverell has been obliterated."

"Then the war is over," said Sajit, trying to sound encouraging.

"The background radiation level is low. Ainverell was destroyed a long time ago. Perhaps even a century." Suddenly, Elloran seemed a child, crying for sympathy: "What shall I do now?"

But before Sajit could comfort him he had remembered his place. He had drawn himself up tall, the way Sajit supposed an Inquestor must always be. Sajit said, "Is there nothing in your training to cover this?"

"I'm only an Inquestor-to-be," said Elloran. "Ton Alkamathdes, my old teacher, would have known. He was half a millennium old or more, and a master utopia hunter. . . ."

"What's a utopia hunter?"

"One who exposes the flaws in utopias, who compassionately brings change and vitality to worlds that think they have found perfection," said Elloran. He seemed to be reciting.

"It sounds wrong."

"What would you know, Sajit-without-a-clan?" Elloran turned to watch the planet, which was growing little by little in the blackness. Then, almost to himself, he said, "Alkamathdes was assigned to rule over Ymvyrsh just before I left on this expedition. . . . But surely he is Kingling here no longer. We were six subjective months on this journey; in realtime, a century has passed. . . . He has long moved on to other things, I think."

They stood in silence for some moments, while the planet loomed nearer. . . .

"Ton Elloran," said Sajit, "if Ainverell has been dead for so long, why were we attacked? Who was it who attacked us?"

"I don't know!" Elloran shouted. "What do you think I am, the galactic thinkhive on Uran s'Varek with all the answers? Listen, soldier boy: We're going down on the planet. We're going to find the people in power, locate the Inquestral tachyon bubble system so that I can return to Uran s'Varek and report on the mission—"

"And what about me? You Inquestors can take your tachyon bubbles and flick across the Dispersal of Man in an attosecond. I have to take my chances with time dilation—"

Elloran said, "The Inquest is compassionate. I will take care of you."

"You can't even take care of yourself!" Sajit said hotly. "You're going to land us conspicuously in the middle of enemies and you're going to get us all killed!"

"What is a life to the Inquest?" said Elloran, but his voice quavered. Sajit thought he saw tears, and he was appalled, that an Inquestor should show uncertainty. He turned his back on Elloran and returned to the other chamber.

Later he tried to play the whisperlyre, but could not find more than a few notes. He came out to watch the stars, and to watch Elloran as he stood motionless in the control room. The planet was much nearer now; it filled half the sky. Sajit found no comfort in the thought of earth under his feet. For him every planetfall had always been a scramble to survive. . . .

*If it were just me,* he thought, *I'd make it, somehow. But with him here, not knowing the first thing about survival—*

And then he remembered that he had thought he had seen tears in the Inquestor's eyes, and he thought, *If an Inquestor can weep, anything can happen. The speed of light can change. We could find a utopia down there.*

Ton Elloran n'Taanyel Tath clapped his hands three times, opaquing the shipwalls, putting a shield of mirror metal between them and the threatening planet.

The lander circled the planet, trying to find the cities. There should have been cities, certainly; when Elloran summoned up holoimages from the lander's memory, they saw cities with resounding names: Tomástris, Dieker, Zhimward, d'Aíhvad, Ang z'Darronderrik, city of the sun, the capital city Undébarang, where floating avenues radiated from a hill-high obeslisk carved from a flawless amethyst that had been grown in the Crystallizing Sea on Uran s'Varek itself. . . . They were all gone, these cities, gone without trace.

The lander's orbit spiraled nearer; they burst through the cloudveil of Ymvyrsh and flew over the land. There were fields that checkered the plains with brown and yellow squares. There were villages, all clustered along narrow roads. Here and there were jade meadows or a crystal serpent of a stream. . . .

The scenery did not change, from one end of the one major land mass to the other. Where Undébarang should have been there was only more of the pastoral landscape. It stretched to the foothills of a mountain range, mist-blue in the distance. And the sky—

Once before had Sajit heard of a sky this blue, and that was in a song about old Earth, before the Dispersal of Man. It was blue and jewel-clear and pure as a ringing octave.

"Do you think—?" he whispered.

"No," Elloran replied coldly. "Earth was never like in the songs. You should know better than that. But no doubt about it . . . this world is suspicious. It's the same from shore to shore, and no culture is really like that. It feels . . . *set up.*"

"But beautiful."

"I fear it," Elloran said. And then he stopped himself short, and Sajit could tell he was angry at himself for having let down his guard in front of a mere clanless soldierchild. . . .

The Inquestor chose a field that lay about where the center of Undébarang should have been, about half a klomet from a cluster of village huts that bordered a winding lane. Softly the lander came down, and they stepped down from the craft . . . Sajit found the gravity quite light; he hardly had to limp at all.

He took a few steps out in the bouncy-soft grass, turned, faced the wall of mist-high mountains, and caught his breath. He saw the rainbows.

They arched out from a point somewhere behind the highest peak, resolving from the mists like cadences of a song; they transsected the sky, radiating from a single, hidden, cloud-high point. . . . They were frozen songs. Chords woven from singing strands of meadow, ruby, tangerine, sky, lapis, topaz, plum . . . peacock-painted bridges, jewel-candy-arcing, heart-stoppingly still.

Sajit felt very happy. He turned to Ton Elloran, smiling, but he saw no responsive smile. "It's so beautiful!" he cried out.

"Too beautiful," said Elloran curtly. "Let's go into the village now."

"What about provisions?"

"I am an Inquestor. They will provide."

Dismay flooded Sajit. "What do you mean, Ton Elloran? Are you mad or something? Here we are on a strange planet with a lander stuffed with food and we're going to walk into an alien village without anything to eat?"

"*I know what I'm doing!*" Elloran had begun walking resolutely down a twisty-curving path half-buried in the tall grass, his shimmercloak flapping and making sparks on the emerald green.

"Powers of powers!" Sajit cried. "Don't you care about your own skin, Inquestor?" *Just like a damned* dorezda, *think-*

*ing he's so important, wouldn't last five minutes on Airang.* He climbed back into the lander, found the provisions shelves, scooped out a couple of handfuls of concentrate packages, found his old bundle on the floor and stuffed it with them. He looked around furtively—street children's habits died hard— and the closeness of the lander's interior oppressed him after the outside. It was then that he realized that Ymvyrsh was a very beautiful world. *And comforting,* thought the boy, hefting the weight onto his shoulder and making for the exit. As he left he glanced at the unplayed whisperlyre, abandoned on the mirror metal floor. It was like a recurring dream.

Half-reluctant, he picked it up. The warmth fled from his fingers.

He ran out into the sunshine. Even the whisperlyre felt less cold. He turned to gasp at the rainbows crisscrossing the blue distance, and then hurried after Ton Elloran . . . and caught up with him, breathless.

"I see you wish to throw in your lot with me," said Elloran looking straight ahead. "That would be wiser."

"No, but I can't just leave you to walk into a—"

Ton Elloran cut him short with a look. They walked on. Presently they came to another field with children at play, pre-warrior aged, six or seven years old. They were running like wild animals; there was shrill laughter in the sunlight. Sajit saw that they never frowned at all. Sajit felt as though a song were about to burst from him, as he had often felt when he was first learning the old songs, a warmth welling up inside. But he only said, "The war is over." It was a strange thought.

They were approaching the cluster of houses. A few peasants walked by, glancing only cursorily at the two of them; again Sajit saw that they were always smiling—a little vac-uously perhaps—in the manner of people who are not used to being stingy with their laughter. . . .

Sajit remembered the streets of his homeworld and was envious.

Elloran was becoming more and more impatient. Finally he went up to a man and stopped him. His blue eyes, gleaming in a wizened face crowned with white wreath-like hair, exuded kindness. He smelled of old earth: pungent, heady, warm.

Elloran said, formally, "I am Ton Elloran n'Taanyel Tath, son of Prince Taanyel, Inquestor-who-is-to-be. I am here to seek the Inquestors-that-rule, to end the war between

Ymvyrsh and Ainverell"—his voice broke a little—"and to bring you peace. Will you give me hospitality and information?"

The old man looked at both of them amusedly and said, finally, "My house is yours, of course. We don't see many strangers here; don't rightly know what an 'Inquestor' may be, but you seem important-looking enough. Be no war here, though. We and the next village are at peace a hundred years, more than that."

*Maybe he's right,* Sajit thought. *Maybe he can automatically get us food because he looks important—or something.* But he clutched his parcel tighter, even though reason told him that this wasn't Aïrang.

But Elloran seemed annoyed. He was talking to the peasant as though he were an imbecile: "Then who rules here, if you don't know what an Inquestor is?"

The man said (without ever losing his jovial countenance), "Rainbow King rules here, of course. Lookit, over the mountain tops."

Sajit stole a glance at the distant mountains behind him, with the color-arcs poised above the mistveils.

"Yes," the old man went on, "Rainbow King. Come now, guests, and eat. Journey from next village made you weary, I'm sure."

"Wait!" Elloran shouted after the man, who had already begun to stride towards one of the squat huts. "Who is the Rainbow King? Is he an Inquestor?" But the man was out of earshot.

Sajit said, "It's a beautiful world. Why ask questions, Elloran?"

"You stupid soldierchild," Elloran said impatiently. His anger seemed so out of place here. "If this is really the way things are, why were we attacked? Who's trying to fool whom? What would Ton Alkamathdes have done? I wish I had his guidance—"

The warmth of this world stirred in Sajit again. He remembered the smiles everywhere, the jewel-glitter of rainbows, the laughter . . . He wanted to embrace the world. He wanted to forget Alykh and Ont and a dozen stinking worlds and the endless overcosm wars. "I don't care what you say! I only know what I see, and it's—it's a utopia!"

"That's just what I'm afraid of," said the boy Inquestor, and Sajit had never seen anyone look so worn with grief.

Sajit liked the house at once—it was so different from the one on Aírang, the peeling, dust-thick house with the painful memories. This one had four detached L-shaped structures surrounding a central atrium, plain whitewashed walls immaculately clean, leaning roofs neatly thatched, and the air faintly citrus-fragrant. They were shown to their room—one of the four structures—wide windows overlooking a dale where primitive autoplows moved ponderously, working the land. . . . Then they went into the atrium, and sat on the furry floor, which curved to support the contours of their bodies.

"Forgive me," the old man said, "if my family and I do not eat with you. We have already eaten, of course."

The family had gathered: a wife and two husbands, two children, drably dressed but brightly smiling; they seemed normal, dignified. The children rushed out to play, the wife and husbands left, and the old man departed after a moment and reentered with food: a tray of fresh *shorreth* cheese, baked *yunaki* with the plumage still showing in a vivid blue ring around the drumsticks. . . .

"You see," Elloran said, "wherever one goes, they still cannot deny food to an Inquestor." Sajit began to feel foolish for having dragged the concentrate packages along. The world of the Inquestors was clearly not the world of the streets.

Sajit looked at the old man, whose benign expression seemed unchanged, and said, "And where is it that your Rainbow King dwells?" He thought it must be some kind of folk belief.

"In the mountains. Far. Where all the rainbows meet, stranger. Dangerous, you can't go there—be pteratygers in the mountain peaks. . . ."

"Oh, come on, there are no pteratygers on this planet. Only on Uran s'Varek—" Elloran stopped short. He seemed to be thinking, very hard. Then, abruptly, "Do you never stop smiling, powers of powers?"

"Why should we? Everyone happy here."

Sajit laughed. "Why shouldn't this planet be a utopia, Ton Elloran?" He reached for a *yunaki* drumstick—

The old man seized the tray; without another word he left the atrium and entered one of the L-shaped rooms.

"What's this?" Sajit cried angrily. "What have we done to make you take away the food?"

There was no answer. Darkness was falling, a little at a time; through one of the four passages out of the atrium they could see the rainbows still, vivid in the graying sky. Sajit saw that Elloran had become very pale; something was in him that Sajit could not touch. The air chilled a little. He was hungry.

"Well, you should at least thank me for having the presence of mind to bring these." He shook out the bundle. Elloran's hand shot out and grabbed one of the packets. *I've been selfish*, thought Sajit. *This boy's been starving and he's too proud or too preoccupied to say a word.* And now he saw the rainbows stained with the crimson of the twilight, and he wondered what kept them in place. Surely they were not natural.

Elloran said, "They don't eat. But they have food, and they *pretend*."

"Let's go to the room now." Sajit got up; tiredness weighed him down for the first time, and he felt the limp a little. He bundled together the packets and the whisperlyre—they had enough food for a couple of days, if they didn't gorge themselves. They turned to go into the guestroom—

"Look!" Sajit heard Elloran's urgent whisper. "Look, through the entry opposite the mountains. . . . Do you remember the autoplows, digging up the field in the valley down there?"

Sajit nodded. They crept up to the entry and stood there a moment. A moon had arisen, hauntingly like the old descriptions of the moons of old earth, and the fields were eerie black, flecked with mirror metal. . . .

"Look carefully!" said Elloran. "Do you see it?"

Sajit strained. He saw the autoplows move into a pool of moonlight. They were not plowing now. They were going back, smoothing out the earth, patting it down, restoring it. Sajit could tell that by morning there would have been no progress. It was all an illusion. Chill claws of fear clutched him. "What'll we do?" he cried, too loud, stifling himself too late.

"We wake them up. We get answers. We find out who is doing this—"

"But—"

Elloran had already stalked toward the L-shaped structure into which they had seen the stranger go before. He banged the doorstud with his fist. It shot open—

"Wake up, in the Inquest's name!" he shouted. His voice sounded shrill and small in the huge silence. Moonlight fell into the room. Blocking the broad stripe of light was the peasant, his face a silhouette. "What's the meaning of these illusions?" Elloran screamed at him. "Who are you trying to delude? Why was this world made to look like a utopia? Why did you destroy the Inquestral mission ship? Who is the ruler of this planet?"

The old man didn't answer. He seemed frozen in place.

Sajit looked deep into his eyes and saw only mirror-blankness. A light wind from the open window played with the old man's hair, but the face never quivered. . . . Sajit shrank back and found himself backing into the woman. She didn't move. The whole family was gathered in this room like disused dolls on a shelf. . . .

Sajit shivered. He had never feared the *dorezdas* with their brash talk and their gullibility, or being abandoned on strange inhospitable planets, or warships streaking through the overcosm. . . . He turned to Elloran. "What'll we do?"

Elloran said, "I must complete my mission."

Sajit followed him out of the room and into the atrium; away from the room and the strangely still family he could breathe a little easier. Elloran flicked his head towards the mountains, now a black wall blocking the starlight and buttressed by the rainbows, drained of their jewel colors now, ghost-bridges arcing in the dark. . . .

"We can't go there!" Sajit said. "That's probably the most dangerous place on this planet. After what we've seen I'm ready to believe there are pteratygers in the mountains—"

"Aren't you interested in knowing how millions of people, hundreds of cities, have vanished without a trace?" said Elloran. "I know I don't have to bring peace to this world anymore. It is utterly at peace. It can't be anything else, since everything is returned to its starting point every morning. But now"—and Sajit was startled by the boy's intensity—"I must hunt down this utopia, Sajit-without-a-clan. Ton Alkamathdes told me that man must dream of utopias always—but to imagine that one has *achieved* that goal . . . is to deny life. The Inquest is built upon this one axiom, Sajit. The quest for the eternal dream, the quest and the never finding, are the heart of the Dispersal of Man. . . ." His eyes were closed and he seemed to be quoting.

"Well," said Sajit, "Let's find the lander then."

"We can get some food from there, enough for the journey."

They had begun walking now, and the house was a hundred meters or so behind them, and the mountains seemed no nearer. This was a world without displacement plates. . . . People walked everywhere.

"Where is the lander?" Sajit said. "I can't see it, it's too dark."

"It's gone!"

The grass was flattened for about twenty meters square. Moonlight silvered the grass-strands. "This world doesn't have any transportation system," said Sajit. "You'll have to go back to the village—"

Elloran had begun walking in the direction of the mountains. The grass seemed to swallow him up. Amid the tall blackness the shimmercloak rippled. "Come back!" Sajit screamed. "You're crazy!"

The boy walked on quickly, not looking back. His eyes were fixed on the mountains. If he wanted to find the Rainbow King it would have to be on foot, all the way. "I won't go," Sajit was yelling into the air. "My foot hurts and you don't know what you're getting into. I don't believe in your philosophies. I just want to eat and sleep!" He limped after Elloran. The path was just wide enough for a boy to wedge himself through soft grass-stalks. "I don't care about your mission, I just care about me! There must be someplace here that isn't full of—" He remembered the room in the moonlight with the unmoving, deathlike family.

Elloran stopped in the distance. "You're right. It's my mission, not yours." He turned his back to Sajit and went on walking.

"Wait!" Sajit thrust hard against the ground, ignoring the limp. Pain lanced his foot as he caught up with Elloran. "I've got all the food."

"Come on."

They went on walking for an eternity. Every step stabbed his foot; he was dizzy from sleeplessness. He heard Elloran muttering, "There must be a displacement plate somewhere, this is supposed to have been one of the most industrialized planets in this area, they must have been industrialized enough to blow up Ainverell. . . ."

"And someone must have disposed of the lander, somehow," said Sajit, out of breath. "It's incomprehensible."

Ahead were the mountains with the rainbows drained of color. They trudged on. Sajit was so tired. Elloran never slacked. *Why am I following him?* Sajit thought. *Just because he wears a shimmercloak? Just through force of habit?* Ahead of him, only the shimmercloak shone, the pink blushing against the dark blue, strangely gaudy in the darkness. The stars of the Dispersal shone on them; the sky was star-thick except for where the ghosts of rainbows made arches of mist. *We'll never make it anywhere*, Sajit thought. He wondered what death would feel like.

After a while—a couple of klomets, it felt like—the pain in his foot was continual. The grass had thinned and the ground was stubbled with sharp stones. Sajit stumbled, whispered, "Powers of powers! I can't go on. Just leave me here—tomorrow I'll be well enough to forage for myself. . . ."

Elloran looked at him, expressionless. "No. We'll rest."

"What about your infernal mission?"

"The Inquest is compassionate."

"I hope the Inquest burns!" he shouted, unable to control himself. "Can't you act like a human being instead of a servocorpse?"

"The Inquest is compassionate . . . and I do not want to go on alone," Elloran said, looking away. Sajit felt the boy's loneliness and was moved.

They stumbled on for a few more meters. The ground became very smooth—they could not really see what the terrain was—and when they sat down it contoured itself to their bodies. They must be in the foundations of an old house, long since swept away in whatever metamorphosis it was that had changed Ymvyrsh from a war-torn world to an illusion of paradise. The moon had set, and they could hardly see their goal ahead of them but for the jagged eclipsing of the starfield, the serated black horizon.

"Do you want some food?" Sajit was emptying the bundle.

. . . jangle of wirestrings, whisper of shadow spirits. . . .

"You still have that thing?" Elloran said, reaching for one of the packets.

Sajit picked it up. His fingers felt cold immediately. Cold, so cold . . . for the whisperlyre was powered by heat from his body, and the more passionate the song, the colder became the singer. It was thus that musicians were taught the power of their emotions.

Instinctively he clutched the whisperlyre to his thin chest. He felt the warmth drain from his body. The strings were like siphoning ice. He snatched away his hand and felt the heat ooze back. But no. The way to beauty was through darkness. That was what the strange *dorezda* had told him, the one who had left him the whisperlyre. He wedged the lyre firmly in his arms, against his heart, charging it with the heat of racing blood and the energy of his life's pumping. A burst of dissonance. He plucked a few notes, touched the tuning studs to find the *pelog* mode of the ancients. . . . The jangle resolved into rainbow resonance misted with sighs. . . .

A song surfaced, fully crystallized—the first song he had ever learnt from the *dorezda* who had taken him off planet and then dumped him on Ont like an old whisperlyre that has lost all its music. . . .

> *eih! asheverain am-planzhet ka dhand-erúden,*
> *eih! eskrendai: pu eyáh chitarans hyemadh. . . .*
>
> *ai: when man dispersed we wept for the dead earth;*
> *ai, we cried: where is the homeworld of the heart?*

At first he was thinking as he sang, *I shouldn't do this in front of an Inquestor who has probably heard all the best singers in the Dispersal, who don't run out of breath in the wrong places*, and he didn't pay much attention, so his voice cracked easily. It was a breathy, impure, poignant voice with little conscious artistry. After a while he was able to ignore his companion and to sing only for himself—not the way he used to sing, eyeing the purses of passing strangers—and it was beautiful in the alien night, and full of pain.

Elloran was saying, "You could be good, if you were trained. Didn't the Inquestors see to it?"

"I ran away," Sajit said testily. He was surprised that Elloran had been listening to him. Elloran looked away, avoiding conflict. The semi-sentient shimmercloak shone in the pastels that even Sajit knew meant *safety, pure air, healthful environment*. The song had frozen Sajit's chest, and the breeze made him shiver. Elloran said, "Yes—the homeworld of the heart. That's what this planet feels like, you know. My shimmercloak feels it. The meadows. The mountains."

"Just words, Inquestor." He had never met anyone who really thought about the words of songs. . . .

"It's a cruel, grotesque parody of a utopia," he heard Elloran say. "It could be a test. Maybe two Grand Inquestors are playing *makrúgh* and they have a wager on me." Sajit didn't really listen; Elloran often talked about things he couln't visualize. . . . Grand Inquestors. Or Uran s'Varek, a planet *full* of Inquestors. Louder, Elloran said, "Do you think we'll ever find it?"

"What?" Sajit's eyelids were heavy and he didn't feel like talking.

"The 'homeworld of the heart', *chítarans hyemadh* in the hightongue."

"Who's looking?" murmured Sajit through his tiredness. "A twenty-thousand-year-old song that beggar boys sing. . . ."

"Look at the trouble they've gone to, to create this place!" Elloran's voice was intense. "*And I have to destroy it*. Without vindictiveness. Only with compassion. If you were an Inquestor you would understand these things, soldier boy."

"Don't brood," Sajit snapped. More kindly, he said, "Go to sleep." He let the whisperlyre slip from his arms and the warmth ooze back into them. The breeze played over him. *I scolded an Inquestor!* he thought suddenly. But he wasn't alarmed. He felt almost happy. Perhaps it was the certainty of hopelessness. The soft wind played like an afterwhisper, resolving the dissonance of the day's terror.

They each took up a corner of the floor space, as far as possible from one another, each treasuring his aloneness.

In the morning, under a dazzling sun, they scratched at the earth a meter or two from the roofless floor, and they found a displacement plate.

Sun-drenched, the sky glowed celadon blue over the plate; Elloran stood where they imagined its center to be, eyes closed. It was hard to make out the patches of mirror metal under the overgrowth of moss and bramble. Before them, the mountains and their rainbow archways, unchanged from the previous day. Elloran was subvocalizing commands to the displacement field mechanism; Sajit hoped that it still worked.

He moved up to stand beside the young Inquestor, bundle slung over his shoulder. Without warning, an odd dislocation—

They were still in the same place! But no . . . Weren't the mountains a little nearer? He tried to move but found that his feet were tangled in brambles. They'd moved forward perhaps a couple of klomets, and the landscape was almost the same, and everything that had grown over the displacement plate had been flicked in with them.

"Progress!" said Elloran. But he was disappointed when he saw how much further the mountains were. "Let's go on walking. We'll be able to uncover another plate soon if we follow the standard patterns. . . ."

They walked for another four hours or so before they uncovered the next one. It was not a standard system, or else some of the plates had been destroyed by time or design. They stopped for a meal—that was the end of the food—and flicked on to the next plate.

Two days went by. The mountains did seem a little nearer. Hunger gnawed at Sajit, but he did not see the Inquestor tire at all. They slept, or tried to, by night; hunger kept Sajit awake. There was water sometimes, from a stream; but they seemed to have passed the agricultural lands now, and there were no wild animals they could have trapped and eaten even if either of them had known how. *Why am I going along with him?* Sajit kept asking himself. He found no satisfactory answer; and the pain in his stomach blotted out everything, so he stopped asking. Around them, the countryside was beautiful as ever. And ahead—

The rainbows hung, hugging the black mountains, taunting them. Sometimes Sajit would sing, but it made him too cold, and he would stop in mid-phrase. And Ton Elloran never looked back. An Inquestor was not like a normal person, Sajit thought. Even the young ones were different.

On the third day, they found a plate that was scrubbed clean, a dissonant silver island in the green sea. When Elloran leapt onto it he cried, "It clicks well, it understands all the subvocalizations!" Sajit saw that he was smiling, a wan little smile, and then Elloran called out in a big voice, "Rainbow King, your reign is ending! The Inquest has come!" and they flicked out and—

They were standing on a ledge, overlooking a tapestry of green fur quilted with fields and embroidered with wavy rivers, and the wind on their faces was cold, and underneath his tiredness even Sajit felt an exaltation creep up. . . . "These paths are constantly used," he said. "There *is* someone in the mountains, someone at the end of the rainbows. . . ." They scrambled for the next plate, only ten meters away against a bare wall of fine-grained schist, and then burst up into a higher level. There was a rainbow directly overhead, a cartwheel of colors fused into the intense blue sky. He gave a wild yodel of joy, the mountains echoed like a well-tuned whisperlyre, and then they crossed the brief plateau and gazed over an abrupt chasm that cradled an emerald serpent of a valley, raced to the next plate and were over the chasm on a ledge with a sheer rockface ahead—

"There are no more plates," said Sajit. He felt dismay as though awakened from a dream of soaring.

Elloran vanished behind an outcropping; he had gone to find a displacement plate. "It can't just end like this!" Sajit heard him murmur, and then he turned around, his back to the tall wall that blocked their path, and saw—

A swoop of shadow. A momentary eclipse of the sun . . . then a flurry of pink ringed with sunlight, diving, piercing the rainbow. . . .

*A pteratyger!* he thought. His heart leapt at the sight. It swerved out of the firehalo of sunlight, pink feathered wings oustretched, motionless. The fierce feline features were frozen, inconstruable. And then, darting from behind the first one like silverdoves, only impossibly far away, a whole exaltation of them, circling, spiraling behind the leader like links in a gene-strand—

"Elloran, come quickly, there are pteratygers!" Sajit shouted. He turned for a moment and ran toward the boulder where he thought his companion had gone. He stood there, out of breath with joy, and then Elloran was pointing, wild with fear, "Sajit, quickly!"

He whirled round. They were wheeling ahead, near enough to see the glow of ember eyes. And then one broke loose and plummeted towards Sajit, wings erect, claws glistening.

It was so beautiful! He froze for a moment, then the soldier in him thrust loose and he dilated his eyes and glared the laser-glare and subvocalized the secret command and—

*Burst of flame, pink feathers drifting, sunlight. . . .*

—the circle shivered, abruptly reformed as a V-line of angry pteratygers arrowed at his face—

And then stopped again. Reformed in no discernable pattern. Sajit saw they were looking past him now, as though someone had given a command.

He stole a glance behind.

Elloran had emerged completely from behind the rocks. His shimmercloak flapped in the wind. For the first time that day Sajit was sick with hunger.

Elloran said, his voice a whisper in the wind, "You dare to assault me, pteratygers, creatures of the Inquest?"

The pteratygers circled uncertainly; a few broke from the flock and swerved up into the wind, rainbowing over the rainbow. Sajit stared at this boy who did not know the simplest thing about self-preservation and yet could face a pteratyger and say simply *how dare you*. Then one of the creatures swooped swiftly onto the edge, facing them. Sajit stepped back involuntarily.

"My lord—" said the pteratyger. A plaintive, screech-edged voice like a songpipe with a broken reed.

"You are far from Uran s'Varek now," Elloran said. "You serve the Rainbow King?"

"Yes—" The cry pierced the wind and Sajit retreated again.

"Why did you attack us?" asked Elloran.

"The soulless one—he should not have penetrated—beyond the rainbow barriers—the King's domain—must be rendered inoperative—"

"Don't harm him!" Elloran hissed. Sajit flinched.

"I do not understand—you are not the King—yet wear the shimmercloak—I am a mere animal—I obey you—"

"Where is the King?"

"In Irísbarah—the rainbow castle—"

"There are no more displacement plates," said Elloran.

"What's a soulless one?" Sajit blurted out, sick with fear.

"I don't know!" Elloran whispered. Sajit froze. Then Elloran said, "Take me to the Rainbow King!" He spoke firmly but his voice cracked on the last word. The pteratyger did not notice the Inquestor's uncertainty. Sajit stared at its face. The teeth glistened like icicles. Then Elloran said, "No. Take me to—where the soulless ones are rendered inoperative. . . ."

"Powers of powers, Elloran, are you trying to kill me?"

"*Be quiet!*" Sajit was cowed into silence now, the reflex of obedience to the Inquestral word taking over. Even now when they had been through so much. To the pteratyger Elloran said, "I will take the soulless one with me."

"As—you—command—" And then it roared, a thunder with a tinge of meow in it, and came nearer, and crouched down. Elloran mounted without a word, and beckoned for Sajit to get on behind. Sajit took a few steps and caught the creature's foul breath. He could guess what it must feed on. Taking hold of himself, he swung himself over the furry flanks and dug his knees firmly into its body. A heavy purr shook the animal's body. Without warning—

The pteratyger turned to face the sunlight, flapped its wings resoundingly and sprang into the wind—

A moment of burning nausea. And then the pteratyger righted itself and began to climb, hugging the mountainside and slicing through the bitter-cold air. Sajit's terror turned to exhilaration. When he looked behind he saw the mountains they had crossed with such struggling, huge crag-topped tombstones bursting from the lush green earth. They sundered a rainbow, sending shiver-shards of color streaking and swirling. They were only holoimages, then, those rainbows. . . .

"Why does the pteratyger obey you?" Sajit had to shout to hear himself.

"They were created a thousand years ago by an Inquestor on Uran s'Varek, genetically altered from earth animals. They were to be part of an immense game of *makrúgh*, you know. They are impelled to obey the shimmercloak—they aren't very intelligent animals."

"What's a soulless one?"

No answer. The pteratyger roared again, its cry shattering the wind's whine, and they soared. The ripple of the animal's muscles under him made Sajit tingle.

Suddenly Elloran cried, "Sajit, you must sing for me, you must—" and he gripped his arm so tightly that it hurt. The touch unnerved Sajit. Inquestors did not cling to soldier boys like children in need. *He has needs,* Sajit thought, and it was not a comfortable thought.

Gently Sajit freed his arm. He shook his bundle, uncovering the whisperlyre, and the fabric swirled away into a speck. Wedging the whisperlyre firmly between them he sang, very softly, the song about the dream of utopia: *"Eih! asheveraín am- plánzhet ka dhánd-erúden . . ."* He thought: *We're going to get killed now, I'm sure of it.* He threw his heart into the song, and the meaning of the words became vivid for him for the first time . . . *"Shénom na chítarans hyemadhá . . .* We yearn for the heart's homeworld . . . *u áthera tinjéh erúden . . .* where sun touches earth . . . *zirsái yver tembáraxein kreshpáh . . .* and rainbows gird the mountains of darkness . . . *zpúrreh y'Enguéstren tinjéh . . .* and the Inquestor touches the begger child. . . ." The wind gouged the tears from his cheeks.

His arm still burned from Elloran's desperate grip. He understood his companion a little now. For a moment they had touched, like in the song, as though the utopia for which all men yearned had come already. . . . It had not felt like an Inquestor's hand. Only like another boy's.

*If this is a false utopia,* he thought fiercely, *how could this have come about?* And impulsively—with the cold of the whisperlyre gnawing at him like hunger—he reached out to clasp Elloran's hand. Elloran stared straight ahead, so Sajit couldn't see his face; but for a moment he thought he felt a responding warmth. Maybe not. Maybe it was only the flush of flesh against the cold.

They thrust through the stinging wind, upwards, ripping through moist veils of mist, bursting over a sea of cloud, and then Sajit saw what lay ahead. The source of rainbows, set on an island peak in the sea of mist. . . .

Irísbarah. The rainbow castle.

Lucent mother-of-pearl pagodas rose like conch shells wrenched inside out, their spires crisscrossed with arcs of color, crystal-bright against the brilliant blue sky. They soared high against the sun, then dove in a time-frozen glide towards the castle.

"Look!" Elloran pointed to a railinged platform set on top of a high stone column. "It's a receiving station for a tachyon bubble system!"

Sajit could hardly contain himself. "Then there's an Inquestor down there! And—you're an Inquestor, and that means you can arrange to have him send us home, alive, with our bellies full! With a tachyon bubble we can be home today!"

*. . . But there's no home for me,* he remembered suddenly. *Only the war.*

Elloran didn't answer. What was wrong with him? Look at all they'd come through! And now they'd found what they wanted, hadn't they?

They circled the castle a few times. He could almost reach out and touch a pagoda. Then they swooped. He closed his eyes and dreamed of the home he'd never had. But Elloran didn't speak, and Sajit saw that he was in the grip of a terrible tension. "What's the matter with you?" he shouted.

"Don't you understand anything?" Elloran screamed in anguish. "Everything has gone wrong! An *Inquestor* made this world. He made a dead world of utter beauty and he embalmed it so that it would never change. He's a heretic—a false utopian—a madman, and he's down there and he has power to explode a planet to watch the fireworks! An Inquestor gone insane!" He was shaking with rage.

Sajit asked him no more questions. They hovered over a firewall braceleted with menacing, motionless guards, and he heard the relentless clap of the pteratyger's wings and gave up trying to understand.

The pteratyger took them to a ledge under the castle's foundations, artificially smooth. They scrambled down and when Sajit turned to face the clouds he saw the pteratyger already diving through a gap in the forest of rainbow arcs, flashing into the sunlight. His eyes smarted.

"Come on!" Elloran said urgently. Sajit turned to see a cavern with an irising gate that had just responded to Elloran's subvocalized command. . . .

The gate clanged shut. Darkness. A pungent, chemical air. Windlessness. Silence,

"Are you there, Elloran?" he whispered.

The light touch of the Inquestor's hand, brushing his shoulder. Again the feeling of dislocation, of unreality, of being touched by a person of such power. . . .

"Do you see anything?" Elloran said. The voice startled him.

After a while he could make things out. People, hundreds of people. Not breathing. Standing against the walls, shoved into piles, motionless. Elloran moved towards a pile of bodies. He touched one gingerly. Sajit flinched for him.

"They are all dead."

Sajit said nothing; it wasn't sinking in. "Come on." Holding on to each other, they pushed on into the half dark. They found another door.

The light blinded him for a moment.

Then he saw that they were on a railinged balcony that circled a chamber big as a starship, hollowed out of the rock. There were bodies scattered across the mirror metal floor in stacks, like leaf-heaps in autumn: old men, children, women. Machines on silent hovercasters darted from body to body, sorting, spraying, restacking them in other piles. . . .

Across the hall, doll-sized in the distance, more heaps of sprawling bodies, arranged by age, sex, height, physical attributes.

"Let's go down," said Elloran.

They found a stairway spiraling down to the floor. Sajit gazed upward to see the fan-vaulting of stone rainbows that was echoed in the mirror glitter of the floor. Slowly they walked across the room. It must be three hundred meters across. Each step re-echoed as in a temple. Now and then a machine would scuttle up to them, react to Elloran's shimmercloak, and scurry off.

"Servocorpses," whispered Elloran. "A servocorpse factory."

Sajit had seen them before, these dead men reanimated into grisly servants, usually walking a few steps behind one of the *dorezdas*, one with a taste for the exotic, the expensive . . . he already knew what Elloran must be thinking.

"All the people on this planet," he said.

"Yes," said Elloran. "They're all dead."

Another displacement plate—

Valleys of dead bodies, unprocessed, unembalmed, still reeking, suspended in huge storage fields . . .

Rows of blank-eyed children, their limbs wrenched off by war machines, row after row of old men emaciated by warplagues . . .

Cosmetic rooms, skeletons plastifleshed into life . . .

A bridge over another chamber where the dead walked round and round in an eerie procession, smiles soldered on their faces . . .

More displacement plates . . .

They crossed another bridge over a chasm of crematoria, choking with the smoke of incinerating bodies. . . . They passed dressing rooms where dead bodies stood stiffly to be decked out in new tunics bright with rainbow dyes and where metal arms patted their hair into shape and rouged their cheeks. . . . The whole mountain was a labyrinth, level upon level, peopled with the dead.

It was the silence that was most appalling. All the machines moved noiselessly. And the people, beautiful in death, did not breathe. . . . Then they were other rooms where autosurgeons were hard at work, clipping cyberinputs into place, and there were rooms where the dead ones walked in circles, their muscles twitching to the movements of unseen strings, and, finally, rooms where the dead ones—row upon row of them—stood talking to the nothingness: *It's a fine day. The crops are good this season. We welcome you, visitor.*

And they found another room where holoimages monitored the ring of clean displacement plates in the foothills. They watched a fresh servocorpse, a young man laughing as the wind made his fresh clothes flap, appear on the plate, run down toward the village, his face flushed with mechanical joy. . . .

"Somewhere in this mountain," said Elloran, "is a machine that runs everything on the planet. A thinkhive of such power that only an Inquestor could have requisitioned it. . . ."

"At night they turn them off," and Sajit, remembering the room of living statues. *Not-living* statues. "And they don't really eat, but they have food, make-believe food, and make-believe agriculture. . . ."

"The thinkhive is programmed for utopia, is primed with the things men yearn for but cannot have. . . ."

"No wonder the planet seems like old Earth—the lost homeworld of the heart. . . ."

"Myths, myths, Sajit-without-a-clan!" Elloran chided. But without anger. "If old Earth ever was, if the Dispersal of Man ever really took place, do you think it was really a paradise from which we fell? The breaking of joy is the beginning of wisdom."

They watched the monitor for a few moments. It showed the empty fields, the sky, the sun setting.

"Everybody's dead," Elloran said tonelessly.

It was too big for fear. Sajit could feel nothing at all, not even the ache of emptiness. Even his hunger left him.

"The war's over," Elloran went on, "and now I have to go and deal with whoever it is who has made this. . . ."

He moved towards the displacement plate. Sajit knew he was going to go into the castle. "Don't do it!" he cried out. The sound rebounded like a broken whisperlyre. But he knew it was no use. He clutched his instrument and followed Elloran, hypnotized by the boy's eyes, the weary eyes of an old man.

A courtyard. Guards pacing. Sunset. Ahead, a towering portal flanked with iridescent columns, massive gateways inlaid with mother-of-pearl.

Elloran and Sajit stepped off the displacement plate. Guards wheeled, weapons pointing. They were surrounded.

"Laser them," Elloran hissed.

"But—"

"They're already *dead!*" Elloran ducked and Sajit opened his eyes wide and whirled, squeezing the power from them with the subvocalized words—

Sizzle, bisected bodies snapping, thudding.

"The castle." Elloran walked to the gates; they dissolved. They stepped into an Inquestral throne room.

It was a giant's domain. Flagstones, fire-etched marble from Ont, each four or five meters square, stretched out like a *makrúgh* board. Columns topped with firefountains ringed them. Their footsteps shifted and echoed like the voices of ghosts. . . .

"Rainbow King!" Elloran shouted. His own voice returned, echo-rich, taunting. Above them a mobile of rainbows twirled slowly, layer upon layer of them crossing the hall's high ceiling, which glowed all over with soft prism-fringed light. "Rainbow King! Come out and meet your Inquestor and Envoy of the High Inquestors, messenger of Uran s'Varek!" Only echoes. It was as if they were inside a gigantic whisperlyre.

At the end of the hall was an empty throne.

"This is it, then," said Sajit. It was hard not to whisper. "This is the end. There's no one here."

"If we go out now and find the tachyon controls still working, I should be able to get us away from here," Elloran said hoarsely. It seemed so unsatisfying, to come here, to reach the lair of the Rainbow King, and to find only an empty castle. . . . Sajit could not understand his own disappointment. Why should he care? It was not his mission. It was not his quest.

"Let's look around a little more," said Sajit. They approached the foot of the throne, and he pointed to a displacement plate. They looked at each other for a moment. Sajit shrugged listlessly. "Why not?" They flicked out—

Another vast room, a perfect sphere a hundred meters high, walled with thousands upon thousands of interlocking hexagons, like a honeycomb . . . each hexagon a two-dimensional monitor. The surface of the sphere was all gravidown. Slowly they walked around. In the monitors—

Smiling children. Startling sunsets. Aerial views of villages, pretty patterns of white flecks in the greenery. Laughing old men telling tales around a table. Skies festooned with rainbows. Flocks of silverdoves, star-bright in the clear sky. A million eyes looking out on the planet of the dead.

In the center of the sphere, sitting in a hoverfloating throne, was an old man.

Elloran was white.

The hoverthrone drifted towards them. Sajit saw the old man's face, parched and pale under a wisp of white hair. And the eyes . . . Where had he seen such terrible, haunted eyes before; such weary, sunken, despairing eyes?

"Loreh, Taanyel's son. My old pupil." The old man's voice was barely audible, as if he had not spoken for years. "After all this, they send me you. . . ."

Elloran said, "Ton Alkamathdes, I am Ton Elloran n'Taanyel Tath, Inquestor-who-is-to-be. You have broken the law, Ton Alkamathdes. You've created an illusory utopia. For what, Alkamathdes? You've"—his voice cracked, and Sajit was dismayed for a moment that he might burst into tears—"you've gone against everything that you taught me yourself, Ton Alkamathdes! How could you betray us all like this?"

"Loreh, Loreh"—Sajit saw Elloran flinch at the old man's use of the diminutive— "They were killing each other! There was so much hate here! All I did was wipe out the source of their hate, the other planet. . . . What was wrong with that? We've destroyed a thousand planets for less. . . . Now they don't hate anymore. Now they love each other, all my children, and they live in paradise."

"You're a heretic—setting yourself up as god—killing without compassion—you're insane!"

"Insane?" Alkamathdes laughed, a dry, rasping sound like leaves in the wind. "I'm perfectly sane. But the Inquest, the Dispersal of Man, the human race—ha! ha!" He raised his hand and the throne came nearer still, hovering only a few meters from the two of them.

"I weep for you," said Elloran. But he did not weep.

Alkamathdes smiled, a twisted smile. "I took their murderous, selfish passions upon myself, Loreh. How can you say I was not compassionate? They did not have to kill anymore. I gave them freedom from their human condition. . . ." He gestured wildly at the scenes on the monitors. "My eyes, see! I see the joy in the world, and I am content that my children love me." He rose and stood at the foot of his hoverthrone, and Sajit saw that his shimmercloak was tattered and threadbare and had ceased to shine.

"I repeat the formula for your release from the Inquest, Alkamathdes, in the highspeech and the lowspeech," Elloran said steadily. "Listen and understand. *Den eis Enguéster! Din rilacho st' Enguestaran! Evendek eká eis! Enguesti tembres! Enguesti dhandas!*" His voice rose. "You are no Inquestor! I release you from the Inquestors! You are alone forever! You are dark to the Inquest! You are dead to the Inquest!" The throne dove towards them like a pteratyger.

"You think you can stop me with words, with official formulas, Loreh? What empty ideas have they been feeding you? Look at me, I'm your teacher, your master. I know what is good for you. I'll send you home. Just keep quiet about this—"

"You had our ship destroyed!"

"Of course, of course, had to protect my children from you utopia destroyers. . . ."

*"Laser him, Sajit!"* The old man had raised up a hand to summon something—

Sajit glared at the old man and tried to subvocalize the word but the shimmercloak rippled through the tatters and he couldn't bring himself to—

"He's calling his dead guards, he's going to kill us!" Elloran screamed. Sajit raised his whisperlyre and threw it with his last strength at the old man's head, thinking *I can't be doing this. I can't be attacking an Inquestor*—

Monitors splintered. Broken whisperstrings jangled. For a second the old man tottered, defying gravity. Then he crumpled from his throne. Sajit looked away.

Before the tears bleared his eyes, he saw in the monitors—

Children toppling in heaps, men and women collapsing in

mid-action, machines grinding to a halt, a lone child plummeting from a treetop with a frozen smile—

The monitors went blank. The whole machinery must have been cued to the old man's brain patterns. He had linked with the thinkhive and now both were dead.

Elloran strode over to the limp form, crouched over the ragged body, and tore the shimmercloak from the body, ripping the fabric with a fierce, childish anger. He was screaming, "You betrayed me, Alkamathdes! I believed everything you taught me and you betrayed me!" He hammered the corpse with his fists again and again, like an automaton, until he was worn out, and Sajit realized slowly that he had killed an Inquestor.

Then Elloran drew himself up tall and straightened his shimmercloak and came to Sajit. He had composed his face now, and Sajit knew that he would never lose control of himself again. It was when he looked in Elloran's eyes that he remembered the eyes of the dead Inquestor. They were the same eyes, eyes of power and of tragedy.

Elloran said, "Now we can go and find the tachyon bubble system."

Sajit went to find his whisperlyre. It was broken beyond repair, so he laid it over the body and drew a fragment of faded shimmercloak over it. It had been the last link to his childhood. "There'll be others," Elloran said gently. "Now listen."

They faced each other in the huge chamber. A million blank hexagonal eyes stared at them from all sides. Sajit glanced at the body and shied away from it. Elloran said, "Sajit, I hunted my first utopia. I am no longer an Inquestor-who-is-to-be. I have reached my power now. Do you know what that means, Sajit? Do you know what power means? This shall be my first act—" He held his hand out over Sajit. Instinctively Sajit knelt. "I name you to the clan of Shen, soldier Sajit. You are free from the wars now. I hope you'll be a great musician one day."

Sajit rose. He glowed with quiet elation. He wanted to embrace his companion, to thank him, to share this joy. But he couldn't.

Now they could not be friends. They could not touch. The illusion of utopia was over. The homeworld of the heart was for poets, for dreamers. Not for survivors. Sajit understood this.

So all he said was, "Thank you, Lord Inquestor. It's what

I've always wanted." Then, impulsively, he added, "You have so much power, you Inquestors! You can make planets that conform to men's dreams, you can make my dreams come true. If only I were like you—"

In the huge chamber, over the Inquestor's body, they almost touched. Then Elloran said softly, "You don't understand, do you?" He sounded bitter. "It is *I* who wish—"

He stopped himself. Sajit knew that there were things Inquestors may not wish. That was how things were.

After a moment, to break the silence, Elloran said, "Shen Sajit, one day"—he laughed shyly—"I hope you will teach me that song."

"It will have to be soon," Sajit said, "before my voice changes."

But he knew they were just acting now, clinging to the last moments of the utopia as the ear clings to a whisperlyre's shimmerfade after the song is done.

# 6

As Jenjen walked back, through the unfamiliar corridors of a palace more vast than the capital city of her home planet, she thought of her own childhood, and of her first encounter with Elloran in the place that celebrated darkness. Could the two of them be the same man? Could the Ton Elloran of countless legends, worshiped by some as a god on Essondras, be so human as to envy a mere childsoldier?

But she knew the answer. She had seen it years ago, in the Inquestor's eyes. She had always known of the canker in the heart of paradise.

And she thought, too, of the first time she had seen Rememberers, and how her parents had panicked and grown paranoid. . . . They should not have been afraid, she thought. Radicals like Zalo talked of the Inquest as though it were something terrible, but could a world ruled by a man like Elloran really be the victim of an evil repression? It seemed unthinkable.

I ought to stay here, she thought as she reached her chamber. As she started to subvoke her entry code, she heard a burst of music on the air . . . a choir of neuterchildren, snatches of words, the mirage-like afterecho of a whisperlyre. What were the words? It sounded like the one Tievar had quoted in the story, a song that yearned for paradise forever lost. . . . How many centuries ago had the story taken place? It had the flavor of myth, even though she had spoken to one of its protagonists, and sensed in him undimmed that selfsame longing for an ancient beauty. . . . And she thought, If they can still have such feelings, they have not relinquished their humanity. There is good in them. Perhaps I will be happy here.

The wall irised to receive her. The room was warm; in a corner stood the lightloom. A ruddy light swathed it; now and then, in response to some subliminal subvocalized thought of hers, it sent small stars flying outward, in bursts, over the room. I *shall* be happy! she thought fiercely. For she needed to believe that there was goodness in the universe, and that the way of shadow was not for her.

No, not the darkness. So long as she could still feel the yearning. She went to the lightloom, in that moment bursting with new images that she had to explore immediately. . . . It had been a tiring day, but the lightloom's warmth revived her. She worked on little things, filigrees of reds and oranges and deep browns, warm colors.

She remembered how she used to work far into the night, how Zalo, sweaty from his exertions at the theater, would come stand and watch her for long silent stretches. . . . Sometimes he would tell her of some new technique to make the dead men dance, some new way of applying makeup that Master Karnofara had taught him. Other times he would just watch. She would weave in warm colors for him, to show how happy she was just to have him stand there. His love was warm too. Warm. The tingle from the lightloom's wombwarmth would be with them all night long. Sometimes she would let him slide in beside her, into the forceknitted sanctum at the lightloom's heart. . . . Zalo was the only one whose presence had not violated that private world. And they would make love, slowly, cushioned in the red-gold lattice of light.

Why did they have to quarrel so often, even on the day before her departure? He was always full of strange, unworkable ideas. "A single person *can* make a difference!" he would tell her. "A single person could even topple the Inquest itself!"

And she'd laugh, but she would look around furtively, just in case it was true and a thunderbolt would come crashing down. . . .

The strains of Sajit's music filtered into her room from somewhere far away. She could hear the watery resonance of whisperlyres once more. How cold they must be, the lyre-players! she thought, remembering Tievar's image of the little boy Sajit, and his instrument sucking away the heat from his body. The music swelled a little. . . . They must be getting even colder now, as their song grows more intense, she thought. And drew the lightstrands thick around herself, as if for comfort.

Could I have been like Sajit? she wondered as the music faded and tiredness began to overcome her at last. If I were not able to bask in this endless warmth, this joy, if my art wrenched pain from my body, could I still make beautiful things?

For many days this question nagged at her, and she could not disentangle it from her thoughts. It was a part of herself she had never had to face before.

# TWO

## The Book of Shapers
## and Visionaries

hokhté inchitrás eih Enguéster
mérans peraiuéuris shtendá eluktierá?
neyáh: luktaín ke atheramýrah
núkt' eyáh ening vás;
kat lúkti chitrá tembára makhásh.

—ek shéntraran Sájiti


Did you think, O High Inquestor
You had reached the day's brightest moment?
Ah no. In the light of a million suns
It was night that you saw;
For the heart of light is a mighty darkness.

—from the Songs of Sajit

I

It was soon after her childhood encouter with Ton Elloran
than Jenjen began to be afraid of dark places. Although her
parents were loving and indulgent, the small house in the
forty-ninth arrondissement was not without its terrors. There
was, for example, the alcove in the heartroom, where the sym-
bols of her father's profession were kept—he was a minor attendant of the planetary thinkhive. There was a message disk
inscribed with curlicuish highscript, a gift from some ambassador. And after that traumatic day at the mnemothanasion, the
niche had carried another memento: the head of Jenjen's great-
grandfather, emaciated and parch-dry from an obsolete mum-
mifying process. Blue crystals had been set in his eyes to dis-
tract from the frayed hanks of hair and the wrinkled
complexion. Now and then the head, keyed to the thinkhive of
the residential complex, would nod or shake warningly or utter
some aphorism.

A darkfield could be drawn up over the alcove. Whenever
she woke up, frightened, in the middle of the night, the first
thing she would do was creep into the heartroom, keeping her
eyes averted the whole time lest his wrathful gaze fall on her,
and subvocalize the command to opaque the alcove. But then,
when she returned to her sleeproom, she would grow even
more frightened, because the pallid blue glow cast by his crystal eyes would now be gone. Should she go back into the heartroom and bring back the ghostly light and risk seeing that
grisly preserved head again? Or remain in the ever more terrifying darkness? The conflict sometimes kept her awake all
night. She never dared confess to anyone, least of all her parents, that she was scared of so commonplace a relic.

57

# 2

Only once had she dared mention her fear to her father. He had taken a fancy to the idea of bringing her in to his office one day. . . . She was about twelve years old by then, and already proficient in the simpler forms of lightweaving. . . . And she remembered being awestruck at the palace of the oligarchs, wondering if she would actually get to meet one of the rulers of Essondras.

"But, Jeni," her father said, "the oligarchy's just a joke. The thinkhive controls it all, and the thinkhive is answerable only to the Inquest."

They were strolling down a cloister formed from tunnel-trees; the trees were in bloom now, and now and then furball rodents scurried back and forth across the flagstones, their paws white with pollen. "How pretty," her father said, trying, she thought, to change the subject. "See how the jitrilla nests in the female branches and sallies forth to gather the juicy twatwe berries from the male. . . ." Perhaps, she thought, I should tell him I'm no longer a virgin! He'd turn purple with embarrassment.

I'd better change the subject. "A joke, Father? The oligarchy?"

"Old farts glued to their hoverthrones!" She saw that he didn't even look around anxiously as he said this; it must be a safe thing to say. It must be true.

His office was an airy place, nothing but a space in an orchard, bordered with trees, curtained off by an impenetrable forceshield but still giving the illusion that they were in the midst of nature. The orchard was on the side of a hill on the outskirts of Ikshatra, the suburb farthest from the sea. All the way down the hill were offices, all blending inconspicuously with copses or rocky outcroppings. At the foot of the hill you could see the city proper. She looked around wide-eyed; the walls of force were quite invisible. Only the utter windlessness betrayed her father's imprisonment.

A few people looked up from desks—square forcefields built over bushes and flower-patches—and greeted his father: "Rejoice, Dwa Jarrys. And this is your daughter, Dwawe—"

"Jenjen," she said, feeling very grown-up, and bowing smartly.

"Show them your tricks!" said Father. She subvocalized to the pocket generator she had had sewn into a fold of her tunic, and did a few simple passes, made gold droplets drizzle in the air, made silver-blue sparklets, wove a fine mesh of color in the air and set it ablaze with a flick of her wrist. . . . They were all applauding. Except . . . a janitor? He was just standing there, gaping strangely, dull-eyed.

"Don't you like it?" she asked him in a wounded, little-girl voice.

He stood there and—

She suddenly realized what he was. She'd never been this close to one before. She started screaming. The fire between her hands flared, sputtered, send dazzleshowers all over the room. Her father grabbed her, tried to quiet her, tried to explain to the others, "We don't have one in the house, she spends all her time at the lightloom, she just isn't used to staring a servocorpse in the face—"

And later, on the way to the displacement plates nestled beneath a grove of spiraltrees, she told him about how scared she was of Great-grandfather's head in the memory-niche back at the house.

He held her tight and said, "You poor poor innocent . . . we may not be that rich, but we have to cling to a few vestiges of class. Your mother and I have been angling for one of the family heads for years."

"But why do you have to have it around? It scares me, it just scares me. With the blue light and everything. I don't like dead things, dark things."

"Would you rather our ancestors were turned into servocorpses, like poor old Baskethead, our janitor? We got him from the Arm for fifty gipfers. Nobody loved *him* enough to treasure his memory. . . ."

"What's the Arm?"

A look of alarm in his eyes for a split second. She was becoming very familiar with this look. . . . Grownups always looked like that when they said something. . . . "Unorthodox," Father had called it once.

"Child, you're a brilliant lightweaver already, but you're quite backward sometimes. I'll show you something." He pointed up the mountain. All she could see were trees: dark trees, bright trees, here a line of trees with salmon-colored foliage, near the crest of the mountain. She looked where he pointed, but couldn't make anything out. "No, Jeni. The pink trees . . . You see, like a wood within a wood. . . . It's shaped almost like a human arm—"

"A pretty crooked arm," she said peevishly.

"Well, what do you think it is?"

"Offices, I suppose! Part of this whole thinkhive-serving contruction, I don't know."

"That's the Arm." He whispered now; she had to strain to hear him. "It's a servocorpse factory. But sometimes it's more. People disappear sometimes, just like that, and many sleeps later they're on the corpse market—"

"Why would anyone disappear?" she asked.

He didn't answer.

"You mean, if they're bad? Like if they say something bad about the High Inquest?"

"Of course not! The Inquest is compassionate. It would never soil its hands with such petty trifles. . . . But there are those who serve the Inquest with . . . unnatural fervor." He looked around shiftily again. Suddenly she understood what it was that all those grown-ups feared would happen if they were caught saying something "unorthodox." She wondered what it would be like if she lost her father, if he were to vanish one day . . . and she were to see his corpse sweeping a street corner or vending candy by the Blue Canal. Suddenly she was thankful that she had the academy to spend her days in, a safe haven, full of light and free of nightmares.

Once, as an adult, she'd been tempted to reveal her irrational childhood fear to Zalo. It was when he invited her down to the makeup room in the basement of the theater, and she saw them laboriously painting the face of an old man, lying spread-eagled and quite dead on a display board. It was dark in the room. Cold, too; she shivered.

"Look," Zalo was saying, excitedly, "we're trying a new kind of luminous paint for the grief lines. What do you think?"

They were daubing the man's brow with a pale blue phosphorescent mush. . . . The cold light took her back to her parents' old house and those sleepless nights. . . . She looked away.

He said, "Jeni, what's wrong? Oh, I know some people find it a little distasteful. . . ."

Looking away from him, she said, "Have you ever heard of the Arm?"

"Why, of course, we get all our corpses from there. . . ."

"All right. I don't expect you to inquire into the techniques of my art, and I'm certainly not going to look into yours anymore. I'm going home."

He looked at her in a baffled sort of way, and went back to his work. As she left, she wondered how he'd been so stupid as to miss the connection between the Arm and his inane anti-Inquestral babblings. She didn't see him for many days after that, and he never understood why.

# 3

Only when she had left Essondras behind did she dare speak of this childish fear again; and it was to Ton Elloran himself. Later she would remember how strange it was to be confessing these intimate memories to a stranger, and one so unthinkably far above her station, and not to the man she loved. But at the time it seemed not so strange.

He had called her to supper; she found him in an inner throneroom. It was not a formal hall like the first throneroom she had seen, with its crowds of suppliants and its singing seraphs hovering overhead. This room was simple, though its subdued opulence spoke, in its own way, of untold wealth. Its walls were faced with Ontian marble, its gold veins etched by that planet's treacherous firesnows; a single firefountain in a cage of force formed their dining table, and the couches were of finespun shimmerfur. A sleek allurosaur crouched at the Inquestor's feet, lazily lapping a bowl of milk laced with zul. There were other Inquestors too: one a young woman with snow-pale hair and eyes like milky opals. A steward showed Jenjen to her couch; quickly came two serving boys, one to annoint her hands and the other to dry the attar with a small artwind-crystal imbedded in his palm.

The guests hardly acknowledged her presence. At one point she heard one Inquestor hiss the word *history;* silence fell suddenly, and all turned to Elloran, who had been petting the catlizard. He looked up sharply and said, "There will be no *makrúgh* at *my* dinner table tonight!" And the other Inquestor, shamed, tried gracefully to change the subject.

" . . . and even if the Inquest itself should fall, powers forbid—" came a voice from the other end of the table.

Again silence fell abruptly.

"We are certainly grim tonight!" Ton Elloran said. "But such a notion is hardly new anymore."

And they began to talk about things she had never dreamed possible. Apparently there was a schism in the Inquest now; Ton Davaryush, a heretic, had spawned a Shadow-Inquest, and his disciple, Ton Kelver, had gone further than any of them had imagined. It seemed absurd, this talk of revolution and war within the Inquest itself, and at first she did not listen. There were so many names to remember, and the issues seemed so irrelevant to a woman of some backworld.

Until the Inquestrix of the opal eyes, who was called Ton Siriss, said: "And what of Essondras? What possible use could the death of Essondras mean to the minions of Karakaël, anyway?"

Jenjen started.

Siriss said, "Look what I've done. We should not be discussing such a thing in the presence of an Essondrish native. It is unseemly, and most uncompassionate."

They were all watching her now. "Come," said Elloran kindly. "You are new here, and we can hardly expect you to accommodate yourself instantly to our ways. We must seem alien to you, callous even. . . . Let us talk of other things."

And she saw him, how stooped and sunken he was now;

and she knew why Tash Tievar had told her the story of Elloran and Sajit as children. She looked into his eyes and, knowing that, in a past long since orphaned by time dilation, he too had once been a child, she lost her fear. In her heart she thanked him.

"Well, speak, young woman. We're not going to have you executed," said another Inquestor.

"My lords . . . this place has been a maze to me . . . but lately I have been learning much from Tash Tievar. I have heard of a great musician named Shen Sajit, for instance. . . ."

All at once she was painfully aware of a dead silence. "I'm sorry, I should not have spoken, perhaps I have intruded—"

"It is well, Ir Jenjen," Elloran said, very seriously. "It is not good for me always to hide my grief; is that not so? Sajit is long dead. One cannot mourn forever."

"Tell me, Jenjen of the Clan of Ir," said Ton Siriss. "On your world, how do you commemorate the dead?"

And she told them of her great-grandfather's head, and of her childhood terrors. She relived those night fears vividly; when she was true she felt strangely liberated. She was no longer embarrassed to be among these people.

One by one (among the Inquestors one seemed always to speak in turn, like polyphonic voices in a musical fugue) they commented. Some thought it was a grisly custom; one, who called himself an historical anthropologist, suggested that it was an effective status symbol, indicating as it did that the family was of sufficient rank not to have to sell its venerable ancestors to a servocorpse factory. "And in a culture as baroque in its uses of servocorpses as yours—"

"—Why, they actually use them in plays, instead of live actors!" said an Inquestor with distaste.

"Live actors?" Jenjen had grown up with necrodrama, and for the past months Zalo had been relating their plots interminably. "You know, that had never occurred to me."

Her remark occasioned some mirth; she could not quite understand why.

"Among the Inquestors," said Siriss, "we have our own system of *memento mori*. And who is to say that ours is any less macabre? I would say that there is a certain honesty, an *integrity*, in keeping actual corpses at home. . . ."

"Ah yes," said the anthropologist. "Your Rememberers."

Somewhere far away came a chime, and a plaintive afterecho like the mieow-roar of a pteratyger. The allurosaur's wattles quivered; it got up and began to pace and paw at the shimmercarpet. "What a serendipitous remark!" Elloran said, not without irony. "I believe it is time for our daily dosage of guilt."

He clapped his hands. One of the walls deopaqued; behind, against a curtain of mist, stood Tash Tievar.

Jenjen was astonished to see him; even more astonished when he began his narration. He told of a system named Shendering, long *fallen beyond*. But although he chose vivid images for his remembering, it was not the same as when she and he had sat privately in the remembering room together. He spoke as his duty bade him: not as a poet, but as the past's mirror.

Yet, when Tievar spoke of the mountain wind that swooped down on the willows of Issirin, and the vermilion road that speckled the system's chief planet, a smile flickered on Ton Elloran's lips, and Jenjen saw that he was moved. But some of the others could not wait for Tievar to finish.

"More zul!" cried one Inquestor.

Another said, "Just like you, Elloran, to ruin a perfectly fine meal with your talk of dead planets."

"The Inquest falls," Elloran said quietly. This statement triggered another sullen hush. "It is good that we should remember not only its brutality, but its ideals, its compassion, its splendor." Then, turning to Jenjen and Tievar, he said, "Come with me, you shortlived ones. I'll show you my own personal reminder of death. As for you others—"

Some rose from the table in anger, strode to displacement plates, vanished; others, including Siriss, followed. The mistveil behind Tash Tievar parted. Behind, another throneroom; at its center, in a column of light, a galaxy spun from dust.

"Tell them Tievar!" Ton Elloran cried. "Let it not be said that I have no heart!"

To Siriss he said: "And know, Sirissheh, that I understand your loss." Jenjen knew from this that the Inquestrix had lost someone she loved. Then Elloran turned to Jenjen and said, "And you . . . know of the perils of loving what you cannot have. You have feared darkness so long only because you feared your own capacity to love—"

"I do not understand, *hokh'Ton*."

"Tell her the tale, Tash Tievar."

Tievar began.

\* \* \*

The dust (he said) came first: dormant, unstirring, hugging the hard crust of Aëroësh for an aeon or more. The tempests that had ground it out of the stone were forgotten; now, weather-shifts later, the winds were stilled and the heat stifling and rasp-dry.

Time-frozen, blood-dyed by the red sun that Aëroësh circled, the dust ocean stretched from eye's end to eye's end, crimsoning with distance and melting into a brown-red sky.

From the earliest times the thinkhives of the Dispersal of Man had known of Aëroësh, but had deemed it too distant and too inhospitable for Man. . . .

In time came disturbances, tugging at the Inquestors' power. The Inquest moved planets to make room for a war. And the people bins went out, towed by convoys of delphinoid shipminds that pinholed through the overcosm beyond realspace, each one of them stasis-stacked with the survivors of murdered worlds. For in its compassion the Inquest was compelled to save what people it could. And so men came to Aëroësh: scavengers, dispossessed, clanless, despairing. Their cities sprang up from the rockface under the dust, domed with forceshields, linked by klomets of burrow-tubes. They were fragile bubbles of humanity, buried in the soundless depths of the dust-dead sea.

And then Aëroësh changed. Surges of power erupted from the cities. The dust rippled. The forceshields hummed. The ion wind came, and the dust woke at last, in slow spiraling storms, a thousand klomets broad, gusting, sweeping the plains, like an army without a foe. There were no mountains to scour, no people to eat alive. The storms were impotent.

And the people of Aëroësh were untouched by them. They lived far down, in the cities with skies of dust. At times they forgot that the rest of the human race existed.

In turn, the Inquest ignored them. The Inquestor who ruled over Aëroësh held sway over a dozen worlds; he never visited this one. And as for tourists . . . what did the planet have but dust? And who could love the dust?

The dust waited, gusting in darkness and light.

"Come," Elloran said to Tievar. "This is not a time for cold expositions. The guests have not followed us; it is not a formal remembrance. Look, the woman Jenjen is half bored already. And I mean to convince her of my humanity. . . ."

"Well then, my Lord," the old man said, "I will try to put

into my words the very music of Shen Sajit. For now I must describe this palace Varezhdur in which we now stand. . . ."

# 4

# The Story of the Dust-Sculptress

The palace! A dance of golden spirals and glitter-burnished spires, easing into orbit around Alykh, the pleasure world. And there in the throneroom tiled with azurite and ringed with columns of cold blue flame, the Princeling Elloran, Inquestor, Hunter of Utopias, and Lord of Varezhdur and all its Tributaries, watching the crescent of Alykh burning in the blackness and listening to the cool music: flutes, watergongs, whisperlyres, shimmerviols.

He too was watched. Shen Sajit, master of the Prince's music, reclining against the curvewall of the sunken orchestra pit, was not bothering to listen to his own composition; he had heard it a hundred times already.

With a clap the Inquestor summoned Sajit. Sajit approached him, sunken in his throne with his shimmercloak strewn over the gold steps patterned with a sequent frieze of quartz-eyed pteratygers. The music went on, not needing direction.

"You seem so tired, so remote," said Sajit. He could do so directly because when they were boys he had saved Ton Elloran's life.

"Wouldn't *you* be? We've just come from another war."

"Yes. You commanded the migrations of a dozen people bins. Very tiring work. Yet you showed no emotion at all." Try as he might, he could not conceal the irony in his voice. For a moment he remembered—

*Chasing the people bins into the overcosm, slow dance of the black ships against the glittering firelights of the space between spaces, and then the last people bin vanishing like a dust-mote drifting from light into shadow . . . and a single tear on the Prince's cheek.* Sajit remembered thinking: *Perhaps he is human! How should I know? We are the same age, and yet his face is far more youthful than mine, except for those gray eyes radiating all the ancientness of the Inquest's power. As well befriend the mountains or the stars,* he had thought, cautioning himself against feeling too much involvement with the Inquestor.

"Look at it," Elloran said, interrupting Sajit's reverie. "Alykh, the pleasure world—"

"Where we'll go down to Aírang, city of cheap love," said Sajit, "and we'll ride the varigrav coasters and drink sweet zul and dance in the gem-paved streets, until—"

"Until we have forgotten all our pain."

*We'll be* dorezdas, thought Sajit. *And Ton Elloran will never see the Sewer Labyrinth or the husks of dead palaces where live the thieves and the beggars and the ugly and the dying, those who call Alykh their homeworld, who eke out an existence by fleecing the* dorezdas *with their eyes on the stars and their minds on the problems of the rich and their pockets lined with arjents. But I will know.* Could it really have been twenty years since a filthy, bone-thin boy had fled the city, clinging to the tunic of a broken old wandering dreamsinger?

"You were born here, weren't you, Sajit?"

*Aírang. Home.* "Yes. But now I'm a *dorezda* with fine clothes and a clan-name and, a place at an Inquestor's court—"

He remembered home as a hovel in the rubble and he turned his mind to music, trying to forget.

Lazily the railinged floater fell towards the city, Ton Elloran standing apart from the others, alone even amid his dozen attendants. A delicate *fang*-scented vapor gauzed them. *You're burying your pain, aren't you?* Sajit thought. *Burying deep inside yourself the memory of the war.*

From a corner of the floater, a quartet of whisperlyres played and a boy singer sung softly of a lost love he could never have known; for Ton Elloran never went anywhere without his own music, he could not bear the silence. Below them, the city—

*Aírang of the* dorezdas!

Pillars of klomet-high varigrav coasters, etchveined Ontian marble knuckleduststudded with amethysts, darkstriping the purple sunset . . . jousting giant reptiles clawing the sunlight and pawing a screechy thunderdust over tiers of cheerers . . . Aírang of the tower-tall buildings warpwoofed with jewelthreads of streets and echo-rich with laughter. . . .

They reached the guest-hostel of Ton Exkandar, Kingling of the Alykh system, a high tower of brick and vine, wound round with a spiral balcony. As the floater eased onto the dais that jutted from the topmost turret, Sajit spoke to Elloran.

"Let me alone into the city awhile, Inquestor."

Ton Elloran turned. "But Sajit, my music—"

"This is my homeworld." But as he said it it rang false.

"Of course. It must have been twenty years." Elloran paused to straighten his shimmercloak, which glowed faint pink against the dark blue fur. "Of course you must go, Shen Sajit." And then, "Will you let me come with you? Will you show me what this city really is?"

"You don't want to know."

"I'm tired of wearing my mask of compassion," Elloran said. "I've pried a trillion people loose from their worlds like so many barnacles. . . . I'm losing touch, Sajit!"

"Yes. Maybe so."

The floater was still now. The sounds of the city assailed them: hawkers' shouts, the strumming of distant dreamharps, the whoosh of the rich men's gaudy floaters—some mere circles of metal that wave their way through the forest of towers, some with great caparisons of peacocks' wings and gilt, sailing majestic through the violet sky, some with crimson-cloaked trumpeteers sounding brash sennets. . . . Sajit waved to an attendant who dissolved the darkfield that englobed the Inquestral floater. Seeing the glitter of the shimmercloak, a man cried out and the traffic jam of floaters parted suddenly. A ray of mauve-dyed sunset fell upon the square below the parapet; people wriggled like little worms. A gate irised in the turret to admit Elloran's party. As Elloran stepped in he tore the shimmercloak from his body, cursing. . . .

*Who can understand Inquestors?* Sajit thought. They drifted slowly down the airtube to the surface of Alykh. He glanced at his own clothes—the short cloak of cloth-of-iridium trimmed with clingfire, the kaleidokilt of the clan of Shen with its semisentient buckle of two mating flamefish—and thought: *I've become one of the very things I used to despise, the people whose pockets I picked and whom I used to beg from. . . .*

And beside him Elloran floated, frozen-faced. Others fell

above and below, streaking the mirror metal of the air shaft. *What does he know?* Sajit thought bitterly. He remembered the burning planets and the people packed in their people bins, and the Inquestor's impassive, soft-spoken commands. *He's blown up planets, but he hasn't stood at the gateway of the Sewer Labyrinth and smelled the stink of the dead. . . .* And he pitied Elloran then. He must always be alone, after all, and have slaves for friends and feel compassion instead of love and play the Inquestral game of *makrúgh* instead of living relationships.

At the floor of the shaft, about to step into the street, he thought: *Perhaps I should show him those things.* The windstream ruffled his hair and he pulled his cloak tighter. Sunset came swiftly on Alykh, and he knew it would be night now, a night more garish-gaudy even than the day. "Here," he said, "you don't want to be without your music." He pulled a songjewel from a fold in his kilt, snapped it awake, and placed it around his master's neck. It was a quartet of shimmerviols, and Elloran smiled a little. A door dissolved; Aírang's noise assaulted them. Sajit stepped onto the street and turned to Elloran with a twisted smile. "My home," he said, with an ironic sweep of the hand.

He led the Inquestor through a glass-cobbled square where revelers skied the bright night sky on threads that were yoked to pteratygers, their pink-feathered wings flapping as they soared and wheeled. . . .

"Where are we going?" Elloran said.

"I'll show you," Sajit snapped, ignoring court protocol. But Elloran did not seem to notice.

"Artists," he muttered, and Sajit felt a ghost of their old friendship for a second. They found a displacement plate at the corner of the square and Sajit leapt onto it, not waiting for his master.

They stepped through a corridor of an indoor theater, masked actors moving solemnly to a slow heartbeat of a drum and sing-songing in piercing artificial voices, dead husks of men perhaps, animated by hidden thinkhives to imitate the dead classics, and the audience murmuring in languid unison. . . .

"Come!" said Sajit urgently. Elloran followed behind, not observing that the servant had taken the lead. For a moment Sajit thought, *I'm pushing too much, he's always allowed me to speak freely but he's not my friend, he's an Inquestor.* . . . But recklessness seized him.

. . . an orgy-field drenched in *fang* vapors, the field itself thrumming softly to the rhythm of a hundred lovers . . . a shrill street opera . . . a slave market . . . the varigrav coasters looming high in the distance, with specks of people as they plummeted on antigraviton fields, swarming like fireflies. . . .

And then darkness.

And silence, save for a whisperbuzz of shimmerviols from the Inquestor's songjewel. "Are you afraid?" said Sajit. There was a stale breeze in the darkness, tainted with a tang of death.

"No."

"Do you want to see where I grew up?"

Elloran didn't answer. "This is the Sewer Labyrinth," Sajit said, "that runs beneath the city. We used to play here. Come on."

They passed through twisted tunnels, and Sajit, growing used to the darkness—there was a faint phosphorescence here—saw Elloran watching everything, memorizing everything . . . the stagnant canals, the old bones, an old man with gouge-yellow cheeks, staring listlessly from behind a frayed wisp of blanket, the children who ran after them throwing stones and jeering. . . .

"I was one of those," Sajit said. They emerged into a street, barely manwide, a displacement plate that didn't work, buildings strung together from sheet metal and old starship hulls. Striding fiercely through the garbage, Sajit made for his old hovel, knowing that it could no longer be there, that buildings sprouted and withered overnight here in the slums of Aírang. "I would have died here if I weren't a survivor."

They threaded their way through endless reeking alleyways, and Sajit realized he would never find his old home. He was angry, and he wanted to be cruel.

Above them the sky glowed, now flourescent green, now garish pink. . . . The lights of Aírang were all that the hovel city needed. They reached Rats' Valley, hemmed in by two hills of refuse, nicknamed for the rodents that scurried pitter-patter through the dark and preyed on the babies, dead or discarded, half-buried in the rust and dust.

They stopped. A cloud of dust made Sajit cough. Finally Elloran said, "What do you want of me, Sajit?"

"Powers of powers, Inquestor! I just want you to admit

you're human too, I just want you to step down from your mountain of power and touch the people you kill by the billions. . . . Look!" He kicked up a flurry of dust and dried excrement. "I was born out of this dust, Elloran! And you came out of a Prince's palace. Yet you destroy planets, and I make songs." He turned away. He had broken all the bounds of propriety. In public it would have meant certain death.

"You too, Sajit," Elloran said at last. To Sajit's annoyance he did not seem angry. "There are times when I think you almost understand, but . . ." He tore the songjewel from his throat and flung it into the debris. A single clank and it was gone. "Are you satisfied now?"

"You *asked* to be punished, Ton Elloran."

"Yes. Yes." The Inquestor turned back and began walking back to the slum and the Sewer Labyrinth. Was he angry? Sajit could not read him. Perhaps they had quarreled, if a person could be said to have had a quarrel with an Inquestor. Sajit let him go. He didn't know whether he had made his point or not. He was tired and he wanted a woman. *Why not?* he thought. *I'm a* dorezda *now.* With a flick of his mind he turned on the tracer at his wrist so that Elloran could find him if he needed him. Perfunctorily he flicked the dust from his clothes a little, and then he headed towards the whores' quarter. The stinking streets went by in a blur, and when he reached the first of the operational displacement plates the squares of the city went by, their colors jangling dissonances. . . .

"Master, master . . ." A wheezing voice. Sajit turned. Standing by a pillar of flame, the old man beckoned him. The face was indecently withered; he had probably let it age in the old way as a grotesque tourist attraction. "You want a girl?" Sajit didn't answer, and the old man came closer, bowing himself in two. "I have such girls, master, such girls, and for a mere demi-arjent they will lull you with song and yield to your masterly touch. . . . You do not speak, master! Is it boys you favor? I have such boys also. . . . Do you want pain and punishment, do you want strange alien creatures perhaps? I—"

"*De zon dorezda!*" Sajit snapped in the local lowspeech.

"You are no *dorezda!*" the man said, not switching to the lowspeech. "I see you have learned some of our words, excellency. You come here often then. . . . For one of such discernment as you, I have other things. . . . Lo . . ." He snapped his fingers and summoned holosculpt miniatures out of the thin air. Women wheeled and dissolved into other women, and all had the perfect body and the perfect face that marked the Alykhish pleasure girl, the bodies rebuilt each year before they became too worn. . . . "But sir," said the pimp, "I see you are interested, and yet you don't speak. Don't be embarrassed, master! Perhaps in your palace you dare not speak your desire, from modesty or from compassion, but here there is nothing one dare not desire, nothing your demi-arjent will not buy. . . . Of course," his voice fell to a sly whisper, "there is a surcharge for death."

"Powers of powers!" Sajit cried. "I speak my mother's tongue and you flatter me for picking up a few foreign phrases! I come looking for a woman and you show me images of my mother!"

"I see," the old man said, ill at ease now. "You *are* a son of Aírang, I see that, Excellency! Come. Follow me. I have just the thing. I know your types! Made it good, gone freeloading off the High Inquest. . . . Now you feel guilty about it all! Ha. Abuse. That's for you, abuse. But I'll make it beautiful for you—is that a deal?"

Sajit said nothing. He felt nothing but his own blind anger. His mother must have worked for one of these leeches. Did she feel any love at all for the dorezda who spawned her son? This was the world that made him, and he hated it with all his heart, and even this homeworld would not accept him as its own, but would cast him as a mark for pimps' duplicity!

I will give Elloran a new song tonight, he thought. An ugly, bitter song. I will sing about darkness, and how all our dreams come to nothing. This is as far from the homeworld of the heart as a man can get. He wanted to punish Elloran, because they would always be slave and master, however much Elloran deigned to befriend him.

Shrugging, he followed the man as he hobbled toward the fiery pillar. The pillar parted. They stepped into a cool atrium. Above their heads was a still holosculpt caelorama: a cloudless sky, red as blood. The atrium's floor was dust.

And at the atrium's center, in a startling shaft of white light, swirled a slow nebula of dust. . . .

"Not a mere whore-without-a-clan, Excellency!" the old man was saying. Sajit ignored him, entranced by the strange dust-sculpture. It was like an ancient song, pentatonic, strophic, nothing to it at all, yet redolent with ancient truth. The day's events seemed insignificant beside it.

"It's unbelievable!" he said. "Who could have shaped such a thing? From which Inquestral court does it come?"

"Didn't you hear him?" A woman had stepped out from behind the dust-sculpture. "I am no clanless whore." He saw at once the beige hair streaked with turquoise. The field that held the dust in place charged her hair and made it stream behind her. The hair was her only luxury; she wore a rough brown smock, as though she had stepped right out of the Sewer Labyrinth, and her face must have been unrefurbished for at least two years; it even sagged in places. "My name is Dei Zhendra," she said, not looking at him. "Of the clan of imagers. I am a dust-sculptress."

"Beautiful, no, Excellency? Classic as the ancients were, before the days of cosmetics and artificial faces? No? Mature, like a gruyesh fruit left to ripen and grow juicy in the sun?" He nudged Sajit suggestively in the ribs.

"Get out!" said Dei Zhendra. Sajit whirled: the man was gone. Somewhere outside a beggar boy was singing; in the back of his mind Sajit could not help criticizing the singer's phrasing and intonation.

"Why . . . why are you doing this? Selling yourself . . . You could be at any court in the Dispersal of Man. How can you demean yourself, Zhendra? I will buy you free!" She was beautiful, not as pleasure girls are beautiful, but beautiful also because of what she had done. He could not bear to see her so degraded.

She said, "What is freedom, Excellency?" There was a bitter mocking in her voice. "Are *you* then free? I sell what is my own. Does your body belong to you? Are even those gaudy clothes your own? Let Zhendra teach you about freedom, courtier who does not know himself. Come to Zhendra the whore."

She led him behind the dust nebula and he saw sacks of dust piled neatly against the far wall. "Dust is expensive when you are free," she said. "Not every kind will do, you know. At your feet is the common dust, a gipfer, a sack, useless, useless, useless. It will not bear the static charge you need for *this*." As she spoke motes sparkled and died. "As you see, the best dust is not to be found everywhere. It comes from the other end of the Dispersal of Man. From a planet called Aëroësh."

"In an old dead tongue, aëroësh means *dust*."

"It is a beautiful dust. A dust of tiny silicate chains, charged and polarized, that seem to yearn for one another, that flow and interlink like a living thing. . . ."

"And for this . . . this breathtaking creation . . . you've found no sponsor, Dei Zhendra?"

"Sponsor!"

"I am a musician. Ton Elloran is a good man, and—" Though he had been angry at him before, he told her what he himself wanted to believe.

"But music is sweet . . . . as is your self-inflicted slavery, my fine musician. I and my dust . . . Who can love the dust?" She laughed then, a terrible, despairing laugh. "Three sacks I bought last year for five hundred arjents, and the pimp takes eighty percent. . . ."

"But it's wrong!" said Sajit heatedly, even as he was drawn to the woman, seeing deep inside her an echo of himself.

"You too are a whore," she said. She pitied him! He could not bear it. Yet he knew that what she said was true. He knew suddenly that he loved her.

She laughed. "You poor poor man, standing there searching my soul. You're like a child. You *did* come here to fuck, didn't you? Not to gape. Get them off, Excellency, I don't have all day. I've dust to pour."

"Zhendra—" Why did he suddenly feel mawkish, like an adolescent? He reached for her, but he felt no passion at all. Just the desire to get her out of here, to show her how he'd striven to claw his way out of the garbage heaps of the Sewer Labyrinth and sail the starstream itself, and how she could do it too, if she trusted him. . . . Why did she reject him like this? Courtiers were not used to being rejected by peasants. Shouldn't he just throw her a few coins and leave?

"But you do nothing," she said. At last her features seemed to soften. "Come." She whisked away her smock and flung it aside . . . so casually, so gracefully. . . . Her body, sagging as it was from lack of somatic renewal, was a work of art.

"In the dust?"

"I love the dust." She laughed again; she threw a handful of dust at him. He ducked. She trickled dust on the crease between her breasts. The dust was exciting her, he could tell. At last he felt aroused, and knelt down beside her, tearing at

his loincloth. "Come to me, you Inquestral plaything. . . .
Come to me, come to me. . . ."

Footsteps.

The dust flew wildly for a moment—

Elloran stepped into the room, his shimmercloak churning up more dust. "Sajit . . . I am sorry. I don't know why I
eavesdropped on your tracer, why I came here—"

Sajit bit his tongue. The woman had risen now. He could
not show his anger in front of a strange woman. One could not
intrude on an Inquestor's dignity.

But Zhendra did. "Get out!" she shrieked.

Elloran walked slowly around the dust-sculpture. Then he
looked long and still at the woman, shaming her to silence. But
she did not fall on her knees and abjectly beg his pardon, as
Sajit had seen thousands do. She clung savagely to her foothold
on freedom. It was this that Sajit loved in her, he realized. He
struggled to contain himself.

Could Elloran be trying to hurt him deliberately? But an
Inquestor must be compassionate! That was a law of nature!
Elloran smiled the wan smile that the two of them shared.

"You have taste, Sajitteh," he said. "She *is* beautiful."
With a shock, Sajit realized he was actually going to take her
away from him. How could that be? Surely Elloran could not
be jealous. . . . "I am drunk on sweet sweet zul, Sajitteh. I
have abandoned this cursed compassion for tonight. A slave
you called him, Zhendra! I at least am not a slave, eh? Not to
any man. Only to the whole Dispersal, only to all mankind!
Oh, you should pity me. . . . Would you like a palace of your
own, girl, and a sack of dust a day?"

"You're buying her!" Sajit blurted out at last.

Elloran shouted: "Well? Shall I drag you away from this
creature who reminds you so much of your lowly origins?
Would you like a planet for your own? I have dozens! I have
Ymvyrsh. I have Eldereldad, Ménjifarn, Kailása, Chembrith,
Muralgash, Gom, Aëroësh—"

Sajit saw Zhendra's eyes widen, star sapphire-blue, heard
her gasp—

"Whore!" he shouted. "Elloran, she's just using you! Or
you're just using her to get back at me, because you can never
really create beautiful things! You're playing some kind of hideous *makrúgh*—"

"Enough. I do not play *makrúgh* with underlings," said Elloran.

"Then I am lost," Sajit said, wheeling to face the whirling nebula. The dust twisted slowly, sparks shifting from shining to shadow. "You have won. As you must always win. You are the Inquestor. I will always serve you. But you cannot make me love you."

Varezhdur the golden palace circled the pleasure planet until the days of the Cold Season trickled away. It did not grow warmer or colder, of course; the names of the seasons were legacies of a lost past. The palace grew too: a wing for the woman of dust, a maze of chambers twistier than a conch shell's innards, a forcedome outside the walls where a nebula of dust grew daily beneath the starstream that it echoed.

Hour after hour Elloran would watch her. On the mirror metal floor lay countless strands of dust, formed and charged and ready to be activated into the pattern with a deft wrist-flick. From a recess in the floor Sajit's music would play. His music was harsher now. No more the shimmerviols and the whisperlyres, but the clang of kenongs and klingels and glass-shatterers beneath shrill highwoods. Zhendra labored, scooping up armfuls of the charged dust and flinging them into the field, sometimes diving into the cloud to draw out swirls of dust with her charger, sometimes deactivating a whorl so that motes fluttered to the floor. She did not notice the music. She did not seem to notice the Inquestor either. Away from the dust she seemed only half alive; enveloped in it, dancing in the dust, she seemed to become part of it, to become a single, breathing organism with it. Sajit envied her her freedom. He knew that even when she slept with the Inquestor she could not feel like his possession.

As the Cold Season ended she came instead to him, seeking variety perhaps. Sometimes he would know that she had just come from Elloran, but she never said anything. He didn't question his good fortune. Her lovemaking was violent; always she wanted to lead the way. Their bodies were flaming and yet he would always know that her mind was far away. He felt like a dust-mote that had veered too near the sun. Perhaps he was in love.

In the Season of Mists the palace moved into orbit around Kailása. In small floaters they would chase the sunlight, skimming the clouds, pausing to hunt the fierce lighthawks with their ten-meter wings leaf-bright with chlorophyll as they grazed off the brilliant sunlight; or to trap the firephoenixes as they mated, shrieking, in mid-air. When they tired they would change direction and follow the night, playing zigzag races through the rifts in the Mountains of Jérrelahf. And when they tired of that too they swung south and rode the flying sea-serpents in the Pallid Ocean and harvested the honey-eggs that floated on the waves cracking them open to quench their thirst. Or north to ski on snowslopes dyed scarlet by hardy bloodalgae. Always the Inquestor would ride, alone but for the music and the master of music, and Sajit always played the new harsh music, not wanting to give his master the sorrow-drowning sweetness that he craved. Since that evening not long after the last war when they had both found Zhendra, Elloran had not lost control of himself. He had not said a word when Zhendra began visiting both of them, for an Inquestor could not hang on to material things. Sajit knew that Elloran was hurt. He *had* to be. Unless Inquestors really were like automated thinkhives and not like human beings. . . .

*Admit your hurt!* he would think silently, whipping up the musicians to a maenad frenzy. But Elloran would stand and watch his courtiers cavorting on the waves or in the snow, and sometimes he would even smile.

And after, when they were too tired even to float and watch the circling of lighthawks or phosphorleafed forests quivering in the double moonlight, they would leave this un-populated world and go back to Varezhdur to do what had been obsessing their thoughts all the while. . . .

The nebula had grown to the height of three men; twice the forcedome had been expanded. The dust had come from Aëroësh at staggering expense, by tachyon bubble. An extrava-gance only an Inquestor could command, for it was said that whole suns died to fuel those specks of realspace that flashed instantly from world to world, bypassing even the over-cosm of the delphinoid shipminds. The gesture had maddened Sajit even as he wanted her to get her dust in time.

She worked and Elloran watched her, both oblivious of the increasing dissonance. Angrily Sajit clapped his hands for silence. "Will it never be done?" he shouted. Zhendra worked on. But Elloran whirled and cried out, "It must never be finished! I never want her to finish it!"

For they both knew what she would do when the nebula was done.

It was said that a man could be lost for years in Varezhdur and never know it. But now the whole palace revolved around that single throneroom with its galaxy of dust; it seemed that Varezhdur's labyrinthine vastness had shrunk to a circle of light in a single chamber. Varezhdur was geared to Elloran's whim; false nights fell at his behest, and day lasted as long as he felt awake. But now the days stretched on and on like a polar summer. Sajit would hear the palace servants grumbling about it sometimes. In the palace of another Inquestor, they might not have grumbled, for fear of sudden devivement; but Elloran was not one who reveled in cruelty for its own sake. . . .

One evening, attending the Inquestor at the hour of retiring, he asked Elloran why he had felt impelled to take Zhendra away from him.

"She did not belong to you in the first place," Elloran said. Sajit slipped behind the gauzemist that encircled Elloran's sleepspace, to give him the illusion of aloneness; in actuality, they were in a huge hall where guards kept watch, musicians played soothing melodies, and stewards, ever mindful of their master's needs, strolled nervously. Through the mistveil Sajit saw only Elloran's shadow, tall, wavering.

"You never gave me the chance."

"Oh, Sajit. Am I not allowed to be human at all? Should I not fear transience too, and death? Tell me why *you* are so obsessed with her." Elloran's shadow blurred; it was edged with shimmerdust. "I will tell you. We both see what we can never have."

"What is that? Freedom?"

"You should not mock me, Sajitteh," the Inquestor said gently. "Do you think I am free? Duty fetters me more tightly than you can imagine. And man's guilt, which we Inquestors, in calling the game of *makrúgh* into being, have taken upon ourselves. Do you remember the song you used to sing, about the homeworld of the heart?"

"Yes."

"In her own way, my friend, she has found that homeworld. . . . But it is not as you or I imagined it, with angels singing and breezes wafting and the brooks and meadows oozing contentment. No, it is a harsh homeworld, and one that exacts a terrible price. . . . But it is hers, hers alone, and we will never touch it. That is why we lavish love on her, why we quarrel over her, whom neither can possess. Do you understand that?"

"No! I think you just want to teach me a lesson, you've seen me grow proud, perhaps, because I am your friend, you want to knock me back down into the Sewer Labyrinth of Alykh. Do you think you can win my loyalty with casuistry?" Sajit had gone too far again.

"We do not choose what we are. I must command, not woo you, Sajitteh. Beware. I'm not just in one of my moods, friend. There are things we both must learn."

"It's all very well for you to flagellate yourself—I understand, it's part of your High Inquestral complex or something. But why me?"

"Is it that I cannot banish from me all feeling for you? For an Inquestor, the way of compassion means the renunciation of love—do you not see that? The greater compassion means we must steel ourselves to tear down civilizations, to load whole planets' populations into people bins and scatter them chaff-like through the overcosm—can you not understand how it must hurt me? But I should not speak this way to you. You cannot understand."

"No, *hokh'Ton*, I cannot," said Sajit. And abruptly he left the bedchamber of his Lord.

Ton Elloran was a consummate player of *makrúgh*. With that single war he had deflected the wars of the Dispersal away from his own sector, with only a planet or two destroyed; now they could expect peace for a few years.

The Mist Season became the Season of Rains. The palace Varezhdur came to Chembrith, the chief world of Elloran's principality. Two whole continents were covered with the thinkhives that coordinated the worlds Elloran ruled. Another continent housed the starships sent from far Gallendys. And the fourth contained the cities: Angesang with its twisting walls you could see even from space, writhing like copulating snakes; Táthenthrang with its rainbow-tiered terraces, hanging over the Lake of Octagons; Ghakh of the thousand pyramids, with its university; Dhandhesht where were stored the holo-ramic memories of dead worlds. Solitude turned to the business of government. Diplomatic receptions on floatislands

hovering over the Lake, where spectacles of times before the
Dispersal were enacted over the waters to the strains of thou-
sand-man orchestras. Fierce games of *makrúgh* played over
interstellar distances, convocations of Inquestors, stiff and
sternfaced in their shimmercloaks, sipping zul in small palace
chambers. New programs for the thinkhives to mull over.

For Sajit there was new music to write; every event, every
new inning of *makrúgh*, was to be accompanied by new music.
Elloran seemed insatiable. He worked as though a demon
drove him, almost courting the heresy of utopianism, for he
assured by his diplomacy that war would be allayed far longer
than the Inquest usually thought suitable. Sajit alone knew
what was driving Elloran.

In Varezhdur, the nebula was almost completed.

He and Zhendra made love in a room in the high citadel of
Táthenthrang, on a hovercouch that drifted in time to a sad
slow consort of hidden shimmerviols. But she was ever more
remote now, living in her own imagined world, breathing the
dust-made starlight. When they finished he sent the hovercouch flying beyond the balcony, high above the Lake of Octagons. They sat and watched the city, each in his own little
silence.

"I hate this city," Zhendra said. "There's no dust here at
all. In the morning come servocorpses, scrubbing the stones of
the city even where there is nothing left to scrub. It's inhu-
man."

From the lakeshore to the horizon the terraced levels of
the city stretched, each coded in a rainbow color. It was beautiful to Sajit, and tragic too, because Elloran had caused the
city to be built in memory of the Rainbow King.

Zhendra said, "That's why I'm a dust sculptress, you
know. I see the towers and the monuments, the palaces and
the ziggurats, and I see the dust on the streets . . . and I know
that when the palaces have crumbled the dust will still remain."

*She's opening up to me,* Sajit thought wonderingly, *in the
only way she knows how.*

"I love you," he said uncertainly.

"Ton Elloran will not let me leave after I finish the sculpture," she said. "But I must . . . I must go to Aëroësh. I must
embrace the dust. You must make him. . . . He has promised

to send me, but you know an Inquestor need not answer to a promise. . . ."

"What influence do *I* have?"

"He trusts you. You did him a lot of good, by bringing him down to the slums of Aírang."

"I turned him into a vindictive monster."

"That too." She looked away. They were circling low over the lake now, sometimes even getting a little wet. Some children in a skiff watched them curiously, voyeuristically perhaps, for Chembrith was a modest world where lovers did not often embrace in the open. Then Zhendra said again, "Aëroësh, Sajitteh. Remember Aëroësh." He could not tell whether she loved him or not. Certainly she had never said so, but he could easily put that down to pride. But she could just be using him as a way to get to the dust world.

"Aëroësh," Sajit repeated listlessly.

The long peace surpassed all their expectations. The Dry Season they spent in Ménjifarn, where the lives of the flora and fauna were counted in minutes and seconds. They watched vast groves of flowers shifting their colors as they died and bloomed afresh, like klomet-wide kaleidoscopes; they watched the birds that soared but once to mate, then plummeted in feather-fluffy rains and cotton-candied into the soft earth. Forests sprang up and toppled, and the only humans were miners who manned the metal mines of the fever-lush equator. Varezhdur did not linger, but pinholed further through the overcosm until it reached Gom, where they finished the season with a deep space fireworks of exploding asteroids.

Not nearly soon enough, it seemed to those who attended the Inquestral court, the palace returned to orbit around the planet Alykh, for the Cold Season had begun. Neither Sajit nor the Inquestor would descend to the world below, and so the palace was mostly empty. And Sajit's music remained harsh, and grew ever more shrill and violent as the nebula neared completion. Now they watched her all day, as she worked until she dropped, hardly eating or sleeping. Her cheeks were hollowed out now, her eyes dead; she might have been one of the dying in the Sewer Labyrinth of Aírang. And the uglier she grew, the more beautiful became the nebula of dust, almost as though she had bequeathed it her own beauty in the final days of breathing life into it.

It was done.

She walked towards the Inquestor on his throne. Sajit saw from the orchestra pit that she could hardly stand. He stopped the music. She whispered "Aëroësh," so softly it could have been a leaf in the wind, and then she stumbled to the displacement plate and dematerialized from the room. Sajit thought she was going to die. He walked up to the Inquestor and looked at him for a long time. His gray eyes were lifeless as polished stone. Half-Alykh filled the blackness beyond the forcedome. Neither of them would look at the dust sculpture. But Sajit knew it by heart anyway; though his eyes were closed, he could visualize it perfectly from memory.

It was about ten meters tall and wide, and it echoed the stars around them, and it drew the stasis-field-power from starlight itself, like a lightsail of ancient times, drifting from star to star. Sajit said, "You must do as she asks, Elloran. You promised, and an Inquestor must always speak truth."

"What is truth?" Elloran shouted. "Truth is defined as what an Inquestor speaks!" He flung a chalice of zul down the steps. It clattered, rolled to the base of the dust-sculpture, forcing Sajit to glimpse at it for a moment. . . . "What is love? Is what you feel love, Sajitteh?" Sajit flinched at Elloran's public use of his child-name.

"You *are* jealous!"

"You dare speak like this to me. . . . You to whom I have opened up my very heart. . . ."

A long silence. In that silence, Zhendra's words on the day of their first meeting echoed and re-echoed through Sajit's mind: "You too are a whore! You too are a whore!"

"I too will leave you!" Sajit cried. "I too will have this freedom!"

"Freedom! Love! Truth! Words, words, words. The stars and the dust are eternal, but words are like the wind." Elloran could not meet Sajit's eyes. At last he said, "The peace has lasted too long. Next year I will play *makrúgh* for a war."

With those words Sajit knew he had given tacit assent not only to Zhendra's true desire, but also to Sajit's impetuous demand. Sajit did not know what to say. At last he stuttered, "I would give you enough time, of course, my Lord, to find a replacement. . . ."

"No, no. You cannot be replaced. You are as much a part of Varezhdur as I am." And Elloran spoke no more that day.

When Zhendra had recovered, Elloran sent her to Aëro-ësh. It was a world he never visited, at the far edge of Varezhdur's tributaries. She went with nothing but her tools and a little money, and an Inquestral seal-disk that he had pressed into her hand, insisting it would grease the wheels of the planetary bureaucracy. Of the parting words between Zhendra and the Inquestor, Sajit never learned anything.

But she did come to his chambers shortly before she was due to leave.

She stood before him: haggard, the sheen gone from her hair. He said, "Which of us did you love? Or was it just a ruse to find your world of dust?"

She said, "I cannot say." And kissed him softly but without passion. She was wearing only the slumsmock she had come to Varezhdur in.

An hour later, Sajit watched the tachyon bubble as it passed through the shipwalls to begin its journey through the unseeable tachyon universe. . . . A sun died to fuel its voyage, if the saying was to be believed.

Elloran commanded that the forcedome of the stardust nebula be opaqued and the displacement plates that led to it deactivated. No one would gaze on Zhendra's creation. . . .

In the throneroom, Sajit relented and played a sweet soothing music, but Elloran demanded the ugly music back. Sajit did as he was told.

Then he went down to Aïrang.

Quickly he found the whores' quarter, with its winding alleys flanked by flamepillars in garish colors, sodium-yellow or copper-blue or potassium-purple, behind which the pimps lurked like cockroaches, avoiding the brilliance of the night sky. He went from pleasure girl to pleasure girl, each one as perfect as the last, devouring them like sherbets. There was no pleasure in the aftertaste. They reminded him of his mother.

When he returned to the palace, he found that war had broken out in a distant sector, and Elloran had allied himself with the Inquestor who styled himself loser. *Makrúgh* again, played with a vengeance.

The seasons whirled.

The Mist Season in Kailasa, where they found a new sport,

dividing the courtiers into armies arrayed in antique costumes and staging mock battles over the Pallid Ocean with honey-eggs for ammunition and floaters for starships, with many giggles as the eggs broke and dripped sweet liquor on their faces. . . .

The Rainy Season in Chembrith, where a new holodrama that purported to represent the first contact between the Inquestrix Varushkadan and the alien Whispershadows was all the rage with the diplomatic set. . . .

Then back to Ménjifarn in the Dry Season with side trips to Gom and Eldereldad and the newly broken utopia world Kiritekanyah, with much gossip about Ton Elloran's coming promotion, perhaps to a larger principality, perhaps even to Grand Inquestor or to become Kingling of a single, important principality like Gallendys or Vanjyvel or the secret world of the tarn crystals. . . .

There was talk of secession from the Dispersal by a renegade Inquestor, kiloparsecs away, at the other end of the Dispersal . . . a heretic named Ton Davaryush. But such things were spoken of only in whispers; for it was well known that Davaryush had been Elloran's friend.

For all these rumors of revolution, life changed little in the court of Varezhdur. Except that Sajit felt impelled to demand that Elloran stick to his word, and allow him to leave.

Elloran only said, "I will miss you," and nodded. Could he not show any emotion anymore? But Sajit had to admit that Elloran was all Inquestor, showing none of the human weakness he had evinced before.

He joined a show-satellite and played background music—just himself and a quartet—for a troupe of rope dancers. It was said that he played for Rax Nika, the greatest dancer of them all.

He journeyed to all the sites considered the most beautiful in the Dispersal of Man: the firesnows of Ont, the iridescing rains of Kenkereng, the wardances of the wild men of Arut, the remains of the Earthdawn Nova shrouding the Flower Cluster of Chitarandaranda.

And on a world called Eirendeh he visited the Institute of Dust Sculpture itself. There he saw apprentices shaping the dust into small tableaux and using miniaturized fieldmakers to snap them into shape. Everyone was speaking of minimalism. But he saw nothing to compare in grandeur with Dei Zhendra's work. Perhaps it was true that she had had the Inquestral vision.

On Eirendeh they fashioned pretty shapes, intricate patterns . . . but no one had sought to encapsulate the whole Dispersal of Man within the contents of a sackful of dust. Zhendra had been a visionary. She had raised dust-sculpting from curiomaking to an art.

And five years passed. Five subjective years, that is; perhaps, in realtime, decades.

He had not forgotten her. No. But he thought he could forget Ton Elloran.

But one day, sipping zul in an alley on some backworld whose name he later could not remember, he overheard some young people at the next table talking about theater, of all things. Necrotheater. They were being waited on by servocorpses; it was one of those worlds where such creatures were ubiquitous.

As he quaffed his zul, he eavesdropped idly on their conversation: ". . . the part of the boy Inquestor is animated by Karnofara, one of the brightest new talents around. I could have sworn, when the boy and the young singer sprang up on those pteratyger, they were alive! And when Sajit sang his song—

Sajit perked up at the mention of his own name. . . . Presently he realized that they were discussing a play on a "mythological" subject, *The Legend of the Rainbow King*. He started to interrupt them, to correct some detail—"That's not how it happened!" When suddenly he remembered something. . . .

When they were children, stranded on that terrible planet of servocorpses . . . when they were riding the pteratyger up to Rainbow Castle . . . before he knew that he would strike down an Inquestor with his harp and kill him . . . in the few hours of true innocence remaining to them both . . . Sajit had sung the song of the homeworld of the heart, and Elloran had reached out to clutch his hand in fear, in desperation, in need. I must go back, he realized.

But when he came back it was as though a single breath had elapsed. Somehow he had hoped that things would go back to the way they had been, before Zhendra, before *makrúgh*. And though Elloran seemed to accept him as before, Sajit could not bring himself to admit that he owed Elloran any more than duty demanded. And always he thought of Zhendra, of the unanswered questions.

Varezhdur had grown, of course. The chamber of the dust sculpture was sealed and unreachable; it no longer hugged the skin of the palace and faced the starlight. It was buried under a tangle of gold steeples linked by coils of corridors. Atop the steeples sprouted a bright new amphitheater for grand recitals.

The seasons whirled again. There was no news of Zhendra, for the planet Aëroësh could not be reached quickly through the overcosm; a delphinoid shipmind might make the trip in many subjective years, and time dilation would take a terrible toll. But Sajit didn't want to admit that he had lost her completely. He wanted to hear her say that she had loved him. More than Elloran. That was the crux of his self-inflicted torment.

One day he was playing a new song in the new amphitheater, scored for a child's voice and a single whisperlyre. The words, in High Inquestral, were:

> *dáras sikláh sta lúkten z'ómbren;*
> *af chítaras seréh chom áish,*
> *chom dáras fáh.*

> The stars circle from light to shadow
> and even our hearts will become as dust
> as the stars have become. . . .

With an imperious wave Elloran dismissed the orchestra and summoned Sajit to his new throne. The amphitheater was larger than the old throneroom, and more austere: no carvings covered the ceilings, no pillars of flame adorned the walls of plain white Ontian marble. Sajit walked the hundred paces from the pit to the throne, a circular reclining throne of white clingfire stuffed with kyllap leaves. He was thinking: *Why must he surround himself with such immensity? Does he want to extinguish himself, like a single dust-mote in the emptiness of space?*

"My Lord," he said. Elloran struggled to produce the beginning of a smile; Sajit saw that his eyes had become lined. He had abandoned cosmetic renewal. . . . He was *trying* to age, he who had the choice of living far longer than those without power.

"You're still thinking of her!" Elloran laughed drily.

"I want to go to Aëroësh, Elloran. I want to see what it is that makes her love the dust."

"There's been no word for years. And if you take a delphinoid ship to Aëroësh there's no guarantee that she won't be dead when you arrive. You know how the pinhole-paths through the overcosm are; space and time lose all meaning, and Aëroësh is too far by objective time for a single lifetime's journey."

"You're toying with me, Inquestor! You know I'm going to ask you for a tachyon bubble."

"Yes, I know." He seemed to sink back even further into the clingfire softness. "Tell me, Sajit . . . why is it so important? But I already know the answer, Sajitteh."

"I will not hear it from you."

"I know. Since coming back you have withheld from me your friendship. You no longer believe me. For you it was five years—but do you know how long it was for me?"

"You are almost immortal! You should not speak of time."

"She's dead, Sajitteh." But something in his voice told Sajit that he was holding something back. "I know you won't believe me. You're still fooling yourself into thinking in terms of romantic passion. . . . But there is a choice. You can learn the truth from me, or you can go. I will not stop you. Yet—though I can refuse you nothing, in memory of what you have been to me—you should tell me one thing: why must I kill a star to send you on a mission of unrequited love?"

It was hopeless. "You're an Inquestor," Sajit said bitterly. "You can't possibly understand the love of ordinary people. How can you feel such a thing, you who can pulverize planets with a single word?"

"Sajit, Sajit, I'm not trying to obstruct you, I'm trying to tell you that it's useless. . . ."

"Let me see for myself."

"Sajit, you're too proud to see the truth about this love of yours. . . ."

"You're still competing with me! You with your hundred palaces and your dozen worlds stocked with slaves and your tachyon bubbles and your—"

"I never competed with you. You flatter yourself, that I would condescend to play *makrúgh* with you. Yes, I'll send you to Aëroësh. May the powers of powers protect you."

Sajit closed his eyes then. He wanted to remember Zhendra the way she was when he had first seen her. He knew of the beige hair streaked with turquoise, the eyes like sapphires in cold light, the haunting, taunting voice, the strained remoteness of her when she dreamed up her nebula of dust. . . . He knew all this but he could not conjure up her image. All he could see was the dust, swirling, whirling, so beautiful you dared not gaze at it for long. . . . The dust did not swirl for him. It did not need him, or anyone; for in eternity they would all be dust.

"I want a floater to the surface, and a guide."

. . . . a city of drab stone, squat buildings set upon honeycombs hollowed from rock, beneath a forcedome that kept out the sky of red-brown dust . . .

"Are you crazy, sir?" The official shivered and offered Sajit a glass of mulled zul. They were in a small evenly lit room of brown rock, reclining on awkward couches of cushioned stone. The official was an elder of the city, disturbed and not entirely delighted at the command to entertain a dignitary from the court that theoretically held sway over the forgotten world. "The dust," he said, "is treacherous. It would kill anyone who went out in it. We do not love the dust here, Shen Sajit. Why, six years ago a woman came, a courtier such as you, sir. She courted the dust—"

"Where is she now?"

The official shrugged. "Your lives are so different, you courtiers. When you are bored of your luxuries you even seek out the deadly, the ugly, the horrifying. I imagine that she sought her own death for some reason that we Aëroëshi are too unsophisticated to understand."

"Was she—"

"Zhonya, Shondra, some name like that . . ." He downed his beaker of zul with a single swallow. "In any case, I strongly advise against it. What could possibly be interesting about huge clouds of dust that sweep the plains and would scour and devour everything if there were anything to devour? So what if they sometimes seem to take on lifelike shapes, to mimic starswarms and nebulae as they gust without purpose across the barran lands?"

"They mimic nebulae?" Sajit said faintly. The beaker

slipped from his hand. A servocorpse silently removed it and wiped the stain from the polished rock. "Then she's alive! I must go up there now!"

The official laughed. "Give me ten sleeps, maybe more, to find someone foolhardy enough to guide you. It may be that we have a forceglobed flier that can withstand the storms, somewhere in the city. But it will have to be repaired. We have no reason to go out on the surface. We can see the dust from here." And he pointed out of the window, out at the sky.

Sajit trembled, unable to answer.

Erupting from the dust, the floater burst into a scarlet sky. It was an incredibly ancient device built by some hobbyist, perhaps never really meant to fly, that thrust through dust and atmosphere by flinging out a jet of smoke-tinged blue flame. Sajit was not happy with it, even though a darkfield had been added to it and englobed it completely except for the opening for the jetstream. He strapped on his restrainer too tightly and tried to push back as far as he could into the seat cushions. The guide, hardly more than a boy, sliped the vehicle into an airstream and let it coast, raising and lowering its wings according to some mystic-seeming pattern. The flier steadied itself, and Sajit dared to look down.

"I want you to follow the first dust-pattern that you see," he said.

The guide shrugged. He was being well paid, and understood well the idiosyncrasies of the rich. They flew against the sunlight; when Sajit looked through the ring of round windows he saw endless bleakness, brown unbroken flatness. The dust seethed a little, like water beginning to boil, but he saw no works of art. . . .

"A storm, sir!" the guide shouted. With a wrench he flung the flier into the sun, darkening the field to avoid blindness. Sajit saw nothing—

And then, at the very limits of the horizon, a small smudge shivering like a frightened rodent—

"Follow it!" he whispered urgently. Zhendra must be there. At the heart of the dust. The flier gathered speed, nauseating him.

The dust raced towards them. Without warning they were soaring over it, and Sajit could make out what it was . . . the arm of a gigantic spiral galaxy that whirlpooled over a hundred square klomets. His heart almost stopped beating. "Go into the nebula!" he shouted.

Outside the roar must be like a thunder of lifting starships. Through the portholes nothing could be heard. The dust shifted and sifted like in a dream, too huge to comprehend. *She must be in there,* he thought. *How can I make her understand?* "Can you fly this thing in patterns?" he cried.

"How, sir?"

"The smoke stream! I want you to burn letters into the dust!"

"I can't go into the nebula, sir! I'm not crazy!" The boy said. The flier veered wildly in the wind, losing speed. Soon the dust would swallow it—

"Let's go back!" said the guide.

"Is there a lifecraft aboard this flier?"

The boy nodded. "Take it," Sajit said. "Go back. This thing can't be so rickety that a veteran of the overcosm wars can't at least maneuver it. . . ." Without a word the boy scurried away. In a moment Sajit saw the small pod thrusting through the dust storm like a lost insect. The boy had not been paid to die, after all. He could not force him. . . .

The flier spun in the storm, Sajit eased over to the control panel and subvocalized his instructions to the flier's little thinkhive, hoping it was advanced enough to obey him. . . .

The flier leapt! And swerved! Sickness churned his stomach as the smoke trails formed into *zhash*, the first letter of Zhendra's name, blue fingers of color against the mud-red—

Again and again, leaping and swerving, the gee-shifts pushing him into his seat and flinging him outward against the restrainers, *zhash* after *zhash* in two-klomet-high figures of flame—

He felt the craft weaken against the wind. The voice of the vehicle's thinkhive broke the raging silence:

*I am not programmed to deal with such stresses! Please reduce density of programming, pending restoration of flier stability*—

*Zhash!* against the tossing tempest—

*Zhash!*

*Zhash!*

The thinkhive's voice—*I am unable to continue with present programming. The craft is now out of control. I cannot hold the forcefield. Environments will interface in a few seconds—*

Sound now, dust hail-pelleting the portholes, whooshing of the storm, ahead, the eye of the nebula unmoving in the turbulence—

*I'm going to die.*

He was falling. He could not survive. And then there was a frozen moment in which seconds stretched like elastic, and his head was light as though the air were drenched with the drug *f'ang,* and the dust was cramming his nostrils but he couldn't feel it—

And then he saw her. The eyes glazed, icy, the cheeks gaunt, the hair straggly and lusterless, the worksmock torn, the nebula whirling around her, engulfing her and yet coming out of her, just as on the day she had finished the sculpture at Varezhdur—

*I'm hallucinating!* a small voice inside him whispered.

"Zhendra!" he shrieked, reaching out to embrace the emptiness—

Silence.

A chamber walled with dust, sourcelessly lit. Sajit struggled to his feet and looked around him, half-consciously straightening out his kaleidokilt. At first it seemed as though the walls were motionless; when he stared he saw the chalk-white dust shift almost imperceptibly. The dust was whirling but time itself seemed to have decelerated to a crawl.

And then she materialized.

A woman made of dust. . . .

All dust the hair-strands, dust the eyes, dust the hollow cheeks and sunken limbs, dust the billowing gray smock. Sajit stared at her, not knowing whether to believe his eyes.

"You've become—"

The woman of dust did not speak. She pointed ahead, to the wall: when Sajit turned he saw letters forming out of the dust, words. . . .

*I am the Zhendra you once knew, Shen Sajit of the court of Elloran. I am the Zhendra you once thought you loved.*

"You can't be! I came all this way—"

*Don't be unhappy, Sajitteh.* Sajit saw the woman smile a little. Specks of dust rained from her lips. *I have found what I wanted. I have found the secret of the dust of Aëroësh. . . .*

*Do you want to know what I know?*

*The dust has been waiting here for aeons, Sajit. Dust is very patient, you know. There were semi-chains of silicon, almost-cells of dead stone, waiting for the breath of the ion wind. When the storms came they linked a little, waiting for consciousness. Then I came. I came alone into this wilderness with my little charge-generators and field-generators and my silly little plans for artistic immortality. How stupid I was! The wind tempted me. When I gave myself to it, it was waiting. . . .*

*It ate away my body like a fire, Sajitteh. And copied it in silicon. And the dust storm made itself slave to my mind, and it found consciousness. . . . We are immortal now.*

*I have given the dust life. I am no longer human, but I am all art, conscious yet created. And I sweep over the dead plains, my body like the galaxy itself, filling the dust with the joy of being alive. . . .*

"Parasites!" Sajit screamed, longing for the woman with the beige hair streaked with turquoise. "They've taken away your soul, everything that made you beautiful. . . ."

*What was there to take, Sajitteh? I was a nothing woman, a whore among a million whores that garbaged the streets of Airang. I thought I had a vision—but how can a dead thing have vision? My soul was all I had to give. I dropped it into the dust as a crystal into a saturated solution, and I became one with the dust I loved, I became the soul of the dust. . . . You should not pity me. You have your music, knit from tragedy and love, and Elloran has his makrúgh, but I alone have become a planet's breath, its mind, its life.*

"Didn't you love me at all, then? Did you use us, Elloran and me, merely as stepping stones?" As he said this Sajit understood at last why he had come. He wanted above all for her to tell him she had loved him. He wanted to know which of the two she had favored. . . . He too had used her. To torture Elloran, whom he envied and loved, and to punish himself for accepting his own slavery. . . .

A tear of dust fell from the dust-woman's eye. Her hair seemed to ripple, though there was no wind.

Behind her, the dust said: *I loved you, Sajit. I loved Elloran. But there are some things far greater than love, when you are no longer human. You could stay here and merge with us, you know. You would know music more perfect than the most accomplished consort of shimmerviols. But . . . though I proffer you this choice, you are to learn from this that there are no true choices. We do not choose what we are. Tell me, did you truly love me?*

"Of course I loved—still love you," Sajit said.

*No. You do not. Your inner conflict never centered on me. It was Elloran, to whom you had given your whole life, with whom you quarreled; I was a pawn, nothing more. Do not try to convince yourself that you give to Elloran only out of duty. It is him you have always loved from the heart, not me. You have turned your whole world inside out, only to discover that you cannot flee from yourself.*

And Sajit wept, for he knew that he had finally learned the truth: freedom is an illusion, and the freer a man seems, the more fettered he is in fact. Perhaps even truth is an illusion. He wept until he was senseless. And the eye of the nebula lifted itself, and the storm shifted until it hovered over the topmost of the tubes that led to the city far under the dust, releasing him, unconscious, at the city's entrance. And then the storm fanned out until it made a nebula a thousand klomets wide, larger than a man could ever see except from high up in space.

And the dust danced for itself, heeding no man.

The laserdrill shattered the last of the seals and the Inquestor and his musician stepped into the chamber that had lain buried beneath abandoned halls and towers and spiraling corridors, unseen for a dozen years. The darkness was almost palpably intense. Their footsteps rang, half-muffled in the hugeness, violating the silence. The air was stale, dusty.

"Thus," said the Inquestor, "we bury our quarrel." He clapped his hands. At once a light-shaft lanced the darkness, a swath of light from floor to ceiling—

The dust, heaped on the mirror metal floor, stirred a little, as the thinkhive that controlled the dust-sculpture searched its memories for the paths that the specks must travel. Silently, the nebula shivered into being out of the cloud, whirling to life. Then the dust danced, always moving yet always one, as the stars have danced since the beginning of time. The arms revolved slowly around a dust-core that blazed in this somber dimness. Fiery dust-specks stippled the imitated sky. . . .

A microcosm dancing with itself. Complete. Alone. Resplendent.

They stood for a moment, too awed for words. Then Sajit said, "I must make a new music to go with this dust. A solemn music, a pavane perhaps." His words pelted the silence. They were unnecessary words. The music, shifting through his mind, said everything.

They walked towards the dust-sculpture, two very small people against the vastness.

"I have received a new thought, Sajit," Elloran said. "The thinkhives are buzzing with it. It comes from a far region of the Dispersal of Man, and here the thought is only a faint one, but it is this: The Inquest falls, Sajit. It will fall soon—in a millennium or less, perhaps. Even though the Fall may never touch us here in our palace of gold."

"It's a terrible thought!" Sajit said, unable to think it clearly.

"No, it's not," said Elloran. Then after a moment he said, "We'll organize an expedition of art-lovers, and we'll go down to Aëroësh and see the dust. She would be pleased, wouldn't she?"

Sajit said—for he had only just returned from the dust-world, and had told Elloran nothing—"How could you have known?" He tried to read the Inquestor's face, tried not to show his own startlement . . . but he saw only a cipher. "You knew and you did not warn me?" He felt anger for a moment.

"Could I have stopped you?" And now Ton Elloran had found his throne in the half dark, and he was dusting it with a fold of his shimmercloak. The gesture was a sad one, curiously touching. "You have forgotten so much, Sajit. You who have known me since I was a child, before I destroyed my first utopia. . . .

"Do you really think I am not human? Do you really think I can't feel love, pain, the rejection of those I trust, hate, envy? We dare not express these things, we Inquestors, but once I did so, and to a mere soldierchild without a clan. . . .

"You left my palace when she left, Sajit. You were gone five years. Don't you think I ever longed for her? Don't you think I was ever hurt that both of you had abandoned me? Do you think I never needed to go to Aëroësh for myself, to see for myself, to be convinced for myself that my love was a hopeless one? Sajitteh—" He stopped for a moment. In the pause, another strain of music coursed through Sajit's mind. "I heard those answers too, Sajit. And at least we have this now. We have both touched the edge of her terrible joy, and it has changed us."

"Elloran—"

"Enough." Elloran's voice had an unwonted tenderness. "At least we will always have this galaxy of dust." He mounted the throne, carefully lifting his shimmercloak for each step of sculpted gold. Then he sat back into its cushions and faced the swirling splendor.

It was then that Sajit understood how deep their loyalty to each other had always been. Even if the Inquest did crumble around them, this loyalty must still stand. . . . He knew he would always be Elloran's servant, giving music of his own free will, giving love even. . . . The dust was the great leveler, making the palaces and slums one.

As always, he waited for a command.

"Go on," said Ton Elloran, "I know you are bursting with music, and you must set it down before it slips away."

Sajit hesitated still. Elloran needed comfort, that was clear. He couldn't bear to leave him alone yet. The stars of dust shone, animated by a woman now transfigured, they shone and shifted and drifted and sifted and made silent music—

"Go!" Elloran whispered harshly. "You are not to see me weep. I am an Inquestor."

Sajit turned his back on the dust-sculpture. The stillness was pregnant, like the hush of a crowd in the second before the first note of a new composition. He walked away from the Inquestor's throne, remembering Zhendra's thought:

*When we are gone, the dust will still remain.*

# 5

When Tash Tievar finished the tale, the throneroom was deserted. Jenjen had not noticed the departure of Ton Elloran. But now, alone with the whiterobed Rememberer in the huge hall with the dust-storm nebula at its heart, she felt as though she had intruded on some private grief.

"Why has he left us?" she said.

"He could not bear the remembrance," Tievar said. "And it is forbidden to him to weep. In spite of the revolution, he is still all Inquestor. . . . If all of them had been like him, the war would never have begun."

He turned his back on the dust-sculpture, bidding her follow. She did not know where they were going; they seemed to be plating randomly through the palace. Here there were honeycombs where lived the thousands of palace retainers; here were great empty halls, that had doubtless once served some purpose, but now lay dusty and untended, their walls frayed clingfire, their floors cracked stone. There were murals and friezes, their power sources long depleted; some were unnaturally still, others yet jerkily animated or with gray lacunae in their holosculpt projections.

"Where are you taking me?" she said at last.

"Nowhere. We are weaving through Varezhdur's life, my daughter. In the weaving all is one."

"That's what my mistress of the lightloom always used to tell me. But I never wanted to be the end-product of an ancient tradition. I always wanted to be singular. That's why I'm uneasy and angry over the Inquestor's decision to name me to the Clan of Ir."

"And my story? Did that not show you Elloran's heart?"

"There was so much in your words. The Inquestor . . . he's so ancient now, not like in the story at all. Surely the story is but a blurred reflection of that remembrance. And I'll never understand all the details of your stories. There's so much I've never seen. Each convolution seems to open up vast new vistas. . . . Yet to you they seemed like commonplaces. The firesnows of Ont. The great cities of Chembrith. That zul-shop where Sajit found out that they had turned the story of his childhood into a myth. . . . Was that not Essondras? I heard Karnofara mentioned. But Karnofara is an ancient man, last in a line of many Karnofaras, all corpse-dancers. It could then have all happened centuries ago. . . ."

"It could have. Or on another world. The Dispersal has a million worlds, and necrodrama is not unique to yours, I'm sure."

"You say you have shown Elloran's heart . . . yet I am more confused than ever before. And angry. I think that he was cruel. Did he truly love Sajit? Or Zhendra? Or was it only a game?"

"I do not know. It is said that Inquestors do not possess love as we know it."

"And the dust-sculptress—did she use them, after all?"

"It is a mystery. There are as many interpretations as there are listeners, Jenjen. But you, the artist, whom do you side with?"

"I'm more confused than ever before. What is this story meant to teach me? That I must accept the geis of darkweaving that Elloran has laid upon me? That I must bear this burden solely because I was born a slave to him?"

"We do not choose what we are."

"Oh, Father Tievar—who chooses for us?"

"Let me tell you the story of Rax Nika, the web dancer. Perhaps you will learn from that. You think, like all young ones, that art is a burst of song, a spontaneous rejoicing, a celebration of the soul's liberation. But that is only the beginning of art, daughter."

"And who was Rax Nika? I heard you mention her name in Sajit's story; you said that, in the time that he parted from Elloran, he had background music for her on a show tour, and that she was the greatest rope dancer of all time. But what is rope dancing?"

"I will tell you all. You will know, Jeni"—and she was curiously moved that he had addressed her by child-name, assuming a sudden intimacy—"about how all the weaving is one. You know, from the stories of Sajit and Elloran, how much can hang on one man's whim. But can the fate of all the Dispersal of Man's quadrillions be that fragile? Could it all hang on a single person: not even an Inquestor, but a child perhaps, a dancer? Listen, Ir Jenjen. . . ."

# 6

# The Story of the Web Dancer

She was poised in the pause on a leap's edge, toes nudging the rope-slack in the tight circlet of glare, pressed between a breath and its release—a girl of eleven, alone under a billion unseen eyes.

*This time—*

Nika flexed her toes swiftly for the first triple somersault of her career. She gathered in all the strands of tension and compressed them, *hard,* into a knot of neutronium deep within herself, then released it all at once, exploded outward at the ends of her limbs, *gave* into the perfect curve of the movement—

And slipped!

There was a moment between falling and fallen. A moment drawn out and still. A moment of cutting clarity. In that moment her gray eye saw—

Image boxes slamming to the ground, lens-jewels splintering, fire cartwheeling over instrument banks, doorways dominoing over monitors and shelfstands, and—*It wasn't my fault I slipped! she thought. Something collided with the show satellite! There's a war going on in this system and we should never have chosen to record here but they said we were neutral and performers can't be touched because they come under the protection of the Inquest!*

—technicians were running amok; alien uniforms of different sides flashed across the floor; bodies cascaded like flocks of birds, someone in a booming voice declaring this quadrant of space now occupied, performers with mouths open staring at the slaughter, screaming—

She closed her eyes then. *I'm going to die!* she thought,

not caring anymore. *I'm just going to be a chance victim of someone else's war.* . . . And then she wished her hair was streaming above her, not cropped to a centimeter's length, but then she remembered why she had cut it off, and she felt a yawning emptiness inside her and wanted to die.

—rope flopping snakelike, writhing, tangling her feet, and—

*I don't care!* she thought fiercely. *I'm Nika of the clan of Rax and the show never stops, never never, never—*

The vault of the show satellite cracked. Through the air-shield the stars shone . . . and another ship, huge, with none of the gaudy local markings, was growing rapidly, blacking out the starlight.

*Who could they be?* she wondered, in the split second before the forceshield slapped her into blackness.

Nika opened her eyes. *Why am I still alive?* she thought.

"They're all dead." The voice was gravelly, the accent strange. "Don't think of them anymore. Be at peace with yourself."

Silhouettes of two men; and behind them . . . She could not tell where the room ended and where the wild dance of laser-bright lights began. Flametongues whipped against blackness! And darting between them, neckerchief swirls of purple, crimson, cerulean, cadium-yellow, ultramarine, bursting out and fading into darkness.

. . . *We're in a starship!* For they were in the overcosm then: that *other* space, of strange dimensions, where *far* becomes *near.*

"Dead?" She faced her captors. *How much time has passed?* She could still feel the tightrope slipping from her feet and the utter helplessness—

"Dead," the gravelly voice echoed. "We won't harm you, girl. We saved your life."

He was good-looking, bland, overdressed; his body-jewels gleamed in the rainbow fire of outside. She disliked him at once. The other one, though: severe, old, dressed from head to foot in a single shimmercloak.

*An Inquestor!* So somehow, power was involved. A lot of power.

It wasn't the first time Nika had been whisked away from

everything she knew. *I'm so tired*, she thought . . . She wanted to cry. But she knew she would not. She had vowed never to cry again.

"They are all dead, your friends," said the Inquestor, not unkindly. "Some might have survived a month or two . . . but time dilation has taken care of *them*. We intercepted a local battle to pluck you out."

"But the Inquest doesn't interfere in local wars!" she said. When that evoked no response, she cried out: "I could have *done* it!"

"Done what?" said the first man.

"The triple somersault!" she said. "The climax of my career, recorded on crystals for a billion eyes."

"Career!" the young man scoffed.

"Don't mock her," said the Inquestor sharply. "Kaz Amar, go back to your astrogating." The man bowed, departed quickly. "You're a child yet," he said when they were alone. "Let's not hear talk of crowning moments of careers, Nika, not for another century yet."

Nika felt rage gathering inside her. *I'm not a child!* How dare they patronize her! They had taken away everything: her homeworld, her friends, the nomadic life of the show-satellites, flicking from system to system . . . and they had plucked her away from her supreme achievement.

She felt the rope slipping beneath her feet again. She would have struck out in fury—

Then she heard inside herself the voice of Iliash, who had trained her: *Push your rage inwards! Let it collapse like the aftermath of a nova, into a ball of neutronium! Harder, harder. . . .* The voice pounded at her memory. . . .

"Nikkyeh—" the other began consolingly.

"*Nika.* I'm not a child." How dare he presume to address her by a diminutive, when he was neither lover nor friend.

"Good, you have personal dignity, spirit," said the Inquestor, appraising her.

"Take me *home!*"

The Inquestor stood impassive. He towered over her, a darkened doorway set into the wall of light-swirls. "Nika—"

"I won't stay here! I have to get back to homeworld. If I train hard I can make the panhuman games. You don't have the right to kidnap me." But she felt her past slipping away, she saw that she no longer believed in homeworld or in herself. . . .

"Nika," said the Inquestor. "You are a Rax, and we have need of a Rax. You've grown up thinking you're nothing special, just fit for the circus; your body too small for a warrior, your intellect too unschooled for a thinker. But you are one of the most valuable people in the Dispersal of Man. You're not ready for all this yet. You should have had more time, more training. But we're desperate."

"For what?"

"Listen. I am Ton Exkandar z Vangyvel K'Ning, Inquestor and Kingling."

"Ruler of my homeworld . . ." Blurred images of infancy whirlpooled.

"Yes. Don't say I didn't have the right to kidnap you." He paused. Behind, fireworks burst from a sea of ink. Fire-ripples laced the darkness. *Why is he trying to justify himself?* Nika thought. Then: *He's vulnerable.* She wanted to trust him, but—

"It is incredible that we should need you!" he burst out. "That I should gatecrash a petty war, like a space pirate, a common kidnapper—"

"But why do you need me?" She was bewildered, angry, frightened. "Did you destroy the show-satellite just to get *me?*"

"No," said Ton Exkandar, "we intercepted the local war. You *had* to be saved."

*Am I that important? I'm only a girl? What sort of game am I a pawn in?*

"And now I'll never do it. . . ."

"Do what?"

But Nika had shut him out of her thoughts. She had turned away from him; and now she watched the shifting, soundless patterns, letting them soothe her, hypnotize her. . . .

She imagined an infinite rope stretched all the way across the overcosm, and infinite Nikas, reflections of herself, leaping, upending themselves in a swift tight arc of movement, whirling down to touch the rope with the gentlest of touches. . . .

And slipping.

It was closed-loop holotape of the memory, each time no less terrifying.

How could she fight these people? She didn't know who they were and what they wanted. And she had fought too many people already to become what she was. She was tired! Drained!

"And now I'll never do it," she said, shuddering.

She would not let them put her into stasis. So there would be three subjective months in the overcosm, and there was nothing to do.

In her quarters there was one curved gray wall that could be blanked and that gave a view of the madness out-side. When she was awake she lay on her pallet and watched.

They had put up a series of ranked transverse bars for her to practice on. But she wouldn't touch them. She didn't even look at them. Because they made her suspect her whole child-hood had been manipulated, had been drawn toward . . . something no one would tell her about.

There was nothing to do but remember. And this she did, in the moments before sleep, or after staring herself into a trance while the colors danced. . . .

She was six and the children had all gone to war. She had run all the way from the orphanage to watch them, to stand by the wall and see the ships rise like a flock of silverdoves and cross the faces of the far, cold suns of Vangyvel.

Mother found her weeping under a whispertree. It reached out a furcoated metal hand to the child's brow; and the tree sang as the breezes of Vangyvel touched its flutelike leaves, a soft random counterpoint. . . . "Don't cry," said Mother in its consoling mode.

"I want to go, too!"

"So you shall, so you shall . . . but right now you're too small. Too precious, too special," it said, increasing its sympathy-tones in a steep gradient with each word.

"There's something wrong with me! I know it, I know it!" She began sobbing again, with the utter, end-of-the-universe hopelessness that only children know. For a while now she had not grown at all, and her bones were thin and hollow. "I'm a mutant or something! Isn't that why I'm in an orphanage?"

"Of course not, child, you're very special, only I can't tell you why yet. . . ."

*And the froglet will become a Kingling!* thought Nika, bitter. Mother was programmed to lie to her. After all, it was only a machine. The tree seemed to copy her sobs, mocking them, the way the other children always did. . . .

"I'll never cry again!" she said passionately. "I'll do something with my tiny body that no one else will be able to do!"

"That's my girl."

"All right, Mother. Nikkyeh will go home now." They stepped toward the displacement plate and commanded the coordinates.

That was the day she had first felt the emptiness inside, yearning to be filled. And had thrown anger into it.

Later she threw herself into dancing the rope. She had to be good at *something!* And she was. Her sense of balance was *unnatural*, everyone said. Which was true.

She could spin like a gyroscope down half the length of a slackrope. She could do it slowly, making them blue from holding their collective breath, stretch out the tension to its elastic limits, then reverse in a flash, stifling the gasps of relief.

Rax Iliash was her teacher. They brought him in, encouraging her. He was older, about twelve or so she judged, but small too, like her. Two years he spent pushing her. He knew so much, he who seemed just a child.

The moments when she released all her anger at being different, all her frustration at not being normal—into achingly beautiful parabolas of motion across emptiness—these were her moments of joy. Finally they made crystals of her dancing, and they became nomads. The homeless life of the show-satellites pleased Nika—what had home meant but children's mocking laughter?

On initiation, she too had received the clan title of Rax. She and Iliash were the only two either of them had ever heard of. She never took part in the initiation; the Inquestor of Judgment had merely handed the title to her. . . .

"But am I not to be tested?" She was suspicious as always, of everyone except Iliash.

Worried, overworked, the eyes had looked right through her and he said: "Daughter, you are Rax. We cannot waste you." *What did that mean?*

Once she and Iliash had gone to the zoo world and wandered around like tourists, gaping at the pseudoenvironments: the firesnows of Ont, the methane fogs of Brekekekex, the rivermountains of Ellory, the amber skies of Lalaparalla . . . and the beasts: lobster-things, fire-things, cloud-things, balloon-things . . .

Two innocents, they walked hand in hand. Between the forceshielded habitats were corridors of a manworld environment.

They came to a cave where a crystal creature slept. The crowd lurched forward as it woke.

Suddenly a burst of anguish issued from the cave and hit Nika, almost physically. "Did you *feel* that?"

"Yes. Yes." His gray eyes, so like hers, were troubled. The crowd was unaware of anything; they bent down, almost touching the forceshield, murmuring "Oh, how cute. . . ."

Iliash's hands almost squashed Nika's. Waves of pain crested and ebbed. "I can't stand it!" she said. Then, crying out: "It's a mistake! That's a sentient creature! You can't cage him!"

Curious stares, laughter. She was being mocked again! She was almost fainting with the pain. Iliash pulled her and dragged her along the path, away from the crowd.

Now they reached a field, with ten-meter-high cornstalks under an ink-blue sky. Iliash was saying, "Nikkyeh, you and I have this empathy. It's one of our special things, an empathy with alien beings. You and I are *tailored*, Nikkyeh! The Inquest has some purpose for us."

She clutched him to her. But they were just two children, and nothing came of it.

Soon after the show-satellite left for another system, Nika began to train for the triple somersault in 0.5 gravity. No rope dancer had ever done it before. She worked with a fierceness not usually found in children. She had to fill the void inside her! She was hungry for training. . . .

And so she forgot all about the Inquest's special purpose. It seemed so irrelevant. She was far from Vangyvel now; and the Dispersal of Man comprised a respectable percentage of the galaxy.

But when she was nine Iliash left the troupe.

She went to say goodbye to him. They were on a desert planet, a dreary planet of endless red sand under a sapphire sky. Iliash stood—strange how he had never grown at all—beside two tall figures in shimmercloaks. Inquestors! And behind the three—

It was a sphere. It was totally black, featureless, perhaps ten meters in diameter. It appeared to have no substance. It was as if a portion of the sandscape and sky had been blotted out, had simply ceased to exist. It was a tachyon bubble, of course. Inquestors used them to travel instantly through space. Never ordinary people. The overcosm still required subjective time of the traveler, even though it was, in effect, faster than light. The overcosm had its own overcosm, and it was through these highest planes that the tachyon devices traveled, short-cutting the short cuts.

It was black because it was not even part of the universe. And only the Inquest could use them, because of the devastating energy waste, and because it might lend too much power to the lower clans.

Nika was afriad. *Two* Inquestors! A tachyon bubble! So Iliash had to be important, somehow.

But he was just a kid!

She looked at the boy whose gray eyes so resembled her own, who shared her clan-name, whom she was about to lose forever. Would they come for her, too?

"You're all I have, Ilyeh!"

The two Inquestors moved impatiently. There was not much time.

"Ilyeh." She held his hand tight.

"Nikkyeh," he said, "I've learned what the Inquest made us for. Now I'm going away to do what I have to do. . . ."

She raged impotently. *Push it inside yourself, the neutronium ball!* "I love you, Ilyeh," she said. (*Do I?* she asked herself.) "When we're older, if time dilation hasn't made us too far apart in age—"

"Don't talk about what can't be!" he said. His eyes looked wistful yet hopeless.

"What do you mean?"

"You and I—" He stopped suddenly, turning to see whether they were watching him. "We don't have puberty. We don't grow. How old am I, Nikkyeh? How old do you think? I'm *eighty-seven!*"

Nika chose to ignore this; she could not believe it. "You can refuse to go," she pleaded.

"They made us too well," said Iliash. "They made us so we'll *want* to do this, they put the love of it in our bones. . . ."

"Of *what*?" she said sullenly. "There's nothing I love more than you!"

"There is, there is!" He turned to go. The two Inquestors had faded into the tachyon bubble, and one of his feet had already vanished into the blob. She felt abandoned, lied to. He was like Mother after all.

"What do you mean?" she shouted. "What is there that I love more than you?"

"That triple somersault!" he said. He blew her a kiss, wrenched himself around and leapt into the bubble. It winked out. There was no trace of it on the sand, only three sets of footprints that led to the same spot and vanished. . . . She turned away and began to walk toward the landing craft.

Now she felt truly empty. Even Iliash, whom she had trusted, had finally betrayed her.

*The triple somersault!* The cruelty of it! How could he make fun of her like this?

But it was true.

That was the day she cut off all her hair, disgusted with herself. And determined to think of nothing at all but the triple somersault, to feed all her anger to the triple somersault!

"Why don't you use the bars?" Exkandar asked, gently. It had been two months; and—abandoning her past in despair— Nika had grown her hair again. It was long now, and black as deep space.

"When the birds aren't happy, they don't sing."

"As you wish."

"Why do they all treat me so condescendingly here?" she said, sounding suddenly frail.

Exkandar said: "You're indispensable; they're not. They're afraid of you, really."

"But why?"

"You'll see."

She watched one swirl of green flame as it slowly transformed into a crazy spiral and melded into the blackness. *"You'll see! You'll see!* Do you people never tell anyone anything?"

"Nika, I don't know that you could take it yet. You're too young. I counseled against all this—"

"Well, give me a clue!"

"All right," he said heavily. "We need more starships. There is to be a war, a war with aliens. . . ."

"That has nothing to do with me. Performers are neutral."

"Wait, listen to me!" (*How tired he sounds!* Nika thought.) "How do starships work? You should know that."

Nika laughed. "They're navigated through the overcosm," she said, "by an astrogator who is in communion with a delphinoid shipmind—" When Exkandar did not answer, she went on, "Delphinoids are giant creatures who are all brain. They're captured on . . . some planet, I don't know. They perceive the overcosm directly. They're cybernetically implanted into ships by means of . . . some crystal or other . . ."

"Yes," said Exkandar. "There are semisentient crystals that can concentrate and focus particle streams into the overcosm."

"But they never told us, in school, where the crystals come from."

"And there is your clue," said Exkandar, and would say no more.

Nika thought it over. She had been tailored—gene-tailored—for empathy with alien minds, for minimal physical development. They needed starships. The ships needed crystals. *It doesn't make any sense!*

Exkandar said, "I want you to keep practicing. Use the bars, Nika." She saw them, light finger-thin poles of some flexible polymer, stretched from wall to wall in ranks of increasing height. For a moment only she wanted to rush up to them and spring into action, leaping from one to the other until she could dance on the highest pole . . .

"No," she said. *Am I punishing them or myself?* Exkandar took this as a dismissal and left. And Nika wondered at this, that her word could command a Kingling and Inquestor.

Then, making sure she was unobserved, she flashed up in an easy bound onto the first rung, then from one ranked bar to the next as though they were steps in a pyramid. When she reached the highest one, she tiptoed swiftly along the bar, her weight hardly flexing it at all. Her mind wandered. . . .

She caught her balance. *Out of practice!* She remembered how she had fallen, and then the bar slithered from under her; quickly she grabbed with her hands and pulled herself up again. . . .

*Oh no. They've ruined me.*

There was a new kind of queasiness in her stomach. *I'm afraid!* she thought, startled by the new emotion.

In a few days they reached a nameless planet that intersected a nexus in the tachyon universe. It was a blizzard-swept place, without inhabitants save for the nexus station crew, all of the clan of Nartak, another one Nika had never encountered.

The two of them came down in a lander to await their tachyon bubble. High overhead, it materialized, blotting out more and more of the snowburst as it descended, sinking through the domeroof as though it were thin air. There was a humming; another Inquestor, also in a plain shimmercloak, emerged from the black blot.

Disappointment showed on the stranger's face. "Only one?"

"We could trace no others," said Exkandar quickly. "And this is a youngling of eleven."

"It's a catastrophe!" said the visitor. "Come, both of you." To Exkandar: "Is she prepared?" He toyed with his shimmercloak.

"She doesn't know anything," said Exkandar. "The circumstances of her presence with us were . . . traumatic; I thought it best—"

"Yes, yes." He blotted out. Exkandar pushed the girl ahead into the bubble; once inside she could not tell she was *inside* at all. They moved, suddenly, into the air, and Nika felt no excitement or wonder, only the same deadness she had felt since her capture. But just before they blinked out—

*This is where they took Iliash!*

She closed her eyes and remembered his face, as though she were looking into a mirror: the eyes that reflected her own, the boyishness that, she now knew, concealed long experience.

She smiled . . . for the first time since the attack on the satellite . . . and clutched the memory of his face to her, determined never to let it slip.

Bleak. Gray. Bleak. Gray.

It was an impossibly tiny planet, with a horizon that dropped too soon, like an asteroid's; its diameter was only fifty kilometers. There was a core of neutronium, the size of a wine-goblet perhaps, denser even than the degenerate matter of white dwarfs, they said. Or perhaps a seething soup of quarks, or perhaps compressed all the way into a black hole. . . . Whatever it was, it gave the planet a surface gravity of 0.78.

She hated the planet!

It had crazy naked crags, gray and featureless, that erupted out of gray, mirror-still lakes. The sky was gray too, an even, impenetrable gray like Iliash's eyes, like Nika's eyes.

Nika and Exkandar hovered in the floater over the mountains. "It's artificial, this planet," she said. It was obvious. But instead of wondering at it, she detested it.

"Yes," said Exkandar, "but not built by us. Not by humans. By a race long extinct. A world built to order, built for the breeding of the tarn crystals. We haven't worked out every variable. We can't duplicate what this world does! The neutronium core, for instance—we don't know how vital that is. If it is, we can't replicate it at all."

The floater swooped toward the frighteningly close horizon, whipping aside to avoid the crag. Nika heard a quiet rumbling, almost beneath the threshold of hearing. "What's that sound?" she asked. And felt herself *drawn* to the sound somehow, attracted by it. . . .

"The mountains are in heat."

"Oh." The two days she had spent here had only compounded her bewilderment. Something brushed her face. She started to strike out at it in annoyance. . . .

She looked up to see a monstrous butterfly, with a wingspan of perhaps a meter, hovering ahead. She let out a little scream, more in surprise than fright.

The animal hovered. The resemblance to a butterfly was only superficial, she saw. It had uncountable tiers of wings, each paper-thin and translucent, refracting light into a thousand colors. There were two legs, crystalline and muscular at the same time . . . and a small, oval head with six or seven eye-like organs. From the head sprouted paper fans—they looked like fans—that glittered imtermittently as they caught the light. . . . The wings moved, vibrating faster than the eye could see, and then were suddenly still as a wind sprang up to support the creature. The fans rotated nervously, catching at sunlight; there was little of it here, for the sun was perpetually hidden in veils of gray cloud.

The creature watched the floater and its occupants for a long time. They were buoyed up by the same air current.

*Angel,* thought Nika, *fairy, creature of myth* . . . Her heart almost stopped beating. Something in the void inside her responded to it. . . .

Suddenly the creature shivered all over, spread its wings, vibrated them, a shimmering aurora of lights splashed across the grayness, a whir of wings, a dazzling soaring into the cloudbanks that left an afterimage like the ghost of a rainbow. . . .

*So beautiful!* "If only I were like it," she said, "and not trapped the way I am."

"It is a farfal," said Exkandar. "The farfellor are the larval forms. . . ."

"Of what?" she said as they rounded another precipice and skimmed a lake of deathly stillness.

"Of the tarn creatures."

"There are beasts, then, living in the mountains?" She tried not to sound too interested, but in spite of herself . . .

"No. They *are* the mountains."

Nika whipped around in panic, upsetting the floater for a moment. She saw the tortuous crags, straddling the horizon, twisted shapes that strained toward the ashgray cloud-veils. . . .

"Whoever built this planet was far superior to us, in technology, in bioengineering . . . tarn crystals, the things that focus the minds of delphinoid ships, are the unfertilized ova of these mountains," said Exkandar. "The adult forms are static, vast, silicon-based; photosynthesizing silicon chains from the gray sunlight and from the silicate-rich crust, the salts dissolved in the lakewater. Perhaps their roots even reach down to the neutronium core—there are unsolved anomalies in its particle emissions—and draw on its energy. We don't know exactly how it works, just that it's a very lucky thing for the Dispersal of Man, a secret stumbled on many millennia ago which has kept the human race in contact with itself, which has stabilized and enriched our culture. . . ."

*So that's how the Inquest keeps control of the Dispersal of Man,* thought Nika. *And it's such a precarious secret, too. They're so* vulnerable. *Without the crystals, war and commerce would both cease.*

*But what does it have to do with me?*

"The clan of Rax . . . we are collectors of tarn crystals, then?" she said. *It's humiliating!* she thought. *To scrabble in the rocks, when I could have been the Dispersal's greatest rope dancer.* It didn't sound possible.

"Let's float onwards." He blinked, and Nika knew that he was keying the floater by means of a brain-implant. Soon they soared above the lake and swerved around a peak, with the horizon gaining on them. . . .

They reached a plateau encircled by a wall of stubbier mountains. A flock of farfellor swooped by the mountain-face and swung upwards, in a perfect arc, like a necklace drawn up by an unseen hand.

The floater came to rest near the edge of the plateau and they stepped down. The rumbling came again. "Is that what you meant, when you said the mountain was *in heat*?"

"They have cycles. Now look ahead of you."

Nika obeyed him. For a moment she had forgotten she was a prisoner, destined for an unknown and probably unpleasant fate.

Gray statues of farfellor stood on the plateau's edge, staring out over the emptiness at the ring of tarn creatures. Nika went up and touched one, tentatively; its touch was cold as marble. Now two or three farfellor, circling overhead, swooped down in a wild glittering and landed beside them, and stopped moving. As she watched, veins of grayness grew and spread across the color-lattice of wings, across the crystalline legs—

"They're dying!" she gasped.

"No, metamorphosing . . . in a few years, a century perhaps, another tarn creature will grow here. There is an active phase of reproduction. After that the mountain is quiet, and never moves again; it might be dead or dormant, we don't know. Are they sentient, Nika? You were bred for empathy with aliens. . . ."

She listened for the cries of other minds. But she could not tell. There could have been a voice, but it was a murmur so distant that it might have come from another world. "I don't know."

"None of you ever know, for sure."

*What an alien world!* And she was so alone in it. She pushed ever harder at her fear, hoping it would contract to nothing. "But where are the other Rax? Where is Iliash?" She knew he was witholding something. "Why us? Do we have to die to get your precious crystals out of the mountains, is that it?" For a moment Nika longed for the touch of Mother's fur-coated iron hand. . . . *But I mustn't be a child!* she thought. *Must fight* . . .

"It's hard for me to tell you, little one. We Inquestors—" Exkandar paused, choosing his words—"are above all compassionate; at initiation we are selected for this trait. I can't bring myself to—"

What could it be that upset him so? Nika could imagine only death. Panic pounded at her. She sprang up and bolted for the floater. When she reached it he had already caught her.

"No, it's not what you think!" he shouted. "Come, let me finish what I have to show you." And again he seemed so vulnerable that Nika felt for him; though she knew that she was the victim, not he.

Some forty kilometers on there was a peak, especially huge, going right up through the clouds. They flew into a small building, open on three sides, built into the foot of the mountain; steps were carved into it, and there were other houses, a small village. People—guards or workmen—in blinding bright tunics, were milling around the hallway. When they saw Exkandar they bowed; when they saw Nika they gaped.

At the end of the hall there was a tiny passageway, circular, maybe a meter wide. It led to total darkness.

*It's a tunnel!* she thought. *They're going to force me in there and make me dig around for the eggs.* . . . "You can't make me go in there!" she said, hysterically. "The other Rax are lost in the tunnels, aren't they? You bred us small to make us live out our lives in there? I won't do it! I'm a rope dancer, I need the open—"

Exkandar stared at her incredulously, then burst out laughing—for the first time since she'd known him.

One of the workers said quickly: "Lord Inquestor, she doesn't know?"

The mountain rumbled a little. The workers fell on their knees and seemed to be deep in prayer.

"They don't know the truth," Exkandar whispered to Nika. "They worship the tarn creatures. They're the egg-collectors, they gather them as they roll down the oviducts—that's what the tunnels are—and they'll worship you, too! We've set it up as a religion to conceal what the eggs really are. . . ."

"Then what *is* my role?" Nika was exasperated beyond

endurance. "What happened to Iliash? Didn't you bring a Rax named Iliash here?"

Exkandar took her by the hand. "I'll show you now."

At the entrance they boarded the floater and wafted upwards, following the gradient of the tarn, hugging the surface. Nika strained to see some crack, some irregularity of color or texture. There was none; it was all one gray.

They glided on to a perch of the cliff-face. The Inquestor jumped off and motioned her to look. At first she saw nothing—

Then—

Growing out of the cliff edge, flung out taut over the chasm until it disappeared into the grayness, was a tightrope. Nika ran to the edge, got down on her knees and leaned over to touch it. It felt . . . made for her. The slackness of it was just right, the pressure just enough. A stadium out in the wilderness, on an unnamed planet!

Something inside her responded at last. She yearned to walk the strand. . . .

Her eye ran along the rope, and she saw faint lines alongside it, crossing over it, above and below. . . . Mostly, the lines were invisible, until the light fell just right, until the wind tugged gently on them.

She put one foot forward, and remembered—

Rope slipping from under her, wild vertigo of burning machinery and people aflame, whirling—*I've been kidnapped! I should be angry! I shouldn't do anything they want me to do!*

And fear. The fear that had come to her for the first time, unbidden, when she had tried to practice again on the ship. She tried to swallow it up, kneeling down and caressing the rope, pulling at the tension. . . .

Exkandar explained. "These strands are the tarn creature's nervous system. When it is in heat, the larval forms . . . and you . . . will feel it calling you. The farfellor fly over and dance lightly on the strands, stimulating the sleeping mountain. . . . After a while, sometimes half an hour, sometimes half a day or more, the eggs are released, one by one, sliding down the tunnels to the oviduct-mouths. The dancing farfal sends out empathy-signals all over the planet, and thousands of farfellor flock to the tunnel mouth to fertilize the eggs, making tempests with their wings, breaking the sides of the mountain in their urgency. . . .

"And after, they are too exhausted. They have spent everything; their fertilizing fluid, their reserves of energy—for farfellor do not ingest—and with their last strength they fly to a plateau, become rooted and dormant, await the next stage of their cycle. Thousands of them will eventually merge into a single mountain—"

And suddenly, Nika saw what he was driving at. "*I* have to dance on the webstrands!" she cried out. And it came to her at once, how she had been manipulated at every stage in her life.

"Don't blame us, Nika!" Exkandar said, anguished. "If there were another way we would have found it. But we need *unfertilized* ova! And if the dancer does not send out signals to the other farfellor, the eggs are not fertilized. We tried using robots and androids and altered animals . . . but nothing works except a human being, reaching to impulses given off by the alien mind, small, perfectly in control of his body—"

"Can't you slaughter them as they attack the mountain? Can't you set up forceshields?"

"The mountain senses if there are any obstacles to the eggs reaching the air freely. That's why the temple is open on three sides. We tried braving it out, assaulting the storm with missiles and projectiles. But often the eggs would be damaged, their crystalline alignments warped; and usually one farfal would get through. And one is enough to fertilize them all."

Bitterly, Nika said, "And when we've danced on the ropes, and given you your priceless eggs—what then? Do we die? One day, do we fall off? Do we slip?"

"Accidents are common. I won't lie to you. And it is necessary to keep the number of Rax small and separated from one another, until they are needed . . . and now you are the only one. You see, the farfellor . . . *compete* with the web dancers—"

"I have to fight them off?"

Those beautiful creatures were deadly then! They were her enemies. . . .

Exkandar was silent.

"And what happens afterward. . . ?"

Nika saw that he was disturbed; she knew that there would be more, and not pleasant, information. Furiously, she turned away from him. How cleverly they had trapped her!

She looked over the precipice. Now that she knew what to look for, she could see many of the strands, silvery-white, crisscrossing one another in strange, irregular grids, stretching out to invisibility.

"I won't do it! You can't force me!"

("There *is* something that you love more than me!" Iliash had said.)

The ropes shifted and swayed in the soundless breeze. *I want to! I want to!* her mind cried out. *I could tiptoe out, ever so lightly, I could press my feet in and spring up, high, high, high, do the triple somersault, here, hovering over the emptiness—*

"Curse you, Inquestors!" she said. "You made me too well!" And she trembled with longing and revulsion.

"Yes," Exkandar said.

Built on stilts over the largest lake, the House of Rax must have been able to house a hundred or more web dancers. Nika was lost in it. Even her private room was as large as a moon-hopper.

She threw herself into practice, which was in a varigrav gymnasium larger than the whole show-satellite had been, with silklike strands stretched over the protective forceshield. She was too immersed to notice the empty corridors hung with imagesongs and lightmobiles, the tape libraries smelling of overscrubbed disuse. But she had time to ask questions.

To become angrier.

She needed that anger, as fuel for the web dance. She had no love, no hope. Anger was all she could dredge up from inside the great emptiness.

She learned that the Rax were cloned (in both sexes, purely a cosmetic difference) from a centuries-old blueprint tissue, and that they were released into orphanages one at a time in worlds as distant as possible from one another; that a recent radical mutation of the tissue culture had almost wrecked the system, that samples had been taken from her in her sleep to rectify and perpetrate the system. That explained partly why she was the only one there now; also, there had been a rash of accidents. The Inquest was desperate indeed.

The mountain god took its toll in human sacrifice.

She learned that replacements for her were being tracked down all over the Dispersal of Man, and that after this breeding season she would be free to leave. Not because of charity.

She would be burned out. Her empathy-circuits would be ruined. Web dancing made a ruin of the mind and the body . . . but they would let her go. She could be a dancer still . . . with a different set of memories.

They would destroy her memories completely—not just the planet, the web dancing, but everything, just in case. Yes, she would truly be free.

Or dead.

But perhaps Iliash was out there among the stars, a ghost of himself with a different personality . . . and Nika became angrier. *I'll dance for him!* she thought. *I'll make him see me!*

*If I'm angry enough I won't be afraid.*

In her mind she tumbled again from the rope, she heard the screaming and saw the fire flash. Iliash had told her: *Anger is good. It's the next best thing to courage. But push it all inside you, coil it up so it'll rush out when you need it most.*

She tumbled in the gymnasium, too, onto the springy forceshield. *It's hopeless, I'm not ready.*

She learned that they had tried to set up a forceshield under the tarnweb, but the mountain had not been fooled. It had sensed an irritation in the environment, and the ova had not come.

She became angrier.

They implanted fingerlasers on both her hands and keyed them to subvocalized syllables. Now there were sounds she could never even *think* again. For hours she danced the high ropes, flicking death at farfal-robots. She learned very fast. Of course: she was made that way.

In her room she lay and gashed the walls with the fingerlasers, and when she came back the walls would always be repaired, umblemished as before. She grew angrier then, and in between practicing she lay and brooded.

Beyond her fear of slipping, beyond the anger—she saw herself, running free on the highrope, whirling against the wind, her body a perfect song of curves and arches, a still hurricane-eye of the wild elements. . . .

*It's not just the thought of slipping,* she told herself in the darkness before sleep. *I'm not a cog in their machine! I hate them for making me want this, for manipulating me this way! I want to be just me!*

But she had sworn never to cry again, that time so many years ago. And she had never broken that oath. So she swallowed everything and woke up knotted with anger.

A few weeks later she found a holosculpture library in a circular room where half the wall could be deopaqued to show the lake that curved and dipped so abruptly into the mountain peaks. They were both so gray, she thought, the landscape outside and the silver walls inside. No wonder the workers wore such dazzling colors. She watched the lake; it never rippled, but cast a perfect echo of the gray sky.

*I'm almost angry enough—*

A worker, in crimson-and-blue swirled tunic, was waiting deferentially. "May I help you, little miss? I am Ynnither, librarian of the House of Rax. The computer indicated you were here."

Nika was annoyed that her solitude had been broken so callously. "I have to be alone! I'm going to break my skull on the rocks, for the sake of the universe or something, and I can't be alone!"

"Is there something you would like to see, a particular holosculpture? Before there was so much work—"

Perhaps he could tell her something. "What about *before*? You have holosculptures of the others, of the Rax before me? Of a Rax named Iliash?" For a moment she panicked, dreading what the answer might be.

There was a rumble—

"There now, miss, that'll be the big one calling for his mate," said the worker. "It'll be your time soon."

". . . Iliash?" She was adamant.

Ynnither said, "I remember him all right. He was the daringest of them all. To the last he was daring. Cocky. A legend to us."

"Show me."

Nika heard the hum of machinery, and the view-walls opaqued. He appeared in mid-air, about a meter from her face, suspended in mid-leap. His hair floated above him, caught in that moment.

She walked closer to the holosculpture, ran her hand through emptiness. How she longed to be a part of that frozen moment. . . .

The gray eyes looked back, full of defiance.

"We have the sculpture in kinetic too, miss," said the worker, and turned to adjust the machinery.

All at once Iliash finished his leap, in the middle of the

emptiness, in one impetuous curve. Nika thought, *Not as refined as I would be. But how achingly beautiful!*

He vanished, leapt again, vanished, leapt again—with the playback in the kinetic mode, there was wind in the picture, ruffling the waves of hair; and as he landed the face broke into a smile at once triumphant and fragile.

"He was your friend, miss?"

*Was?* Realization shot through her, and she felt outrage . . . outrage . . .

"He was the greatest web dancer we have had. You should have seen him in life! We often watched on the monitors in the eggroom. He's dead now."

She stared at the leaping figure till her eyes burned.

"A farfal got him, miss, on the very day he was scheduled to return to his homeworld. He needn't have danced the web that day; they'd told him it was enough. But he was wilder than usual, ran like an animal across the ropes—how we mere mortals envy your powers!—and then he shouted, '*I'm going to try for that triple somersault!*' And he stood on the rope and steadied himself for a tremendous leap. The farfal swooped down and dislodged him. They never found all the pieces."

*So you're dead!* she thought. Blood was on her hands and she realized how hard she had clenched them. *Control your anger, roll it into a secret place inside you so you can throw it into your leap—*

And Nika knew that she was ready. The rage had built up inside and was ready to explode. The void inside her was full.

The rumbling came again, and Exkandar was standing beside her. "You must come now, Nika. The mountain is calling for you. . . ."

In the back of her mind she felt an alien presence, tugging at her, hungry and passionate. She did not have to be told what it was. She has been bred for empathy with aliens' minds. It was the call of the tarn-creature to all the farfellor. Then they deopaqued the wall and she saw the mountain peaks jutting out over the lakeface, and her heart gave a funny leap and she let out a cry. And understood the ugly, dissonant rumbling. . . . It was a song!

And she felt tears rushing. Choking them back, she said, "I can't help what I am, after all. Even after what you did to Iliash, the only person I've ever loved, and the others."

"Come!"

"Did you think this would make me feel like a superhero in a kid's holoplay, rushing in to save the Galaxy from the evil aliens?" she said, exulting. "I'll dance the webs—but not for your precious ships. I'll dance for Iliash, who died for my somersault. I'll dance for the perfect leap! I'll dance for ME!" And she was proud of what she was, and of her importance.

And she looked the Inquestor—a Lord of the Dispersal—full in the face, and saw . . . humility. And pitied him at last.

The rumbling called her, thrilling her. She saw flocks of farfellor, responding likewise, flashing across the sky.

And, against the mountain peaks and the steel sky, the ghost of the boyfigure with the bright gray eyes tumbled and leapt, tumbled and leapt, over and over, with consummate grace.

After about twenty meters Nika opened her eyes.

She had been testing the web's tautness. With every cautious step she had felt the strand bend itself, accommodate itself to her weight. It was a thing alive, that strand. Not like the lifeless ropes of the show-satellite, which her own body gave life to. Here was a rope she was almost in communion with. . . . But she did not trust it, not quite yet.

She looked. Below was Exkandar on his floater; if she tumbled, he would catch her if he could. There were other webstrands, their ends lost in the grayness. The grayness was overpowering. Space and distance were swallowed up by it, so that she seemed suspended in mid-nothingness.

*Love me. Love me. Leap for me. Dance for me.*

It was a voice not quite sentient that sang in the back of her mind, more the voice of an animal in need, broadcasting distress signals. "You poor mountain," Nika whispered. "You're just a pawn in their game, like me. Yes, I'll dance for you. . . ."

She took a tentative leap forward, landed lightly on her right foot, spun around.

*Love me more! More!*

The voice tugged at her, yearned for her. . . . She whirled once, twice, each time leaning harder into the silkstrand, catching herself miraculously just at the instant she would have tumbled.

"That's right, Nika, slowly, cautiously," prompted Exkandar's voice, reaching her via a head implant. She shrugged the voice off contemptuously. They didn't know anything, these people who used the tarn-creature's eggs to control the Galaxy. Right now there was only her and the mountain, alone together.

A light wind sprang up. She took four more steps, then narrowly avoided a tumble, overcompensated for the wind, almost tripped again, flung out her arms wildly and steadied herself in a moment. Above the rumble came a high whistling, mixing with the wind sounds.

She looked up, pushing down harder with her toes and keeping her arms outstretched for the balance. A flock of farfellor broke through the cloudveils, a dozen or more of them, swooping, converging on her—

*Mustn't panic—*

She remembered the rope slipping from under her over and over but the whisper of the mountain touched her, calmed her. . . .

*Dance more, dance more, why do you stop?*

The fighter convoy moved in to cut them off. About fifty meters above her head, a projectile volley exploded the flock into wild flurries of color. The farfellor screamed, a heart-rending high-pitched keening that became part of the whistling wind. *Poor creatures*, Nika thought for a moment. *Sacrifices.*

But *I'm going to ignore Exkandar and the farfellor and the Inquest and the fate of the galaxy now. I'm just going to leap high, leap perfect, leap*, she thought.

*Leap for me, love me!*

Impetuously, she cartwheeled across to the next strand, ran swiftly along it, leaping back to the first strand, making singing arcs in the air.

"For the sake of all of us, play it safe, girl!" she heard Exkandar say. And laughed at him. . . .

One of the farfellor had not been killed. It hovered over her, vulturelike, waiting. Nika ignored it, until it swooped down and knocked against her face. Angrily she whirled around and bisected it with her fingerlasers, watching the iridescent pieces fall forever into grayness. . . . She turned back to the web dancing, feeling the pull of the mountain, *loving* the mountain.

Suddenly the sky was alive with the flapping of farfal wings! A sea of colors crashed across the sky, and the convoys were everywhere, slaughtering. Farfal bodies plummeted like rain. Projectiles zinged and boomed. Nika closed her eyes, reaching for the strands with her nerves, with her mind—

And leapt up, somersaulting! In her mind's eye Iliash turned with her. Her feet touched the strand and she steadied herself with relief. She laughed again, feeling the mountain's joyous response. And whirled again, arms out, like a top, with the wind flushing her face and her hair flying.

*I think I can do it—*

A shudder went through her, a release of rapture, thrilling her. . . .

The mountain was giving birth! She knew it, she could feel with it, she could feel the eggs falling down the long tunnels toward the foot of the mountains.

"You've done it!" Exkandar cried. "We'll come and get you now—"

"No!" she cried. "I think I can do it!"

"Do what?" She saw the floater climbing up after her. She ran along the web, further out into the emptiness, using the bounce of the web to propel her even faster. . . .

And then, in a moment when she found herself quite alone, she wound up all her anger and all her love, everything that was ever pent up in her slight body, and *compressed* it into a core of neutronium and then exploded, hurled herself upwards—

*Iliash! You should see me now!*

—defying the planet's pull, higher than she could have thought possible, and somersaulted, with the world and the farfal colors kaleidoscoping about her eyes and the windstream burning her—

*One—*

*Two—*

*Three—*

And touched the web, giddy with triumph and joy.

". . . all right," Exkandar's voice was saying. "Don't move, we'll come for you. It was a fantastic crop. You've done well by the Galaxy. . . ."

She laughed again, a peal of laughter that scorned Exkandar and all his kind. "I've done well by me!" she shouted, her face flushed. "I've done the first triple somersault on a rope *ever*! I've danced free under the open sky with the wind singing and the mountain loving me. And I'll never forget this! I'll show you! You can erase my memory, you can discard me like another used-up tool, but I won't forget! Not ever, not if I live a thousand years.

She had come to the arena again, a grown woman still shaped like a girl, to dance the rope dance. It was the Highfest of Vangyvel—which, they had told her, was once her homeworld—and it was the nameday of the Kingling Exkandar, who would actually deign to attend. But this meant nothing to her. She stepped onto the slackrope.

There was no forceshield. She despised safety. . . .

The tiers of crowd rose to the roof of the dome. In a breath darkness fell, and she was alone in a pool of light.

She danced. She danced with a kind of crazy joy, a wildness that always drove her audience to a frenzy. But all this was routine; the climax was yet to come.

She did some dazzling footwhirls; and then, suspended only by her feet, twisted her body up the length of the rope, accelerating to the music. The crowd was deafening now, the waves of sound egging her on, pounding at her. . . .

And then she stood in the middle of the nothingness, prevented by a thread from abrupt death. She stood frozen for a long while, while the crowd grew silent, pondering.

Her gaze fell on the royal pew and met the eyes of Kingling Exkandar, aloof, his Inquestral shimmercloak topped by the iridium crown.

*Odd,* she thought, *that face. . . .*

And she closed her eyes in the ritual of the triple somersault, imagining herself away, far away, on some made-up, impossible planet:

> *Gray lakes, still as mirrors—*
> *Colors, sluicing the gray sky, threatening—*
> *Wind, caressing her—*
> *Mountain peaks, jutting from a too-near horizon—*

What was the memory? From what scene in her sketchy past had it come? It would always surface before the great leap. She seemed to remember that once, ages ago, she had filled the void inside herself with anger, not with love. . . .

And she pressed her body like an arrow into the bowstring

and sprang upward as the wind whistled and creatures like butterflies flashed against an alien sky—

And landed!

The crowd's silence broke into thunder. The strange planet sounded deep into her unconscious. She had been perfect.

*Perfect!*

As she looked out at the crowd, only a trace of the phantom memory lingered, a voice not human, crying out for her compassion—

*Love me. Dance for me. Leap for me. Love me.*

# 7

For many sleeps after Tievar told her the stories of Shen Sajit, Dei Zhendra and Rax Nika, Jenjen was in the grip of an almost unbearable rage. Often Zalo had railed about the Inquest's interference, the Inquest's stifling stranglehold over the Dispersal of Man; but Jenjen had thought that he was merely trotting out one of the radical political theories fashionable among the young; she herself, who had the lightloom with which to create whole universes, had seen no sense in such talk. After all, there was nothing one could do about the Inquest. The Inquest was like the sunrise, like the inland ocean that ceaselessly eroded the shoreline of Ikshatra; how could you fight it?

But as she sat laboring with light, she began to understand how insidious those stories had been. She kept comparing herself to the three artists in the story. . . . Did she really know the fanatic independence of Zhendra, for whom even humanity was a small sacrifice for art's sake? Did she have Sajit's capacity for love and defiance? Could she be like Nika, created specifically for a role for which art was only incidental, yet investing it with all the fire of her tiny body? Could it be that all that Jenjen had done had been mere prettiness?

At times she stared at the lightloom, not wanting to touch

it. And when she sat down to weave, it no longer held her totally secure in its wombwarmth. No place was safe anymore.

The palace still orbited Essondras. Sometimes, going to one of the many observation chambers, she would watch her homeworld revolve, a blue-white cloud-crystal in the great blackness. Now she truly understood that the Inquest's might could smash her world, for she saw it as the Inquestors saw it: a small globe, toy-sized, a bauble in the endless night.

She knew that she wanted none of the High Inquest now. *I will make light,* she told herself fiercely, and gritted her teeth and settled into the lightloom in her sleepchamber.

But after many hours' work winding and twisting the laser-filaments into kaleidoscopic matrices, she saw that darkness had stranded itself into the tapestry she wove. Here a whorl of light, but darkness was at its core . . . here a knot of pitch-black in the texture of finespun scintillance. She grew angrier.

She tried to sleep: whenever she closed her eyes she saw once more the head of her great-grandfather grimacing from the memory-niche. Or the cold blue light that emanated from his eyes, the light that was but a veil for devouring darkness—

She stormed from her sleepchamber.

"Where is the Inquestor?" she shouted.

And there came an inner voice from the thinkhive of the palace: *He is alone, my Lady; he is in the throneroom of the galaxy of dust; he is mourning.*

"I must see him!" she cried. She walked down corridor after corridor: here were varigrav stairwells where down became up, here were tubes of force that threaded the needle towers of the palace, here hallways guarded by deathmasks and peeling mummies, here gardens, here aviaries, here storerooms—never locked, where dust gathered over holosculptures and kaleidolons and tortuously-worked intagliates.

Finally the voice returned: *Ton Elloran n'Taanyel Tath, Inquestor and Kingling, will see you now. Find the nearest displacement plate. I will lead you to him.*

She found it, endured the familiar queasiness of displacement, and stood before Ton Elloran's throne. Behind him whirled the galaxy of dust. Before him were the golden steps that led up to his seat. Around him gloom: the hall carpeted with faded shimmerfur; grayness immured the two of them as they faced one another, each isolated in his own puddle of light. It was just like that day of her childhood, when they'd stood in the inner room engulfed in a powerful darkweaving. The Inquestor passed his hand through the sculpture of dust; the dust billowed, settled again, each mote a star.

"You are angry," he said.

"And why not?" she said, challenging him. "I've seen your pomp and your splendor and your heartlessness, and I feel helpless!"

"Tievar told you the story of Rax Nika?"

"Yes! Yes! But I'm not like her. You didn't leave anything to chance with her; you fashioned her very genes so she couldn't possibly resist doing what you wanted. Don't you feel any guilt? I wish that I had stopped my ears. Perhaps, Lord Elloran, if you would only tell me that these are not true. . . . I know you are a man of compassion, yet such things the High Inquest has done in compassion's name—"

"Alas, child, I cannot undeceive you." He did not meet her eyes.

"Tell me it's not true."

"What is truth? I have sanctioned the story; and truth may be defined as that which an Inquestor speaks—"

"But if the High Inquest is truly that fragile . . . if its hold over the Dispersal of Man is truly as tenuous as this . . . then to speak of revolution—"

"Be silent! I am forbidden to hear those words. I have not heard them. They were never uttered."

There was an uneasy silence in the throneroom.

At last, Ir Jenjen said, "I know, Lord, that you cannot unmake a clan-name. But I can't accept what you've lavished on me. I must go back to Essondras. This can never be home to me. I have to go back to my art, my family, my lover. I beg you—"

"You wish to return. We have still not left the orbit of your world. It is easily accomplished."

"You will not force me—?"

"Such hubris, young woman!" And suddenly Ton Elloran laughed, a laugh both kind and bitter. And he went on, "They never understand, these volatile artists." He must have been thinking of Sajit. The thought crossed Jenjen's mind: *I am reliving history for him, aren't I?* "I think you are beginning to understand why you have been brought here. Go now, my child. Return to your homeworld. Use what you have learned. Already you move along your destined path, and when I return for you you will be ready for the great thing which will be demanded of you."

"Demand nothing!" she cried. "For the sake of all the artists of the Dispersal"—it sounded absurd, melodramatic, even as she screamed out the words—"for the sake of those you've squeezed the lifeblood from, for the sake of Dei Zhendra and Shen Sajit and Rax Nika, whom you destroyed—I must defy you."

But then, when the Inquestor smiled on her, she knew also that underneath her rage and hatred there lay a kind of love. It was a memory of that childhood meeting. How could Elloran be all those evil things? It was so complicated, too complicated. All she had wanted was a lightloom to warm her and keep her safe and hide her from the dark. . . . And now darkness was creeping into her innermost of sanctums.

Later, when they came to escort her to the shuttle that would bring her back to the spaceport of Dar-Ikshatron, she felt a twinge of remorse. Because, like Sajit, like all Elloran's servants, she had been touched by . . . something godlike in the Inquestor. She was torn.

And when she stood once more beneath familiar stars, and saw her lover waiting for her beyond the forcebarrier, and the lights of Ikshatra streaking in the bay . . . she knew that there was something unfulfilled inside her. She had left a piece of herself in the golden palace that sailed the overcosm. She loved her home—of course she did, she reminded herself sternly—but she knew that her return to homeworld was only a reprieve, and that one day she would have to go back; she would have to face and learn to conquer her newfound anger, her hate, her long-repressed longing for the shadow side of things.

# THREE

## The Book of
## Rememberers and Warriors

*chom vízhvila antháh*
*et ashevráih z dhendáih eká;*
*níkin shtáh peránthanda z perdhándanda*
*et táshas za ekdeáih.*

*xa, hokhté Enguéster, xa*
*vain ishprán es-detún,*
*kat k'nám jivýten dhánat' ney'vió:*
*em-shtendút imnézna.*

—ek shéntraran Sájiti

As a flower blooms but to scatter its seeds and die, so must a planet ripen and perish, that it may yield its Rememberers:

It is thus, O Inquestor, that you have given us hope. No longer is death the purpose of life. Remembrance has become it purpose.

—*from the Songs of Sajit* **jit**

**I**

They made much of her. She was invited into the homes of Essondras' oligarchs; receptions were thrown in her honor; there was a retrospective exhibition of her artwork, an honor rarely accorded women twice or even thrice her age.

It was some time before she began to notice a kind of diffidence in their manner towards her. She first saw it in Zalo, who had always been so quick to anger or to burst out laughing. One day, as they swooped over the city by floater, she started to make fun of some of the more pretentious art critics, and of the new biomaximalist structuralism. Instead of laughing, Zalo actually took her seriously.

"Perhaps you're right," he was saying cagily. She was so astonished that she lost control of the floater; before its thinkhive kicked in, they lurched, almost flip-flopped. "What's the matter? Did you forget how to drive?"

"But Zasha, how could I possibly have been serious when I said that Gramstrewash paradigmaticizes the pancontextual structure of the light filaments' ontological—"

He began to laugh now. But for a second, just a second . . . he'd hesitated. "Powers of powers, my love! I've only been gone a few sleeps. . . ."

"But you've talked with Inquestors," Zalo said. "How can I know *what* you mean anymore? You've said seven incomprehensible things since we set off on this little ride."

"Zasha, Zasha." She threw her arms around him—after carefully subvocalizing for the floater's autopilot to take over—and although he seemed to return her warmth as passionately as ever, there was something. . . .

"You're apart now," Zalo said, very seriously. Just then the

129

floater swerved skyward to avoid a tower. "You're not one of us anymore. I know you want to be; that's why you came back, isn't it? But you'll never be happy here. Perhaps we shouldn't see each other again. . . ."

"How can you say that?"

"Karnofara has entrusted something very special to me," Zalo said after another such quarrel. "I'm to animate Ton Elloran in his necrodrama *The Rainbow King*." A little awkwardly, he asked her, "Will you come?"

They kissed and made up.

She was watching the stage from the balcony designated for the corpse-dancers' friends and relatives; as a result, there were many afficionados seated around her, and she was regaled with shop talk throughout the performance. The first few items were essentially circus acts: journeyman necrodramatists trying out new choreography numbers and testing new techniques of voice control.

Then came *The Rainbow King* . . .

From the start she knew something was wrong—when she saw the boy-corpse that represented young Elloran cross the stage, his face illumined by ghostlight. She had seen that face before. A boy's face. Briefly. Where could it have been? And long ago. It nagged at her memory. The eyes; they could not be the right eyes, corpses had eyes of precious stones, not human eyes . . . but the lips she remembered well. When last she saw them they had been talking of . . . What was it?

The boy-corpse danced a solo; from his mouth came words, intricate poetry, exquisite artifice. The shimmercloak was wrong, of course. . . . He had worn a *white* robe! That was it. And looked warily about, as if afraid of being caught. . . .

Could it have been he? Gava. The name came to her suddenly. The young rememberer she'd talked to when she was ten years old and lost in the mnemothanasion. He'd been afraid of saying something . . . unorthodox. Gava. But he must have died very soon after they spoke. That was years ago, she thought. He must have died as a child. It was not a very comfortable thought, the idea that the human shell that walked the stage beneath had once been living, had once talked to *her*. Her discomfiture at this colored much of what she saw in the necrodrama that followed.

\* \* \*

After the show she met him in one of the many zul-shops that lined Angkhoshti Avenue. What a sad street that was—a tourist trap without any tourists. Though she had never yet seen another city, she had traveled far beyond Essondras in the shipmind of Tievar's telling. The zul-shop was not one that she frequented regularly, though it was a haunt of the necrodrama set, as could be seen from the fact that as she sat down a servocorpse shambled forward to take her order: a pitiful zombie, reconditioned, doubtless, from the junkheap of a theatrical supply house.

"Anything," she muttered, drumming her fingers on the hovertray. The corpse regarded her with bloodshot compound eyes and backed politely away; a bug in its circuits made its neck crane at an improbable and menacing angle.

Zalo came out and embraced her. "Jeni, Jeni." Other necrodramatists were with him. Most were made up to look like fresh cadavers, as was fashionable among afficionados of corpse dancing. "What did you think?" he said breathlessly, beckoning for a hoverseat. "Wasn't it grand?"

"Well . . . there was something rather upsetting. I *knew* one of the corpses."

"Well! Which one?"

"His name was Gava. He was a Rememberer."

"Oh, let's see now . . . oh yes, my Elloran. A superbly preserved little fellow, don't you think? Though why a young kid like that would end up being sent to the Arm—"

"The Arm! But that's just a servocorpse factory. . . ."

"A factory for the"—Zalo looked around—"politically dangerous."

So it had not been mere paranoia, she thought, when Gava had glanced anxiously about for spies. "How do you know?" she demanded hotly. "And why would a mere boy pose such a threat anyway?"

"The Rememberers are somehow close to the Inquest. I don't know how. You would know better than any of us. Among them, I daresay unorthodoxy isn't viewed as tolerantly as it is beyond the walls of the House of Tash." He laughed nervously, trying to cheer her up. "Look at me, for instance! I don't see anyone rushing to arrest me. And I say ten unorthodox things every day before breakfast . . . Anyhow, enough unpleasantnesses. It was you who always told me that you can't do anything about the Inquest. So let's talk about art! Did you like the play or didn't you?"

Still seething inside, she took a sip of pale blue zul, served up in a human skull. "It was not true," she said.

"Not true? Not true? We're talking ancient myths here, darling. The child-Inquestor and the child-musician defeating the forces of darkness and establishing the utopia for which all mankind yearns. That's what the myth of the Rainbow King is all about. . . ."

"It's not true!" She gulped down the fiery-ice intoxicant. "You made your corpses dance with such uncanny elegance, Zasha. . . . You gave boy Elloran's corpse such demure beauty. . . . The orchestra played such pretty tunes for Sajit's music. But I've heard Sajit's music, Zasha . . . and it's diamond hard beneath its softly shifting harmonies. . . . And I've looked into the face of Elloran."

She became aware of a great silence in the zul-shop. They were all waiting for her, the woman who had hobnobbed with the gods themselves, to speak. "They didn't build a new utopia, Zasha," she said. "They *hunt* utopias, these Inquestors! They hunt them down and shatter their people's dreams. That is the truth in the story of the Rainbow King. I've heard it from Elloran's own Rememberer—"

The silence went on, frozen, appalling.

At last Zalo said quietly, "Then you're for the revolution?"

The hush dragged on. She drank down more of the zul; quietly a corpse refilled her skull with a more potent concoction: reddish-brown, fuming, bitter. She said, "I didn't know there was a revolution."

Someone's voice from another table: ". . . the armies of shadow are coming to Essondras."

"We'll kill them!" another's voice. "We'll drag them from their hoverthrones and cut off their balls."

"But . . . how can you fight . . . *that*?" She pointed upward, past the deopaqued ceiling, to where the stars shone. "And they aren't evil, you know. It's all much more complicated than you can ever know. . . ."

"Traitor!" Zalo cried, ashen-faced.

"I'm high on zul and I'll say what I please," Jenjen said. "I've stood in the throneroom high over your heads and heard how the Inquestors play *makrúgh* and make words *fall beyond*. But I've also seen their grief and their compassion . . . and that they are themselves torn by a terrible schism, and that they are the hunters of utopias precisely because it is they who most yearn for utopias! Oh, there's so much you can't understand yet, Zasha, you with your big talk about blowing up the Inquest. . . . You're as bad as they are! You'd be no different . . . and maybe worse, because you haven't lived for millennia, haven't experienced for yourself the long pageant of human misery over which the Inquest must preside—"

"Are you one of them or one of us?" said one of Zalo's friends, a brash woman wearing nothing but a wire tiara, her naked body caked with necrocosmetics. "What's your position on the Inquestral question?"

"That you're just a bunch of fools . . . dreaming up your own never-never-utopias. . . . The Inquest's death will come from the Inquest itself, if it comes at all. . . . They're the only ones with the means of changing things, the awesome power." Suddenly she wondered why she was defending the Inquest so staunchly when she had been flinging curses at Elloran himself only a few sleeps ago.

"So! You've been upstairs a week, and now you disdain us mortals!" said the woman. "You, the great expert on galactic relations! Come on, Zalo, it's useless." And she grabbed Zalo's arm and pulled him out of the zul-shop, leaving Jenjen gaping.

# 2

In the night, after many sleeps, he came to her. She saw that he had been weeping; because she did not want to hurt his pride, she did not mention it. But because she too was proud, she would not speak first, but sat stubbornly at her lightloom, deftly spinning the lightstrands with one hand and sifting them into different colors with the other.

"There's a lot of dark, isn't there?" Zalo said. "I mean, in the tapestry. I mean, not to criticize, but it's rather unusual for a lightweaving to be so . . . so dark. Dark, that's it." She ignored him. He waited.

She subvocalized more commands to the lightloom's

thinkhive. *How dare he say that!* she thought, calling for gaudier colors from the generator. . . . Crimsons, ceruleans, vermilions streaked across the wall, dissonant, hurting her eyes. *No!* she thought, and abruptly the colors faded, leaving only lines of black against the pale glow of the background lighting.

"As I said," Zalo said, "dark, dark. Something's wrong with you, Jeni. And you're not sharing it with me, and it hurts."

"How can you understand? You badmouth the Inquest on one hand and perpetrate comfortable, brainwashing myths on the other."

"Powers of powers, they're the only myths we have! That's why I never cared to learn the Inquestral highspeech. . . . I couldn't stand to see my precious myths proved illusions!"

More darkness, crawling crablike over the whorls of color.

"And anyway, why is it the Inquest has become so important, anyway? I thought *we* were more important than some shadowy authoritarian figures. Do you know something I don't know? Are they about to destroy our homeworld or something? Speak to me—"

"Do you know the story of the Rainbow King?"

"Of course. Everyone knows that story. I've been working on it for months, animating that young boy's corpse. All Essondras has seen me dance that corpse . . . in person or by holovision."

"I will tell you what really happened," she said. And she told him. And though she had not Tievar's art of weaving realities out of words, yet the tale itself was moving.

"I will never tell that story," Zalo said at last. "It will make people uncomfortable."

"You'll get drunk and babble about revolutions, and you'll go on putting pretty lyrics on the lips of corpses."

"I guess you'll go back to them," he said.

"Yes." Only then did she know it was true.

There came a day—she had not seen Zalo for many, many sleeps—when she found herself returning to the arrondissement where stood the exhibition hall of the darkweavers; she found herself entering the vestibule, where the woman who had once stood guard and who had scolded her for disturbing the Inquestor now sat, stooped and palsied, by the cloakroom collecting gipfers from the charitable. Many of the darkweavings were gathering dust; they were no longer black, but spangled with light-flecks, like starfields.

She had put on the cloak of writhing, holographic darkness that members of the Clan of Ir were entitled to wear; because of this, the guards had deferred to her, and the curator himself had come out to exchange pleasantries. But she had been curt with him, and he seemed pleased to get out of her way.

And now she reached one of the inner exhibits. . . . She remembered it vividly now, for it was in this room that Ton Elloran had quizzed her about what the darkwalls' captions read, and she had stood puzzling out the highspeech words. She stood in front of one for a long time . . . brushed away some of the dust with a sleeve of her tunic. And suddenly, just as before, she glimpsed something beyond its darkness. It was as though she were in a pitch-black labyrinthine cave, and though she could see no way out, though the exit must be immeasurably far away, yet some stray lightray from it had invaded her field of vision. It was dark and not dark. Each strand of darkness was woven from a thousand colors. She stared transfixed at the field of absence of color. For many hours she gleaned nothing save that first fleeting lightflash. But then came a darting streak of some faint color, then another, then another, until the whole tapestry was shot through with ghost-light. It was like . . . the light from the crystal eyes of her great-grandfather's mummified head as it filled the heartroom of her parents' house and filtered past the open doorway of her childhood sleepchamber. That moment returned in all its terror. She screamed—

Blackness, all-concealing.

A voice: "I thought I might find you here."

She whirled round. It was Ton Siriss who stood there in a swath of light, the Inquestrix of the opalescent eyes.

"We are leaving Essondras' orbit now, Ir Jenjen. There is a great game of *makrúgh* to be played. The Inquest itself is at stake, perhaps. But this time we will be gone a long time. Perhaps, when you return, you will find your friends aged or even dead, though you yourself remain young."

"Where is Ton Elloran?"

"Come. You will see him. Perhaps it will be the last time. . . ."

And without hesitating for a moment Jenjen agreed to go.

"I have to understand," she said. "I have to find some version of the truth for myself."

"Ton Elloran knows and understands."

And when the shuttle breached the clouds of her home-world, and she saw Varezhdur glitter against the glow of Essondras' atmosphere, in the light of many moonlets, Jenjen tried to weep for her world and her lost friends. But she could not.

"Why so silent?" Ton Siriss asked her.

She said, "There is a kind of darkness in my heart, a void, an abyss. And my past is sliding into that darkness, as inexorably as light into a black hole. I'm afraid, Inquestrix."

"Yes." Ton Siriss did not speak for awhile, then she said abruptly, "So am I."

"You, Inquestrix, afraid?" Did they know already of this talk of revolution?

But she did not elaborate, and it would have been unseemly to question her.

# 3

There was confusion in Varezhdur when she arrived. The thronerooms were crammed with suppliants, neuterchildren, oligarchs in many-tiered robes and hair haloed by flamedisks, here and there a whiterobed Rememberer; she could not hear Sajit's music over the din. She searched for Elloran, thinking it her duty to report that she had returned; he was nowhere to be found, and the thinkhive of Varezhdur did not see fit to reveal his whereabouts. And Ton Sirris, who had said little during the brief shuttleflight, paused only to give Jenjen a wan smile before she disappeared into the throng of a throneroom's antechamber.

No one had even shown her to her room. She found it by herself, plating from corridor to corridor, falling into the familiar rhythm of displacements. Nothing had been touched. The lightloom still was there. A floatbed rose up from the furfloor when she raised her fingertips.

She had longed for Varezhdur all the time she was down on Essondras. She had felt its music in her bones, and her dreams had been haunted by its eerie light. But now that she was back . . . Somehow she had thought they would play triumphal music and shoot off fireworks for her reconciliation with Varezhdur, but instead there was nobody to greet her at all. Perhaps Tievar would know the answers. . . .

She found him in the old Chamber of Remembrances; it was as if no time had passed at all. The same woman was whispering in his ear; she looked up, saw Jenjen approach, quickly plated out of the room.

"Ah, you're back, Jeni."

He studied her for a moment; doubtless he was etching her face in his memory, in case some Inquestor should ask him to call her to mind. "And you've come to the chamber of Tash, where I rule, to ask me about the commotion in the palace."

"Tash Tievar, I'm so confused—"

"It's always this way before a departure. There's much to be done; the astrogators have to link minds with the delphinoid brains that control the palace's pathway through the overcosm, and the Inquestors must spend many hours brooding about imminent games of *makrúgh*. That's what this journey is about."

"But where is Ton Elloran?"

"He seeks aloneness; he sits by his galaxy of dust, listening as the palace thinkhives play back Sajit's old songs and cense the chamber with scents of ancient memories. Soon he is going to go on some journey. He won't tell anyone where it is. But he has already named his successor. And I . . . I know where his odyssey leads. To the gray spaces, to the silence between the stars. It is in a song of Sajit's."

"His successor?"

"Varezhdur will fall to Ton Siriss k'Varad es-K'Ning, whom you know already."

"But what about me?"

"Doubtless he has some purpose for you. Then there's always the revolution. That's what this game of *makrúgh* is all about. The Inquestors will take sides. Some will opt for the Shadow Inquest, which subscribes to the heresy of possible utopia and seeks to bring it about by scattering chaos. Or they will join those who insist on maintaining the status quo. Or, like Elloran, they will be neutral. It is hard for Siriss . . . for Ton Keverell, who leads the armies of shadow, and Ton Arryk, who follows the old ways. . . . They have both been Siriss' lovers. At the heart of this conflict that will splinter the Dispersal of Man there stands a personal tragedy, a love triangle."

She could sense a story in him. She waited. . . .

"We are going to the Shendering system, Jeni. There was a world there once; now there is only its satellite, Kilimindi, presided over by the Inquestor of the Million Masks, Karakaël. I lived on Shendering once. . . ."

"You, Father Tievar? I've just realized that, in all the time I've known you, you have never told me a story about yourself."

"That is not my gift. But I do enter, peripherally, into the tale of Shendering and Shendering's destruction. Did you know, Jeni, that Elloran had a sister once, and that sister a Rememberer?"

And Tievar told her a story of Rememberers, and how the Clan of Tash lived; and of Elloran's childhood and maturity. And the tale illuminated much of what she had been told before; for she came to understand how the Inquest needed the gift of remembrance, yet feared it. And she was moved.

# 4

# The Rememberer's Story

In the huge chamber, dwarfed by their gilded hoverthrones, a boy and a girl sat quietly by themselves. The boy was utterly still, numbed. Beneath them, shrouded in shadow and ceremonial vestments, lay the corpse of their father.

The girl sprang up from the throne. The boy did not move, but followed her with his eyes. She clapped her hands, dissolving the dark walls to reveal the dying city below.

Tall walls crumbling into cindercrusts. Streams of liquid light that shattered the milky-glass clouds, so artfully crafted by a generation of cloud-sculptors—light that struck the twisted towers and the jeweled minarets and made them vanish in puffs of smoke. Fire chasing fire in the labyrinthine gardens.

There was no sound; the forceshields screened out the screams. But the boy could make out people at last, tiny dots of people . . . insects being flushed out of their nests. He forced himself to watch. Towers cracking open like ripe fruits, seed-pod people tumbling, snapping into flame, sizzling, plummeting. . . .

Quietly, his sister was saying, "We should have gone out with the people bins. There was plenty of warning."

"Father's dead."

"If they find us here they'll separate us, assign us to different clans. The Inquest won't let us grow up together."

He leapt from his throne then, hugging the dead Princeling. The body was ice-cold, stone-hard. "I want to die," the boy said.

"Yes." Their eyes met over the body. Glint of a dagger drawn suddenly from the girl's kilt. The old traditional weapon of the city's ruling house. No painless euthanasia for a prince of the blood. He saw her smile sadly. *We're only nine years old!* the boy was thinking. *This can't really be happening to us.* . . . They were matched twins, destined from birth to share throne and bed. For thousands of years the Inquest had not touched their world, had ruled it from afar. . . . And now came war. What they had fought over no one knew, but the planet's fate was sealed. In an orbit around one of the moons the people bins waited to collect the survivors, to time-freeze them in stasis until an unused world could be found for them.

"Quick, the dagger," he said. "Before we change our minds."

"No . . . One more look . . ." She rose and turned to the wallshields. Smoke blotted out the suns. And now, bursting through the darkstriped clouds, a tower-string of childsoldiers riding their mirror-flashing hoverdisks. Never breaking their formation, like links in a chain that hung from the sky. The children all whirling, whirling endlessly, twin lances of light bursting from their laser-irises, spinning disks of deadly light. . . . Buildings sawn instantly into toppling chunks! Sliced people tumbling into heaps on the streets! And the fire—

"They're coming closer! Let's get it over with!" the boy whispered, hoarse.

"But I must see this—I must never forget—"

"What for, sister? It's over. What do you mean, never forget? It's over!"

Then they hugged one another, not passionately but ceremonially, as kings do. He seized the knife from her. "I'll do it first."

The noise burst on them. The shields were broken. The knife slipped from his hands. Tendrils of smoke curled in through the dissipating shielding. And behind the smoke were dozens of the childsoldiers. They wore black war-tunics. Their eyes—their weapons—glittered crystal-gold. Their faces were hard, pitiless.

They were here. It was too late to observe tradition. "Why?" the girl was screaming. "Why did you come here? We had such a beautiful world, we harmed no one—"

An explosion drowned her crying. They clung to each other now, no longer playing their tragic roles. . . . Now they were just two frightened children. He squeezed his eyes tight shut, trying to wish everything into a bad dream. And then he felt gentle, old hands separating them. He opened his eyes. A shimmercloak rustled, blushed pink against deep blue. . . .

The Inquestor smiled. His sister's hand felt cold and dry, like smooth stone. He released it.

The Inquestor spoke. His voice was so quiet, so authoritative. "The Princeling's children. Why was I not told?"

An underling's voice: "Lord Inquestor, we did not know—"

"No matter. I am glad we have found them, and they are alive. It would not have been compassionate, to have abandoned them here. . . ."

"Let me die!" the girl cried.

The Inquestor only smiled. At last he said, "I cannot do that. I cannot kill you without reason . . . no. I will take you with me, assign you suitable clans, let you go forth into the universe from which your world has secluded itself for so many centuries." The boy could hardly hear above the crackleroar of the burning city. "Oh, do not be afraid, Kerin and Elloran, daughter and son of Prince Taanyel. Don't try to follow your father into a foolish death. . . . The Inquest is compassionate, and will provide."

"It isn't fear that make me cry," Kerin said. "It's anger."

The Inquestor had already turned his back on them, expecting them to follow. "Loreh, Loreh . . ." she whispered, calling her brother by his child-name. "Don't ever forget what they did to us! Don't ever forget who you are! They can't make us forget! Promise me, even if we're separated by a thousand parsecs—"

Through his tears, the boy nodded. The smoke hid her from sight. Death had spurned him, and now he was all alone.


The Shendering system was unremarkable. . . . There were hundreds of such backworlds in the Dispersal of Man. There was the little moon, now a sliver, but sometimes a pale peardrop, gleaming in the glitter-dark of the planet's night. The planet itself, cloud-shrouded, water-blue, its land-masses a startling green threaded with silver rivers and peppered with the fragments of the great vermilion road. The big moon, far off, pockish and jagged, where rockworms slithered, covering a millimeter a day and living off the cold light from the small yellow sun. . . . It was not a world to interest the great and powerful. "But a fine world," Tash Tievar said as the learning craft of the House of Tash made another pass over Shemberas, the Singing Mountains.

Some of the younger children gasped; Tievar could not suppress his smile. Once he too had seen his homeworld from space for the first time, when he had first been named to the Clan of Tash, the Rememberers. . . . but that was eighty years ago. *I remember too much*, he thought, and turned to the business at hand. . . .

"Watch the world," he said. The children were silent, clustered in a semicircle on the mirror metal of the ship's floor; all the forceshields had been deopaqued, and it seemed that they floated on a mirror-disk in the midst of empty space. "Now, all together, eyes closed. . . .

*Eyes closed. Wringing remembrances from the inner darkness. The daily training of the Clan of Tash* . . . "Good," said Tievar. "Now tell me what you saw."

Kerin, a highborn girl, displaced from her native world by an Inquestral war, for whom the Inquest had found a home in the Clan of Tash out of their infinite compassion, said, "Father Tievar, I remember the world hanging between the two moons, three shells on a peasant's necklace."

"Nice image. Your future master will like that."

"I don't want a master!" the girl cried out. Such an outburst was not suitable, for all that Kerin might have been a Princeling's daughter.

"Be careful," Tievar said as gently as he could. He avoided her eyes, not wishing to single her out. The girl had only been on Shendering for a few months, and already she was his favorite. He turned to watch the half-world wisped with hover-haze and wreathed with a million stars, matching it in his mind with remembrances of other worlds, other times. . . . "I know you have endured much pain. The Inquestor who gave you the name of Tash knew you would have Remembering in you, because of your father's suicide, the destruction of your country, your world, would be branded indelibly in your mind as a Rememberer's Remembrance is branded. . . . But there are also things that a child of Tash must forget if she is to do what is ordained. . . . Come, I don't wish to scold you. You are doing well here." He watched the girl as she stood for a better view; she wore the plain white tunic of the Clan of Tash well, as though it were a costly robe. *If only she knew how much I understand her pain,* he thought. He wished he could tell her about his love for her, how he felt for her what a father feels . . . but it would not have been right. The memory of another father still burned inside her, and he knew better than to touch such a remembrance.

Now all the children were doing their remembering exercises, and the small craft sped swiftly from the world, aimed at the greater of the two moons. *They resent this training,* Tievar thought, *because they believe they will never have to use it. But I have been Rememberer for an Inquestor once already. Only his death released me. And in all that time he called for me perhaps a dozen times. Powers of powers, what use are we really?*

"Be ready," he called out. "We'll hit a displacement field in a few minutes." Suddenly they were through; the perspective had changed in an instant. Now is was Shendering that was distant, a fierce crescent of blue fire behind the craggy rim of Dhaëndek, the dead moon. A collective catch of children's breath . . . "The exercises. Don't forget why we're here."

"It must be so cold there," said Kerin. He thought he felt a twinge of longing in her voice. But she was too young, surely, to long for coldness. . . .

. . . And then the last moon, Kilimindi, hardly more than a rock, but within it, hollowed out of the dead basalt, the palace of the absentee Inquestor who governed the system. The little moon's surface was made smooth by the Inquestral architects, checkered with square fields of ice to look like a *shtezhnat* board warped into a sphere. Tash Tievar compared the images with his remembrances and found them true.

But now the children were clamoring for stories, and he wanted to remind them of the high seriousness of their purpose, so he went on with the lesson in earnest.

"Your services may never be required," he said, "but if they are . . . if a time should come when, through a game of *makrúgh*, this planet must be destroyed. . . . They will summon us. The Inquestors do not like to destroy planets, children. Their purpose is . . . we cannot really understand it. To preserve the balance of the Dispersal of Man, to protect us from stagnation . . . But there is a House of Tash on every planet. We are all like aliens here, shunned because of what we represent. When war comes we will know first. The people of Shendering—as many as can be saved—will be packed into people bins and towed by convoys of delphinoid shipminds through the not-space between spaces, the overcosm, waiting, for centuries perhaps, for a new world to become available. But a few of us will be chosen, we who Remember. For every Inquestor who has taken part in the game of *makrúgh* must acquire one of us, to remind him—in perpetuity—of the planet that he has caused to die. . . . The Inquestors value compassion above all things. That is why we exist, so that they will never forget that they must have compassion." He stopped suddenly. He had seen something that did not accord with his remembrance—

Kerin was saying, "They don't seem to have learned very much about compassion. I saw rivers of white fire gush through the city streets—"

But Tievar was not listening. He had seen something . . . something he hoped he would never see again in his life. A serpent-string of silver cylinders. Slowly they were circling the moon, flashing briefly in reflected light before the darkness swallowed them . . . and streaks of delphinoid ships, darting among them like corkscrew comets. *No!* Tievar thought. *It can't be*—

A chill shook him, a dread he had only felt once before in his life.

"I think," he said, "that the lesson is over. I think we

should return to the world now, to the House, get a little refreshment. . . ." his voice wavered. "We will be having visitors soon—"

A babble from the children. "Visitors, Father Tievar? Who?" Tievar closed his eyes, subvocalizing instructions to the craft's little thinkhive. The craft shuddered, shifted, did a momentary stomach-wrenching gravity change. The moon was behind them now. Tievar did not want to look back, but something impelled him—

"The visitors, Father! Who are they?" It was the girl Kerin.

"Inquestors." Even without looking he felt the girl freeze. She was remembering her past. A world in ruins. Well, she would have to forget it now. They would all have to forget a great deal before year's end. . . .

"It's time, then! And I've only just come from one war-wrecked planet, to find that I must—"

"Do not weep, Kerin. You will not have time for weeping now. We'll all have to intensify the work, have longer remembering sessions, more field work. . . . There won't be much time."

"I am not weeping!" Kerin said defiantly, and Tievar decided not to look too closely.

Instead he watched the people bins. From this distance they seemed like little silver pellets, beads perhaps, a bracelet around the moon. . . . The starships stormed like phosphorflies. It was hard to believe that each people bin could hold millions of people, stasis-frozen and stacked in racks. . . .

*What did they want with this poor, insignificant planet? What crisis in the Inquestral game of* makrúgh *had forced the war to move to this sparsely peopled quadrant of the Dispersal?* Tievar watched the children. Many were silent, wondering about the future. Some were chattering with excitement. Perhaps they would be chosen! Perhaps they would live in an Inquestor's court!

"Father Tievar . . ." It was the voice of the girl Kerin.

"Yes?" She had drawn him away from the crowd of children.

"If you are chosen by the Inquest, will you go, Father Tievar?"

"I'm too old."

"So if they choose me, I'll never see you again?"

"Never. Because I will not go out again. I have been a Rememberer too long. The memories confuse me now, and I long for . . ." he did not want to say death, not aloud; it would frighten the child.

"I know what you mean, Father. I too have wanted to die. To crawl away to a place as cold and dead as the emptiness I've carried inside since Father's death. . . ." The girl frightened him sometimes. She was so intense, her past still burned inside her. She had not yet learned that there are things a Rememberer must forget. And then the girl said, "I will never leave you."

He was moved that she had touched him with her love. But he had nothing to say, no comfort, no platitudes of wisdom. So he turned to watch the people bins and said nothing.

With a flick of his mind, Ton Elloran n'Taanyel Tath dissolved his tachyon bubble and stepped out onto the surface of the doomed world. With him came Sajit, his musician, and a ...usic of tinkle-topped sighs from strings of songjewels that hung about their necks; for Elloran could go nowhere without music, he found the silence too painful. There were too many memories to be found in silence. Utopias destroyed. Planets in ruins. And . . . when he thought too deeply . . . a memory of a small boy, waiting to die, in a dark huge dreadful silence.

It was a forest clearing. In the grass, a few meters of vermilion road, garish against the grass-green; a displacement plate. For the only city on Shendering was Ayn, the Scrambled City, a city shredded into minuscule jigsaw fragments and scattered all over the land-masses, linked by a single scarlet road and by a million displacement plates, the buildings artfully concealed underground, under quilts of jungle overhang, under umbrella-cliffs and ocean floors. . . . Whoever designed the city had not wanted to inflict man's presence upon the planet's wilderness. In Ayn, you dared not leave the road unguided for an instant, or you would never find it again.

Now it was deepest night, and the only light was the soft blushing of Elloran's shimmercloak, a pale pink shifting across the deep blue shimmerfur. Another step and it was a brilliant, flower-fragrant night with two moons shining, a pocked moon and a haloed one. A step later, bright daylight, mist-blue hills; another step, twilight and a brook bridging the red road, winding around boulder croppings . . . and always the landscape peppered with white rosellas, the most prosaic of all flowers. For a moment Elloran felt a sea-breeze, breathed a sharp tangy smell, and then—

The road forked. Flicking an image of the city's layout into his mind, Elloran saw where to turn and what instructions to subvocalize into the next displacement plate. Cliffs loomed, blurred into meadows, meadows shimmerfaded into orchards doused in the bitter fragrance of ripe krangfruit.

"Are we there yet?" Shen Sajit said. "I mean the House of Tash. Although why you choose to come here yourself—"

In the pause, a rush of shimmerviol music. "I had to. Sajit, I had a reason to lose this game of *makrúgh*. This planet has something I've been looking for, for thirty years. . . ."

"For this you're letting it get destroyed?"

Elloran didn't answer. He was thinking of Kerin. How old would she be now? He tried to calculate what effect time dilation would have had on her. . . . She must seem younger, he decided. An image of the burning homeworld came into his mind for a moment, but he cast it away. It was so long ago, and he had lived through so much. . . . *I am an Inquestor now,* he told himself sternly. *My compassion extends equally to all men.* It was different for other humans, even ones, like Sajit, who might have been friends if Elloran had not been an Inquestor. For a few seconds Elloran debated whether or not he should tell his musician of the real purpose of their journey to Shendering. How he had searched the colossal mind of the thinkhive on Uran s'Varek until he had found his sister at last. They walked faster; a river flicked into view, a veldt speckled with white rosellas, a half-house growing from a sheared-off rockface. *Kerin* . . .

The road branched; displacement plates glinted in the thick grass. Elloran selected a turn. Abruptly they were in the House of Tash. A central atrium with a kaleidotinted roofshield, the light-colors dartshifting through whispertrickling fountains, sending pastel ripples across monochrome holosculptures of ancient heroes . . . a cool place, subtle and restrained. He could hardly hear the songjewels' music above the burbling water.

An old man in the white tunic of the Rememberers came to greet them. "Ton Elloran," he said gravely, "I am Tash

Tievar, senior instructor here. You will give audience in this atrium?"

Elloran nodded. A hoverthrone of faded wicker materialized on the displacement plate at his feet. He ascended. "I suppose you know why we are here. The representatives of the Inquest, I mean."

"Who could fail to do so, my Lord?" Was there bitterness in the old man's voice? *Powers of powers, I'm not responsible for the way our universe is!* he wanted to say. *I didn't choose to be where I am now. . . .*

"Know then," he said formally, "that war has come to this sector of the Dispersal of Man, and that in all probability the Shendering system will fall beyond . . . that in its compassion the Inquest has prepared people bins to receive such of this world's inhabitants who wish to avoid the possible annihilation of the world . . . and that I, as spokesman of the High Inquest, do solemnly invoke the charter of the Clan of Tash, to choose a Rememberer for myself." This last he spoke in highspeech, according to formula.

"What selection process shall you require for the people bins?"

"Whatever selection plan was chosen when the world was first chartered."

"By choice, then, with those possessing clan-names having the right of first choice."

"Very well." *What a tired, pointless ritual it seems!* Too many times Elloran had spoken these words and consigned faceless millions to their deaths. *But it is necessary!* Man was a fallen being. To be static was to court a thousand heresies, worst of all the heresy of utopianism. War was necessary! It was the deepest of human instincts! At least, now, war was controlled by the Inquest, war was compassionate, striking only when it must. But to be an Inquestor was to court the most terrible of all lonelinesses. Elloran wondered if this old man understood the pain of it, the terrible war between guilt and compassion that every Inquestor strove to conceal deep inside himself.

Tash Tievar stood silent, waiting for another command. "The Rememberers. I must have Rememberers, Tievar. Twelve Inquestors took part in this game of *makrúgh*, and none must ever forget. . . ." When was the last time he had summoned a Rememberer? A decade? *Next season, when I return to the palace . . .*

"Pick whom you will, Lord Inquestor."

"Let lots be drawn, or use some other fair method. It doesn't matter to me. Except . . ." He tried to keep his voice steady. "Except for myself. For myself I wish to requisition the girl named Tash Kerin."

Why had the old man turned so pale? "What's the matter?" Elloran said.

"My Lord—she is so new here, so untrained—I did not know that you Inquestors knew so much about us, knew our very names and the planets on which we were stationed—"

"Fetch her." There. It was done. The old man stepped onto a displacement plate and was gone into the next room. Perhaps the next room was on the other side of the planet; Elloran did not know how fine the scrambling of the city was.

He commanded Sajit to call forth an eerie music from the songjewels, like the call of ancient cetaceans in the ocean of mythical Earth. It whined above the trickling of the iridescing waters. And suddenly she was there—

She didn't speak. *She's so young—*

"Kerin."

"Lord Inquestor?" Elloran saw a slip of a child, her blond hair cropped unbecomingly like a peasant's, her eyes wide, dark, fierce. She did not avoid his gaze the way commonfolk should. He was proud of her for this, for not forgetting who she had been.

"Kerin—you're so young, still—it must have been only yesterday for you, the childsoldiers ravaging the city, the burning world, keeping deathwatch over our father—"

And suddenly she knew. She shrank back from him. "You've become one of them! Loreh, you promised never to forget!"

"Kerin—" He reached out, wanting to touch her, and it was as if she was in the past still, a ghost, taunting him, his fingers slipping through her . . . but it was only that she had darted behind one of the fountains. It gushed from the ceiling, defying gravity by means of a Shtoman varigrav device, cloaking her with spray-mist. "I know this is hard for you to accept, Kerin. I had no choice. They named me to the clan of Ton. They said that my past suffering would enable me to feel compassion. I had no choice!"

"You wanted to die! You grabbed the dagger from me, you were so eager!" Her voice was a shrill shriek, lost in the echoing rush of waters. She did not look at him now. She backed into the shadow of a huge holosculpt tableau, her face crisscrossed by shadow-horns of a mythical beast, her white tunic burning amber-mauve-emerald in the light from the skyroof's kaleidolon.

"You don't know how I've looked for you."

"I don't care! You've killed our father all over again, you traitor—"

"I have golden palace now. Its name is Varezhdur. The palace flies from star to star. I am a Kingling with a dozen worlds. I have worn the shimmercloak of the Inquest for fifty years, and all this time I have searched for you, and all this time your starship sailed the overcosm, with a half-century squashed by relativity into a single year. . . . I have told no one, not even Sajit whom I trust more than any man. . . . For you I played *makrúgh*, to get you back I picked this planet to die—"

"You don't look sixty years old."

"We never need to age. You can share this too, you can share all of it—"

"You're an Inquestor. You can make me do anything. If you requisition my services as Rememberer I have no choice."

"I will not force you, Kerin." It had all been for nothing! Elloran clapped his hands for louder music, hoping to deaden his grief. Percussion thundered and thudded. "Isn't there any way we can start again?"

She came towards him then, disrupting the fountain and sending the spray flying. She was saying, "There is an old man here, a teacher, Tash Tievar. . . . He has been like a father to me. I have promised to stay with him always. To stay here, and perhaps be killed, if need be. . . . I've been prepared to die ever since our world died at the hands of the Inquest. I will go wherever he goes."

"Then I will requisition him too. There's no problem there."

"You say you would not force one of us?" She laughed then, an angry, desperate laugh that he had never heard from her in all their childhood. She had changed so much. Again Elloran had the uncanny sensation that she was only an illusion, a shadow-revenant from the coffined past.

"No," he said, "I will not force one of you. Compassion, not compulsion, is our way."

"Tash Tievar will not leave, Ton Elloran," said Kerin. "And so I will not leave; my honor binds me, and the Inquest, I know, understands honor well."

He stood speechless for a moment. In coming here, in revealing his emotions so nakedly, he had violated everything the Inquest had taught him. How could the Dispersal of Man be held together if even Inquestors ignored the trappings of degree, broke caste, pleaded with underlings? He wanted to be a brother, not a Kingling dealing with a subject, but . . . for him it had been fifty years. He had expected gratitude, not resistance. Not that Kerin would play *makrúgh* against him— and win! He had forgotten how alike they were.

"At least . . . at least . . . I'm your brother, Kerin—"

"I have no brother," Kerin said softly, bitterly. "My brother was killed by the Inquestors last year, the year they devastated my homeworld." And she walked back through the fountain, vanished from the displacement plate. From the songjewels around his neck came a burst of martial music, inanely cheerful.

There was still time, some days at least, before the war would come to Shendering. Tievar thought it was best to continue as he had always done. Today he led the children away from the road a little. They stood in an open field flecked with wild rosellas. The children clustered around him, wildflowers themselves, he was thinking. "Close your eyes now. Perceive the fragrances. Separate all the scents until you can enumerate them all, every blade of grass, every flower. . . ."

He took Kerin aside then. "You did wrong, little daughter, to mock the Inquestor, to link your fate with mine."

"I can't help it, Father!" and then she told him everything that had passed between her and Elloran. "How can I go to him now, knowing that he's callously killed this world to get me back?"

Tievar touched the girl's cropped hair for a moment. He did not know what to think. He was disturbed that an Inquestor would move a world to fulfill his own emotional needs. Inquestors were supposed to be beyond such things. *And she is so like him in her own way,* he thought, *dragging me as a pawn into her conflict with him.* . . . He left her abruptly,

turning his mind to the remembering exercises. He had the
children singing monotonous, mind-stilling chants now, lulling
all the senses except for the sense of smell and the touch of the
breeze.

Then, without warning, a different music came—

Harsh resonanceless highwoods shrieking through waves
of shimmerviol and whisperlyre like exotic fish skip-skimming
the waves. It was Ton Elloran and his friend, the silent musician.

"My Lord—"

"Go on, Tash Tievar. It is not our intention to interrupt
your little lessons." Uneasily, Tash Tievar muttered a few more
instructions. The apprentices were too rigid, too wound up by
the Inquestor's presence, to be able to concentrate on Remembering. Pointedly Kerin took up a position as far away from the
Inquestor as possible, squeezed her eyes tight shut, feeling
nothing but the wind and the fragrance.

Elloran did not seem to notice Kerin. *Of course,* Tievar
thought, *he would not go so far as to show his emotions to us,
the shortlived.* Instead, the Inquestor chose to ask questions
about the planet, and about remembering.

"The city," said Tievar, "is practically a myth to most of the
world's inhabitants. Who would notice a patch of vermilion in
the middle of a hundred or more square klomets of countryside? And the city is well scrambled. . . . At times the road
even touches the surface of the moon Dhaëndek, where
miners try to trap the rockworms for their crystalline stomach
linings. . . ." Tievar saw that Kerin was listening to every
word, despite seeming to concentrate on her exercises. He
went on, "Remembering is hard for most people. There are so
many things that men would rather forget. But Rememberers
are like the rosella flowers, Inquestor, which are so hardy they
can subsist anywhere." He stooped, plucked a rosella; it was a
tiny thing with a thousand prickly-stiff petaloids. He crushed
it; it was pulverized into a million spores, and he blew them
into the breeze. "Each one seems so fragile, doesn't it? Yet it's
been said they would bloom even on Dhaëndek, living off the
sunlight and drawing sustenance from the rocks, toughening
themselves against the almost zero cold. Memories will come,
no matter how we fear them . . . like the spores of rosella,
clinging to your shimmercloaks, even to the hulls of delphinoids as they breach the overcosm, until they find new

fields to bloom in. . . . And in a day they are dead. But did you not see, as you came along this branch of the road, which alternates winter and summer with every step, that there wasn't a landscape without a few of them? Even the mountain peaks glassed in with cold?"

"You are a born Rememberer," Elloran said. "A true artist. You make the humblest things sound beautiful . . . if only you would come with us."

"Inquestor . . . Your sister has told me everything." He noticed Kerin pricking up her ears. But he had to say this! "Perhaps you were not a good Inquestor—"

He saw Elloran stiffen. "Please." He tried to stay unruffled, even though such forwardness might mean instant death. "But I see now that you are human, underneath it all. Because of this, and because of the way Kerin has linked her fate with mine. . . . I have decided not to stay on Shendering and die. . . . I love the girl, Lord Inquestor, and I won't see her throw herself away in a needless gesture. I am old and my life would have been useless but for this."

"Thank you," said the Inquestor. Not a word more; it would have been unseemly for him to express fulsome gratitude, Tievar knew. They turned to find Kerin—

"No!" she was screaming. "First my brother and now my second father—you've both betrayed me!—I don't want any part of this miserable universe of yours!" The children's chanting wound down to a pathetic murmur. Tievar saw Elloran's face, ashen, appalled. There was a second of stasis, and then—

Kerin was sprinting for the displacement plate, trampling across the meadow towards the taller grass that concealed the vermilion road, now her head was bobbing up and down in the wavy green—

She was gone. A cry escaped Elloran's lips. *I pity him,* Tievar thought, and the thought was strange. . . . How could you pity a man who had calmly arranged for the destruction of your world? "Quick! We must follow her—if she leaves the crimson path, there's no way we'll find her again—" he said.

They ran for the plate. The Inquestor and the musician and the old man. The children following in a huddle.

Touching the path—

Nightfall. A branch in the road. The girl's shape, shadowslim, flitting to the left.

Snow. Rainbows bridging the mountainpeaks.

Summer. Beach. Autumn. Dead-leaves freckled with rosellas.

Darkness. Jungle. Twilight. Taiga. And then—

"We've lost her." Sajit was speaking. They had run perhaps only a hundred meters down the road.

"Powers of powers!" cried Elloran. "Fifty years I've searched for her . . ."

Tievar was breathing heavily. He was too old for this. Through his exhaustion he heard them talking—

"Her gene-pattern. Must be in the planetary thinkhive. They'll have monitors all over the planet, surely they'll trace her. . . ."

Elloran. "No, Sajit. This world has no such amenities."

"We could use troops. We have enough extra ships crammed with childsoldiers."

"The war is due soon. It's hopeless."

"Inquestor—" Tievar spoke up. The two turned on him, waiting. "I am a Rememberer. Perhaps I may speak more freely than most. I know this world well—it is my duty—and I have known the girl these past few months as well as though she were my own daughter. Perhaps I can trace her. Let me try to find her, Ton Elloran. Give me a few days, set a deadline before you rain the fire-death on this world."

"Yes. Yes."

"Three sleeps then," said Sajit, taking his master's arm. Elloran said nothing; but he nodded once.

And Tievar said, "But—and I say this as Rememberer— you must realize that though you are Inquestor you are only a man. Man is a fallen being, is he not? Perhaps you will learn from this, that you cannot always get what you want, even though you burn down the moons from the sky." *Powers! I don't mean to mock him. . . .*

"You ignorant idiot!" Sajit cried in a sudden passion. "Do you think he doesn't know this already? Do you think he isn't burning from the pain inside himself, from which he can never escape? Do you think the Clan of Ton is for sadists and mass-murderers?" Elloran still said nothing, but waved him to be silent.

The Inquestor and his musician stepped towards the displacement plate. In a second, Tievar and the children were in silence, for the music of songjewels was gone. Tievar and his apprentices stepped in a different direction. A blizzard, bitter-cold, assailed them. "Remember this cold!" he shouted over the howling wind. "Remember it all your lives!" He closed his mind to the cold, trying to think of Kerin and where she was likely to have gone.

Thousands of parsecs away, a golden palace danced against the stars as it orbited a rich world. There were wings and corridors and arches and towers and klomet-long comet-tail streamers of beaten gold. And in the palace's heart, a throneroom. And in the throneroom, swirling slowly in an artificial lightfield, a galaxy made of dust. A dust-sculpture. It was the most private of Ton Elloran's thronerooms.

The tachyon bubble materialized, dissolved. Elloran and Sajit were alone together in the vast hall.

"I've failed!" Elloran cried. "Sajit, more music—"

"Wait." Elloran allowed himself to be helped into his huge throne, with its firefur cushions stuffed with kyllap leaves, with its wide steps of sculpt-friezed gold. He stared at the dust nebula.

Elloran wished, sometimes, that they could have been close friends, that he could have told everything long ago. But it was not in the nature of things.

Sajit said, "Why did you try to do it this way? Why the game of *makrúgh*? Couldn't you just have sent a tachyon bubble for her and be done with it?"

"I've forgotten so much," Elloran said. "What it is to be a normal human, in utter terror and awe of the Inquest. . . . It's been so long! I played *makrúgh* because it is what I'm used to, because to be devious has become second nature to me . . . I thought she'd be impressed! That I had done all this for her! And now I've killed her!"

"Perhaps not. In three sleeps—" But Elloran would not answer him.

With a wave of his hand and perhaps a subvocalized command, Sajit summoned a soft music of shimmerviols, the sweet voices of neuterchildren weaving and twining long wordless melodies. "Drown me in it!" Elloran whispered.

Sajit had come up with him to the throne. Even with his friend so near, Elloran felt terribly alone. "You should have told me," Sajit said. Elloran looked at his face, more aged than his own that had been frozen in an ageless youth. Inquestors did not talk about their past, about the time before donning the shimmercloak. It was so deeply ingrained. . . . An Inquestor must seem to have sprung from nowhere, like a god. . . . Couldn't Sajit understand? He could not rush in and acknowledge the girl to be his sister before a whole planet. Such knowledge of an Inquestor's humanity could hurt the Inquest—

"Sajit, the Rememberers. All of them. Now. Order them awakened. Here, at once."

"Elloran—"

"Obey, curse you!"

Presently they came. It had been night in the palace of Varezhdur—night and day fell at the Inquestor's whim—and they were half-asleep, dazed at being admitted into the Inquestor's secret place. There were a hundred of them or more: old men and women, children, people in their prime, all with their white tunics hastily pulled on, their hair disheveled and their faces streaked with sleepiness.

"Remind me!" said Elloran.

They begun. They talked of a triple world, of a gas giant glowering in the sky through the silhouettes of tower-tall trees. Of a hot world with cool bubble-houses shadowed by smouldering sulphur-clefts. Of water worlds where the humans built dark slimy houses in the bellies of sea-serpents. Of beautiful worlds, shimmering blue-green or russet or amethyst in the void. . . .

"Remind me! Remind me!" Elloran screamed.

. . . of old men playing *shtezhnat* by the sea. Of children with forcenets in the mountains, straining to catch the leaping flamefish from volcanic lakes. Of a young thief slipping into the shadows, clutching the cut-off credit-thumbs of a dead merchant. Of bands of women hunting for snow-phoenixes among the glaciers. . . .

And Sajit was whispering to him, "Why torture yourself more? Make it stop," and Elloran could see the pain in the musician's face, but he couldn't stop—

. . . of last days. Of crisp-burnt birds raining onto the fields. Of fire flushing corpses from the catacombs. Of child-soldiers whirling blazing death from their hoverdisks—

"Stop!" Silence fell. Elloran remembered at last, that memory he had tried to forget for fifty years. He did not weep; he was too drained. The people of the clan of Tash stood uncertainly, waiting for a new command.

"How long have I been listening?" he asked Sajit weakly.

"More than a sleep, Inquestor." Sajit was always careful to speak formally when they were not alone, and Elloran was grateful for that. "They must be tired, Lord Inquestor."

"Yes. Dismiss them." It seemed that he only blinked once, and they were gone. *Phantoms*, he thought. *The past returning to haunt us—by our own command. . . . It takes a certain masochism to be an Inquestor. . . .*

"I'll rest now," he said when he was alone with Sajit. "Command a soothing music for me. And after, after . . . We will return to Shendering to see the end."

"Do you have to torment yourself so?"

"I have no choices. I have relinquished all my freedoms. I am an Inquestor."

At dawn Tash Tievar rose and followed the vermilion pathway out to the field where he had last spoken to Kerin. The wind was gusting sharp, making the grass dance, churning up the dead rosellas. Even as his mind raced, trying to think where Kerin might have gone, he was drinking in the wind and the whispering meadow, fashioning a future remembrance. . . .

He squatted on the grass, alone. At the House of Tash, the chosen ones were being readied; the rejected ones were already leaving en masse for the packaging houses to be prepared for the long journey in people bins. He closed his eyes, making his mind blank, an empty message disk, as a Rememberer must when he is preparing to summon up a vivid remembrance. . . .

*Kerin*—

She had come to the House of Tash a girl on fire, yet speaking always of the bleak and cold. A memory surfaced like a sea-mammal for air—

*I too have wanted to die. To crawl away to a place as cold and dead as the emptiness I've carried inside since Father's death. . . .*

He saw her as she said those words. In the learning craft, looking out into space. And then he saw—

Dhaëndek, a dead rock whose shadow fell over Shendering, dead craters made glitter-faceted by borrowed light. *It must be very cold there.* The twinge of longing in the voice.

Tievar opened his eyes. At the zenith Dhaëndek shone

still, a moon-ghost softened by sunlight, half-hidden in amber dawnlight. The wind made a miniature hurricane of husked rosellas, freckling his hair and shoulders.

*It has been said that they would bloom even on Dhaëndek—*

He roused himself. There were places when the crimson road went through caverns or underground chambers. There were places when you suddenly felt a stomach-twisting lightness for a moment, almost as though . . . They said that the pathway touched the moon, but only Rememberers, well-trained and cautious ones at that, would leave the pathway for the treacherous places beyond. . . . Kerin was a good Rememberer. He had trained her well. She would have noticed.

Quickly his mind traced over the thousand branches of the road. The city's maps showed only what the city would look like if it were not scrambled; so long as you stuck to the road, you would not need to know the road's locations in true space. He would have to go by memory, by following the twists and turns in his mind until he recalled the queasy-making stretches of the road. . . .

Resolutely he turned now, stepping onto the displacement plate subvocalizing instructions to its mechanism.

The light gravity hit him at once, and the chemical-rich odor of the air. The road—only three or four meters of it—was in total darkness; only the displacement plates at either end glinted. No walker along the road would have bothered to notice such an anomaly; it would have been dark, one would have pressed onward to one's destination. After a few minutes, when his stomach had stopped groaning, he left the road, bumped into a wall, groped his way along it for a while, found a door that accordioned open when he touched the stud. . . .

A village square. Overhead, a roof of rock. Houses hewn from the living stone of Dhaëndek. A few people, dressed in rags, wandering about.

"Please could you tell me—" A woman saw him. She pointed. Screamed. Made some gesture to ward off evil. The square emptied abruptly. Tievar walked on. It must be a village of those who hunted the rockworms on the surface. The hostility he understood. The clan of Tash was evil-omened. No one wanted to see one now, when news of the world's end must surely have reached even Dhaëndek.

Mocking laughter. Tievar whirled round—

A woman was watching him. She was middle-aged, swathed in a shapeless smock, grinning. "Cowards, the lot of them," the woman said. Her voice was raucous, grating on the nerves. "I know you're looking for the girl."

He started. "You've seen her?"

"Perhaps. A miner sees a lot, they say. You have to, to catch the worms before they notice you and lash you to smithereens."

"Where is she?"

"What's a cityman like you coming asking questions of us countryfolk that don't even know how to get to the city? I tell you, I'm not superstitious. I don't believe you whitecoats herald the end of the world. What would anyone want with Shendering, for powers' sake? Take the girl—"

"The girl! Quick! You'll be well paid."

"Keep your credit. I suppose you'll tell me to sign up for a people bin next. It's all a ruse, I say, to oppress us simple people. The girl . . . She stood here for a sleep, two sleeps, and everyone shunned her. Except me. Don't believe those stupid stories, I tell you. The chatter of hermaphrodites. I'm a miner with a clan-name and I didn't earn it listening to nonsense."

"The girl!" Tievar said desperately.

"I took her to where she wanted to go. Out in the middle of nowhere, past the last of the wormhordes. She was crazy, said it was time for her to die. Well, that's her business, and I only did her a favor."

"Take me there!"

"If the worms don't get us first." She laughed uproariously, thinking the prospect very funny.

The woman's name was Beren of the clan of Var. She led him down empty streets—Tievar got the feeling that they had only just become empty at his approach—and to a little rock-hollowed house where she threw him a pressure-skin and slipped into one herself. It was an organic, semisentient device that hugged his body, constricting but invisible save for the air supply in its belt. A hoverplatform outfitted with strange gear waited on a displacement plate. Beren sprang up, beckoned him to follow, without waiting subvoked the command and they were on the surface—

Barren. Bleak. Craters within craters. Jagged mountains, a menacingly near horizon, and half-Shendering and distant Kilimindi shining dimly, casting soft twin-peaked shadows.

And the silence. Tievar had never known such silence, even at the most profound levels of remembrance-concentration.

They sped over the pocked, gravelly terrain. Now and then the floater mechanism kicked up a dust-flurry and the dust-motes took a long time falling. "Are there many rock-worms here?" he subvocalized, hoping the skin had a con-versing device.

"Ha!" a thin whisper in his ear. "We mine them. . . . Mostly they just sit and photosynthesize, but if they sense dan-ger they'll lash out once with their tails and . . ." another laugh, converted by subvoking into a strange cough-grating sound. "If we get them right we spray them with liquid water"—she tapped some of the strange apparatus on the floater— "and this freezes instantly and keeps them still long enough for us to slit their stomachs and gather the carbon crys-tals, *huge* ones the size of a baby's head—"

"Carbon crystals?"

"Diamonds. They come somewhere in the middle of their digestive chain—"

Tievar let the woman chatter on. Her mouth never moved, as his did by accident whenever he talked; he was not used to subvocalizing whole conversations. The tinny buzz of her speech continued, and he listened, because if he did not he would think of finding Kerin's corpse, lying frozen in a crater. He was terrified to think of it. And then—

A sliver of white, running out of a crater wall's shadow—

"Kerin!" he cried out, forgetting the airlessness. There was no sound. But she must have picked up the subvocaliza-tion on her pressure-skin. She twisted around, saw the floater, ran—

The floater skidded over a stray rock, righted itself, Tievar propped himself against a railing, they raced towards her, he subvoked her name over and over, and then—

"Where is she?"

"In a shadow somewhere," the woman said. "Shall we go back? Her air supply will run out soon anyway."

"*Kerin!*"

And then, in his ear, a quiet voice. "It's no use, Father Tievar. I made a pact with my brother, and I'm going to fulfull it even if he never does, even though he has gone over to the other side. It's no use, no use. . . ." He thought she was sob-bing. "I'm going to do something beautiful first, though. In a few seconds I'm going to dissolve my pressure-skin. Didn't you once say that the rosella might bloom even here, in the coldest land? Yet the people who live here wouldn't think of testing out such a theory. But a million spores are clinging to my body, to my clothes. I give them to this dead world, a gift from my dead heart."

He saw her darting out of the shadow—

"No!" he screamed, his voice helpless in the big silence. "She's going towards that glacier," he subvoked to Beren.

"That's no glacier! There's no glaciers on the surface, you ignorant cityman. That's a—"

A rockworm was slithering down a craterwall. It was like a crystal tunnel with a thousand icy segments. It was a hundred meters long or more. And Kerin was running straight towards it.

And the floater was off! Rising with a suddenness that toppled Tievar onto the platform, racing towards the rockworm. And then Tievar saw the creature's innards through its transparent exterior, quivering contructs of tubes and globules like an ancient chemist's laboratory, and the octahedral diamonds, fist-huge, rolling slowly around. . . . "*Kerin!*" he tried to shout. How could she not notice—

A scream, transmuted by the skin's device into a strangled whistle—

The tail, coiled on the other side of the crater wall, whipped out. Kerin sailed upwards—

"Quick! Do something!" But Beren had already commanded the floater. It sprang up, swerved to avoid the backlash, Tievar saw Kerin falling, slowly, slowly in the moon's low gravity, and then—

The monster reared up, glittering. He saw crystal plates rippling slowly, the inner organs pulsating crazily—"

"If she's already opened her pressure skin," Beren said quickly, "*open yours*. Seize her, tight, hold her to your opening. The skin may adjust to hold you both—"

They soared! Tievar felt a stab of terror as they crashed the creature, prying loose a shower of crystalrock, and then swung away to avoid—

Curve of the crystal tail, then—

A hundred nozzles, spraying mist over the creature! Making it shudder to a standstill, crusting the crystal surface with fine ice—

Kerin, crashing onto the speeding floater. "All in a day's work," said the miner. But Kerin—

"Something's wrong with her!" Tievar clasped her to himself. The skin was undone. At once he dissolved the skin that was hugging his chest, clutching the girl to him. Her eyes were stiff and open as if in death. The cold of vacuum seared him for a moment, and then the skin grew taut around them both. He felt cool blood wetting his chest. She had only been exposed to the vacuum for a few seconds, but a little while longer and . . .

"Kerin . . ."

She did not speak. The floater came to rest a few centimeters above ground, and Var Beren was already seizing the opportunity to slice open the immobilized rockworm. The vibrosaw was efficient, spewing crystal guts and diamonds all over the stony ground. And Kerin was stirring. . . .

"Why are you punishing me?" clasped together in the same pressure-skin, they could speak to each other now.

"You were punishing yourself, Kerin. Sometimes we see people only as what they represent. Your brother was a symbol of those who had dispossessed you, who had driven your father to suicide. But *he* did not do those things, Kerin. It is Dispersal of Man itself, the order of things, that causes such things to happen. . . ."

"I don't believe it," Kerin whispered. "I can't accept that things *must* be as they are. I want to fight them, I want to destroy them—"

"Understand yourself," said Tievar. "You think you ran away because you were angry—at me, at Elloran. But you can't punish the universe by killing yourself. That's a child's way. And you are fast becoming a woman, Kerin. This is the only universe we will ever have. You have made a beautiful gesture worthy of a Rememberer, but now you must understand why you tried to destroy yourself. . . . It's because you were angry at you, not *us*. Because, with all your hatred of the Inquest, you could not burn away your love for your brother." She did not answer him, but he knew that it was true. He held the girl tightly, shielding her. And then she pointed towards the dead rockworm, to where Beren was approaching with a forcenet stuffed with diamonds that she would never be able to sell now. She pointed feverishly until he saw what she wanted him to see—

In a cleft between two rocks, some meters away, a rosella

was budding. They wasted no time, those hardy little blooms, adapting to anything. Tievar smiled sadly, storing the Remembrance; but Kerin's face held no expression at all.

Kilimindi. The stronghold of Ton Karakaël, absentee Kingling of Shendering and a score of other systems.

A huge arena-hall, a disk englobed by forceshields that let in the starlight. Its floor appeared to be dark blue grass; in fact it was carpeted with the living fur of shimmercloaks, and now and then it would blush pale pink against the ultramarine. A dozen Inquestors and their guests had gathered here. There were fluttering shimmercloaks, there were three-tiered head-dresses topped with still-living featherskins cloned from peacocks and calliopteryxes, nude hermaphrodites with kohl-blackened eyes and nipples rouged with paste of powdered rubies.

Elloran had not wanted to come to this grand display; but his absence would have been unseemly. And the music of Sajit had been demanded; he could not, in all propriety, have failed to oblige, since it would have been commented on if he had shown rancor at losing the game of *makrúgh*.

It seemed a very artistic notion—to organize the disposal of the people bins into a grand fireworks with music. After all, once the planet's millions were in their temporal stasis, nothing could affect them at all—why not use them to make pretty effects? They would never know of the indignity they had suffered, when they awakened a century or two from then, on a new and perhaps hostile world.

Elloran looked over the familiar scene. He didn't want to play this game anymore.

A thought touched him. *One day the Inquest will fall*. . . . He flicked it aside. He dived into the throng, making trivial conversations, feeling the awful aloneness that all Inquestors feel.

Sajit's music began: a sennet of a thousand brasses, relayed from an auditorium in the palace of Kilimindi. The room they were in began to move away from the moon; the conversation was stilled for a split second, and then continued as though nothing had happened.

And then Elloran saw the people bins. Their tops funneled in readiness.

"Number one," the announcer said. "Exploding flowers."

A swath of light played over the blackness. And suddenly it was full of people! Time-frozen in fetal position, scattering like dust-motes in a wind . . . The people bins swooped now, scooping them up like chaff, making swift swerving passes by the arena so the Inquestors could have a better view—

"It's beautiful, so beautiful, is it not?" said a young woman in a shimmercloak. He knew her to be Ton Zherinda, newly elevated to the Inquest. He nodded abstractedly. It *was* beautiful—and he needed beautiful things around him now, so that he might forget that he had murdered his sister, his birth-matched bride—

"Number two: phosphorflies over the Mountains of Jér-relahf. . . ."

The light-swath darkened now. A new explosion of frozen people, this time each one coated with glowstuff, so they were like human meteors pelting the darkness, and now the people bins extended klomet-wide nets and swooped down to catch them as they flitted by. Thunderous applause now; everyone chattering wildly, wanting to know the name of the artist so that he could be engaged for the next game of *makrúgh*.

The Inquestrix, hardly a woman yet, still stood by him. Perhaps she was not yet at her ease among these jaded people.

"Vultures," he said. "Vultures!"

"What do you mean, Lord Elloran? Are you insulting these people as a means to begin a new round of *makrúgh*?"

"No! I—"

And they were clustering around him now. "No!" he said. "I don't want to play now—"

"Brilliant!" an old man was saying. The Inquestors circled round, ignoring the fireworks now, while the rest still watched them in awe. "To begin a game by protesting a lack of desire to play—"

He was trapped. He looked for a way to escape. *There must be a way to break the circle—*

And then an announcer said, "A craft is approaching. The display will begin again shortly. A craft of the House of Tash is approaching."

Inquestors muttered among themselves; the guests grumbled, complaining about the interruption. In a few moments they were materializing on the displacement plates. Each one was in a fresh white tunic. Each one found the Inquestor to whom he had been assigned and went directly to him. Suddenly there was silence. And, in whispers that were meant to be heard only by their masters, each Rememberer began to tell the story of Shendering. Outside, little towcraft whisked by, gathering the stray frozen people that the big bins had missed: for the fireworks were an aesthetic event, not a murdering one.

Elloran waited. Already the mood of jaded exhilaration was gone. Some of the Inquestors had gone off to far parts of the room with their Rememberers, brooding, moved. It was in these little ways that the Inquest tried to discourage the pride that came with awesome power, the hubris of almost-godhood.

And then there was Tash Tievar. . . .

Elloran ran to the displacement plate, ignoring all seemliness. When Tievar stepped off the plate, *she* was there.

She came to him. She began to whisper in his ear as the others were doing, but he waved her silent.

They turned to watch as people bins drifted away. Behind them was half-Shendering, heartbreakingly lovely, doomed.

"Don't say anything, sister," said Elloran softly. "The Dispersal of Man is a brutal universe, and if we believe in it completely we will be crushed, like insects, like rats, like star systems. . . . But we are humans, and they cannot crush us completely, they cannot crush love. . . ." He did not dare touch her.

She was the ghost that had haunted him these fifty years. Now the two sides of his life were one, master and victim, and he could no longer tell which was which.

At last he remembered the past without pain.

She did not smile. Instead she reached into her tunic and handed him something.

A rosella.

He stared at it for a long time. Then he cupped his hands and crushed it and blew the spores out into the chamber. He thought he saw her eyes laugh a little.

Then he said, "Full circle. Again we keep deathwatch together." And hugged her hard to him, bursting with grief and joy.

# 5

"Now I have told you," Tash Tievar said, "of the games the Inquestors play as they hover, vulture-like, on the periphery of the wars they themselves have conceived. But oh, the wars themselves! The Inquestors become so involved in the intricacies of *makrúgh* that they seldom notice the wars themselves, the dying, the displacement of lives, the despoilment, the despair; or else they turn away for fear of besmirching their precious compassion."

"Have you seen wars, Tash Tievar?" Jenjen asked. She was thinking: And what if Essondras were chosen, one day, to *fall beyond*, like Shendering? What if Zalo were quick-frozen and packed into a people bin with a million other souls? She had a vision of the necrotheater burning, and the corpse dancers fleeing, and the corpses themselves twitching, out of control, aflame in their grisly newfound freedom. . . .

He went on as though he had not heard her. "And the heartsick beauty of the childsoldier armies, with their dark and glittery panoplies, their topaz-slitty eyes, their keening, ululant warcries—"

"Tell me, Tash Tievar," she said. For she did not yet wish to leave the Chamber of Remembrance and face the Inquestors, and know that they were preparing to play games of life and death. . . .

And Tievar told her another tale of Sajit. It had happened, he said, one of the times that Sajit traveled across the Dispersal of Man, away from Ton Elloran, seeking, like all artists, the unseekable.

165

# 6

# The Comet's Story

. . . the child's eyes, amber-clear, deadly . . . "When I die, *hokh'Shen,* I want to be a comet."

"A comet." Shen Sajit, wrapping his kaleidokilt around his waist and readying his array of musical instruments for the second half of the concert, watched the childsoldier they had assigned to guard him: lithe, slender, the black hair matching exactly the midnight of his tunic, the short cloak thrown sharply over his shoulder at just the regulation angle, the gravi-boots, iridium-laced, glistening. "Why a comet, boy?"

"Because they experience the tumblejoy, Master Musician, when they appear in a planet's sky as harbingers of the firedeath."

"You've lost me. Things have changed since I was a boy here, a childsoldier myself, when I swapped my eyes for the killing laser-irises and learned to inflict the whirling-death on cities. I don't know why I came back."

For a moment the childsoldier seemed to lose his reserve. "*You* were here once, you the most famous musician in the Dispersal of Man?"

"Is it strange to you than someone can survive the years of childsoldiery?"

"I have never thought of it," the boy said wistfully. "Were you really here? You must be a thousand years old."

Sajit smiled a little at this. "Almost."

"Why did you come back?"

Idly Sajit touched his old whisperlyre; the strings stole warmth from his fingers, adding it to their resonance. He looked at the room they had given him behind the small stage that was used for the childsoldiers' assemblies, for making announcements, for meting out punishments. It seemed little different from the grubby rooms of his childhood: first as a whore's son in Aírang, then here in the childsoldiers' city, impressed by the Inquest into the trade of killing. He wished he had not come back. From the minute he had set foot on Bellares, the barrack world, he wanted to go back to Elloran's palace, to be again among beautiful things.

"I asked for a leave of absence from my Inquestor," he told the boy, "so that I could better remember certain flavors, certain smells, certain colors. I am writing a new music for him, you see." But now that he had seen he did not think he wanted to remember these things. He had not expected the years to have softened the past's ugliness so much. He wished he could tell the boy about Varezhdur the golden palace that flew from star to star through the light-mad overcosm; of the gardens within labyrinthine gardens, of the long dark corridors lined with holosculptures of weeping pteratygers that slowly flapped their wings in the wuthering artwind. But it was useless to talk of such things. Doubtless the boy would be dead in a year. Instead, he simply said, "Over there, the amplijewels—hand them to me. Here. And the belt with the buckle of mating flamefish. And . . . what is your name, boy? You've attended me three days and I'm tired of calling you *hey, boy.*"

"N-narop," said the boy. Then, bursting out, "You asked my name! They never ask me my name." He looked away, embarrassed.

Sajit was dressed now. He gestured for the hovercushion to decend toward the floor; the boy Narop made to lead him by the hand. Sajit said, "No, no, I'm really *not* a thousand years old, you know." The boy shrank away, afraid of offending. For Sajit came as Inquestral envoy, and a word from him could mean instant death, just like that. Sajit knew this too well. Things weren't that different after all.

A displacement plate was set into the floor; Sajit saw a small insect crawl onto it and vanish. As he made to step out of the room he saw the boy, anxious, unsure. He beckoned him forward. *I was like this once,* he thought. He tried to drown out the memory in the strains of the music he was about to perform; but it kept surfacing. "What did you mean, Narop-without-a-clan," he said, "when you said you wanted to be a comet when you die?"

"You know, a comet."

"A comet comet?"

"Yes. An angel of death. You know. They build them here.
I think they'll show you the factories so you can report to your
Inquestor."

"Comet? Angel of death? Some new weapon then?" For
he remembered no such thing, and he had thought the boy
meant some pretty conceit, some childish daydream.

The boy said, smiling ingenuously, "Maybe they didn't
have them in your time, Shen Sajit. But *we* all dream about
them. If we are fierce in battle, if we are unwavering in our
loyalty, they reward us after we die by making us into comets. I
thought it was something they always had."

"Where is the factory?"

"By the hospice, where they take the childsoldiers to die.
It all makes sense." For a moment his citrine eyes glowed like
hollow fire, and Sajit was afraid. He knew that a glance and a
subvocalized command was all that the boy needed to slice him
in two, more cleanly than any knife. If done well there
wouldn't even be much blood; the burn's intensity would cau-
terize the vessels. . . .

*The words of the song,* Sajit thought. *The homeworld of
the heart . . . the homeworld of the heart . . .* But somehow
his heart wasn't in it. His mind saw vivid nightmares of war: of
ships burning as they struck the atmosphere of a doomed
world, of severed children littering the steel-gray of a starship's
hold. These things had all been real, real as the gold that bur-
nished the palace of Elloran the High Inquestor; to the boy
Narop they must be the only reality.

Impulsively he said, "Have you thought about . . .
beyond the wars? The time after, if you survive?"

"No, Shen Sajit. I'm afraid to think such things. I don't
want a clan-name. I want the tumblejoy. They say that a comet
feels it, that it's the finest feeling you can have."

"When they take me to see the comets, Narop-without-a-
Clan," Sajit said, "will you attend me?"

The boy nodded. And the old musician clutched the whisperlyre to his chest, gasping at the sudden chill as his body
heat funneled into it and fueled its whispering resonances,
and he stepped onto the plate, his eyes closed; and as he
opened them he saw the clashing lights and heard the familiar
murmur-roar of the crowd, and his voice came to him at last, as
he knew it would.

\* \* \*

They had cheered him, worshiped him; now the performance was over, and Narop had escorted him to his quarters, and he had slept fitfully; and when he awoke the word *comet* was on his lips. For he had dreamt of an army of childsoldiers turned comets and given the power to soar the night skies of a doomed world.

As he sat up and the floor contoured itself to support him he felt strangely old. Once he and Ton Elloran had been boys together, friends even; now Sajit was aging while Elloran had not even begun to feel the touch of time. And when I am gone, he thought, he will go on and on, and he will forget me, because there is so much else that he must do. He must play the great game of *makrúgh*. Sajit knew the doctrine by heart: man, a fallen being, needed wars to prevent stagnation, to prevent the heresy of utopia. But the Inquest, in its compassion, had taken all the guilt of war upon itself. Even Sajit was not without guilt, living as he did in the shadow of the High Inquest; his music was much in demand as an exquisite backdrop to some of the bloodiest *makrúghs* ever played.

That was why he had come to Bellares: not to escape the beautiful, but to understand the ugly. For one gave rise to the other, and they were inextricably woven in the tapestry of birth and death.

He heard breathing behind him. He turned. It was Narop, the childsoldier he had talked to before, and a woman he had not yet met. She wore a robe stitched from the skins of a dozen species of snakes. He recognized it as a sign of the Clan of Aush, whose special provenance was the linking of art and war.

"I am Aush Keshmin," she said. The voice: low, breathy; she could have been a musician, Sajit thought, evaluating it automatically. "Your childsoldier-in-attendance tells me that you have expressed an interest in our comets. I'm flattered, naturally, that an artist of your stature should throw a passing glance at our fledgling military art. As director of the comet project, I have had the honor of being involved in every stage of the design. . . ."

"I told him I wanted to be one when I die," Narop said eagerly.

Keshmin silenced him with a quick glance. He cowered for a moment, and then stood sharply to attention. "That day will come sooner than you want," Keshmin said, "if you don't learn to quell your impertinence!" Then she turned to Sajit, all smiles.

Sajit watched the boy. He was stiff as a statue now. Only a slight quiver of the lip revealed his terror. "Leave the boy be," he said to the woman.

She said, "As you wish, Shen Sajit. But you cannot be too hard on the creatures. They are not bred for compassion, as you people from the fancy courts of Inquestors. We drain the pity from them the day they first come here."

"I know, Aush Keshmin," Sajit said. "I know."

The military artist looked at him curiously for a moment. He said, "I have been here before."

"I see." She would not meet his eyes now, but shied away from him as if he were tainted.

"Perhaps, Keshmin, you will guide me now?" Sajit was buckling his kaleidokilt now, leaning his arm on Narop's shoulder. "I want so much to learn what it is you do. My Inquestor will want to know everything."

"Undoubtedly he already does, for it was from his palace that the conceit originated: the comet as death-angel."

"My master no longer plays *makrúgh*," Sajit said. "It must be some other Inquestor." And already, in his mind, he was wondering who it could be: was it Siriss of the white hair and opal eyes, or cruel-mouthed Ton Satymyrys, who thought only of arcane pleasures, or Karakaël, the masked Inquestor, whose face no man had seen in a hundred years? These and many more met in the gardens of Elloran's palace to play the deadly game.

"Be that as it may," Aush Keshmin said, "come now." She began walking toward the only displacement plate in the small room. Sajit had the distinct impression that she was hiding something, some inner sadness. He did not think that she would have chosen this field, though one could not argue with the Inquestral granting of a clan-name. It was the only way to escape from being planetbound, from being a peasant, from meeting a childsoldierly death.

He followed her down straight gray corridors that cut across each other at right angles. He could not tell them apart, except that some had holosculptures of starships poised for attack, or companies of childsoldiers with the cloaks flying and the killing light streaming from their pitiless eyes. Some corridors were so long that Sajit could see no end to them, for the walls seemed to converge into distant pinpricks of light. They said nothing for a while; the boy was rigid, fearful of being rebuked again, while the woman's face was set into a mask, revealing nothing.

Finally, Sajit asked, "Are we below ground or above it?"

The woman laughed. "What does it matter, Shen Sajit? You are in hell. That's what matters. Tell that to your Inquestors."

But presently they reached an air-chute, and Sajit followed the soldier and the artist as they jumped into it and floated upward. The walls became less gray, almost translucent; finally they were completely deopaqued, and Sajit saw that they were in the sunlight over a chessboard landscape, fields walled with barbed wire, cities of steel whose towers knifed the violet sky.

A floater awaited them, and in a moment they were slicing through the planet's dense, fragrant air. Sajit looked out over the fields, and he saw sights from his childhood. Here a battalion of childsoldiers on hoverdisks whirled in unison, the killing light darting from their eyes, kindling distant targets and toppling tall towers of a pseudocity. Even from this height he could hear the shrill war cry: *Isha ha! Isha ha!* It was a sound all humankind feared, a pure sound, pitiless, yet strangely innocent, for how could these children truly know what it was they did? They whirled over the fields like locusts. Sajit ached, knowing how narrowly he himself had missed the final tumblejoy.

And presently they came to a starport that haunched out over a hill; and they took a shuttleglobe out beyond Bellares's atmosphere. And in all this time, since her bitter outburst, Keshmin had not said a word; the boy was frozen in a posture of attention; and Sajit stood watching the sky as it shifted imperceptibly from violet to dark blue to starry black. At last he saw where they were headed; a hospice, a vessel of bubbles and spikes, growing in the distance. Such places, he remembered, were often beyond the atmosphere, for some battle wounds were best treated without the encumbrance of gravity.

Suddenly Narop cried out; the woman did not chide him. He pointed up. Sajit looked.

Beyond the hospice, three comets arced, one over the other, their tails twining in a braid of light.

He looked from boy to woman. Keshmin looked uneasy, as

if fearful of his reaction. "It's breathtaking," he said at last, and for the first time she smiled, and he could see a certain beauty behind the stern lips, the care-sunken cheeks.

"I designed them," said Aush Keshmin.

And the boy repeated, "When I die, *hokh'Shen*, that's where I'm going."

Inside the hospice, Sajit was led into an atrium upon which the stars shone through a deopaquement of its dome high ceiling. Two fountains, fire and water, played on either side of them; it was all very restful. A crying, like a birdchoir in the dawn, pervaded the huge chamber. It came from the tier upon tier of levels that opened onto the atrium. The hall was so vast that the levels seemed like shelves, and the beds of dying children like boxes of toy soldiers; it was because it came from so far away, and from all sides, that their deathcrying was transmuted into the singing of birds. When Sajit looked up, he saw the three comets dance through the skywall.

"When they are about to die," Keshmin said, "we bring them here, we set up their deathbeds under the cometlight. . . . It seems to ease their pain. Will you visit with our dying?"

Sajit nodded. Already he wanted to leave, to return to the palace; but there was something about this woman. With every look she taunted him. He followed her; the childsoldier walked behind, each step the perfect regulation width. A displacement plate took them up to one of the floors; in pallets against the walls, as far as he could see, the children lay dying. He followed as Keshmin went among them, whispering a word to one, holding the hand of another.

"Yes," she would say, replying to a hoarse question. "Yes, you've been very loyal. They will choose you, I'm sure, they will, they will; you'll be up there in the sky, zooming and zinging among the stars." The words seemed to come automatically to her, a ritual formula.

She was saving it for the fourth or fifth time when the child whose hand she was holding actually started to die. Sajit saw her, a pitiful rag of a little girl. . . . How old could she have been? Seven? Eight? As he watched, the girl's eyelids began to flutter uncontrollably, and colors shifted on the holoscreen where a monitoring thinkhive was displaying her vital data.

Aush Keshmin seemed to be listening to something, then to issue a subvocalized command with a flick of her mind.

All at once, a forceglobe formed about the dying child's head, abruptly severing it. As Sajit stared, dumbstruck by the sudden horror, the globe floated upward to a displacement plate in the ceiling. The eyelids were still fluttering, the mouth half opened in a silent scream. Sajit looked down at the headless corpse; a hundred metal tendrils had slithered into place about the neckstump, cauterizing, sucking away the blood.

"What does this mean?" he shouted. His voice echoed about the four walls of the great atrium. "What have you done to the child?"

Aush Keshmin's voice was distant, cold: "Don't shout, Shen Sajit; you'll disturb the others. Tonight we will see the girl dancing in the starlight. We're talking about a new kind of weapon, you know. A weapon that feels rage and wants vengeance, a weapon with a soul. That's what our comets have, you see! Better to serve the mysterious purposes of the High Inquest. . . ."

"But the girl—"

"Her brain, Master Musician. It has to be fresh if it is to be at the center of the comet's consciousness. . . ."

Sajit looked from the woman to the childsoldier Narop. Through the hall the deathsighs of a thousand children echoed, like windchimes, like the tuning-up of a distant flutechoir. There stood the woman who had designed this twisted artifact. He marveled that she showed so little emotion at a child's death. Perhaps her mind was dulled; perhaps the single death was insignificant beside what that death could inflict, the death of millions more. "Do you feel no compassion, then?" he said.

"Compassion, Shen Sajit? That's for Inquestors to feel. My duty is to my art."

"A cold, bleak art."

"But there *is* beauty in it, musician, a grace of heartache in the slow arc of death."

"Show me more, then. I must see it all." The woman frightened him more and more. When he'd been a childsoldier, though, so long ago, he had thought he could fear nothing. She is so desolate, he thought, so hopeless, and yet she still believes herself an artist. What if *I* had been commanded by the Inquest to be a maker of toys of death? Could I still live with myself?

Aush Keshmin said, "You will see all, of course. That is your privilege as Inquestral delegate."

"Yes. Narop, come." He turned to look for the boy.

Narop was standing at the very edge of the tier. His gaze was fixed on the deopaqued ceiling and the starstream.

The three comets had shifted now. They were chasing each other, their tails radiating out in a catherine wheel, blurring. Now the comets broke loose from their tight circle and they began to soar and dive like porpoises in a sea of night. Now they flew in tandem, tails swerving in triplicate.

The child stared at them with such terrible yearning. . . . It was this longing that frightened Sajit most of all. For a moment he had recognized it in himself, but had dismissed the thought, had buried it in a mass of irrelevances, for he could not bear to admit the longing to himself.

And now they were in a starship and leaving Bellares behind. It was beautiful, this planet of killing children, when seen from afar, Sajit thought, as he watched the patterned lightstreaks crisscrossing the planet's mistlayer, blue-white and fringed with violet where the sun's diamond peered through it. The woman Keshmin never met his eyes, but stared outwards, through the deopaqued screens that showed the three comets. Behind them were delphinoid warships.

"What is this?" he said. "You're taking me to a war, woman?"

"And why not? You demanded to be shown everything. Look at the comets. Soon we'll leave Bellares behind. As the sunlight fades, so will their streams of luminescent almost-vacuum. Soon they'll be dark and cold, like the hearts of the Inquestors that cause the wars to happen."

Sajit listened in silence, awed by the image. She went on, still avoiding his eyes: "But they won't be as cold as those mindless chunks of ice that orbit every star. . . . Each one has a precision thinkhive that controls its every movement, and each one is animated by a vengeful spirit . . . the brain of a dying childsoldier!"

"They are alive, then."

"Alive and not alive, master musician," said the military artist. "They're in a state of half-awareness, a kind of hypnosis, perhaps. These are brains that burn with loyalty to the Inquest. They see and hear through powerful prosthetics. They speak to us only when we give them machines to speak through. Soon the thinkhives will forge a dark corridor through the tachyon universe, and we will be in the vicinity of the world to be destroyed; the comets will catch fire from the sunlight and will dance their doomsayings over the chief cities of the world that is to *fall beyond;* then, at my signal, their dance will reach fever pitch, and they will fall upon the cities and crush them. It is beautiful, isn't it?"

Sajit said, "What is the world?"

"It is called Korith."

"Why will it *fall beyond?*"

"That I don't know. It's the will of the Inquest, of course, and in their compassion they have arranged for the people bins to carry off most of the population. We don't question the Inquest, Shen Sajit; we're soldiers. Come, do you wish to see more?"

They flicked by displacement plate into another chamber. There were strange instruments here, and forcecases that held human brains linked by wires to control panels. The walls were all deopaqued, so that it seemed that they rested on a platform drifting through empty space; and above their heads the comets swam still, their tails dim now.

"Why are we here?" Sajit asked.

"The control room," Keshmin said. And she summoned a hoverchair and was soon bent over some controls, while Sajit stared at the brains that hung in the air, forcebubbled, quivering a little. "Look!" As Sajit looked around him, at the spectral starscape, he saw the stars shimmer strangely; he felt a queasy, dead sensation crawling up his throat from his stomach. He knew then that they were preparing to break open a tachyon corridor, to breach the space between spaces. For this was war, and war must be fought instantaneously; it could not wait for the leisurely pace of pinholing through the overcosm. As he watched, a wedge of blackness parted the starstream and grew wider and wider, as though the sky was a skin and the darkness a surgical incision held open by forceps; and they were accelerating towards the cleft. . . .

And abruptly, it closed behind them, and they were in another region of space; for now the band of the starstream stretched up and down, and a red star dangled from it like a cherry.

"The Korith system?" said Sajit.

"Yes," said Keshmin.

As she spoke the three comets soared into existence overhead, having made the crossing in the starship's field. Sajit saw other dephinoid ships too, full, he knew, of childsoldiers. A pearl of a planet ballooned abruptly out of the dark. "Korith?" said Sajit.

"Yes. And now the dance will begin."

The comets were one, three-tailed now, arrow-aimed at the half-world. Awed, Sajit watched. Now the tails broke free of the strand and they whirled, blinding-fast, like a catherine wheel. Now the three separated, swam like flamefish through the black. Now they arched as one, now three, now one, now three. . . .

"They will be seeing them now, on Korith," said Keshmin. A grim smile stole over her features. Sajit watched first the woman, then the boy, whose eyes shone with longing. He thought: I have never hated the universe so much.

"What are you thinking, master singer?" Keshmin said. "You don't have to tell me. You think I'm tainted, don't you? You despise me."

"How can you call this art?"

"And you, *hokh'Shen*! What about you? It's you who lull the Inquestors' minds after they have decreed these worldburnings, isn't it? It's you who envelop your masters with beauty, so they no longer understand about death that falls without reason from the sky."

"No!" Sajit trembled. This was a sorry woman, a vicious, callous woman. . . . How was it then that her words rang true? He turned away. "Give me a private chamber. I will not watch this war. I'm going to compose. Attend me, boy."

"Coward!" Aush Keshmin hissed after him, as his feet sought the displacement plate.

Narop led him to a spartan square chamber walled with metalfrost. He sank down onto the yielding floor. There was a whisperlyre there, and a starharp of concert size, the seven frames of strings fanning out from the controlseat like a silvery asterisk. The grayness of the room rested his eyes. The boy stood guard.

Presently he said: "What do think of all this, then, Narop-without-a-Clan?"

"That your kind, master, are too delicate for war."

"Delicate! Delicate!" Sajit shouted. "No, don't be afraid, don't shy away like that. Shall I sing you a song of space battles, of heroism and courage?"

"If you wish, *hokh'Shen*." And the boy settled back against the dull wall to listen.

Sajit performed, as much for himself as for the boy. But the words of the songs seemed empty. Presently curiosity overcame him; he thought of the three comets and their cold stardance. He ordered the walls deopaqued so he could see them. Once more the night engulfed them, and they saw the comets: writhing, twisting, zigzagging over the darkside of the crescent planet.

And behind the world, a fleet of delphinoid ships, waiting to rain destruction. Like a swarm of phosphorflies.

Then came an alarm. A metallic screech, earsplitting. "What is the matter?"

A voice: *Alert. Alert. Stations. Stations.*

"What is the matter now?" The alarm woke old memories in Sajit, memories he had thought buried forever. Once, once only, he had escaped a shredded starship—

"Come boy," he said. The boy—he could see that the boy was clenching back terror—preceded him to the displacement plate. They stepped into the control room of wires and floating brains—

"What has happened?" Sajit cried. "I am an Inquestral ambassador. Are we being attacked?"

He saw Aush Keshmin now, white. Her lips hardly moved. She pointed at the deopaqued ceiling.

A comet had broken loose, disrupting the pattern. It was making its way towards the fleet.

"It has awakened," she said. "Malfunction of its life-support. . . . It has decided to attack *us*!"

"Why?" Sajit whispered.

"It was a terrible idea. To give them consciousness. There was always the possibility. It's gone mad, Shen Sajit, mad!"

"Retreat, then! Abort the mission."

"And the other comets? Their programming is set. The Inquest will not be pleased."

"How long do you have?"

"A few hours yet, *hokh'Shen*."

"Hours. . . ."


Aush Keshmin played with control panels. Lights darted across holoscreens. "I am opening a communicating channel," she said, "switching on the comet's eyes and ears so we can hear its thoughts . . . *now*."

And then Sajit could hear it, a faint, kittenlike voice, like the edge of a wind—

*Ma . . . ma . . .*

"What does this mean?" he cried.

*Ma . . . ma . . .*

"By all the powers of powers!" Aush Keshmin said. "The child was not quite dead enough. It has woken from its trance state. It's afraid. It's found something it doesn't like. But that's impossible! We select the children for the utmost loyalty to the Inquest. They are screened, tested, psychically probed to the limit—"

"But what is it saying?"

"Why, it's crying for its mother, of course. Childsoldiers often do that, the first day or two of training."

Sajit hated her then. He knew that the woman cared only for the chill beauty of her deathdance, and not at all that a child was in pain. He tried to remember the pain himself. He saw himself fleeing down the flame-twisted corridors of a dying starship. For a fleeting moment it was more real to him than all the splendor of Elloran's Varezhdur.

And the woman was saying, "We will have to destroy them all."

But Sajit said, "Will you not find out what kind of child this was? Its name? Its former homeworld? Perhaps there will be some information you can use."

"Very well," said Keshmin stonily.

*Ma . . . ma . . .*

Sajit remembered the voice now. His own past. Once he had had a mother. How long ago? Time dilations had taken their toll, and she must be lost in the far past.

Keshmin was subvocalizing instructions to the central thinkhive of the ship now. For a while they heard nothing but the whining of the little lost voice. Then came the thinkhive's voice, metallic, echoey: *The comet is now insane, Aush Kesh-*

*min, was once Yryan-without-a-Clan, son of a merchant of Korith—*

"You fool!" shouted Sajit. "You sent a childsoldier against his own homeworld! In my day such a thing was never done!"

"You don't understand! That's no child out there, it's a machine, malfunctioning . . ."

Out of the silence came the childish voice: *Mama . . . Bad men are coming. . . . They want to kill you. . . . But I'll stop them . . . stop them. . . .*

"I will communicate with it," Aush Keshmin said. "Listen, child of the tumblejoy! Resume your programming at once! Or you will be destroyed!" She spoke these words to the air; communicators were relaying them into the mind of the comet.

*It's trying to tell me to kill you, Mama. . . . It's bad, bad, bad; I won't listen. . . .*

"It's useless to reason with it!"

For a while they stood, master musician and artist of death, hating each other. Finally, Sajit said: "You cannot make it understand, Keshmin, that its mother is long long dead. How can you make it understand? You yourself cannot understand. It fears you. You are evil to it. No, *I* must go to it, Aush Keshmin, because though I seem now almost as high as the Inquestors, I was once like this Yryan."

"It is safer to destroy the comets and return," Keshmin said sullenly.

"I am an Inquestral ambassador, and I demand to visit the comet. We still have time. Through Ton Elloran n'Taanyel Tath, my master, I assume responsibility."

"You meddling street singer! You'll use this, no doubt, for one of your melodramatic songs, to ease the stomachs of Inquestors at dinner parties."

"Say what you want. I have the authority."

*Why did I say that now?* he thought. *What masochism is it that impels me to pursue the ugly, the anguished? But I must go. It's my past that calls me. Ghosts must be faced and exorcized.*

Aush Keshmin turned to summon a shuttlecraft.

The pearl-world wheeled above them, ravishing, doomed.

They did not speak; their anger walled them from each other. But from across the silence of space, the comet cried for its mother.

. . . space now. A shuttlecraft. The comet's tail rearing up, dividing the night with its swath of radiance.

At first Sajit had insisted on going up to the comet alone. But it was true that he needed Keshmin's technical aid; and he wanted the childsoldier there too. He had an overpowering desire to strip away the boy's illusions, to show him the degradation behind the dream. He did not know why he had this urge. It was almost criminal to open the boy's eyes, to let him see the utter hopelessness of the universe. Sajit was angry and bitter.

Presently the band of incandescence filled the whole screen. It was a million klomets long, this dust-tail, and thinner than most vacuums; and yet it glowed. When they entered the tail the darkness barely changed; only before and after, in the plane of their flight, was a barely perceptible shining. And in the distance, the head: a snowball of frozen gasses with a child's soul at its kernel.

And all the while, as they were approaching, the craft's thinkhive relayed the crying of the comet.

"How much time?"

"Two hours. Then, whether you will or no," said Keshmin, "ambassador or not, you will die, because I have ordered the comets aborted. Do you understand? I obey instructions, Shen Sajit. I do not have whims, as you palace parasites do. Your whim may kill the three of us."

"Quiet! Think of the planet's millions. They will die too."

"We saved as many as we could. Already the people bins have left with as many stasis-packed humans as could be persuaded to leave, threading the overcosm like a million segments of silver centipede."

Grimly, Sajit looked ahead. He clutched his whisperlyre to his chest; at the last moment he had brought it from his room on the starship, needing a sense of security.

They landed. A forcetube dug its way out of the snow. They put on pressure skins; Sajit felt the strange isolation as the unicellular skin warped around his body and his whisperlyre. They plated from the craft; Sajit felt the gutwrench of near-weightlessness. Ahead was the tube of nothing. They walked to it over the icerock peppered with methane snow. Though the pressure skin shielded him from the cold and fed him oxygen, Sajit felt another kind of chill. It was the silence between the stars, the utter aloneness. Once starpilots had sailed this silence, and known nothing of the overcosm.

In moments the three were following the forcetunnel deep into the heart of the comethead. There was a little cell there, lined with instruments and walled with gray metal. "Can he see us?" said Sajit. For now that they were at the seat of the comet's soul, they could no longer hear its projected voice.

"Not yet." Keshmin touched a stud; all at once the child's sobbing burst into the chamber. "After I subvoke a few commands to the thinkhive, you will become visible to it."

"Stay out of its line of vision," Sajit whispered. He dared not raise his voice. There was a presence here, a thing undead.

Woman and boy stepped into the shadows. He felt their eyes on him, but tried to forget. To concentrate. In front of him were semiorganic machines, spirals and corkscrews of metal fanning out from growths of lichen; and a circlet of mirror metal. His own face stared back at him.

"Make him see me," he whispered. And he called the dead boy's child-name: "Yrieh, Yrieh."

A swirl of mist in the mirror; then a holosculpt image of the boy's face, culled by the thinkhive from its repertory of remembrances. . . . eyes of burning amber . . . thin pale lips . . . a mane of midnight hair . . . he could have been the twin of Narop-without-a-Clan. "Listen, listen, Yrieh. Can you hear me? Can you see me?"

The boy's voice, echobent, tinged with metal: *Who are you? . . . Are you my mother?*

"A friend."

*You're from the bad people. I'm not turning back. I'm going to kill you all, all, all.*

"It *must* be destroyed!" Keshmin whispered urgently.

"Be quiet! Don't let him hear you," said Sajit. To the boy: "I am Sajitteh."

*. . . one of the childsoldiers?*

"One of the childsoldiers."

Tears streamed down the cheeks of the ghostface in the mirror. *I woke up. . . . They tell me I'm dead. . . . I'm not dead. . . . I'm awake. . . . I've got power, kill-power. . . . Bring me my mother. . . . Or I'll kill the whole fleet, I'll kill, kill, kill. . . .*

"Why, Yrieh, why?" Sajit said. He could hardly contain his anger. "You can tell me."

*You'll understand? . . . not like the others.*

"You must make him turn around. Or put him back to sleep," Keshmin said, "so that the comet can be operated automatically."

*. . . Whose voice? One of them?*

"No, Yrieh," said Sajit. "Listen. Your mother's gone, child."

*No!*

"Are you afraid?"

*Yes. Afraid. I woke up in the dark. In the dark, falling towards my homeworld.*

"You didn't feel the tumblejoy?"

*Joy? Joy?*

"The wild joy of the dance of killing? Surely they taught you that?"

*Joy? I feel alone, alone, and cold, cold, afraid, afraid.*

"Go to sleep."

*No! Then I'll never wake up again.*

How could he deny that? Never had Sajit felt so angry about the cruelty that the Inquest inflicted so casually, every second of its existence, in the name of the High Compassion. Sajit searched his mind for a solution. Either alternative meant death for some. Both were death for the child-comet, a second death. *Should I lie to him?* he thought. *Tell him his mother's coming to him?*

He pulled out his whisperlyre from his tunic. "I will sing to you," he said. "Then you won't be afraid anymore." And he played a few notes, feeling the lyre suck the warmth from his chest, hearing the plucked sounds echo.

The spectral eyes watched him, wide with innocence. He reminded himself that those eyes had killed. As, once, his own had.

He sang a lullaby. Once his mother had sung it to him. But that was in another time, and could not be brought back. He sang.

> Sleep, child, sleep;
> The Inquestors are watching you
> from their far heaven.

*The wings of pteratygers are fanning you.*
*The war is done.*
*Your mother's arms are warm.*
*Sleep, child, sleep.*

As Sajit sang he began to weep. He could not help himself. Often he had wept in concerts; this was part of his art, something that moved audiences, that could be controlled. Not this. He wept for his own lost childhood. He wept for his Inquestor, Elloran, who had drowned himself in beauty so that he might not feel the pain. As he sang the whisperlyre stole all his body heat, compounding its resonance with it. He was so cold. But still he sang:

*The war is done.*
*Your mother's arms are warm.*
*Sleep, child, sleep.*

And the wraithface in the mirror closed its eyes and was beautiful in sleep, and at peace.

Sajit said, "I have taken away his pain. That is my art."

He turned to his two companions. Aush Keshmin was shaking, nervous; she could not meet his eyes. He seized her by the chin and forced her to look at him. "Now, death-artist! Do you see what you've done? You turn children into monsters, but in their hearts they have not lost their innocence utterly. They are not beasts."

Keshmin said, "I didn't know that before. No. I did know. But I buried what I knew. I knew that any clan-name was better than none. Please, master musician, take my name from me."

"The comet will function properly now?"

"Yes. It will fall on Korith and destroy cities."

"And do you rejoice?"

"How can I?"

And then Sajit turnd to the boy Narop. He stood in the wall's shadow, shuffling his feet. "Look at me, Narop!" Sajit cried. "Is this what you want to be when you die?"

And suddenly, appallingly, the boy began to cry. He was only a little boy after all. Sajit saw the crumpled sable cloak and the iridium boots, too shiny, and knew them to be toy armor for toy soldiers. . . . "Don't cry," he said tenderly. To the woman he said, "Don't despair." And to both: "Where there is bitterness there must be beauty too. It has always been so, and always will be. I will free you."

For he knew now why he had been moved to come to Bellares, to the place of his tormented childhood. . . . It was as the woman had put it. To make a song to ease the stomachs of Inquestors, she had said. That was true, but not the whole truth.

They returned to the craft, and thence to the starship. Sajit did not choose to watch the end of the dance of comets, nor the death of Korith. He had seen such things before. He knew what he would see from far in space: a sudden vaporous burning in the planet's atmosphere, a patch or two of brilliance . . . an eruption of diamonds on the surface . . . and the chain of people bins, spiraling into space like a necklace, seeking an entrance to the overcosm where they would sail the centuries until another world was found for them.

But when he left for Varezhdur, he took Keshmin and Narop with him. And they were with him when he was ushered at last into the throneroom of Ton Elloran, his master, whom trillions called *the compassionate one*.

The gold, the gold . . .

They passed through hallways with gilt-burnished walls, inlaid with highscript poems in lapis lazuli, Sajit's own poems . . . groves of goldplated arbors crisscrossed with streams that glittered with gold dust. . . . The woman gaped, sullen at first, uncomprehending. . . . The childsoldier cried out in delight. . . . and Sajit saw that they had reached the corridor lined with a hundred reliefed pteratygers of Ontian marble, and he knew that he was home. And in a moment they were in Elloran's throneroom, built around Dei Zhendra's great galaxy of dust. A shimmerviol music played from a hidden alcove, and the chill pure voice of a neuterchild was singing one of Sajit's own songs.

Sajit looked at his master, who sat, closed-eyed, on a great throne.

"Elloran," he said.

Abruptly, the music stopped.

Elloran opened his eyes. How old he was! Had Sajit been gone that long, then? "Elloran, I'm home."

"Who are these?"

"The woman was once a maker of deathtoys. The boy was once a childsoldier. But Elloran, they are not what they were made to be! They have poetry in them." Sajit came closer to the throne. He saw his master's face: how tired, how world-weary. The shimmercloak itself dwarfed him, and the huge throne of gold. And he beckoned Aush Keshmin and Narop-without-a-Clan to him, but they cowered behind him, not daring to stare at the throne's brilliance.

"Oh, Sajitteh, Sajitteh," Elloran said, "always the redeemer! You'd save the souls of everyone in the universe, if you could."

"And what of it?" Sajit said, his anger bursting out at last. And he told Elloran what he had seen. How they'd been making dead children into deathweapons. How one had awakened in terror and gone mad. And how he had lulled it to sleep with an ancient song, and given it an illusion of peace. "Why do you let these things happen, Elloran?" he cried out.

"Tell me, Sajit. Were they not beautiful, these comets, when they danced?"

"Yes. That was the most terrible thing."

"Is there not pain in everything beautiful. . . ? It is true that I let this happen. But once, long ago, at a game of *makrúgh*, you were singing us a new song as we played at burning worlds. Do you remember the words? Perhaps not. You have written a thousand songs. Here, though, are lines from the song:

> *What if the stars had life?*
> *What if the comets felt anger*
> *As they burned across the space between worlds?*

"It was your song, Sajit, that gave rise to the idea—"

"No!" cried Sajit. "It was your players of *makrúgh* who twisted my meaning into a cruel conceit!"

"Sajitteh . . ." Sajit saw terrible sadness in the Inquestor's eyes. And because he loved his master, he could not be angry.

"I know," he said, "that you too are trapped by the Inquest's doctrine. You are compelled to maintain the stasis of the Dispersal of Man, and to create such little wars as may be necessary to give the illusion of movement; it is thus that you preserve the balance between utopianism and progress."

"You could almost be an Inquestor," said Elloran, jesting to hide the hurt.

"You don't fool me. You too are a victim, imprisoned by your own power."

"Yes. Yes."

"That, Elloran, is the lesson I learned on Bellares, and at the comet's heart."

"And what else did you learn?"

"That we must wrest from the universe every fleeting moment of beauty, of freedom, of truth."

"Old lessons, Sajitteh." Elloran closed his eyes again.

Sajit said to his two companions: "You are free now. Elloran has released you. You can stay in Varezhdur and travel through Elloran's worlds; or you can leave. You will be given money. What do you want?"

Keshmin said, "It's so beautiful here. . . . I didn't know. . . ."

"Can I serve you?" said Narop. "I'll be your slave."

"I am a slave," said Sajit. The thought no longer rankled him. "By all means, then, stay. Drink in Varezhdur's loveliness. When the time comes, you will want to leave, like I did, and face the ugliness again, and perhaps you will want to return. But for now, be happy."

He summoned an usher to find them apartments in the palace. Keshmin smiled at last. The boy was walking on air as they left.

Finally he was alone with Ton Elloran n'Taanyel Tath, Lord of Varezhdur, Princeling of Many Tributaries.

"Well, Sajitteh!" said Ton Elloran. "Two saved. How many more to go?"

Sajit didn't answer; he only smiled. Then he said, "How long was I gone?"

"Forever. It must have been only a few years to you; for me it was a century."

"No wonder you seem old."

"Old! I missed you, Sajitteh." His eyes sparkled. "What was that lullaby you sang to the child-comet?"

"A silly ditty, Inquestor, quite without art. My mother sang it to me once."

"Sing it to me."

"But—"

"Come, Sajitteh! Only chance has elevated me above that child whose soul they planted in a comet. That's why I need you. To remind me that I'm still human. I am, you know. Human. Yes. I, the all-wise, the all-compassionate . . . the burner of worlds."

Sajit sang. Without an instrument, in a soft comforting voice. Just the way he remembered it from childhood, before they took him away to Bellares, to be a childsoldier.

As he sang he watched the Inquestor's face. What worries plagued him now? What problems of planets? He could not tell. But he meant to soothe the pain. That was his art. Illusion, perhaps, but still art.

Elloran slept.

# 7

"So now," said Tash Tievar, "you know of the world of Rememberers, whose life is a long dreaming of things forever lost, and the world of the childsoldiers, brutal and beautiful, whose tiny locust lives sustain *makrúgh* and the Inquest's might. You have heard many dark things, Jeni. Perhaps now you will want to turn back, to unknow that which you know."

"Yes," Jénjen said bitterly. "The first time I came to Varezhdur you told me of those who stood firm against the Inquest, who managed despite the overwhelming odds to dream their dream . . . today, instead, you've told me of defeat. Of planets torn asunder; of children victimized by lies. To think that I came back to Varezhdur rejoicing because I would once more be part of this great beauty! But blood has been this beauty's price."

"Yet they *were* victories: Kerin is reunited with Elloran, Narop and Keshmin are released from bondage. That cannot be shuffled off."

"The price, Father Tievar, was too much. . . ."

"You have reached a turning point, then, in your life, my daughter. But don't despair. There is hope."

"How can you talk of hope? When every hope is crushed beneath the Inquest's heel like a worm, destroyed for daring to crawl upward out of the dark earth?"

"Be comforted. There are more stories to come."

But there was no solace in that promise. So ended the first day of Jenjen's return: in despair and recrimination.

# FOUR

## The Book of
## Three Young Inquestors

*suvítek Enguéster pelái ke shehtráot' varúng
ekeíry; éa ke tálor' kerávishen.
eih kreisnevyúreke Enguéstrek hokhté:
feraváh: ng' eká zýh serés? és kat
nan leluktuarémmyrein kechaikáiske,
krudháns výrein ekbreindáiske, dhánati
shélynein keklaiskáis, veveraipáiske
pa' bráxein zi, és-dénde ke
ney'vió et sha zháksho kalókas?*

—ek shéntraran Sájiti


We two will soon be gone, the ancient Inquestor and the
demented singer; so come, Inquestrix of the cloud-crystal
eyes, to the throne of tragedy. They are all asking: Will you be
the one? Is it you who will cause to be blinded the million laser
eyes, and the fires of rage to be doused, who will shut down
the death-moons and lay down your arms, and say: No more
will I hunt utopias?

*—from the Songs of Sajit*

# I

Jenjen did not return to the Chamber of Remembrances for many sleeps. For it seemed that the more she learned of the workings of the Inquest, the more corrupt their universe appeared. She feared to confess to herself that it fascinated her . . . that she wanted to weave into her artworks not only the wonder but the terror and the violence and the heartlessness. And these were dark things, the things darkweavers wove.

But if she accepted her desire to depict the darkness, would she not be like Rax Nika, who gave her all to the Inquest because the Inquest had fashioned her very genes? Or that poor comet, lulled into mindless slumber so that it could be an instrument of death for millions. . . . There has to be a choice, she thought. We are all given the power to will our own future, and to fulfill it if we can . . . aren't we? That was what they had taught her in school. And that far away, in godlike splendor, lived the Inquest, untouchable and irrelevant. But she knew already that this was not so.

And so she shunned Tash Tievar. But she could not refuse an invitation from Ton Siriss to join her at dinner.

The room was familiar; many of the guests were the same. But there was no Elloran. The throne was empty. A boy with a pteratyger cub on his arm showed Jenjen to her couch; on one side of her was a singer in the kaleidokilt on the Clan of Shen; on the other a man who, she remembered dimly, was an historical anthropologist. His eyelids, painted deep blue, were curiously heavy; his puffy eyes nictated a steady stream of turquoise tears. She had not had an opportunity to study his

191

face before, so awed had she been by Elloran's presence. But now that he was gone, she was far less fearful.

Besides, she knew much more about the Inquest now, and awe was tempered with contempt.

Trumpets and megaconchs sounded: Ton Siriss entered. She wore a shimmercloak more resplendent than her old one; since she was now a Kingling in her own right, her cloak had been grown from a double-yolked shimmeregg. Jenjen saw her eye the throne, as if wondering whether it would be seemly for her to assume it. To Jenjen's relief, she contented herself with the couch on its right.

Jenjen spoke little. The conversation buzzed: inane remarks about art mingled with pointed sallies of *makrúgh* between the three or four visiting Inquestors. Then she heard someone say: "*He* is coming."

There was a brief hiatus in the murmuring: then she heard the words run round the table: "*He* is coming, *he* is coming."

"Who is he?" she asked the singer beside her, who had previously been as talkative as she was taciturn, but who had now fallen strangely silent.

"The Prince of Shadow," the singer said, and turned to toy with a fold of her kaleidokilt.

"And who is the Prince of Shadow?"

Faces turned to stare at her. Once again she seemed to have committed some solecism. "Forgive me," she said softly.

"Do not ask forgiveness," Ton Siriss said, her voice ringing out imperiously over the chattering, silencing it at once. "You can't be expected to know everything. The Prince of Shadow is the most important human being in the galaxy at the moment. That's all. He holds all our fates in his hands."

"Yes, *hokh'Ton*."

Siriss's lips twisted into the semblance of a smile. "You need not call me by that title anymore, Jenjen."

What was going on? Something catastrophic had to be afoot, for the Inquestrix to deny her title. For degree was the basis of all things. But Ton Siriss went on, more kindly, "All things end, do what we may. As Ton Elloran said once, 'The dust and the stars are eternal, but words are like the wind.' Such a word is Kelver, our lord's name; a childish name, the name of a peasant from a backworld; but he is become Inquestor and more than Inquestor; he has become the Prince of

Shadow, and his name is a wind that will blow down the Inquest itself!"

And Jenjen thought: I have heard such rhetoric from Zalo and his friends, but never from an Inquestor's lips. It's true then: revolution has been kindled at the Inquest's heart.

"You've hardly touched your food," said the anthropologist, speaking to her for the first time. "Try the volcanic salmon from Ont! Its roe is worth its weight in iridium."

"Thank you," Jenjen said, not bothering to look at the spectacle of viands and delicacies spread out before them.

"I remember you. You're that darkweaver, one of Elloran's favorites. He had some kind of plan for you, you know. But he's gone now." He pointed ruefully at the empty throne.

"Who is Kelver and why is he so important?"

"Shh. Even here, in this select company, someone may be treacherous. It would be best to ask the Rememberers."

"A song! A song!" someone cried.

"Yes," Ton Siriss sighed, "we should have some diversion in these distressing times."

At last the singer who had remained silent since the mention of Kelver's name rose and bowed to the Elloran's empty throne. "What shall I sing of? Love? I have a hundred love songs; from immortal songs of Sajit himself, to lewd ones penned by my humble self. Betrayal? Flattery? I have all these."

"No, Shen Koressi," said the Inquestrix, "for we all see the great ending circling inexorably nearer. And *his* coming will make it even sooner than we had ever dreamed. When I first heard the words, *the Inquest falls*, I was stunned, I quaked, my heart was numb. Now I can hear them almost with equanimity. Is that not something? But since the end draws nigh, it would amuse me to hear of the beginning. If any of us can remember that far back," she added as a half-hearted joke. It drew raucous laughter; for the tension had been almost intolerable.

"Then," the singer said, "I will sing of the beginning of things."

# 2

# The Myth of Mother Vara

"In a time before time had meaning, before men had scattered as the petals of the rosella to the infinite corners of the galaxy and seeded the million known worlds, another race ruled the universe. They were not exactly men, though their souls were similar to men's; for their substance was attenuated, stretched out over many parsecs; and planets hung like jewel droplets from their bodies. They were a proud people. With a single thought they could smash a world to powder; with another they could span the overcosm and be in all places at once. They were perfect; for in their innocence they knew not their own flaws, and that which they knew was the only truth it was possible to know. And each, as do all creatures, even the most insignificant, had a shadow side and a light, so all was in balance; and so they roamed the silence between the stars, beings neither flesh nor spirit; and whithersoever they went they breathed life or death as they chose, so that planets bloomed and died by the whim of their passing by. And these beings had no names; for language did not yet exist. (And because of this, neither did truth nor untruth. For though I mentioned truth earlier, it was only that men see through the eyes of men, and language is our medium, and the existence of truth and untruth the necessary consequence.)

"It could not be said that time passed in this universe, for time had yet to acquire meaning. Yet I must say that time did pass, for once more I am limited by the perceptions common to us all. And now I will sing a song of the passing of time that was not the passing of time."

And here the singer interposed a song which, though brief, appeared to last forever. Now and then a whisperlyre jangled; but mostly it was a wordless melisma, and each melodic phrase grew from the iteration of a single note, swelled, and returned at last to that hypnotic tonal center. When the last melisma died away, and the shimmerfade of the whisperlyre had ceased, Jenjen felt that she had awoken from a timeless trance. Now Koressi continued her narration.

"In time came the awareness of time; with the awareness of time came the compulsion to change, for time is nothing without change, and it is change that defines time. And it came to pass that the shadow overwhelmed the light; and the spirit creatures, tired of pulverizing planets, turned their attention to the stars. And they began to hunt the stars, to kindle within their cores a cancerous combustion which burst hearts and wrenched them apart and killed them. For the stars were sentient then, and each had a soul on which the spirit creatures could feed. For when time was set in motion, entropy inexorably followed. And with it came the depletion of energy and the wasting away of the Ur-beings—and this led at last to the ravening, vampiric hunger sated only by the release of the massive energy in the hearts of the stars themselves. And as the shadow engulfed their souls, the Ur-beings became ever more bloated with their stolen energy, and shone like quasars, and they cried: 'Who now shall conquer us? For we are the mightiest of the mighty. We will shine forever, and time, our slave, shall stand still.'

"In this they erred. For when time, and therefore language, were brought into being, so there came to exist truth and untruth. But the Ur-beings knew this not, and still defined truth by their own utterances.

"And the stars became angry.

"And it came to pass that one of the beings (the idea of *one* and *many* having come into existence simultaneously with the coming of time) became so full of the substance of the stars it had swallowed that it partook of the stars' unfathomable nature; and thus the stars had their revenge, for the Ur-being said at last: 'Untruth exists after all. And time, which we in our pride thought we had engendered to be our plaything, is in truth our master. And it has determined that we must end. And thus it is that I will hunt the stars no longer; and my spirit-flesh will no longer span the gulfs between the stars, but shrink to the size of a lowly planetary dweller. And I will relinquish all of my Ur-being nature, retaining only one thing: *compassion*, for it is only through compassion that the hunters and the stars are one.' And the Ur-being swallowed all the lesser Ur-beings, and absorbed them unto itself; and absorbed therewith all the stars that the lesser beings had absorbed, and became the entire universe. And it uttered a terrible cry: 'Var! Var!' and gave birth to the universe as we now know it; and their Ur-beings were vanquished. For they had become tiny beings such as crawl upon the surface of planets; and their spirit natures were transformed into whispershadows, which haunt the spaces between spaces. And the stars lost their souls, and in their great despair threw themselves into a black hole at the heart of the galaxy, and extinguished their being. And the new tiny beings were called men. It was thus that the Dispersal came into being.

"And all the worlds of this galaxy revolved around a world that was called *Uran s'Varek*, 'Heaven's Eye.' On this world was the one mother reborn, she who had uttered the syllable 'Var' and given birth to the universe. (For in doing so she had of course given birth to herself.) And because man had now become a fallen being, whose every step in the journey towards death was a dance of pain, whose children were winnowed by warfare, who lived in perpetual darkness and sorrow . . . the one mother was moved. Only one of the Ursouls was left, and that soul a pure shadow, for it was the soul of the world at the center of the universe, on which she had been born, and in this world's heart was the black hole that had swallowed all the stars. And of all the beings in the universe, the one mother alone had compassion.

"And because of her infinite compassion, the one mother seduced the shadow soul until it was stirred by love. But the love of the shadow star was a searing fire; and for ten million years the two made love. For each time that the black hole touched her the mother was wounded; and each wound bled tears, and each tear was a star reborn. . . . And after ten million years the heavens were again ablaze, through the mother's compassion and her pain; but the stars never regained their souls.

"Now there was little compassion left in the universe. For compassion slips away, is subject to entropy; a time will come when it exists no more. But the one mother, who now called herself Vara, after the syllable of agony and joy, having now given light once more unto the skies, saw that man was still a fallen being, and needed guidance. So she gave half her store of compassion to a man whom she named Inquestor. And that man shared his store with another, and that man with yet others. And so were created the guardians of the light, who carry man's guilt upon their shoulders, who have banished the shadow and stand forever watch lest it escape.

"And Vara said to the Inquestors: 'Protect this precious gift of compassion. Nurture it. Let it fall like manna on my myriad peoples. For though despair engulfed the Dispersal of Man, I have given them the stars, and now I will give them hope.' And again she said, 'When you weep, you will weep in secret, but your tears will fall on my million worlds as the water of life. Their hope will be your sorrow forever, till the end of time.' And a third thing did she say: 'Because, when you were beings of spirit, you hunted the stars themselves, as flesh-beings you will hunt utopias. Thus, while you destroyed order in your former lives, it now falls to you to maintain the universe's balance. I, your Creator, say that whereas you once named yourselves Destroyers, I now name you Preservers. And this will be your chastisement and your supreme joy.'

"Thus she spoke. But she was tired now, for she had given birth to a universe and had made love for ten million years. She was spent; and her store of compassion was gone. And having thus exhorted the Inquestors to continue her work, she now sits alone upon a throne on a vast abandoned planet, and has never bestirred herself at all, since the first days of mankind. Some call her throne the Throne of Mercy, but others know it as the Throne of Madness. By night the black hole's shadow-soul haunts her and begs her to renew their love. But she answers him not a word, for she knows that if she speak with him again she must yield all that she has gained, and the universe will be plunged into chaos, and the Inquestors be no more."

# 3

"I think," Jenjen said, "that I'm more confused than ever."

The anthropologist said, "That's not surprising. Myth is a very wishy-washy subject, no?" He turned to the throne and attracted Ton Siriss's attention, and said, "My Lady, our friend here seems to have no idea what our songstress has been talking about. And I daresay many of us are pretty much in the dark, too."

"Well," said the Inquestrix, "perhaps an explanation should be provided."

"If you please, *hokh'Ton*," a lilting, androgynous voice from the far end of the table said, "I have a theory."

"Oh, you," said Siriss. "Very well." Languidly she continued, "For those of you who do not know the insufferably brilliant and insufferably boring Lai Lililas, the palace lexicographer—"

Jenjen watched as a fat hermaphrodite in a shapeless robe rose to address the throng. "It all boils down to the word *Var*," he said, "which, as we all know, is in the highspeech the root both of *vara*, which means *truth*, and *varung*, which betokens *madness*. Why this accident of etymology? Well, this entire myth was fabricated to explain what is essentially an accident: the falling together of two 'a' vowels in the Old Highspeech— the long 'a' and short 'a'—into a single sound. As a result, the two roots have become homophonous. You see what lengths mythology has gone to merely to explain away a felicitous pun!"

There was some polite laughter at this. "Does this explain our neophyte's confusion?" said Ton Siriss.

"If it please you, not in the slightest."

"Well," said the anthropologist, "I suppose *I* must be the one to illuminate these mystic words. I'm sure you're all aware of the Mother Vara cult that has arisen on many worlds, each of which has, as its secret mystery, the recitation of one version or another of this myth?"

"I had heard snatches of it before," Jenjen said, "but our family is atheist."

"Well, it is all but an allegory of the archetypal war between good and evil, of the yearning for a better universe, and so on. This is common to all cultures. Clearly it describes events so fantastical as to bear no relation to reality, yet it is full of images central to human consciousness: I mean, for instance, birth and rebirth, the primal sex act, the postulation of superior god-beings, the dogma of the falling from grace. But in time, and because of various errors creeping in and being perpetuated through constant ritual repetitions, I would suggest that the meaning has become clouded, much as the clarity of a lightweaving is obscured by the gauzing effect of a darkfield. . . ."

"Nonsense!" said another voice. "Because of its prevalence in all the societies of the Dispersal of Man, I submit that it must pertain to a racial memory of genuine historical events—for instance, the seeding of space, in our primordial past, from a single planet."

"Now *there's* a controversial theory!" said the anthropologist, chuckling. "Here, Ir Jenjen, try the broiled kashanthra. I know the color is unusual, but it has been marinated in a poultice of fresh algae and gruyesh vinegar, and is not unpleasant."

"Wait!" said the same voice. "Let me finish! I submit, too, that the spread of this myth over the last few dozen years is essentially subversive: for the myth suggests that the Inquest has lost its compassion, and that, moreover, it is transient, defeatable . . . by the powers of Shadow. . . . Why else would Kelver have taken the name of Shadow for his own?"

At the mention of Kelver's name a hush fell over the dinner guests. No one spoke for a long time. What was it about this one name that provoked them so? Why did the name of *Shadow* inspire such awesome emotions?

At last it was Ton Siriss who broke the silence. She spoke directly to Jenjen, and all followed the Inquestrix's gaze. Jenjen's cheeks warmed, and she cast down her eyes. But Siriss spoke gently, and there was, in her voice, a ghost of Elloran's; from her at-least compassion was not gone. "And you, my friend, do you believe this man's astonishing accusation . . . that this myth has somehow been planted on thousands of planets merely for the purpose of sowing discontent . . . of aiding the rebellion?"

*The rebellion—*

There. The word was spoken. The guests tensed. "My Lady," Jenjen asked in a small voice, "Whose side are *you* on?"

An uproar. Siriss raised her hand for silence. "I wish . . . I wish I knew."

"Then I do not know either. How to answer, I mean. To displease you means death, doesn't it? So I have always been taught. I mustn't speak at all."

"Bah! Do you know nothing at all, then? Do you not realize the importance of the events in which you have been caught up—the momentous words and deeds that will bring the whole galaxy tumbling down? There's only one way to settle this. Call Tash Tievar, the Rememberer, somebody!"

And trembling, Jenjen knew that she would have to face in public that which she had tried to avoid even in private. . . . She must listen once more to Tievar, and learn more of darkness, and stagger ever closer to the brink of personal perdition.

He came, bowed before the company, was told the details of the controversy. He seemed haggard; perhaps they had awakened him from sleep. He turned to Jenjen and gave her a weak smile; she knew then that she forgave him for opening her eyes and making her see distasteful truths. Finally he spoke.

"My Lady, nobles, guests: all your interpretations are correct, as far as they go. But you know, too, that Uran s'Varek, the Inquestral homeworld, is a real place; and many of you know that Mother Vara is no myth, but a figure out of history. Twenty millennia ago, fleeing the rubble of smashed empires, she found Uran s'Varek. What a paradise it was, this sphere that surrounded the black hole at the center of the galaxy! For it gave her the gift of limitless power. The thinkhives of this unthinkably vast world, powered as they were by the deaths of the stars that the black hole devoured, transformed science into magic. A vision could become reality merely by the thinking of it. When the Princess Vara (that was her name in those days) tired of creating crystal palaces and pleasure domes, she turned to altruistic pursuits. She wanted to abolish evil from men's hearts, and restore their primal innocence. And so she created the Inquest and the Inquest conquered and reunited the ravaged galaxy, and peace reigned for millennia. But the utopia could not be forever, and Vara saw her dream come once more apart. So she said, 'To restore men's innocence, we must take all their evil unto ourselves. We must shoulder the burden of their sins.' And she created *makrúgh*, and with it the hunting of utopias. This time the stasis lasted twenty thousand years. For some it was a golden age. For others . . . well, we have all seen the people bins as they sail the overcosm; we have seen the blood that the Inquest daily sheds in compassion's name. And a time came when, by the Inquest's own precepts, it was itself doomed: for it had become a utopia, and it itself its fatal flaw. Vara tried to flee the curse, but she could not. And so she had to work instead for the destruction of all she had wrought. But she was old now; the oldest human being in the galaxy she was. She passed the mantle of rebellion to Ton Davaryush, who is called the Heretic. But Davaryush saw that no man who had been nurtured by the Inquest, and who truly knew its vastness and might, would dare bring about its downfall. An innocent was needed, one who had not yet been touched by the twisted thinking of *makrúgh*, who could be made to see the light and then to infiltrate the Inquest and subvert it from within. And so he passed the shimmercloak to Kelver, a peasant boy. Kelver who has become the Prince of Shadow."

"But how was it," Jenjen said, "that a peasant boy was willing to tackle this task?"

"To answer this question, I must begin by telling you a different creation myth. This myth was manufactured by the Inquest in order to endow a people with an artificial past. The people lived in the innards of a mountain, and they were all deaf and blind. . . ."

# 4

# The Myth of the Windbringers

"You must imagine that these are the words of a seer—if he can be called such, being deaf and blind—among these people. As to the nature of the Windbringer-God, I shall reveal that as soon as I finish this narration.

"'Our darkness,' says the hypothetical seer, 'is not really darkness. When the angels have carried us home, we will perceive as one with the Windbringers.

"'The world is the belly of a cosmic Windbringer that courses through an infinite darkness. Who knows? In the vastness outside there may be other Windbringers carrying little worlds of their own, with their own special fragrances, their own textures, their own warmths. . . .

"'This is how the world was created. First the Sound was distilled out of the darkness. So wet and dry were the first sensations to be distinguished. There was not even warm or cold then. These things were dark to the touch. Then the first Windbringer rose from the Sound. He hovered over the waters, and when he moved the wind sprang up. And then the Windbringer immolated himself. This is the supreme mystery of nature, the act of love that unlocked the universe. His body shattered and the shards that were flung the farthest became hard walls of rock. His bursting breath became the warmth that burned and boiled the water of the Sound; and his blood mingled with the water, and the warmth of his breath incubated the blood and water as a mother's womb a little child unborn. And so men and women rose from the water. There was a terrible darkness and they were afraid. But the force of Windbringer's bursting blew them onto the rocks and then they touched cold as well as warmth, and knew the difference between life and death. And out of the same substance were born the Windbringer's children who fly the thick winds over the Sound, who make food appear on the floors of metal. And when we hunt them it is a sacred hunt, for we bring him home and reunite him with his immolated self. Thus in giving death we give life, and celebrate the universe's mystery.'"

# 5

But even as the old Rememberer's words died away, Jen-jen could feel a subtle shifting in the air, a moment of jarring discontinuity. . . . It was much like the split second of disorientation one always experienced when using the displacement-lattice to cross an unfamiliar arrondissement of the city, but more protracted; there came with it a sharp emotion—she could almost smell it, it was so strong—a sense of sudden bereavement. It jolted her out of the world of Tievar's narrations, and she cried out.

"Do not be afraid," said Tievar. "We have entered the overcosm."

"But why this grief? I have lost no one—" She stopped short, understanding that her journey might now isolate her in time and make her return a stranger to Ikshatra.

"It is not the loss of your friends; I daresay there's a good chance you'll see them one day, though you may find them gray and withered and feel cheated of the time you might have spent with them. As we sail the space between spaces more, and time becomes more and more irrelevant, that grief may deepen, or it may fade away. No, daughter, what you felt, that pervasive melancholy that ran through the mind of every sentient being aboard this palace, was the pain of the delphinoid shipmind."

"The shipmind? It feels pain?" As she looked around her she saw that grief had touched the minds of every member of the party.

"The Windbringers, you see, and the delphinoids . . . are one. Once, the brain that steers this palace through the overcosm was a creature—almost all brain—a hundred meters long, that soared through the dense air at the heart of a vast dark mountain, singing his lightpoems. . . . Though he was deaf and blind to his imprisonment, his mind perceived the overcosm directly. And his giant intellect gave order to the chaos, and out of this order came the lightsongs. . . . But the hunters captured him and gave to him this hellish immortality. They soldered his brain to a starship hull, and built this palace around it, and now, his mind linked by the tarn crystals to the minds of his astrogators, he seeks out the quickpaths between the stars. But he can never forget that once he was free. And he no longer sings the lightsongs that once resounded over the Sunless Sound, so beautiful that when men first saw them they could not bear to slaughter the delphinoids . . . until the Inquest engineered a race of the deaf and blind to hunt them."

"And gave them that creation myth—to justify their slaughter! All because the Inquest lusted for power. . . ."

"It was compassion that moved them at first, Jeni. They believed that in the game of *makrúgh* they could take all men's evil upon themselves, and all its guilt, and its original sin. But

now the power has driven them mad. . . . Then Ton
Davaryush the Heretic, Kingling of Gallendys, was led by two
children to the light on the Sunless Sound. One of the children
was Darktouch, a hunter who was by genetic throwback able to
see and hear, and so not immune to the delphinoid's lightsongs; the other was Kelver, the peasant boy who rescued her
and helped her, out of love, to reach the Inquestor across the
wasteland of Zhnefftikak.

"So Davaryush saw and was forever changed. He strove
for revolution now. But the corruption of the Inquest was so
deep in him that he knew he could not lead the rebellion. For
in its compassion, the Inquest had renounced love, compassion's one true source. Now only a pure innocent, plucked as a
child from some peasant backworld, made to see the light on
the Sound before being corrupted by the Inquest, could smash
the Inquest's power. And so he named the boy Kelver to the
High Inquest; it was his last act before the name of Ton was
stripped from him, and he was condemned to silence."

It was hard to imagine all this at once. "The largest tapestry I've ever envisioned," Jenjen said, "was a single wall of
light."

"But the tapestry of Remembrance goes back twenty
thousand years, to the birth of the Inquest; and it embraces
the million worlds of the Dispersal."

"So that's how the schism started," Jenjen said, somewhat
confused.

"Kelver took possession of the Throne of Madness on the
Inquestral homeworld of Uran s'Varek. And unlocked the dormant power of the black hole, first harnessed by the Princess
Vara at the beginning of history. But while he now possesses
power almost as vast as the Inquest's, it has been at a terrible
price. . . . When you see him, Ir Jenjen, you will understand."

"Yes. They say *he* is coming." And so, at last, I'll set eyes
on him, thought Jenjen, the man that even the High Inquest
fears. She said, "And I've heard another name mentioned,
Tievar. You yourself have talked about Ton Arryk: how he is
leader of those who oppose the rebellion, and how Ton Siriss
once loved both him and Kelver."

But the Inquestrix spoke up: "I will not hear the tale, Tash
Tievar. Even an Inquestor may have enough of pain for one

dinner party. I grow weary; I should have soothing music, not remembrances of my lost loves. . . ."

"I'll tell you about him, too," Tievar told Jenjen. "When you come again to the Chamber of Remembrance." He never asked of her why she had been absent so long; but she knew that he understood, and that she was now ready to return there. "But now why don't you go gaze at the overcosm? Go and demand entrance to the astrogating chambers at the hub of the palace. Since you are Elloran's favorite, you will not be denied. As a lightweaver you have often brought order to a chaos of many-colored light; now you will see light gone mad."

And, after a decent interval in which the party conversation touched on nothing but trivial pleasantries, Jenjen excused herself and went to find the overcosm of which Tievar spoke.

# 6

She inquired the way; a link-boy, his upraised hands coldly aflame, led her through the maze. Nimbly he sprang from plate to plate, so she barely had time to look around her; only dimly did she see the scenery about her jump wildly from corridor to garden to piscine to aviary to holosculpt library to throneroom to refectory to artificial gorges rimmed with mountainmists and lakes of liquid amethyst and rotundas where metal monsters battled at the behest of palace ragamuffins.

Presently the guide took her, by way of a fallopian passageway, to a shadowy chamber. Its walls bled reddish rheum; in niches sat astrogators, of the Clan of Kail or Harren. Their eyes were closed. They sat cross-legged, still as idols. The link-boy said, "We should not disturb them; they have linked their consciousnesses with the delphinoid shipminds that are the eyes of the overcosm. But perhaps we can find one who is off duty."

Banks of spiraling machinery, half metallic, half organic:

waldo arms that spidered along the walls, thrumming thinkhives, and here and there windows of force, through which Jenjen could see massive hillocks of brain tissue, throbbing, sweating in thick gray rivulets.

At last one of the astrogators broke free from his trance; painfully, as though still dreaming a little, he descended the clanging metallic steps that wound up to his niche. He saw Jenjen, clad in her living darkness, and greeted her. "Ah, the Inquestor said you might come here one of these days. A lightweaver, are you?"

She nodded.

"Follow me." She turned to dismiss the link-boy, but he had already disappeared. "My name is Kail Kirian," said the astrogator. "Forgive me if I seem abrupt, but I have been attuned to the overcosm for some days now, and time is irrelevant in the space between spaces. . . ."

"Those brains—" she pointed through the forcewindow at one of them. Attendants with hoses were climbing up and down it.

"They are the shipminds. Don't gaze at them too long; if you're not used to it, you tend to absorb their endless melancholy. Come."

A moving stairway led them to walkways of force that overhung the astrogating chamber. "It's strange," Jenjen said, "that in this palace, where every hallway seems suffused with radiance, that there should be a cavern of such darkness. . . ."

"We all have our little secrets." He was a dour man, she decided, uncommunicative. As they walked he never looked at her, but pleated and unpleated his kilt.

They reached a spherical chamber, an inner wombroom. At first all was dark, "I will give the command to deopaque," he said. "Don't be alarmed."

All at once—

She gasped. Light exploded all around her! Nets of flame, vermilion, cerulean, cadmium yellow, closing in, engulfing . . . eruptions, whirlpools, stipplestorms of brilliant dust, fogs fringed with incandescent, rainbow veils and mirror-metal flickers and phosphor geysers, veils behind veils behind—

As if the universe had become a cosmic lightloom, and that lightloom weaving frantically, without an artist to direct the lightstrands. Inchoate chaos . . . Its brightness burned her eyes. They blurred. She squeezed them tight shut; still the madness raged. When she opened her eyes she saw, like a shadow on a screen, a woman's silhouette against the maelstrom. "Ton Siriss," she said.

"Ah, the young lightweaver," said the Inquestrix. Such wistfulness in her voice. "Your first time?"

"And my last!" With feeling.

"One never grows used to the overcosm. Often I come and watch, to meditate on darkness. . . ."

"I remember, *hokh'Ton*, that Ton Elloran used to meditate on darkness too. When I first met him, he had come to Essondras to view certain darkweavings. . . . But surely you can't think of darkness with all this going on!"

"Truly, Ir Jenjen," said the white Inquestrix, "this *is* darkness, nor can we ever flee it. It is good that, against the raging lightstorm, you see me only as a shadow. Or else you might see me weep."

"Weep, Inquestrix?" she said.

"He has gone now!"

"Elloran?"

"But his spirit haunts this palace . . . in the light from the gold-burnished walls and the airy voices of Sajit's neuterchildren. . . . He will never be truly gone. But it seems that he has left us, to go sail the gray spaces, as in that song of Sajit's. And when we reach the Shendering system I will be crowned Kingling, and assume his principalities. . . . I'm not ready! No one could ever have had *his* compassion, *his* love of the beautiful. Yes, this wilderness of light is just another darkness, lightweaver."

Jenjen did not know how to comfort the Inquestrix. Indeed, it was unseemly that she should even think of offering solace, for in her station she was as far removed from Siriss as a vegetable might be from the sun that nourishes it. And yet . . . just as that day of her childhood, when she had stumbled on old Elloran meditating on dark things in the museum on Essondras. . . . That same pity touched her.

The lightstorm . . . They seemed to stand at the heart of an exploding crystal with mirror-facets shattering. . . . They seemed to be hurled through a pinhole of crimson light, like a leucocyte through a capillary. . . . Lightveins, cracks in the cosmos, they seemed to be spokes of a dizzywhirling centrifuge and yet she knew they were not moving in spacetime at all. "How can you bear to watch it, time after time?" she cried.

"It is said," said Ton Siriss, "that all Inquestors are mad even the truly compassionate ones. In that sense, Kelver's aberration was only one of degree." She was talking only for herself, clearly. Jenjen stood as far away as possible, not daring to intrude, her eyes closed against the madness of light, which still battered her senses.

"It's no use," Siriss said, addressing her abruptly, not unkindly. "The light-mad overcosm is not entirely a physical phenomenon. Come, I will command that the observation deck be opaqued." She clapped her hands. "You will join us for the midmeal, perhaps?" Again she clapped. The lightstorm was not cut off all at once, but faded, slowly, afterimages of afterimages of afterimages. Distractedly Siriss said, "How can I choose? I love them both. Kelver and Arryk, shadow and light."

"But Lady Siriss . . . Ton Elloran once told me to see lights behind the thick darkness of darkweavings. Now I see you standing in the overcosmic lightstorm, and you call it darkness. They must all be one, inextricable." The darkness in the chamber of observation was complete now.

And Jenjen left that place, thinking: *If only I could distill that energy, that madness, into a work of art. How magnificent it could be!*

She had a vision of a grand lightwall, perhaps encircling the inner city of Ikshatra. Now that her Inquestral connections had imparted a certain cachet to her, she was sure that the oligarchs of Essondras would not hesitate to allow her to realize so ambitious a project. She envisaged crowds gathering in the city plazas, stunned to silence by the immensity of it. Only in one other place had see seen whole throngs so moved. . . .

In the necrodrama, where corpses danced out ancient myths, myths she now knew to be untrue.

In her sleeproom she sketched out her grand project in miniature; using the palace thinkhive's memory she summoned up a panholorama of Ikshatra; it sprawled halfway across the room. And, weaving the lightstrands with bright, assertive strokes, she drew in the lightwall . . . from the arena of necrodrama to the ruined palace of the mummified princes to the Blue Canal and the bridge of the hunchbacked pteratyger that straddled it. There, by the palace, she would recreate the exploding crystal effect, the volcanic starbursts, the crosshatching of millions of light-threads.

For days she worked, not sleeping, thnking always of the delphinoids' song. Surely I too can bring order to the overcosm's chaos! she thought. I've seen it too. Can't I do as well as a flying alien brain? It can't be true, what Tievar said: that a lightsong, an artwork, and a couple of people who chanced to set eyes on it, could trigger the change that splintered the million worlds of man!

And thought of the creation myth of the delphinoid's hunters:

"The world is the belly of a cosmic Windbringer. . . ."

Surely, she thought, that is true of Varezhdur itself! For Varezhdur is a tiny world adrift in the overcosm, and its mind is the mind of a Windbringer. She thought of this floating world with its richness and spectacle, and of that other floating world, the closed world within the mountain, the world of darkness, woven from a fabric of Inquestral lies. . . .

She worked hard. Ambition and envy kept her going.

There they were! The whirlpools carapaced with flame . . . the nebulae bristling with phosphorescent cilia . . . veils within veils within veils. It was chaos in miniature. But she knew that something eluded her. It wasn't art yet. She threw herself ever more angrily into the work. There was much to be angry about—anger at worlds devastated, at mankind stifled by the Inquest. And private anger. She did not know which was worse: knowing or never to have known all she now knew.

After many sleeps she realized she had achieved nothing.

My mind has succumbed to the overcosm's madness, she thought. Everything's confusing now. How different from that crystalline epiphany of my childhood, when I first looked into the eyes of Ton Elloran!

She got up from her lightloom at last. As she stood up, shards of light scattered, dissipated, faded into Varezhdur's own quiet luminescence. A last thread of vermilion spiraled from her fingers and was absorbed into the furry floor. She blinked away the simurama of Ikshatra. At a handclap, the lightloom folded itself away. Nothing remained of her tortured labors. She strode toward the displacement plate and gave the command for the Chamber of Remembrance.

*The belly of a cosmic Windbringer* . . .

Tash Tievar said, "But the palace is in turmoil! Surely you have heard?"

"No, Father Tievar. I've been hard at work, though it seems fruitless now."

"A message has come. . . . It is about Shen Sajit."

"He is dead, isn't he? That is why Elloran grieves so much."

"But we have only now found out the terrible news—that his body was shipped to a servocorpse factory on Idoresht. And though Elloran has already departed in search of the gray spaces, Siriss will move planets to find Sajit, and bring him home for a real ceremony."

"What difference will it make?" Jenjen said bitterly. "He's dead, isn't he? The Inquestors had no such scruples when they played the Shendering system in *makrúgh* and caused it to *fall beyond!*"

"Inquestors are not like other men."

"In this, Tash Tievar, they are."

"But you have come to hear a story?"

"Yes. You were going to tell me of how Siriss came to love Ton Arryk."

"Yes. You have heard much of death; now I should tell you of birth, of an Inquestor's making. I am old to tell a story of birth. Perhaps this will be the last story I tell."

"You shouldn't say that. You're the only friend I have in this huge palace."

"You have something of the Rememberer in you, though you are of another clan. I have no apprentices anymore. . . . I hope that one day you'll tell my tales. And that you'll experience a story that you'll make your own, and that the day will come when you stand, gray-haired, where I now stand, and another young one can profit from your wisdom. . . ."

"Father!" And she embraced him; she felt the frail frame quiver a little in her arms.

He said, "The story of how firephoenixes ceased to exist, and were perforce transformed into the stuff of legend . . . the story of an Inquestor's birth; of Arryk, who once held such promise for the Inquest. . . ."

# 7

# The Story of Young Arryk

"They're not sleek, their eyes don't flash, their wings don't glitter with lust-driven fire the way they do in summer, phoenix-herder. What can I do? The game has come early to Kailasa. . . ."

He was startled; it was a low voice, almost an aural after-image of the winter wind. He looked up and saw her. She was an Inquestrix; he wasn't too ignorant to notice the shimmercloak, a whirlpool of rose-streaked ultramarine flapping and churning up the scarlet snow of Kailása's northlands. Her face was white; her hair silk-light, milk-white; even her eyes were white as mist, and in her chin-cleft sparkled a single diamant.

He was a youth, clanless, tending flocks of firephoenixes for an absentee Kingling. Summer had been kind; his village of hovertents followed the great migration across the rift-rich Mountains of Jérrelahf, over the Pallid Ocean where they harvested the flying sea-serpents' honey-eggs, down to the southlands. They had been lazy, haze-bright days when the white-scaled birds soared skyward, screeched, and mated in mid-air amid bursts of blue ether flame.

Winters were hard: he drove the phoenixes, flightless, pregnant, through the northern slopes, his tunic stained a thousand crimsons by the snow. Only the bloodalgae withstood the cold the whole year round; but here the birds laid spore-puffs that would hatch, come icebreak, in blue-brilliant fireworks, and catapult their fledgelings flaming into the sky. He neither liked nor disliked what he did; he'd been born to it. Sometimes, in the summers, unpredictably, the Inquestors came. Kailása was a world set aside for a Kingling's pleasure.

211

Here the Wars within the Dispersal of Man could not come. Nor would the war against the alien whispershadows ever touch his world.

The Inquestrix never took her eyes off him. He was disturbed. The Inquestors were like gods, incomprehensible. Some said they blew up planets for pleasure. It was hard to believe. She was too beautiful, this one, to be a world-burner. . . .

"Come," she said, "don't be afraid." He flushed. He genuflected, the snow-cold digging into his knees. "No, up, up, this is no ritual, we are alone here." And she reached for his sugar-pouch and began strewing the snow with the brown crystals. The phoenixes dived, hungry, and the snow flurried, white and red.

"Look at me, Arryk," she said.

"You know my name—"

"You are Arryk-without-a-Clan, seventeen years old by our reckoning, you herd the firephoenixes for Ton Elloran n'Taanyel Tath, Inquestor and Kingling, Lord of Varezhdur. I've been watching you."

"Why?" Just in time, he remembered his place. ". . . Lady."

"Do not question me." She reached out; her hand brushed his cheek. The cold made him wince. "I have been watching you," she said, "waiting in my web like a spider. Does that frighten you?"

"No. It's strange, though. One doesn't talk to Inquestors." In his confusion he found himself speaking the lowspeech, as he would in the village, but she did not seem to mind.

"I am Ton Siriss k'Varad es-K'Ning," she said. "I am to inherit this world. Elloran has forfeited it in a game of *makrúgh*."

Arryk had heard of *makrúgh*; it was the game that Inquestors played. *So war has come*, thought Arryk. *We'll all die, we clanless people.* He flicked the thought away; it made no sense.

The Inquestrix laughed. "So solemn, Rikeh!" He started when he heard her use his child-name. "This planet won't be touched; it's a pleasure world, too insignificant even to play pawn in the game. This is just a little trinket, a love-gift, because I cured him of his melancholy. Ton Elloran is very old now, boy. He has abdicated. He is giving away all his worlds:

Chembrith, Eldereldad, Gom, even Kailása, even useless Aëroësh. I know this talk is way above your head, Rikeh, but I have a whim to talk. Did you know that I desire you? Your eyes are violet like dawn over the sea on my homeworld, and my homeworld has lain waste for a century. . . . I was there only yesterday. But then I stepped onto a delphinoid ship, I sailed the overcosm, I lost a hundred years in time dilation. I'm sad, Rikeh. Yes, you are beautiful, you child, you innocent. One day I will take you. Perhaps I will destroy you."

He knew she had this power. He shifted his feet in the snow, unnerved, anxious.

"I need you for something else, though, now."

"Yes, Lady."

"The phoenixes." Her eyes burned. "I want them roused, now, in mid-winter. I want a grand hunt in the scarlet snow. Scatter the mating-pheromones in their feed. Make them think it's spring."

"They will die without giving birth, Lady Siriss, and there'll be no young, and our village will lose its livelihood. And I—"

"Don't question me! In its compassion, the Inquest will provide for you; that goes without question! But I must have my hunt." He saw her eyes catch fire when she said *hunt*. "It is a gesture, a move in *makrúgh* . . . . You see, Ton Elloran has decreed that he will play one final round of *makrúgh* before he relinquishes his power. Don't you understand how important this is? I want to disrupt the seasons, to create a beautiful gesture of transience, to set the scene correctly for my next move. You are to be go-between from me to Elloran."

"I—" Things were moving faster than he could understand.

"You are to go to him in his palace at Varezhdur. . . ." Snow whirled in a sudden bloody hurricane. When it settled, a floater hovered there, globed in a darkfield: a gilt staircase angled up from the snow, melted into the blackness. "You may take my floater."

"Yes, Lady."

"Call me Siriss. We'll play a little game, you and I, a game of false identities. Would you like that?" The boy nodded, dumbfounded. "Beware of Elloran! He is very old, very cunning, very wise in the game of *makrúgh*. He is utterly evil. But we can beat him. You and I."

"I?" The phoenixes were running in circles, catching his consternation.

"Even you, pretty child. I have a mind to subvert the natural order of things, to dissolve the difference between us, to invert the seasons. . . . That is how I play *makrúgh*. She laughed a guileless-seeming, quicksilver laugh. "Is that not witty. Rikeh?"

"I don't know." In spite of his confusion he already found himself moving towards the stairway.

"You are tempted, you are tempted. . . ." Siriss laughed again. It was a laugh that affected menace, but Arryk felt, behind it, a curious innocence; he knew that Inquestors were often unimaginably old even when their faces seemed like children's, but somehow he could sense that Ton Siriss was not one of those ancients. That she was a half-child like himself, hiding behind the ambiguity of Inquestral agelessness. But he said nothing; for he knew that from the moment he first saw her he had been treading a tenuous tightrope, courting death with every gesture, every word.

Anyone else from the village would have panicked and run, or thrown himself abjectly on the Inquestor's mercy. But he found himself reveling in the danger.

That, of course, was why she had picked him.

Arryk shielded his eyes: even then they smarted. The sun was rising over a sky of beaten gold. The floor was gold too, burning with reflected heat. In the center of the vast audience chamber there danced a galaxy of dust, stippling the air with dazzlesparks. When he grew used to it, the light became soft. In the distance, through the gauze of star-motes, sat a man of immense age. Nearby, from scattered sunken recesses of the chamber, music played: ethereal shimmerviols blended with whisperlyres and the voices of neutered children. Arryk couldn't speak. Ton Siriss had told him this was the serpent's lair, that Ton Elloran would entrap him with beautiful words and sights, and yet. . . .

Bolder, he walked a thousand paces towards the throne of gold. And now he saw the old man smile at him, serene, his shimmercloak swirling about his shoulders in a tempestuous artwind.

"*Hokh'Ton,*" he murmured, prostrating himself. And then

the old man laughed. Arryk looked up, his eyes tear-blurry from the brightness. It had been a soft, kind laughter.

"Get up, lad. You're from Siriss, I take it; what has she been up to then?"

"I—" Then Ton Elloran stepped down from his throne and touched him and raised him up, and Arryk saw a shrunken, sunken man, half a head shorter than himself. *His touch will sear you,* Siriss had hissed at him. *Keep down, keep low, deliver your message in a steady voice, or he will look at you, long and searchingly, and as he gazes you will crumble into dust. . . .* But Elloran's touch had not burnt him. "The Lady Ton Siriss k'Varad es-K'Ning invites the Lord Inquestor to a Grand Hunt of Firephoenixes," he said, repeating the high-speech message by rote, "on the eleventh day of the week, beginning at dawn upon the Mountains of Jérrelahf and ending at dusk upon the Ruined City at the North Pole."

Elloran was silent for a moment; then he burst into helpless laughter.

"My Lord, what is so funny?" he said, then bit his tongue.

"Believe me, child, it isn't at all funny. But I am old. I've learned to laugh sometimes, for an Inquestor may not be seen to weep; that would be unseemly, you know."

"Shall I bring back a message?"

"No. Wait." The Inquestor put his arm around the boy's shoulder and walked him down the steps, towards the galaxy of dust. Arryk was trembling now. They entered the swirling dust, and the light surged, smarted. "It's only a holosculpture," Elloran said. "My true galaxy of dust is waiting for me, in the throneroom of my delphinoid ship, for when I relinquish the Kingship of Varezhdur." Arryk was feeling more and more uncomfortable. He was thinking, But Inquestors *never* talk about themselves! They're apart from us mere humans. They live for centuries.

*I'm trapped!* he thought. The Inquestors were toying with him, tossing him back and forth like a ball. He put his hand through brilliant emptinesses that were clusters of dust-mote stars. "Look," Elloran said at last. They had climbed to the center of the galaxy on spider-stairs of force that twisted and branched invisibly within the holosculpture. "Here is all the Dispersal of Man." Arryk's heart quickened. "Not much, is there?" the Inquestor said sadly. "The million known worlds, parsec upon parsec of the Inquest's power . . . not even half a single galaxy of dust. It humbles me, Arryk." And Arryk noticed that the old man called him not by his child-name but casually gave him status equal to himself. And this, in its own way, was more disturbing even than Siriss's unseemly familiarity. And now Elloran pointed again, and there was a string of white suns that traced a bracelet around a patch of darkness. "This," said Elloran, "is what she's after."

"Stars, Lord?"

"Not stars, but the deaths of stars. I have declared a last game of *makrúgh*, and she means to win it. She doesn't know that to win is to lose. She's too new to the Inquest to understand yet. It's a symbol, you see. We call this chain of stars—because of their matched whiteness, because of their uncanny formation—the *Vauvenizhi*. . . ."

"That is Old Highspeech, Lord Inquestor?"

"Yes. It means Flight of Phoenixes.

"Oh!" He knew suddenly what it meant. "They are linked, phoenix to star. If a phoenix dies you'll kill . . . millions of people!" And he cried like a little child.

The Inquestor flung the shimmercloak around them both. Stars whirled. The shimmercloak's warmth danced through his body. He heard the Inquestor's voice: "Yes. There are a thousand ways in *makrúgh* of putting a world *beyond*, child. What can I do? The Dispersal of Man needs the constant vigor of change, of war and peace, of pestilence and plenty. Or else it would become a stillborn, stagnant utopia peopled with the dead. But we, the Inquest, have taken away the evil of these things and siphoned it into our souls, and now we alone bear all the guilt. . . . Do you wonder then that we are unhappy, that we long for an end?"

"Can't you just end everything? Give up? Start over?" They sat down on the stairs of force, enveloped in the holosculpture.

"It is too big for a man to change, Arryk. And I, who can crush a planet with a command, am only a man. So we try to make things beautiful. We have our *makrúgh*, we tag the firephoenixes and chase them through the air and bring them down, and when they die their tags send signals through the tachyon universe to the great thinkhives of Uran s'Varek, and war comes to a world of the Vauvenizhi.

"But Siriss . . . misunderstands! The game is still everything to her. She'll burn worlds out of season, she'll rain plague down on infant planets still gouge-cratered by the landings of people bins!"

"Lord, she says she will win at *makrúgh*, no matter what the cost. She says that you are evil, heretical even; that you say things that go against the Inquest. But *I* think—"

"What do you think, Arryk?"

Arryk could not speak. The old man's sorrow was terrible and beautiful. And Arryk knew that he loved this man, in some strange way that he could not understand; that he would follow him as blindly as a phoenix follows its herder. Elloran did not force him to answer, but said, "Siriss has not yet learned that the object of *makrúgh* is not to destroy but to heal. It is not to earn the applause of other Inquestors, but often to earn their rejection, their hatred. It is not to gain power, but to grow in compassion."

"You have to destroy her! Prevent her from playing *makrúgh*!" Arryk cried.

"She must learn," said Elloran. "I accept her invitation. Will you be my messenger to her?"

Arryk did not often think of his parents. They had been killed when he was a small child, crisped and shredded by tumbling firephoenixes during a Grand Hunt. A stupid accident. There had been talk of sending the orphan to the overcosm wars to be a childsoldier and to gain a clan-name, perhaps, if he survived; but the village elders had never quite made up their minds, time had passed, they had grown used to him.

Now the firephoenixes thrust through the red snow with unwonted liveliness. Their feed had been tampered with. In a day they would burst out in flame and drag their misused bodies into the air and try to fly towards the still unwoken warmth of summer. As the village grew near, the tent-peaks peeping from the mountain-rifts, he remembered suddenly— . . . soaring . . . shimmer of sunlight . . . they'd gone ahead, little Arryk in his slingwomb, to draw the phoenixes in a bow-arced line over the mountains, the Inquestors' floaters darted in the distance like haze-twisty dragonflies . . . then *duck! duck! duck!* his mother's swift sharp shriek, the angry phoenix falling, unmasking fire from the sun . . . spinning. . . .

There was the village now. Arryk consigned his birds to their forcecage, camouflaged as a bare crag jutting from the crimson, and prepared to step onto the displacement plate that led to the orphans' tent.

. . . their bodies snapping, crackling in the blue fire . . . ahead, not three meters away, the snowline ending, the scarlet cutting to seamless, endless yellow ocher veldt . . . not crying. Numbed. Sloshing home through the melting snow, thick as blood.

He grew up a moody child; for the most part they left him alone. He did his herding cheerfully enough, and was so little bother that he was easily forgotten.

Yet two Inquestors had confided in him, had told him conflicting stories, and at the bottom of their stories there was only one mutual truth: worlds would die before the Great Hunt was over. *I'm no one*, he thought, *but I alone know what it's all about*. The knowledge did not comfort him; it was cold as the snow.

Maddened, frustrated, the phoenixes were dashing themselves against the forcecage. Arryk turned aside and stepped onto the displacement plate.

She was standing in front of the tent. The village square was almost empty; two or three villagers, trapped by the Inquestrix's arrival, had frozen into genuflections and averted their eyes.

"Are you ready, pretty child?" she said.

"For what?"

"Tomorrow we chase the sunlight." She beckoned to him; he followed her onto a floater disguised by holoart to resemble a whirlpool of scarlet snow.

Inside, the walls' darkfield had been completely deopaqued, so that they seemed to be standing on emptiness, in the air over the snow.

"I told you," she said, "I would take you whenever I wanted."

"Nobody in the village wants me," he said. Not whining; mere fact.

"Shall I force you to love me? I am an Inquestrix." *But I*, he thought, *I own my own soul. . . .*

At a flick of Siriss's mind the darkfield settled around them and the invisible floor of the floater softened. She was like the lighthawks of summer that swooped from sunlight over flaming phoenixes, devouring him. *How she loves the role of predator!* She could not awe him. Because of what Elloran had said. Yet she seemed content to feed on his flesh. . . .

When she was satisfied she blinked away the darkfield and gathered her shimmercloak to her. Softly it blushed, but Siriss's paper-white features never colored, and her hair fell untousled into the perfect swirl of the artwind that kept it billowing in the stifling stillness. She showed him the crystal pendant in her hand. "It's a phoenix-tag," he said, knowing how it spelled a world's death.

"It is a semi-sentient," said the Inquestrix. "We link them with the phoenixes, life for life; when the phoenix falls, the crystal dies. It turns blood-red. Its dying shriek is a sharp shrilling through the tachyon universe; and when the thinkhives on Uran s'Varek hear of the phoenix's death they will precipitate the linked world's death. . . . Thus we show that every act has its consequence, resonating down the chain of being. But enough of these high affairs, pretty boy. You weren't made to understand them. Touch—" She tossed the crystal to him.

"I played *makrúgh* long and hard for this pendant," she said. "Each Inquestor who takes part in the hunt has only one phoenix that he may kill, tagged with his personal tag; and almost all the tags are dormant ones that will not link to the living. They are a kind of parasite, you know. . . ."

It seemed to suck the warmth from him. It was like Siriss herself, like a vampire. "Quickly," she said, "pouch it! If it clings to your flesh for longer than a single sleep, it will be bound to you until you die!" Hastily he thrust it into his tunic.

She said, "I played *makrúgh* with the Lady Ynyoldeh for three sleeps. Elloran has named Ton Ynyoldeh Queen of Daggers for this grand *makrúgh*. From her I gained this concession: that my crystal would be the only living one. And that it would be linked to Kenzh, the most populous system of the Vauvenizhi. And so this gesture in the grand *makrúgh* becomes mine alone, a private metaphor from me to Elloran."

"You're a monster!" he blurted out.

"Surely no," she said, teasing him almost. "How can you call it that? One world is enough to prove my point, and even that world may not die. . . . It would not be compassionate to quicken all the crystals, to risk a thousand stars for the sake of a single gesture. . . ." She sounded remote now. "I will show him that I can play *makrúgh* with consummate elegance!"

"You love him. And he has hurt you." He knew this was true because, since his encounter with the old Inquestor, he had loved him, worshiped him blindly, utterly. He was all an Inquestor should be: wise, beyond deceit, compassionate. If she did not love him she must hate him for not being able to lie to him, for not being able to shake his eerie serenity. If she could only see how her mask had slipped—

But she only smiled at him. "You pretty boy," she said. But he knew they were more alike than she would ever admit, that she was as lost as he, in her own way. They made love again; this time he could sense the child within the beast of prey. And he pitied her. He tried to hold her tight, reassuring, but she shook herself free and stood aloof. She said, "Find me the sleekest of the firephoenixes. One that will not tire, that will soar till we have chased the sun to the roof of the world. I don't want to make my kill and then have to wait all day, watching the other Inquestors and knowing that their hunting is in vain. It's your choice, Arryk. I give you the fate of the Kenzh system. You, a peasant boy, can save a star system if you choose a phoenix swift enough to elude me—and I choose to hunt the ancient way, with a bow and a single homing arrow tipped with shatterstuff. It will be beautiful, no? Like you with your clear wide violet eyes."

His hand gripped the tunic-pouch that held the death-crystal. Even through the cloth the cold stung. *In two sleeps*, he thought, *I've been thrust upward a million levels, from peasant herder to planet-savior or planet-destroyer.* . . . It wasn't right! The Inquestors had their intricate game of power and control; why should they reach down and pluck him out of obscurity, and dangle dangerous truths in front of him, when in another day they would drop him, crushed, back into the snow?

*I have a single chance*, he thought, still clenching the crystal, *to do something important*.

He was going to save the Kenzh system somehow. It was up to him alone—hadn't the Inquestrix said so? The burden was bitter. But for a second there had been a kind of crazy joy to it.

"Go now," said Siriss. A gap opened in the darkfield; snow

gusted into the floater, melted, left crimson stains on the forcefloor.

"I hasten to obey your whim." It was a mere formula of the highspeech.

"Inquestors do not have whims, Rikeh!" For a moment she seemed strangely vulnerable. He turned his back on her and braved the cold, hugging himself so he would not be tempted to finger his new possession.

Arryk and the other herders stood in the man-tall grass that stretched all the way to the Mountains of Jérrelahf, bloody in the snow and dawnlight. Overhead, a lone lighthawk circled. The wind blew from the wrong direction. The phoenixes, primed with tampered feed, screeched against their restraints. The young boy scurried about, shushing them.

Arryk pulled his big white scarf tighter around his neck. It streamed in the ice-prickly wind. He had a secret that could kill him now, and he was afraid. At first he had thought to run out far into the snow, to bury the death-crystal, to flee and try to forget. But he knew that Siriss would still find a way to destroy the star system. He had to find a way to think like them, to understand *makrúgh* a little. To create a beautiful gesture.

And if he was walking a dangerous tightrope a few days before, the day he had first seen Siriss, then now he was walking straight into the furnace. Could it really be that a woman could begin like Siriss, drunk with power and self, and after a century or two become like Elloran?

Arryk thought of a planet dying, of cities bursting into flame, he who had never been more than a few klomets from the village of hovertents. He didn't care if he died by sunfall, if only he could touch her heart.

A cry from the young herders! The sun burst bloody from the black hills! In the distance, a black-and-glitter cloudlet resolved into a hundred floaters, some darkfielded, some open and opulent, where Inquestors stood drowned in the splendor of shimmerfur and gilt. Eight orchestras of trumpets and megaconchs and lyringes and kettlecrumhorns played from hoverfields at eight corners of the sky. The floaters flitted and froze in mid-swerve like hummingbirds. Now the Inquestral assembly was overhead. Arryk saw the young ones gasp. He blinked; the colors hurt his eyes.

The music swelled, deafening. And then, slicing through the clouds, came Elloran's floater: a disk of beaten gold that seemed to shine brighter than sunlight. It tilted, and he saw Elloran, tiny, shriveled, reclining on his throne. He thought he could see Siriss too, standing beside the throne; attendants dotted the floater.

Silence fell. Even the firephoenixes ceased to strain against their leashes. The tiny figure of Elloran was speaking now; amplijewels made his voice echo even down to the ground. Arryk felt a longing that was like pain; he knew he would never see Elloran again.

"Remember," said the voice in the sky—here it was the merest whisper, a shivering of the wind—"that only your arrow, reaching the phoenix that bears your tag, may send the message that makes your chosen planet *fall beyond*. That in our compassion we have commanded that the Lady Ynyoldeh, Queen of Daggers, cause our own tag to remain dormant, so that our joy in the chase be not dampened by bloodlust. There may be some who play the Grand Hunt for destruction; I play only as a gesture." Arryk saw that Siriss had moved away from his throne: was it in anger? He could not tell. Then he had to turn to the phoenixes.

"Rikeh, they won't fly!" a girl cried, as she loosened the jesses from her bird. "It's a terrible thing to do to them—"

The phoenixes stirred now. They'd been starved to make them airworthy out of season. At a signal from Father Garavan, the chief herder, all the children let go at once. The phoenixes ran scattering into the grass, bewildered, refusing to take to the air. "More pheromones!" someone cried. Now they were pelting them with drug-pellets, and the birds were running into each other, squawking in a hideous parody of their mating cry, here and there a burst of blue flame set the grass on fire, smoke tore at his eyes—

Young children with sticks ran through the grass now, flailing at the phoenixes. A thrilling, penetrating shriek rent the air, drowned out the children's chatter. The mating call! They were all echoing it now, a single shrill note. The children began to shout the beating-song in rhythm, trampling the ground and pounding it with their sticks. A single bird half-hopped, half-soared, a streak of white breaking out of the grass-sea overhead—

The villagers were cheering now. The Grand Hunt was

beginning! First one then a dozen then a hundred phoenixes broke through the grass and sprang into the wind with the dawn sun glinting red on their scales and their wings flapping in thundering unison. The doomed birds struggled to soar, to ignore the bitter wind that bore down on them, to breast the unwonted cold. It was a flight of terrible splendor, and the last time for the village. But he knew they'd never forget, no matter what the Inquest did to them.

Now they had formed two ragged formations, male and female, the male birds holding to a cross shape and flapping their wings all at once, all together, the female phoenixes in a fluttering whorl of white already sprinkled with blue flames, and the females had begun to whirl towards the northern mountains with the males pursuing. In a moment the Inquestral entourages, too, had fallen into formation and were following. And the villagers, old and young, were racing for their broken-down hovercars and signaling to the village's navigator to set the tents in motion.

Arryk ran, tripped over a child, his scarf tore free. . . . Panicking, he roped it tightly around his neck and jumped onto the nearest hovercar. At the horizon opposite the mountains, a low dust cloud showed that the village was shifting, gearing up for flight. He was crammed in between an old woman gnawing at a jangyll bone and a squalling child who wouldn't be still. The caravan of cars sped, skimming the grasstops, following the wheeling birds.

In a few hours the Inquestors had broken ranks, their floaters darting, weaving among the birds, thrusting through the eye of the circlet of females. No one was shooting yet. One after another the females burst into flame, the flame was quenched by the wind or the chill, the flames sparked again—

Now a single male broke loose from the males' formation, now more, now strings of males, still flapping in unison, twisted free like a yarnball's unraveling. Now the males were a net around the fire-hoop of the females. One after another, gaining courage, they dove into the thick of the females, seeking their pheromone-bonded mates—

And far above, Elloran's golden disk hovered, bright in the mid-morning sunlight. The sky had become brilliant blue, the clouds dissolved by Inquestral cloud-sculptors, but the air was bracing as ever. Arryk sat crushed into his seat, dazzled by the splendor. He was past caring about his fate now. He was seeing the last flight of firephoenixes, and he was drunk with the splendor of it.

And now they were at the shores of the Pallid Ocean. The hovertent village ploughed ahead, across the pastel-blue water; the hovercars were driven onto waiting rafts that were yoked to the necks of distant sea-serpents, and at a prod from the serpentman's laser-goad the water parted a quarter-klomet across the sea and the serpents rose, coiling, lashing, their scales glittering peridot, malachite, chrysocolla, emerald, jade. Hypnotized by the laser-goads' rhythm, the serpents swam crazed, hugging the surface, their flared fins spinning and fire jetting from their tails, towards the opposite shore where the Mountains of Jérrelahf still loomed, black and capped with scarlet.

Here and there, a bird fell flaming, skewered on a dart; one fell on the raft and the children fell to putting out the flames and quarreling over the meat. Once the whole flock came tumbling, tired, glancing the tallest waves, and the villagers bombarded them with scent-missiles that frenzied them and dredged up the last of their strength so that they soared again, struggling against themselves.

At mid-day they reached the shore. The sun hung high but the air was chill still, and the wind blew stronger, whinnying, pelting them with snow. Quickly the rafts emptied and the serpents were freed; fins whirring, they flew southwards.

Arryk saw that the phoenixes had paired off now, the males catching fire from the females as they mated in the sky; now and then a floater spun by and a blue fireball plummeted. As they neared the mountains, more phoenixes fell, but a mass of them still flew true, arrowed up, angling towards the mountain peaks.

It was then that a single floater, totally englobed in a darkfield, came falling towards them. Nervous, the villagers stopped their cars. Some of the children whimpered. It landed softly, hardly unsettling the snow, and a voice called Arryk's name.

"Arryk of the phoenix-herders, the Lady Siriss summons you to the court of Elloran. You are to use this, a floater from the fleet of Ton Elloran n'Taanyel Tath, Kingling of this world and the principality of Varezhdur. . . ."

The others shied away from him, afraid. *Even if I survive,* he thought, *I'll never be able to come back now.* Those whom the Inquest touched were both blessed and cursed. They would always be feared, envied, distrusted.

*You're truly alone now,* he told himself. A few steps and he was mounting the staircase into the floater; a few moments and he had landed on the golden disk where Elloran held court, and was standing before the throne of the only man he had ever worshiped.

Elloran's face seemed impassive, like a god's, but his eyes smiled. At his feet sat Siriss, her face perfectly composed. But he sensed an unease between them.

"You've chosen your phoenix well, pretty child," said Siriss, edging her voice with scorn. "We are only a few hours from the roof of the world, and I've been unable to kill it. And I've killed a fair number!"

"Yes, my lady."

"The sensors on my arrow have been unable even to detect quite which phoenix . . . what have you done, boy? Buried it? I'll find its burial place and dig it out, stamp on it with my foot until it sends its deathsong to Uran s'Varek!"

"I have not buried it. If I have hidden it where you cannot find it, please kill me, Lady Siriss."

For a moment she seemed uncertain; but the look passed at once. "Come," she said, "sit by me." To Elloran she said, "Do you like my new toy? Are you jealous? Isn't he beautiful?"

Elloran said, "He is beautiful, and I fail to be jealous either of you or of him." And he smiled a quick smile that seemed to be for Arryk alone, as though they were sharing some richly comic secret.

"Enough of this!" cried Siriss, rising. "My bow and arrow!" These were brought to her just as they reached the edge of the fire-cloud of phoenixes. As she took them from the cushion, the arrow glowed an eerie green.

"At last!" she cried. "For the first time, the arrow senses the nearness of its phoenix! You see, Elloran, I was not wrong! The boy—"

"The day is not yet over," said Elloran mysteriously.

What was going on between those two? What was the *real* crux of this game of *makrúgh*? He felt like a pawn again. His life was terribly in danger now, but he was no longer afraid. He felt only a kind of wary joy. It was not a feeling someone of his station should have.

Siriss ran to the edge of the hoverdisk. She aimed, her

body bending taut, echoing the bow in a duo of woman and weapon, utterly graceful; and the shaft flew into the mass of blue fire. A phoenix exploded, a little nova among the fireballs. The arrow swerved, homed into her outstretched hand. She turned, acknowledging applause. He heard her say, "It is the wrong phoenix; my arrow has stopped glowing, it should not have returned. . . ."

When she approached the throne she seemed puzzled. They were crossing the mountains now, and it was late afternoon. There were far fewer floaters buzzing about, though the phoenixes that remained, some scores of them, still flew strong. More and more of the Inquestors seemed to have abandoned the Grand Hunt and were materializing on the displacement plates in the hovering throneroom, adding to the buzz of conversation. "Everywhere around us, Arryk," said Elloran, "they are playing *makrúgh.*"

Shimmercloaks everywhere. Among the Inquestors were lackeys too, and a few servocorpses serving refreshments; there were ladies with mountainous headdresses and gowns curiously wrought from cloth of precious metals or animated with dancing holosculptures of mythological scenes. Their attention was no longer on the hunt, it seemed; only Siriss and Elloran still followed the flight of the firephoenixes towards the north pole.

"If this had been the right season," Arryk said—he could not help sounding bitter—"their mating would reach its consummation at the north pole and the females would drop their millions of spores and we'd be ready for another year. . . ."

"You're sorry that this village's way of life will come to an end?"

". . . No, *hokh'Ton.* I don't feel anything anymore."

"Good, good. When you think you are drained of all feeling . . . it will be time for us to fill you with knowledge. . . ." What did Elloran mean? Arryk sat speechless, cloaked in thought.

Siriss, coming up the steps, said, "It's glowing again!" and ran again to the edge of the disk. Each shot was as perfect as the last; each was greeted by less applause than the last. She was angry now. Coming back, she shouted, "I *will* find the tagged phoenix! I *will* destroy it!" The sun was beginning to set. The mountains were behind them. The ruined city at the north pole loomed ahead; ghostly obelisks of marble blanketed

with crimson, too-symmetrical hills of red that must have once
been domes. . . . "They are tiring! They are going down to
roost, a score or less of them! The chase is ending—bring the
hoverdisk down, I'll get them on the ground!" Siriss shouted.
The throneroom dove, following the birds that flamed still,
blue torches in the gathering dark. At a command from Elloran
a sourceless luminescence played over the throneroom. Again
and again Siriss shot into the sinking birds. As they died they
spattered the snow, their oxidizing blood bleaching the bloodalgae, turning the snow an unearthly white.

Now they had landed, and she and Elloran and Arryk
rushed overboard to stalk the final few birds, and even the
court was roused from its lethargy and began to stream down
many staircases and even to leap the two meters onto the snow.
"You've done well, Rikeh, but I'll win yet!" Siriss shouted, running into the white-stained snow.

And then all the birds were down. Some still flamed a
little. Light from the hoverdisk shone over the court, throwing
long shadows that melded into the looming towers and
obelisks.

When Siriss approached Elloran she was livid. "What
have you done, you old man, you heretic? I won the death-
crystal fair, in *makrúgh* with the Lady Ynyoldeh! How dare
you—" She seemed about to strike him.

It was time. He stepped between them. "I don't understand anything," he cried, "but I won't let you kill a world just
to score points in some arcane game—"

And Elloran roared with laughter. He moved towards the
boy, gently touched his shoulder. Arryk froze, knowing the end
was at hand. And Siriss looked wildly about, unable to meet
Elloran's gaze.

"You stupid girl," said Elloran—so quietly, so lovingly—
"when will you ever learn why we play *makrúgh*? I am many
centuries older than you; through time dilation my life has
spanned millennia more than yours, yet you will not listen. . . . Three sleeps ago," he said, to the whole throng now,
"this stripling Inquestrix challenged me to a game of *makrúgh*.
She told me that things must change now, that day must be
night and summer winter. And I said to her, it is true that
things must change now. But not to become what they are
not. . . . No, they must become more what they really are.
And so I laid a challenge on her: that she should go to a village

of peasants, and find an ordinary child of her own age, and even he would play *makrúgh* more truly than she. . . ." And then he put his arm around Arryk's shoulder and eased the scarf away from him.

Arryk's hands flew to his throat. Elloran pried them loose. All eyes turned to the jewel that clung there, embedded until death now.

Arryk wanted to cry but he didn't. He blinked away his tears. Into the appalling silence he shouted, "But you used me! You didn't care about the world you were going to destroy. I suppose you'll kill me now and your plan will be fulfilled. But at least I know that I'm better than you, even though I'm nobody and you're the highest of the high. Because I cared! And I understand how you loved Elloran, and how he saw right through you, down to the core, and you had to show him you were somehow better. . . . All right, all right. I'm ready now, go ahead, kill me—"

The silence went on and on. He searched for words to pour into the silence but found nothing. *Why doesn't she just shoot me down now?* he thought. The silence stretched on for another moment—

Applause! He turned wildly to Elloran, who only laughed and hugged the boy's shoulders harder. An expression of murderous rage crossed Siriss's face, and then . . . unexpectedly . . . she merely shrugged. And then smiled a radiant smile. And at this the applause crescendoed until he had to put his hands over his ears.

That night the ruined city came to life; servocorpses with torches lined the snowy streets, and the Inquestors feted the end of the Grand Hunt, warmed with sweet zul and roasted phoenixes.

And later still, when the fires were dim, Elloran and Siriss and Arryk walked out into the snow. Arryk and Siriss walked together, speaking little. Elloran walked ahead, a tiny figure in the darkness.

"I'm sorry I used you," Siriss said.

"It's over." At these words they kissed. She was no lighthawk, circling for the kill, but a firephoenix like himself; his heart danced, flaming. Under a snowdrift Elloran was waiting for them.

"This will be your world now," he said to Siriss.

"Yes."

"And Arryk . . . oh, child of my heart . . . you played *makrúgh* today with such elegance, such artistry. . . ."

"But you knew exactly what I had done."

"Well . . . I am very old." He studied the boy with piercing gray eyes. "I have reached the end of my *makrúgh*. I am free—free to relinquish all the power, all the splendor. Not many of us reach the end, you know."

"Father Elloran," Siriss said, and she fell to her knees in the snow, as if she were a mere commoner, "what can I do? I would have brought war to a world I have never seen, just because I envied you your peace, your gentleness. . . . Can you strip me of my clan-name? How can I be an Inquestor without compassion?"

"You have already begun to find it. You knew what it was that you had to learn, but you didn't want to face it, you wanted me to get up and rub it in your face. . . . If you'd really meant to win at this *makrúgh*, why pick *this* boy? You didn't pick a spineless lad who would be so much fodder for your grand plan. No, you sought out a loner, an independent. You made your own plan backfire. And as for stripping you of your rank . . . how can that be? We are what we are. And you are already showing the promise of a fine Inquestor. But you must know that you will always be lonely. Do you know, boy,"—he turned to Arryk, and instinctively Arryk too knelt down in the snow—"how we pick the Inquestors?"

"No, *hokh'Ton*."

"Often among the dispossessed. Among the terribly alone. I was nine years old and a princeling, watching my city razed to the ground by childsoldiers."

"My Lord—" Siriss gasped. "I didn't know. . . ."

"Yes, Sirissheh," he said softly, calling her by her child-name, "just like you." Absently he caressed the boy's neck, his finger lingering on the death-crystal. "I had better see to it that they turn off this thing; we don't want Kenzh to go to war just because you happen to fall off a cliff." He laughed quietly. "And now . . . I have given you a planet, Sirissheh. . . . What do you want, Rikeh?"

In the silence, Arryk listened to the wind. They were standing where the last phoenixes had died, and already new snow was falling, healing the deathstains with new crimson. "Listen, Rikeh," Elloran said. "Today, did you not feel many new emotions? For instance, didn't you feel a joy and pain all mingled, when you knew it was up to you alone to save the distant world?"

"How did you know?"

"Arryk . . . soon I will leave on a long journey. I don't know where I'm going. Away, far, out of the Dispersal of Man. They say that the Inquest is falling, Arryk. But I daresay they'll need someone to replace me. For the time being. What I mean is . . . Arryk, you have played *makrúgh*, and peasants do not play *makrúgh*. . . . I name you to the Clan of Ton. You knelt a phoenix-herder; now rise an Inquestor." He laughed; a short, half-bitter laugh.

"Are you mocking me?" cried Arryk. Were they really all alike, these Inquestors, even Ton Elloran?

"I should mock you? Oh, Arryk, never, never . . . But haven't I told you that to laugh is better than to weep? I believe that the Inquest will fall, as surely as the stars will be as dust; and what will come after the Inquest? I will be dead; but you, perhaps, will see the beginning of the fall. You may be able to guide this fall, to ensure that it does not bring utter chaos. For capricious, cruel, power-lustful as we have sometimes seemed, we have held mankind together well, Rikeh, Sirissheh. Some say that when the Inquest falls its crash will crush the universe; I wish I could show them all my galaxy of dust.

"Don't fight what has to be. I knew you to be truly of the Inquest when you put your own death before the death of an unseen world, when you welded the death-crystal to yourself as we Inquestors shoulder the burdens of the universe. You'll be one of the great ones, child, never fear."

"But—" He stood up abruptly, startled. And now the words came pouring out: "But I want to go with you! I want to follow you wherever you go, to serve you, to learn from you—"

"No. There was a time when I would have needed your love, when I would have drunk you dry. But it's Siriss who needs you."

Panic flooded Arryk. "How can I be an Inquestor? I'm just—"

"*I* became one," Elloran said, shrugging.

"But you're so wise and . . . Did you plan it all, then? Just to make Siriss understand?"

"I'm too old to make plans. Let the young ones play *makrúgh*. As for today . . . a whim, nothing more."

("Inquestors do not have whims," Siriss had said. She seemed to remember that, for she smiled wryly.)

"Wait—" There was so much more to ask. But the old Inquestor was already stalking off towards the city, ignoring them completely.

# 8

"Just like me!" Ir Jenjen cried when Tievar had finished his narration. "Elloran filled *my* head with fantastical new ideas, and then he went off on his private odyssey, and I'm alone, brooding, confused."

Tievar said: "Confusion must come before understanding."

"And Arryk? Did Arryk finally come to understand whatever mystic truth he was meant to discover? 'You may be able to guide the fall,' Elloran tells him in your story. But does he?"

"Alas, Arryk wrestled with the great darkness and in the end he lost. He is a man who had great need of love, and much love to give. He could not face the desolation at the heart of Uran s'Varek; he could not embrace the darkness, make the sacrifice that would free the universe. The Dispersal of Man is a magnificent creation. . . . In its own way it *is* a utopia. Therefore, as I told the dinner assembly when I narrated the history of the Inquest's founding, it *must* fall: the Inquestors themselves are this utopia's fatal flaw, and to hunt this utopia is to say, 'The Inquest falls.' And that, Jeni, Arryk could not accept."

"He didn't have the courage to—"

"It fell to Kelver to embrace the final darkness, to seize the Throne of Madness and become Prince of Shadow."

"But how did Kelver find the strength to do what might topple the Inquest and destroy everything we know? Like Arryk, he was just a peasant from a backworld. How could he even conceive of doing what he did?"

"He was, Ir Jenjen, an innocent. He formed no conceptions. He trusted Davaryush's vision and leapt blindly into the void . . . and unleashed the end of the empire. Poor child! But he had faith. He had love. Those things alone might not have been enough; but he also had a brief encounter with an absolute beauty. . . . He was one of the first, in twenty thousand years, to see the light on the Sound."

"I see, then, that the great rebellion has really come down to a conflict between Kelver and Arryk—"

"We must not forget Siriss. It is the tale of three young Inquestors, daughter. One has chosen what he calls the light: like the bloated Ur-beings of the creation-myth, devours world's souls and glows like a quasar from their deaths, and his light is founded on their darkness. The other—the Prince of Shadow—has chosen to name himself for the darkness. Yet light is the shadow's shadow, is it not? And the third is Siriss, who cannot decide between them and perhaps never will. She will side first with one and then the other. She has loved both Kelver and Arryk, and their mutual hatred grieves her more than anything else."

And Jenjen said, "Father Tievar, I've learned the most important lesson of all from the myths of creation and the story of the firephoenixes. I was moved by the myths—but though they contained cosmic images I perceived them only dimly. They're like darkweavings—woven so intricately, and over such a long time, that they obsure themselves. But your tales of Kelver and Siriss and Arryk have shown me that though we speak of good and evil and of absolutes, it all comes down in the end to only a few people, frail, bewildered, afraid of the dark."

# FIVE

# The Book of the Darkweaver

*xa, xa hokhté Enguéster*
*sha tíhssis shirénzhen in dárein?*
*sha tíhssis on' makháshas greúras,*
*urá in úrein?*

—ek shéntraran Sájiti

Ah, ah, O High Inquestor:
Do you yearn to touch the silence between the stars?
Do you long to touch the great gray spaces
In the space between the spaces?

—*from the Songs of Sajit*

**I**

In time, Ir Jenjen learned to endure the overcosm. But she could never love it. Many of the astrogators seemed to, though; in their mindlink with the delphinoid brains, they were able to perceive the patterns underpinning the overcosm. But there were some things she learned from this that human beings unaided would never see. It gave her new humility. She no longer dreamed of emulating the songs of the delphinoids in her own art.

Time passed; they breached the overcosm; she knew that Inquestors were meeting to play the game of *makrúgh*, but it made little difference to the rhythm of her own life. She had thought once that Elloran must really have died, that this gray space was some euphemism, like *falling beyond*, or that curious word the Inquestors used for death: *devivement*. But she knew now that he had, as the Inquestors said, "walked his personal *makrúgh* to its end," and abandoned the game, and departed the palace in a delphinoid starship towards some destination that he alone knew. Time moved slowly for the Inquestors; though others might long have forgotten the death of Shen Sajit, yet even now the time had come for Elloran's grief, and for his private expiation.

These things touched Jenjen little, for Elloran's memory illuminated every corner of Varezhdur. And her own remembrances of Essondras had become like holosculptures, time-frozen, slipping through her fingers: the niche of her grandfather's head, the quarrel with Zalo in the zul-shop, the theater of dancing corpses, the academy with its apprentice lightlooms. Occasionally, lying in her chamber in a wing of the palace that no one seemed to frequent, she would rehearse some memory; she knew she would be moved—the memories were so vivid—but she was untouched. This made her afraid. Then she would get the urge to wander.

She would get up, throw the cloak of writhing darkness about herself, stalk the corridors of Varezhdur. She no longer feared being lost, though sometimes she would travel in the company of one of the ubiquitous link-boys; it was not a palace that inspired terror. She no longer cared what world they orbited, or whether they sailed the overcosm; Varezhdur was world enough.

Rooms opening up into other rooms, sepals into petals: Here walkway tapestried with cobwebs or with clinging vines buzzing with lugubrious insects. Here a room dissected by muddy streams, where trained flying fish leapt, audienceless, in a precise listless ballet. Halls with fallen columns, dusted with green-tinged copper dust, covered in curlicuish grafitti.

And sometimes there would be other people, also bent on exploration, or looking for gratification; for though Varezhdur was not a palace that practiced denial of the senses, its inhabitants loved secret trysts and mysterious meetings. When she met such others, she would, if she chose, retreat with him or her behind an arras or a pillar's shadow. Love was never forbidden, but the awesome vastness itself forced furtiveness upon them. Jenjen took pleasure in these encounters. If one wandered long enough they were sure to be had, for Varezhdur had thousands of denizens, and many were, like her, forgotten people, chosen by one Inquestor's whim, always cared for, yet, because of the change of regime, never called upon.

Sometimes she would pause in one of the deserted halls and cry out to its echo-rich emptiness. Words of despair, words of exultation; sometimes tag lines from old necrodramas. Or whole conversations she'd had with Zalo long before. For although she'd begun to master the nuances of High Inquestral, and had become accustomed to its resonant cadences, its elliptical syntax, its multiplicity of verb forms, its quaint archaisms, she longed to be able to converse in the lowspeech of Essondras with someone. It was a yearning she seldom dared admit, for fear someone would laugh at her. But in all her wanderings she had yet to encounter a person from her own homeworld.

Until she passed by the Chamber of Remembrance, and saw a procession of white-robed Rememberers streaming in, and the doors irising shut, and a young boy waiting outside. He too was clad in the robes of the House of Tash. They were big for him, and trailed the floor. He was afraid, she could tell, as she watched him skipping the flagstones to while away the waiting.

She heard the child singing to himself, a nursery rhyme of Essondras: *"Ya wo, ya wo, kashatro plassa neni kwocho—" Hey, hey, the kashanthra-bird is weeping in the sewer. . . .* The boy looked up, abruptly. They stared at one another, the white-robed child and the woman cloaked in darkness.

In halting highspeech, the boy asked whom he had the honor of addressing.

And Jenjen replied, in the dialect of Ikshatra, in the same words with which Elloran had addressed her so long ago, with which he had dispelled her fear: *"Keshwelati, dawello; temweminit; ki kiamwati?* Little boy, console yourself. Don't fear me. What is your name?" With a gasp she realized that, with those words, some cycle of destinies was drawing to a close, as a lightstrand could be made with a twist of a trained finger to swallow itself and confuse its beginning and end. . . .

And the boy said, "I am Tash Tarrys. I was summoned from Essondras only two sleeps ago. . . . We of the house of Tash already know, but the announcement has not yet been made in Ikshatra. . . ." He burst into tears. And Jenjen held him as he blurted out his misery. A tall Inquestor with a face like a mummy, and a young Inquestor with violet eyes—Arryk, she knew, from his description—had come to the House of Tash in the eighteenth arrondissment of the city, and they had chosen Rememberers, and told them that Essondras was soon to *fall beyond.*"

"How soon?" Jenjen cried, thinking of Zalo and her old friends and wondering how many years it had been and realizing too that they must once more be orbiting her homeworld—

"I don't know, Lady Jenjen."

"You know my name?"

"I saw you once, my Lady, when I was five years old. . . . You had an exhibition in the hall of the lightweavers. . . . I am a trained Rememberer and cannot forget your face," he added with a measure of pride. "That was seven years ago. . . ."

"So my friends would still be alive!" How long had she been aboard Varezhdur in subjective time? Only a few months? But she had lived through so much, so much! And

seven years had passed at home. But at least she was still remembered. . . . This child proved it! "You remember . . . perhaps . . . a corpse-dancer named Zalo?"

"You know him, Lady?" he said, wide-eyed. "The most
famous of necrodramatists, the one who rewrote the story of
the Rainbow King?"

Seven years . . .

And how long could she have now, even given that they
would allow her to return to Essondras, before the people bins
came and her planet's civilization was wiped out? She had missed
out on seven years, during which time her lover had gone from
apprentice to journeyman to master of necrodrama. And her
parents, whom she had seldom thought about . . . dead, perhaps. She said, "Why are you waiting here, outside the door?"

"I am to be formally inducted into Varezhdur's society of
Rememberers. I will give a brief remembrance of our
world . . ."

As though it were already *fallen beyond*! she thought, angry.

Just then the portal irised open, and Tash Tievar stood
with open arms, welcoming the boy. Timidly he stepped forward. Tievar looked up and saw Jenjen, and in that look a thousand words were spoken—words of bitterness, regret, despair.
A whoosh as the doors were drawn shut.

As if Essondras were already dead! She stood in the huge
antechamber for a long time, weeping disconsolately, like a
child abruptly orphaned.

## 2

Her forays took her farther every evening. She pressed
onward with a desperate determination. She reached the hallway that led to those parts of Varezhdur that had fallen into
disuse; for Varezhdur was a palace built upon palaces, and
some central core of it was almost 20,000 years old. Elloran's
predecessors had not always built with an eye for the whole,
but had decreed a wing here, a spire there, at whim. Yet even

these dim corridors glowed as though in memory of Ton Elloran.

She found a tube-like hallway where *up* and *down* spiraled around and around by means of some gravity-controlling device. She walked on, getting dizzy, until she collapsed onto a displacement plate, giving it no particular command. It would displace her to some random location.

A garden overgrown with weeds . . . The walls, by the magic of holosculpture, created an illusion of vast spaces, distant mountains, a trickling waterfall. She had been here once or twice before to make love to strangers. There was a gazebo with dusty columns that threw bar-shadows across its carpet of malachite and serpentine cunningly stranded to caress her feet damply, like fresh rained-on turf. There was a curtain woven like a light-tapestry, but by machine, an infinitely repeating minimalist design; it stretched across a few of the columns. A good place for a secret tryst. Perhaps I'll find someone here tonight, she thought.

And someone called her name, very quietly.

She turned. It came from a column still topped with antique freezefire, so that its long shadow was speckled with dancing light. "Jenjen, weaver of light and darkness, named to the Clan of Ir by Ton Elloran n'Taanyel Tath."

The owner of the voice: a young man, shabbily clad in a tunic of threadbare clingfire. Green eyes, wide, transfixing. Lithe, boylike, beneath the clingfire. "Who are you?"

"Never mind. I've been watching you. You're not gregarious, like most of Elloran's sycophants. You go everywhere alone, no? I've been watching you."

"Who are you?" But she half-recognized him. She had seen him somewhere. Incongruously she felt as though this were someone she should worship, even though he was dressed like a peasant. Something about those eyes . . . and the face, unlined like a boy's, yet infinitely, chillingly old.

He laughed, a warm, comforting laugh. She hadn't expected it. "Come into shadow," he said. And she found herself obeying. And touched warm flesh beneath the clingfire . . . and kissed him, hungry, passionate. "Who are you?" His face fell further into darkness . . . and her own darkrobe's shadow shielded his features from her. "Who are you?" Only laughter. "Who, who?"

"Don't think of it yet. . . . But I was right to seek you

out, wasn't I? You are ready to turn to the shadow now, aren't you?"

"What do you mean?" How could this man know of her struggle to give meaning to the light-mad chaos? Of the creeping darknesses that had marred her new creations, mirrors of the war within her? "I'll never be a true darkweaver, if that's what you mean. I've tried. But even Ton Elloran can't always be right, can he?"

"No, no," he said, "the other shadow . . . There is one more thing you must see, and then you will be ready. . . . Darkness is not death but the beginning of life. Come, Jeni." She flinched at his use of her child-name, but yielded to the magic in his eyes. "Follow." He took her hand.

It seemed then that he whispered certain words, and that the column melted and they flowed into it. If only she could see his face! But now they were running fleetly down a passage, and wherever they ran the light muted itself and the man's face fell into shadow.

"Why are you taking me here?" she started to demand, but he put a finger to her lips: a coarse, callused finger, a peasant's finger.

"Listen."

And there was an eerie music . . . a voice. It was not an old man's voice, and not a child's, but something else entirely: high-pitched, sweet, utterly lifeless.

"What is it?"

"Listen! You will need to know every nuance of this voice. . . . You will need to remember, with all the clarity of a Rememberer—"

Nothing quite like this voice . . . though there was something familiar about its intonations. The voice sang an ancient song of the days before men found the quickpaths in the overcosm and pinholed through them through the dephinoid minds. In those days, the voice sang, men sailed the slow gray spaces for centuries at a stretch, not knowing what worlds they searched for:

> *den óm verék en-tínjet*
> *in dárein shirénzheh*
> *zenz kel skevúh varúng*
> *e varánde.*

*aivermatsá falláh setálikas!*
*tekiánveras ývřens ká!*

*o-tínjet*
*in dárein shirénzheh*
*sarnáng, varúnger shentráor.*
*eih, hokhté Euguéster, min zhalá,*
*min zhalá, sarnáng,*
*varúnger shentráor, varúnger shentráor.*

"You know this song," said the unknown man.

"I have heard some phrases from it often," said Jenjen, "from the lips of Tievar, of Elloran, of Siriss. *No man alive has touched the silence between the stars, save that he was driven mad, or attained enlightenment. But now delphinoid ships fall through the overcosm, and tachyon bubbles burst through the cosmos; and only I have touched the silence between the stars, I, the mad singer. Envy me, O High Inquestor, envy me, the mad singer, the mad singer.* But where is the voice coming from? That is an old song of Shen Sajit's, isn't it? It tells of where Elloran has gone . . . to seek out the gray spaces, and the silence between the stars. . . ."

"You have learned much. Do you think it's too much?"

"Have I said something wrong?"

"Never, Jeni, never." And stopped her mouth with his. But was this making love? She was drawn to him, inexorably, as to a lodestone, yet it was like a slow dance in the arms of a fire-creature, and she was so afraid of being burned, she dared not approach too close, until the final moments. . . . And through it all the strange song sounded, daunting, haunting. She gave herself to darkness at last. She was on fire but the fire itself was darkness. And behind the darkness she saw . . . she saw. . . .

Far away, lights flickering. Perhaps a door opening in some distant passageway causing light rays to run from one gold wall to another, skimming the burnish. "Do not be afraid, Jeni." The boy-man stood, the clingfire flowed to him, gathered around his slight, hard body. "You must be afraid, of course; you have toyed, unknowing, with the fire from which the Inquest itself is forged—"

"You don't sound like a peasant anymore."

"No. But you shall not yet know what I am. And I have been a peasant."

"Your words are dark."

"There was a wall of darkness once; the Skywall Mountain that rose a hundred klomets high, casting my village into perpetual shadow. When I was a child I watched its black expanse. . . . In my mind's eye I drew great fleets of starships on it, and worlds and galaxies. . . . I dreamed of the stars. I suppose we've all done that. But within the hollow mountain, flying through an ancient atmosphere, was a creature who, though blind, saw in its mind all space and time."

"You come from Gallendys! The world of the delphinoids."

"Tievar has done well." He smiled a little; the smile but skirted his deep melancholy. "But there is one more thing to show you."

He clapped his hands and spoke words even more archaic than the highspeech. A wall opened; a ruddy light flooded the corridor where they now found themselves, though she did not remember stepping into it. And she now saw the source of the song. A fractured memory leaped into her mind: the cold blue light, the head of her great-grandfather, the little girl in the throes of nightmare—she screamed and screamed, until she felt the stranger's arms about her.

It was a corpse.

And she knew who it must be: Shen Sajit himself. In Tievar's stories she had heard Sajit described again and again—as a child, as a young man, as an ancient—until she knew his features better than her own. . . . He had been shipped to a servocorpse factory, hadn't he? Like all dead servants! But now—

The corpse stood in a little niche. A perfumed odor mingled with decay issued from it. Its mouth opened and closed in song, like a machine; its jellied eyes stared unseeing. Its cheeks were sucked in, shadowed, hatchworked with wrinkles. Its white hair stood on end, billowed wildly as though from an electric charge. It was hideous. And yet from its lips came a sweet music.

Jenjen was afraid. Why did she have to see this? Was this, too, part of the destiny Elloran had foreseen for her? She turned to look at the stranger, who wept quietly.

"Why the tears? . . . My Lord," she whispered, intuiting his high station, "it is not good you weep."

"You'll never understand. This man's music was the first thing I heard on Uran s'Varek that gave me consolation. . . . I was far from all I had known or loved. . . . And after, there was not a single moment when I set foot in this palace when I couldn't hear his music. . . . Now it has come to this!"

"How does it come about? It is a prodigy. The servocorpse-making has backfired, the process of reawakening must have been hurried or interrupted, a short-circuiting of the dead man's brain . . . and the corpse repeats the same words over and over, and must be aborted. . . . My lover Zalo has told me that these things can happen."

"Lord Elloran does not know yet that we have recovered Sajit's body, and that it has been trapped within this single song. . . . He will go mad with grief! As all of us have."

Once more the song began.

"Did you know, Ir Jenjen, that the Inquest is falling?"

"I have heard it whispered. . . . But slaves always whisper, even when they know better. How can a thing so vast and all-encompassing be said to fall? It cannot come soon." She thought of Zalo and his revolutionary rhetoric. And of Tievar's tale of Kelver, the Prince of Shadow, who had possessed the Throne of Madness.

"It will come soon! No more will the Inquest renounce love in compassion's name. All the old emotions will come back: love and its dark companion hate, and desolation and betrayal and hope! And a time will come when delphinoids no longer sail the overcosm, and our tachyon bubbles no longer carve pathways through the space beyond spaces. It will be in your lifetime. And I believe that you will play a role in it, you, weaver of light and darkness!"

"Are you one of the . . . heretics?"

"Yes, I am," A sad laugh. Strange to hear an Inquestor make such an admission. Stranger to hear one speak of the fall with such longing. And Jenjen was moved at this, and awed. "And you, Jenjen, will you take the big step with me, will you know your own shadow as well as your light? You have heard of the Clan of Rememberers and their curious secrets. . . . Do you know that there will be a new species of remembrance after the fall? The memories that will bridge the time of shadow that must ensue, the memories straight out of the hearts of ordinary people? We must *all* become Rememberers now!"

"*Hokh'Ton!*" she said, preparing to fall on her knees before him, for she had an inkling of who he might be.

"Rise." And though he did not smile, his eyes sparkled. "You have seen; you must tell. You must go back to Essondras. Please help me."

"You should command me, Lord."

"I do not command, though trillions have cried out my name as though it were a god's. I am not a god, Ir Jenjen. Flesh and blood." And they embraced again: and in the darkness of that embrace she saw reflected all Tievar's tales. She must distill all these remembrances into one fierce, willed, shining truth. Under the old Inquest they had all been like servocorpses, dancing on the marionette strings of unseen masters. But now, but now—

"What are you thinking, Jenjen?" But she could not answer him for the welter of warring emotions.

So he uttered a command that made the walls dissolve; the niche that had held the corpse of Shen Sajit withdrew from their sight; and they stood in a vast nave, at one end of which Ton Siriss sat enthroned, and behind her the dust-galaxy of Sajit and Zhendra and Ton Elloran; and other Inquestors too, not isolated on their massive hoverthrones, but mingling with the throng. When Jenjen and the strange Inquestor approached, the eyes of the nearest ones lit up; the spark spread outward, as a forest fire spreads; they were all drunk on this new joy, the childsoldiers, the kings, the Inquestors, the harpists, the whores, the kallogynes, the mendicants, the merchants, the once-lost. And there came a cry of *Kelver! Kelver! Kelver!* like the rushing of the wind, like the beatings of the wings of pteratygers. The green-eyed Inquestor clutched Jenjen's hand, as if to plead indulgence for these misguided people; hadn't he told her, *I am not a god?* Yet the roar went on. And it was his humility that awed her most.

Now even Siriss came down from her throne. The crowd surged forward. Some were throwing themselves at his feet, stretching out their arms to touch his tattered clingfire. And though the Inquestor protested, even Siriss knelt before him. And Jenjen felt for him an almost unbearable love. Not the love she had felt and would always feel for Zalo, but a thing far greater than herself. For she knew that this man, who held the Galaxy in his grasp, had need of her love, demanded it even. And because he of all Inquestors had dared ask for love instead of fear, they had all given it to him, blindly, fervently. . . . It was this love that would unleash the final darkness on the Inquest. . . . At last she unclasped his hand and fell prostrate before him. This time he did not move to stop her. But she saw that he wept for her, and for all men, tears more precious then the stars.

"You will go to Essondras for me? As my emissary? A long time ago, Ton Elloran saw in you the possibility of understanding. He could not fight for the path of shadow himself, because he was too much of the old ways. But he could seek out people like you," he said, "and hope that they could be made to see behind the darkness of the Inquest's fall. And so, if you accept this mission, the cycle of your existence will have wound round to the beginning, and you will once more see with a child's clarity."

She could barely hear him above the thunder of their worship. Yet she heard too, with her mind's ear, the afterecho of Sajit's song behind the roaring: *Envy me, O High Inquestor, envy me. . . .* And she understood now that though they might dwell in gem-encrusted palaces and command the deaths of millions with a handclap, yet they well should envy the short-lived. They had become servocorpses themselves; *makrúgh* alone, not human feeling, animated them. They could not say—as even she could—*I am free*.

"I'll go! I'll use my art to shout the new truth out over the city of Ikshatra. I must go, because—"

"I am the Prince of Shadow."

*It's taken me this long,* she thought, *to stop being afraid of the dark.*

And she told him, "You've made me brave enough to embrace the dark along with you. Because I know you're not a god, not some creature endowed with superpowers . . . I've made love to you, I know you're human. And *you* braved the great darkness. I haven't seen the light or the Sound, but I can see how deeply it has touched you, and I've caught the contagion of your courage. I'm not afraid—I'm not afraid anymore!"

The Prince of Shadow smiled; and Jenjen saw sunlight in his eyes, and cried for joy.

# 3

She returned to Ikshatra in secret. Her parents were dead now; her first act, after checking in at the academy and determining that she could find lodging there, was to visit the mnemothanasion to retrieve their heads. She did not look forward to the visit, for it brought back all the horror of the funeral she had gone to as a child, when she had met the young Rememberer . . . the boy who had become a servocorpse through the ministrations of the Arm, and who, for all she knew, still danced daily in the theaters of the dead.

It was not as she remembered it at all. It was a beautiful place, tranquil, a complex of soft-curved edifices of white and off-white marble. For though the place where the dead were taken for their funeral rites had been appropriately awe-inspiring, and was intended to instill a measure of terror and solemnity in those still living, the mnemothanasion proper was not considered a place where one should go to experience pain. Each memory-cubicle suggested, by a continuous holo-sculpting of its walls, landscapes alien and familiar: firesnows, needlemountains, umber oceans, starfields, meadows under many moons. She paid the cephalographer the traditional demi-arjent for his services; when he asked her what backdrop she would require for her mnemothanatic meditations, she asked for something prosaic: the environs of her old house and arrondissement: nothing cosmic.

Her parent's heads were displayed on a twin-niched rotating stand; the holoimage made it appear that she was sitting in a garden outside the old house. The illusion was not quite complete, for from next door she heard the shrieks and ululations of a woman in the throes of traditional grief.

She sat silently for the requisite seven watches, her fingers drumming the deliberately uncomfortable restraints of the invisible forcechair. *What do I have to say to these people?* she thought. Eventually, her mother's head spoke:

246

"Jeni. All is well. Be happy. Though we didn't see you for many years, we were comforted, dear, to know you were up there, among the powerful and compassionate ones. We were never religious before, but after you left, your father and I went out and bought a little fetish—a ball of shimmerfur; we put it over in our memory-niche, so your great-grandfather could see it; and you know, his eyes lit up with that wierd blue glow, and a smile actually creased his lips. . . ."

"We're proud of you, daughter," said her father's head, picking up smoothly from her mother's pause; this, then, was one of the cheap models, driven by a single thinkhive the size of an amoeba.

"What should I tell you, my parents? That I stood among the gods and heard their Rememberers talk about how our gods can break worlds in two with a sigh, and devastate star systems with a handclap?"

Her mother's head whirred, then responding in some pre-programmed fashion: "Impiety, daughter! Think of the values that your father and I instilled in you!"

The heads nattered on. They were toys, really. It was ludicrous to suggest that possessing your ancestor's heads was a symbol of socioeconomic prestige, as if to say, "I was rich enough to prevent my parents from being made into servocorpses; you'll never see *my* mother mouthing some dramatist's words in the arena!" Nonsense! These heads *were* servocorpses, animated by the same technology, and just as disrespectful of the dead. What strange, revolutionary thoughts I'm having! Jenjen reflected. The Inquestors chose me well. I will always be a subversive, questioning every handed-down axiom, trying to see through pretension. . . .

She said, quietly, unemotionally, "You're not my parents."

And with those words she broke the spell that had held her in terror of her great-grandfather's head for all these years. And washed away some of the pain of loss.

# 4

At the palace of the oligarchs she applied before the planetary thinkhive for a grant to build a monumental lightwall in the center of Ikshatra.

"It will run," she said, "out of the sea; it will be just a wisp of a lightwall at first, hardly visible; then, cutting as the crow flies toward the city center, gaining and gaining in intensity, until it scales the old Angkhosti Avenue and towers over the National Theater itself. . . ."

*How long?* The planetary thinkhive's impersonal voice.

"There's not much time. . . . Such a project should normally take a year or more, even with the most powerful light-generators on Essondras. . . . But there's no time. I would have to do it in three months, no more."

*Not much time! You know something, then, that we do not?*

"I cannot say, Oligarchs of Essondras." She wondered suddenly whether the oligarchs made any real decisions, or if it was in fact the thinkhive who truly governed.

*It is good.* A softening of the thinkhive's customarily peevish tone. . . . She looked up abruptly. The wombroom at the oligarch's palace, where citizens went to communicate with the Inquestrally-appointed government, was a dank, dark chamber whose walls sweated organic fluids, for it interfaced directly with the thinkhive's mind. But she had often heard the thinkhive's voice over the holovision network; always it had sounded stern, impersonal, uncompromising. *It is good,* the thinkhive repeated, *that the visions of such as you, who have glimpsed the outside universe, should grace this planet's eschatology. You cannot avoid apocalypse, but you can give it beauty, my daughter.* And she recognized that voice—

"Ton Elloran!" she cried, forgetting in her startlement the appropriate honorifics. She continued in the highspeech: "Is this thinkhive possessed by you, then?"

248

A soft laughter filled the wombroom.

"Or have you merely taken on his voice in order to haunt me with memories of golden Varezhdur, which I will probably never see again . . . and to make sure I don't forget the purpose I was sent here for?"

*I cannot answer more, Jeni.* Then, another shift, the voice of Siriss: *We are with you always.* And finally the voice of Kelver, the Inquestor of the shadow, who had demanded and won her love: *Be free, Jeni. While you can, be free.*

And again the thinkhive's laughter.

She walked home through the forest, down the slope of the hill that bordered Ikshatra, remembering that once she had visited her father's office, that he had had some kind of bureaucratic job servicing the thinkhive. She wondered if her father ever dreamt of the deviousness of the thinkhive's mind, or whether he just thought of it as a planetary watchdog, a useful servant.

There was a slight chill this high above the city. She had heard rumors of a strange seeping cold in the city, as though great forceshields were being drawn across the sun in preparation for . . . what? Falling beyond? No one except Jenjen felt any urgency.

She looked up as she reached the rank of displacement plates that would send her back into the city. There it was, at the hill's crest . . . the Arm, a band of flesh-toned foliage. . . . The new chill had killed off some of the deciduous trees and caused unnatural denuding up and down the hillside, and the Arm stood out more starkly. . . . It was a sharp outline of a human arm, and it seemed that it grasped the mountain with an elemental force, strangling it almost.

"I must not see metaphoric images of horror," she told herself. "The real ones would come soon enough." She thought of the great work that she must do . . . and of the great artists in whose tradition she must follow: of Sajit the eternally devoted, always the humanist even in his most cosmic songs . . . of Dei Zhendra, who had turned her back on humanity itself in her pursuit of an absolute beauty . . . of Rax Nika, who, because of what she was, could not help creating beauty, though it served the Inquest's purposes and was forever fleeting . . . of Aush Keshmin, the weapons designer who had made the human comets of death, who had wrung a kind of twisted beauty from instruments of galactic warfare . . . of the Windbringers who sang for no one now, though their song, as it wove paths through the overcosm, held together all the Inquest.

Could she distill all their joy and suffering into a single entity?

As she stepped onto the displacement plate, she heard for one last moment the thinkhive's laughter, echoing across the hillside. It was for her alone: cosmic laughter, perhaps.

# 5

She wondered whether, now that her duties had been discharged, she should go and try to find Zalo. She had taken a small studio near the necrodramatists' quarter, on Angkoshti Avenue, only a few displacement plates down from the zulshop where they had quarreled. She often heard his name mentioned on the street or in shops; he was quite famous now. They were all talking about his new play, *The Rainbow King*, which, it was said, was a shocking travesty of the original legend.

She heard her own name mentioned on the street, too. Everyone knew, it seems, that the infamous Ir Jenjen had returned from a seven-year sojourn among the High Inquestors, and that she was creating a gigantic lightwall that would carve up half the city. But no one had any inkling of what it would be like yet. First she'd drawn a line from the harbor to the center of the city, and outlined the lightwall in hoverlight; then she had had the whole corridor hooded with a lightbending forceshield. People passing by saw nothing of the artwork arching out over the streets; they saw, instead, an unfamiliar blurring of the cityscape, an abrupt, impossible refraction, as though half the city had been submerged in water.

As for herself, she had learned much about the colors of light, and how light could be made to cancel out light, and how images could be woven, one on top of another, until the jumble of their emotional resonances was almost unbearable. But though she now possessed the art of creating lightforms so beautiful as to make men weep, she had heard of the light-poems of the delphinoids. She knew there was something ultimate, something she could never hope to achieve. She saw clearly now what must be done. But for the first month she could not steel herself to face her vision's harshness; so she pottered around, throwing skeins of light at random, up and down. . . .

Her lightloom was a monster; a ten-meter-long contraption mounted on a floater, capable of sending out strands twenty klomets long. She would sit at the lightloom's center, sending the floater soaring high, skimming the edges of the forceshield, watching, on a holographic monitor at the center of her cramped control room, her handiwork unfold. She despaired.

Then there were the days when she haunted the arrondissements that she knew were Zalo's favorite spots: some particular garden, some zul-shop, some museum. She was too proud to go wait at his doorstep, and she did not think he would come to her after those harsh words—they had not been so long ago for her, though years had elapsed for him. Again she despaired, for she knew that her creation lacked one spark that would make it whole . . . and she feared to find out what that spark might be.

But one day, exhausted from fruitless hours of labor, she decided, on a whim, to attend the necrotheater. It was Zalo's notorious play, *The Rainbow King*.

It was only the second or third time that she had watched necrodrama in the flesh; she was accustomed to the holovised, edited versions. Now that she thought about it, the last time she had sat looking down from the artists' gallery, she had been seeing another version of this very story, one that had sparked a quarrel between her and Zalo . . . and now she would see Zalo's version.

Lights: a hush all the way from the mist-wrapped cheap seats down to the skene where the corpses danced. One corpse, aged, his face painted in the gold-and-black pattern proper for depicting bards, entered the skene. Below stage, in the pit, she thought she saw Zalo. But no, he must have changed. . . .

A sinuous dance, each fluid gesture punctuated by ponderous footfalls, and the opening words of Zalo's narrative:

*No use thinking of glory.*
*No use thinking of distant starships*
*That seemed to stand still against the starlight.*

Those words! How familiar they sounded. . . . The language, being the lowspeech of Essondras, was different, but the words themselves . . . Wasn't this how Tash Tievar had begun his tale of the Rainbow King?

And she remembered the quarrel again, and Zalo daring her to tell the truth, and herself pouring forth her remembrance of Tievar's telling—

And she knew then that she still loved him. And at last the vision came together in her mind. For she knew that the revolution had truly begun.

And, finding now the courage to realize her vision, she worked feverishly. She threw into her weaving all the magnificent artworks she had herself encountered: the songs of Shen Sajit, Dei Zhendra's galaxy of dust, Varezhdur itself—

And, lashing together immense strands of light of precisely complementary colors, she wove images of the Inquestors in their cruelty and their compassion; she mixed in all the mad colors of the overcosm, and her imagining of the delphinoids' lightsongs; she made a thousand faces of Tievar, a thousand Sajit's corpses, singing still in death, a thousand of Kelver's captivating eyes.

She looked at her creation; she could only see it in miniature, of course, by holoprojection; only from the Essondras's stratosphere could all be visible. But she knew the Inquestors would see, and wonder, when the time came for her world to *fall beyond*. . . .

"It's finished!" she cried out.

And the thinkhive of the planet, which had, as do all planetary thinkhives, eyes and ears in every corner of its world, heard her words; and it prepared for the unveiling. Since no one had yet set eyes on Jenjen's creation, it alone shared the lightwall's secret.

# 6

She sat in one of the cloudseats at the topmost level of the necrotheater. She could see crowds everywhere: in the plazas, lining the streets, leaning from parapets and skywalks. There must have been a million people in the streets, waiting.

And the forceshield dissolved:

At first, silence. Then the babble: furious, argumentative, cacophonous. She was glad the theater was closed; she did not know whether they would cheer her or lynch her. The roar went on and on. *I don't think I can bear it*, she thought. And closed her eyes and stopped her ears against the roaring, but still it came. Then she felt hands on her hands, prying them loose, and the soundburst blasting her senses—

"Jeni."

She turned. "Zasha. I thought you might find me." He looked at her quizzically. . . . She raised her voice to a shout, "I'm sorry, I know you can hardly hear me above this thundering—"

"I didn't expect this. . . . It is a wall of utter darkness! There it goes, cutting the city in half, throwing great edifices into shadow—"

There. He had said it. Would he accept what she had become? *Darkweaver. Darkweaver.* She could hear some chanting that epithet in the distance, and she could not tell whether they were cursing or cheering. "I made sure the shadows would fall mostly on ruins."

"But it is all meaningless! It's nonsense!"

"You tell me this? You, who single-handedly blaspheme against our most sacred legends . . . for the sake of something as irrelevant as truth? Oh, Zasha—"

And suddenly he laughed. "Of course! The old Jenjen. I only meant, though, that this grand artwork has been billed as the ultimate sensory experience, a depiction of everything that the Inquest means, a holographic interweaving of human and

253

Inquestral history, a monumental spectacle—color, movement, pageantry, music, the dance of myriad lights, the ultimate pyrotechnic display, and then you give us this . . . this
arch of darkness!"

She looked at him long and hard. He had grown older;
this she had expected, of course. He was seven years older
than she was, now; when they last met they had been the same
age. But what she had loved (and what had most annoyed her)
in him was still there: he loved truth, even when it made him
unspeakably angry. So she said, "Not just an arch, Zasha, but a
bridge too. For twenty millennia men have gazed upon rainbows of false hope. . . . But I would show them truth, whatever the price. We've longed for freedom so long we've
forgotten its meaning. And before redemption comes the har-
rowing of hell."

"But all the advertisements—"

"The advertisements didn't lie. All that . . . spectacle has
indeed been woven into my wall of darkness. I am a darkweaver now, after all. I understand why I was chosen to be
one. Do you know why I was so dazzled and fascinated by
intricate patternings of lights? Because I was afraid to love the
darkness. And because I knew I had to. Do you think it's easy
to take all those lightstrands and to weave those patterns with
such precision that they cancel each other out completely?
That's what darkweavers do. Everything I saw among the Inquestors is in that weaving, Zasha. . . . And its sum total is
darkness!"

"But do you know what this means? Some people will di-
vine the truth behind your vision. The oligarchy will censure you:
revolutionaries will look to your darkwall for inspiration—"

"Yes." She felt the sea-tanged wind, making the darkrobe
ripple about her. Down there, in the Square of Inquestral
Compassion . . . Was that a fire, a riot? She could barely make
it out, for her darkwall's shadow swathed over the avenue and
blotted out half the square. Behind, seaward, the darkwall angled down to the water until it was just a triangular slit of
darkness in the ocean. "Look," she said, pointing at the
fire. . . . Another was springing up far to the west.

"What have you started?" Zalo said. She could not tell
whether it was awe or panic.

"You started it too." Fire latticed the streets of a suburb
that ran up the side of the distant hill, in the shadow of the

Arm. Fire sprang up in the ruins of the ancient palace of the oligarchs. . . . It flickered eerily against the underside of the rainbow blackness.

"Yes." He looked away from her. "People will stare for a long time at your darkwall, and they'll . . . start to see things in it."

"Like boy Kelver and the Skywall Mountain." She knew he would not understand her, but he smiled; she knew from this that he trusted her. He did not seem to need an explanation, though she felt she owed him one. But she found herself echoing the words that the planet's thinkhive had spoken to her in Kelver's voice: "Be free. While you can. Be free."

He said to her, "At a meeting of the artists' council last week, the name of the Prince of Shadow was mentioned. Who is that? Have you seen him?"

"His love has touched me. Are you angry with me for that?"

He did not answer, though his silence said much. Finally he asked her: "What is it called?"

She thought of young Elloran stranded in the world of servocorpses that hideously mimicked man's dreams of utopia. She thought of Mother Vara of myth and perhaps of history, who had brought forth the Inquest with dreams of hope, and who now reaped fruits of bitter disillusion. Of the Inquestors who killed in compassion's name, and who, though lived in splendor, had relinquished joy, and who, though they preached of mercy, and renounced love.

And she thought of the slender hope that Kelver now held out for the Dispersal of Man: the way of shadow. The search for the great light that underpinned the darkness as surely as her great black wall was woven from skeins of brilliant light.

And she told him, before they kissed above the roar of the rioting and the glare of fire and beneath the arc of dark hope, "I shall call it 'Utopia Hunters.'"

*shénom na chítarans hyemadhá*
*u áthera tinjéh erúden*
*z irsái yver tembáraxein kreshpáh*
*z púrreh y'Enguéstren tinjéh.*

—ek shéntraran Sájiti

We yearn for the heart's homeworld
where the sun touches the earth
and rainbows encircle the mountains of darkness
and the Inquestor bends down to touch the beggar child.

*—from the Songs of Sajit*

*Alexandra*
*1978–1984*

SOMTOW SUCHARITKUL

## ABOUT THE AUTHOR

SOMTOW PAPINIAN SUCHARITKUL was born in 1952 in Bangkok, Thailand; he grew up in various European countries and was educated in England, at Eton and Cambridge. His first career was as a composer; at the age of 21 he became Thailand's delegate to the Asian Composers' League, and shortly thereafter became his country's representative in the International Music Council of UNESCO. His compositions have been performed, televised, and broadcast on four continents. In 1978 he branched out into the writing of science fiction, producing in rapid succession a series of short stories that won him the 1981 John W. Campbell Award for best new writer. Since then, his novels have included the Locus Award-winning *Starship & Haiku*, the satirical *Mallworld* and *Aquiliad*, and the epic multi-volume *Chronicles of the High Inquest* as well as a collection, *Fire from the Wine-Dark Sea and other Fantasies*. He has just published, as S.P. Somtow, his first mainstream novel, *Vampire Junction*, and is a regular book critic for the Washington *Post*. He now lives in the United States and works alternately on music, books by one alter ego or another, and reviewing. He is addicted to roller coasters.

Coming in the summer of 1985 . . .

# THE
# DARKLING
# WIND

## by Somtow Sucharitkul

Somtow Sucharitkul brings his epic Inquestor saga to a close with this spectacular novel of the revolution that rocked the entire universe.

Read THE DARKLING WIND, on sale in the summer of 1985 wherever Bantam paperbacks are sold.

Somtow

# OUT OF THIS WORLD!

That's the only way to describe Bantam's great series of science fiction classics. These space-age thrillers are filled with terror, fancy and adventure and written by America's most renowned writers of science fiction. Welcome to outer space and have a good trip!

# FANTASY AND SCIENCE FICTION FAVORITES

Bantam brings you the recognized classics as well as the current favorites in fantasy and science fiction. Here you will find the most recent titles by the most respected authors in the genre.

| | | | |
|---|---|---|---|
| ☐ | 24370 | RAPHAEL  R. A. MacAvoy | $2.75 |
| ☐ | 24103 | BORN WITH THE DEAD  Robert Silverberg | $2.75 |
| ☐ | 24169 | WINTERMIND  Parke Godwin, Marvin Kaye | $2.75 |
| ☐ | 23944 | THE DEEP  John Crowley | $2.95 |
| ☐ | 23853 | THE SHATTERED STARS  Richard McEnroe | $2.95 |
| ☐ | 23575 | DAMIANO  R. A. MacAvoy | $2.75 |
| ☐ | 23205 | TEA WITH THE BLACK DRAGON  R. A. MacAvoy | $2.75 |
| ☐ | 23365 | THE SHUTTLE PEOPLE  George Bishop | $2.95 |
| ☐ | 24441 | THE HAREM OF AMAN AKBAR | $2.95 |
| | | Elizabeth Scarborough | |
| ☐ | 20780 | STARWORLD  Harry Harrison | $2.50 |
| ☐ | 22939 | THE UNICORN CREED  Elizabeth Scarborough | $3.50 |
| ☐ | 23120 | THE MACHINERIES OF JOY  Ray Bradbury | $2.75 |
| ☐ | 22666 | THE GREY MANE OF MORNING  Joy Chant | $3.50 |
| ☐ | 23063 | LORD VALENTINE'S CASTLE  Robert Silverberg | $3.50 |
| ☐ | 20870 | JEM  Frederik Pohl | $2.95 |
| ☐ | 23460 | DRAGONSONG  Anne McCaffrey | $2.95 |
| ☐ | 23666 | EARTHCHILD  Sharon Webb | $2.50 |
| ☐ | 24102 | DAMIANO'S LUTE  R. A. MacAvoy | $2.75 |
| ☐ | 24417 | THE GATES OF HEAVEN  Paul Preuss | $2.50 |

**Prices and availability subject to change without notice.**

Buy them at your local bookstore or use this handy coupon for ordering:

# SPECIAL
# MONEY SAVING
# OFFER

Now you can have an up-to-date listing of Bantam's hundreds of titles plus take advantage of our unique and exciting bonus book offer. A special offer which gives you the opportunity to purchase a Bantam book for only 50¢. Here's how!

By ordering any five books at the regular price per order, you can also choose any other single book listed (up to a $4.95 value) for just 50¢. Some restrictions do apply, but for further details why not send for Bantam's listing of titles today!

Just send us your name and address plus 50¢ to defray the postage and handling costs.